Connie May Fowler is an essayist and screenwriter, as well as the author of three previous novels, including *Before Women Had Wings*, winner of the 1996 Southern Book Critics' Circle Award, a US paperback bestseller and a successful film from Oprah Winfrey.

Also by Connie May Fowler

BEFORE WOMEN HAD WINGS

RIVER OF HIDDEN DREAMS

SUGAR CAGE

REMEMBERING BLUE

Connie May Fowler

BANTAM PRESS

LONDON · NEW YORK · TORONTO · SYDNEY · AUCKLAND

TRANSWORLD PUBLISHERS
61–63 Uxbridge Road, London W5 5SA
a division of The Random House Group Ltd

RANDOM HOUSE AUSTRALIA (PTY) LTD
20 Alfred Street, Milsons Point, Sydney
New South Wales 2061, Australia

RANDOM HOUSE NEW ZEALAND
18 Poland Road, Glenfield, Auckland 10, New Zealand

RANDOM HOUSE SOUTH AFRICA (PTY) LTD
Endulini, 5a Jubilee Road, Parktown 2193, South Africa

Published 2000 by Bantam Press
a division of Transworld Publishers

Printed and bound in Great Britain
by Mackays of Chatham plc, Chatham, Kent.

1 3 5 7 9 10 8 6 4 2

For Joy Harris

In Memory of Bob Tavetian

Acknowledgments

I would like to thank my editor Deb Futter for her uncompromising vision and fierce support. Joy Harris for sharing her laughter, her tears, her insights, and most importantly, her friendship. Mayme and Jesse Millender for guiding me through the intricate mysteries of being a shrimper and a shrimper's wife (and Mayme, thank you for the detailed reading and erudite suggestions). Martin Terrell for his astonishing kindness in revealing the haunting details of his wife's death. Bob and Rhonda Heins for borrowed books, for local knowledge, for fighting to protect what's left, and for their hard-fought wisdom freely dispensed over heaping platters of steamed shrimp and Panacea blue crabs. Anne and Wayne Coloney for the chickee and the pocket house. Debbie Logan at My-Way Seafood for the stories, the sustenance, the eagerness to help me get it right. Trisha Lamb Feuerstein for suggesting Candace Slater's wonderful book *Dance of the Dolphin*. Doubleday for believing. Leslie Daniels and Kassandra Duane for their humor and fortitude. Beth Betbeze and Lillian Powell for loving so selflessly. My sister Deidre, whose support is unflagging. Pamela Ball, my co-conspirator in word and deed. And always, always Mika, whose infinite patience, strength, goodness, and grace inform each page.

Here, I came to the boundaries
where nothing needs to be said,
everything is learned with weather and ocean . . .

—PABLO NERUDA

Remembering
Blue

M*attie, Mattie, sweetheart, I love you.*

I*t's* all so surprising. Here we are, staring into the jaws of a new century and I at twenty-five years of age am left to ponder the world as if I were a woman of eighty. My remembrance, my meditation on Nick Blue—who he was and why his life was important—is a simple act by a grieving wife, yet his story cannot be told to the exclusion of mine.

For twenty-two years, I existed as that murky shadow at the far edge of your peripheral vision, a faint reminder that there are those among the living who are exceptional at no level. My head down, my shoulders slumped, my manner of dress benign and colorless, I drifted through life with singular purpose: never to draw attention to myself. Fearing both judgment and recognition, I scuttled along the fringes, noiselessly.

Today, if you pressed me to come up with something nice to say about the old Mattie I suppose it would be this: I was dully efficient.

1

Bookish without being brilliant. Quiet without an ounce of presence. Unflagging in my devotion to sensible shoes.

Enter Nick Blue, a man who didn't have a dull bone in his body. Nick was a dreamer, a pure-hearted shrimper who could hear the wind creak through the bent wing of a roosting heron and who would whisper into that same wind, "Bring me a good haul, tonight, sweet bird."

Despite my reticent nature, Nick's charms were not wasted. The very moment he held me in his gaze, my denial of myself as a sexual being began to crumble. This isn't to say that before meeting Nick passion escaped me. I had desires, dreams, carnal fantasies. But there were problems. One, the episodes occurred at embarrassingly infrequent intervals. And two, they invariably involved extreme flights of fancy during which for a few minutes, an hour, perhaps several weeks, I stoked the flames of a private crush on someone with whom I could never, never, never really have an affair. I was mad for old movies, you see. And I spent a rather unhealthy amount of time daydreaming about the likes of Cary Grant, Sir Laurence Olivier, Robert Mitchum, Richard Burton, and Paul Newman. The pitfalls, I believe, are obvious.

Nevertheless, these secret one-sided romances got me through some rough spots, perhaps even saved my life, at least kept my libido in some semblance of working order because when it came to real flesh and blood passion, I'm afraid that more often than not I possessed an extreme case of cold feet. In fact, mine were frozen to the bone.

I blame my sexual stage fright on my mother. She was a withholding woman when it came to loving me. But she had other priorities. Such as the fact that Daddy was a booze hound who wandered out of our lives when I was seven.

Minutes before he disappeared into the mosquito- and gnat-infested Jacksonville Beach night, he staggered into my purple bedroom with its white eyelet curtains that smelled of bleach and dust, shook me awake, and mumbled in a Jim Beam haze, "Matilda Fiona O'Rourke, sweetheart, I'm leaving. I'm joining the circus. Make sure your mama brings you to see me next time we roll into town."

He kissed my cheek. His day-old beard scratched my face. I looked up at him, blankly, intrigued that my daddy had aspirations beyond his job as a shipyard welder yet also confused at his intentions. *I'm leaving.* Two spare words tossed into the close air of my bedroom as if they held no weight. As if they wouldn't claw at my heart for the rest of my days. As if his presence in our lives didn't matter, had never mattered. I stared into his bloodshot pale eyes. They shone with tears. Or was it excitement? I reached up and touched his stubbled beard. I was Daddy's girl. His little angel. Cupcake.

"Don't go."

"Got to, Cupcake. Time to see the world."

He tipped his finger at me in a drunken salute. Signaling his resolve, he folded in his dry, full lips and squeezed shut his eyes. "You close your eyes, too, sweetheart," he said in a slow singsong voice. "That's it. Keep 'em closed."

I heard him pick up the jewelry box he'd given me just that Christmas. When you opened the lid a ballerina popped up and spun in a perpetual pirouette to the tinny strains of *Swan Lake*. I loved that shiny black lacquer box and its pretty music. But on that night the song sounded warped, too slow. The little gear needed to be rewound.

Daddy said, "Goooood girl. Doooon't peeeek." His heavy footsteps glommed across the pine floor. "Just listen to the music, baby. That's right. Sweet dreeeams."

The door creaked open and he was gone. The music stopped in midnote and I knew the ballerina was no longer dancing. I kept my eyes closed but hung on to the only thing I had left of my daddy: a sour, thin gust of Jim Beam.

I do not know if he said goodbye to my mother or not. She didn't volunteer the information. And I did not ask. In fact, she behaved as if he had never happened. After that night, the words *your father, your daddy, my husband* never crossed her lips.

One afternoon I came home from school and found that all physical traces of him were gone, as well. His clothes. His greasy tools. His ashtray shaped like a bass. Even his collection of sweat-rancid baseball caps. All evidence of him kaput, except for me—that part of him she couldn't erase. My presence was a constant, painful annoyance, the rock in the shoe that wouldn't let her forget.

But she tried. By God, did she ever.

Other than to criticize or browbeat, she rarely spoke to me. I suppose that could be chalked up to her hysteria over being a single mother. But being a single parent doesn't explain her refusal to look me in the eyes or hug me or attempt a normal conversation. Maybe that's what I regret most about my unconventional upbringing. My mother and I never simply chatted. Not once. Maybe she kissed me when I was a baby. But I have searched my memory backward and forward, and for the life of me, I cannot recall one single instance of even the most summary peck on the cheek.

Her relations with men stood in night-and-day contrast to her at-arm's-length handling of me. After Daddy left, Mother spent the rest of her days becoming her own three-ring circus as she chased, entertained, and made a fool of herself over an uninterrupted series of no-good prospects who kept her ceaselessly brokenhearted. She danced for them. She cooked for them. She even shined their shoes. But none of them stuck. It was as though her vulnerability awakened their basest instincts. She was a woman cut from the same gossamer cloth as Blanche Du-Bois—her desperate need for a man led even the kind ones to use her.

I once saw her shimmy for a man. Through my cracked-open bed-room door, I watched—a mixture of shame, revulsion, and fascination keeping me pegged. He sat on our natty brown couch, his legs spread wide, stroking himself as my mother—with an ear-to-ear cheerleader's grin plastered on and panic filming her eyes—shook for all she was worth.

He laughed and said, "God, you're stupid." Then he grabbed her arm, tore off her panties, and shoved her down on him. She grunted and her eyes winced with pain but she kept that smile intact, even when he smashed his lips into hers.

The more judgmental among you might say that she suffered from some sort of sexual pathology. Being her daughter, I can't accept that Pearl Monita O'Rourke's problems boiled down to loose morals, physiologically driven or otherwise. I prefer to think that her aberrant behavior was spurred by a relentless, profound, and yet rather boring bent toward self-destruction.

Though Mother tended to ignore me in favor of her beau of the week, she occasionally tossed me blemished pearls of queenly wisdom which she fitfully conjured during the many hours she spent on that love-stained couch smoking cigarettes and staring into space.

Sometimes her advice ran contrary to her own actions: "Don't ever believe anything a man tells you. They just want their pants washed."

I was never sure whether this was a sexual euphemism or a laundry tip.

On other occasions her words ran true to form: "Don't set your sights too high, Matilda. Don't try to be a doctor when you can marry one. And whatever you do, don't major in English."

Mother viewed anything remotely associated with the English language as a mortal sin—grammar, spelling, literature, punctuation. That's because in the arms of a good book, I could be lost to the world for days. And while Mother didn't want to be involved in my moment-to-moment existence, she believed anything that could keep a child occupied from dawn to dusk and beyond was cause for alarm.

"Books!" she'd say. "They're rotting your brain! Why can't you just go outside and play like other children?"

When I was old enough to know about both bras and sanitary napkins, she decided it was high time for me to leave the nest. "Don't you have any prospects?" she would nag. "When I was your age I was hanging out with my friends, flirting with the boys. You're never going to get married at this rate!"

I would pause from my reading and say, "Mother, I'm only fourteen. This isn't Kuwait."

She'd look over her shoulder, her cigarette poised in the air and her eyebrow angled haughtily—an homage to Dietrich, I suppose—and she'd snap, "Don't you use those big words with me, young lady. You think you're so high and mighty. Well, you're not. You're nothing. You're no better than I am."

Her vitriolic insistence that I wasn't worth squat had its way with me. The last ambition I experienced was in eighth grade. I desperately wanted to be class secretary. The prospect of reading the minutes to my fellow classmates filled me with the sort of joy that causes a person's toes to tingle. But I never gathered the courage to run for that office or excel in any other fashion. It was as though I lived forever in Opposite Day, a world where parents beat their breasts and pulled out their hair if their children met with success.

Mother's desire to live in a beige world unfettered by the pressures brought on by success and achievement wasn't simply because Daddy's abandonment of us had left her stark, raving mad. Not in the least. You see, my mother *believed* in mediocrity. She saw its potential. She thought that if everyone lived life haphazardly and half-assed, there would be no wars. She once said to me, "Matilda, overachievers are the unhappiest people in the world. They have ulcers and bad hearts. They make the rest of us uncomfortable."

Her faith in mediocrity was buoyed by her abiding laziness. Mother's was a life of sloppy hems, dirty floors, smeared mascara, a terrifyingly long succession of Patio Mexican TV Dinners, and inspirational platitudes feverishly ripped out of *Reader's Digest* and left to curl and rot on the refrigerator door.

She did manage, however, to become an Avon lady. She rarely got her orders exactly right and she often forgot to turn in her paperwork, but she could match eye shadows with nail colors like nobody's business. And I, for one, was fascinated by the lipstick samples that came in diminutive white tubes and were, in retrospect, shaped like miniature nuclear cooling towers.

If Mother caught me lingering over even so much as a nail polish she'd say breezily, the glint of a razor shimmering in her voice, "Hands off!" So I'd wait for her to go pick up a quart of milk at Winn-Dixie or to the movies with her man of the hour and then I'd rummage through the samples—Lilting Lilac eye shadow, Perfect Petal blush, Rendezvous Red lip gloss—momentarily believing with all my heart that cosmetics held the key to my future, that they would transform me into a grown-up woman who was as mysterious as she was alluring, a seductress who by the grace of God also managed to be of the highest moral fiber. Joan of Arc, Joan Crawford, and Joan Jett all wrapped into one fabulous package.

After spending a Sunday afternoon in front of the TV watching Elizabeth Taylor in *Cleopatra*, I stole from Mother's Avon-issued box of magic tricks the darkest eye shadow they made. Midnight Blue. Cream-based. I stood in front of my bedroom mirror and smeared it on. Two sweeping half moons that dramatically narrowed into cat-eye points at my temples. With my fair complexion, red hair, and blue eyes, the shadow made me look like a cross between Pippi Longstocking and the Joker. But at the time, I thought I was a knockout. That is, until my mother busted into my bedroom, took one horrified look, and proceeded to smack my face and shoulders, again and again, shouting that I was nothing but a show-off and she wouldn't have it. She just wouldn't.

To this day it annoys me that she was determined to keep all the Avon for herself. But perhaps her behavior was motivated by her sheer love for the stuff. Her favorite scent was Hawaiian Ginger and she'd drench herself in it even if she wasn't going anywhere. When she did make sales calls, she'd plaster onto her small face all the beauty products she could possibly manage—she was a thin tart of a woman—and inevitably her cheerleader smile would be compromised by lipstick-flecked teeth, a sin I vowed to never repeat.

Here's the enduring image I have of my mother: her leaving the house in a bright pink suit she bought at a church tag sale—her lip color the exact shade as her cotton candy blazer—lugging her samples to our VW, teetering on secondhand patent leather pumps, her golden hair falling messily out of the fancy bun she'd just spent thirty minutes fitfully pinning and spraying, sometimes yelling over her shoulder that she wouldn't have to work so hard if I weren't such a money pit.

As you can see, she was not a perfect mother. And even though in her entire life she never once told me she loved me, I have to believe she did. The alternative is too damaging to live with.

My feelings for her are, I admit, tangled. Sometimes untouchable. But when the recriminations, self-flagellation, and anger have waned, I am always left with this: I did feel a certain affection for her. Maybe it was love. Or pity. I'm not sure. But I know that even before Daddy disappeared into the night in search of the Greatest Show on Earth, I desperately wanted to please her, which meant not doing anything to attract attention or draw it away from her. So I kept my dreams to myself, painted my face when she wasn't home, learned to lock my bedroom door, pushed aside the occasional renegade aspiration, and slouched my way through the small secret pieties of inconspicuous survival. I did it for her *and* for me. Compliance was easier than confrontation and far safer than doing anything that might inspire or compel her to become a better mother. And although I understand that the healing and raising of a parent is not a child's job, I regret that I lacked the gumption to try.

Here is the nagging irony: Despite the fact that there were days I wished her dead, bitter hours spent in silent rants during which I convinced myself my life would be better off without her, I was saddened to the core—perhaps even set adrift—when she passed. The woman who gave birth to me in what she termed "a fit of pain so great I can never forgive you" died at forty from a brain embolism suffered while cutting a bachelor sheriff's toenails on our front porch.

There's an ugly truth buried in all of this. I could have left her. Nothing was stopping me, not after high school. I could have found myself a flophouse apartment, leaving her to stew and rot all on her own. But I didn't possess the conviction or the meanness. Despite her refusal to display toward me the merest hint of maternal affection and my eventual leaden acceptance of that state of affairs, I must have needed her. How else can I explain that her death left me feeling profoundly jilted—again? The fact that death chose her, that she didn't knowingly abandon me as Daddy did, was of little solace.

But, as I floundered in self-pity, I did discover some small measure of common ground with my mother. The afternoon I buried her—just as she had done with the knickknacks that had belonged to and defined my father—I embarked upon that most impossible of goals, one which she herself had struggled to attain: a clean slate.

I started by purging my life of Avon. Every lipstick, every bottle of foundation, every pressed or loose powder, every cologne bottle, every tacky eye shadow/blush duo, every brow liner I had coveted throughout my youth—I piled the works into the trunk of her VW Beetle. As I backed out of our driveway, I briefly imagined tossing it into the Intracoastal Waterway but reconsidered, fearing the toxins would leach into the environment, resulting in some nebulous, made-for-TV disaster—a fishkill or contamination of the city's water supply.

Someone in this town must need the makeup, I thought, as I made the turn onto Atlantic Boulevard. But who? What type of person would find joy and hope—as I did when I was a kid—by tinting one's cheekbones a sultry, smoky sienna? Who was that desperate and unloved?

Simply, quietly, while waiting for the traffic light to change, it came to me. Pregnant girls.

I felt oddly defiant as I bumped along the circular oak-lined drive of Our Mother of Perpetual Help's Home for Unwed Mothers. Relieved that there wasn't a nun in sight—imagine the Sisters with all that makeup!—I stopped short of the front doors, threw the VW in park, and waved down a huge-bellied child who was probably all of fifteen. As she waddled over, a mixture of suspicion and misery shadowing her bloated face, I got out of the car and popped open the trunk. Her eyes widened, momentarily sparked by the possibilities offered by moisturizers, pore cleansers, mascara. "Take it. It's yours," I said.

"Everything?"

"Everything."

My next stop was Beach Betty's Used Autos. Betty's son, Petey, told me I should have sold the Bug fifty thousand miles ago and then offered three hundred dollars. I stuck to my guns, pointing out that the upholstery was in good shape, the rust minimal.

"But the brake shoes are worn through."

"Petey, the junk man would give me more than three hundred. Do you want the car or not?" I said, surprised at my boldness.

After less than thirty minutes of haggling, I caught a cab home, five hundred bucks, cash, stashed in the recesses of my book bag.

Getting rid of the rest of Mother's belongings was surprisingly easy. Goodwill sent a truck over and the driver with the aid of his mildly mental but polite partner hauled everything away: her stuffed animals, her minor collection of ruby glass, her bedsheets, her dishes, her beauty magazines, her clothes (many of which she had purchased from Goodwill), her soiled sofa, her exercise mat, her hot curlers, her pastel pumps, her refrigerator magnets, her mirror-surfaced sunglasses, her stationery which she compulsively bought but never used (to whom was she going to write?—she claimed we had no relatives and even fewer friends), her Home Shopping Network cubic zirconia tennis bracelet, her many un-opened packages of panty hose, her rayon lingerie in various shades of plum and aqua, her high school yearbook, her bought-on-a-whim and never used Rollerblades, her brassieres (mystifyingly in six different sizes, cups A through C), her coffee maker, her mantillas which I occasionally caught her modeling in the bathroom mirror but which she never formally wore since she never went to Mass, her nail clippers, her ink-exploded Bic pens, her Swatch. This exodus of inanimate ob-jects went on and on until finally in the space of a single afternoon barely a trace of her was left.

The house was more problematic. I should have sold it but couldn't face the prospect of putting it on the market, and even though I readily accepted money for Mother's car, I viewed any proceeds from the sale of the house as blood money. Other than my paltry life, the house was the only link to my familial history. In terms of being connected to anything beyond myself—which is what religion is truly about—I viewed our two-bedroom, one-bath cinder block as a relic, sacred, and therefore beyond any monetary value.

So I gave it away.

I realize the contradiction, of course. Some people would argue that if the house was that special to me I should have hung on to it. But such reasoning suggests I was proud of my family's past. I wasn't. I was deeply ashamed. I was a high school graduate who worked a minimum-wage job answering the phone for Eternal Rest Funeral Homes, Incorporated and I couldn't name a single relative who had ever once inspired or challenged me to explore my ambitions, talents, dreams.

Add to this the fact that though I didn't realize it at the time, I was in mourning. For a mother newly deceased. For a father I never knew. For the little girl I should have been and the young woman I feared I would never become. Grief is the great jokester—he pulls our strings at whim, spurring us to collapse or run, masking our pain behind a scrim of daily practicalities and then revealing our anguish in such detail it's apparent to everyone but ourselves that we're slightly off. Believe you me, the grieving are sometimes the last to recognize their anger, hurt, disbelief, and confusion for what they truly are.

And so, I thought it was completely logical for me to give our house to the woman who lived next door. Our neighbor for nearly a year, she was a single working mother who, from the vantage point of my living room window, seemed to dote on her three children. A just and practical decision, I told myself over a solitary dinner of canned lima beans. Mother had been in the ground shy of a week and in that time I had determined that there was nothing keeping me in Jacksonville Beach, that there was no reason under the sun for me not to head down the road with my five hundred dollars and seek a fresh start. Slip the chains of the past, I silently lectured. Unburden yourself of the kind of life Mother would have predicted for you.

My plan did not work. The following morning when I pressed the keys into Eloise Johnson's fleshy palm, I did not feel free. In fact, the weight of the past bore down with greater ferocity. I walked away from the house and down the street, toward the pay phone on the corner, feeling stupid, hollow, foolish, knowing Mother had been right all along.

In this dark mood, I took a cab over to the bus station and bought a Greyhound ticket for as much money as I thought I could spare. Twenty-seven dollars poorer and by late afternoon I'd be disembarking in Tallahassee, a city that according to the tourist brochure I picked up off the ladies' room floor was "Florida with a Southern Accent!" The photos revealed rolling hills, moss-draped oaks, and azaleas as lush as crushed velvet.

The town also happens to be the state capital and home to two universities, one community college, and innumerable private institutions. Culinary. Secretarial. Medical assisting. Graphic design. Massage therapy. Acupuncture. Computer programming. Flight. Nail technology. Parachuting. Dance—ballroom to belly. Language. Modeling. Real estate. Beauty. Bead working. Needlepoint. You name it.

But as the old saying goes, Life is what you make it. Even after I'd settled into an apartment and secured a position as a convenience store clerk at the Suwannee Swifty on Apalachee Parkway and purchased from a starving graduate student a third-hand Yugo, I still did not avail myself of Tallahassee's educational opportunities. Nor did I keep abreast with the times. The world of ever-changing technologies—the Internet, Web sites, global communications—these were nothing more than rumors, catch phrases caught in the crab trap of time. My universe was composed of small cans of pork-'n'-beans and nylon roses. My goal was an unsullied job performance free of errors or brilliance. During those interminable eight-hour shifts spent ringing up Winstons, Michelobs, Mars Bars, pickled pigs' feet, and lotto tickets I was ever aware that I was invisible to most of the customers. It was as if the condensation that fogged the refrigeration units' glass doors also obscured me. But in my case, no one bothered to rub away the icy dew and peer in.

I accepted this. I viewed my unremarkable existence as my lot in life. It was as though from her padded cell in Heaven, Mother was still exerting control over my incredibly low standards.

That being said, working in a state of thoughtless anonymity is not as easy as it sounds. Being a convenience store clerk is a people job, after all, and people can be extremely difficult. For instance, if you possess even the slightest sense of self-preservation, you learn within the first week on the job that certain items must be slipped into brown paper bags the moment the customer places them on the counter. Single beers, skin magazines, rubbers, feminine hygiene products. If you fail in this duty you risk the indignant or embarrassed wrath of the overworked, oversexed, and overwhelmed.

Lack of confidence and money may have prevented me from enrolling in any of the local colleges but at night I attempted in my own meager way to compensate. I would come home to my efficiency apartment and take a shower, determined to wash off the store's stink: the stale popcorn, the sweat-soaked dollar bills, the permeating musk of tobacco, the cooked-to-leather rotisserie wienies, and thousands of other nearly imperceptible smells people left behind as their hands brushed my skin in the process of forking over money.

With a loofah and a bar of Irish Spring I would scrub myself in near-scalding water. When I smelled clean and simple again, I would dry off, fix a sandwich, and crawl into bed. There I would read good books and pretend that I was devouring them not because I loved literature but because a demanding, silver-haired, high-voiced college professor was forcing me to study. *Jane Eyre. Wuthering Heights. To the Lighthouse. My Ántonia.* I became each heroine, lived in castles across the sea and hovels on the prairie. It made for a rich, rich life. Some nights the imaginary professor would question me about the texts, and I forever gave brilliant answers and passed with A-pluses. Eventually, I would fall asleep, the book on my chest feeding my dreams.

Come morning I would push aside my reading material and lope out of bed, leaving my imagination tangled in the sheets. Then, as if I were a nun donning a habit, I would slip into my uniform: blue jeans, a clean white tee, and a Suwannee Swifty smock.

Six months. That's how far I was into my new life—which wasn't really any different than my old one except now that Mother was dead her stinging barbs seemed to have full-time access—when everything changed, when the safety and coziness of a life half-lived no longer seemed adequate.

Even widowhood (one of the sorriest of human conditions, a state of being that has much in common with blunt-force trauma) has not been able to extinguish the memories—the crisply edged details—of that day: He wore jeans and a black cotton T-shirt—no jacket—and the clear cold light of the North Florida winter tripped across his dark features as if pushed by the wind. I noticed this about him as soon as he stepped into the store. And also, his arms were huge—not grotesquely so, not like a bodybuilder's—but large enough that his shirtsleeves were stretched taut over his muscles, and I remember thinking that he must do something physical for a living, something which required an excess of upper body strength.

I felt strangely moved by the sight of him, as if I had known him my entire life but also impossibly certain that he was fundamentally different from anyone I had ever met. These opposing at-first-glance impulses could not be reconciled, nor could I snuff out my sudden infatuation. Quickly, before he had a chance to look in my direction and erode my invisibility, as though felled by a bullet I dropped to the floor.

Hidden behind the counter, I grabbed the first thing I could reach—a carton of safety matches—and obsessively began pulling out one small RoseBud brand box at a time, my plan being to repack them. Slowly. I wanted to stay busy. I wanted to remain anonymous. I wanted not to look like a lunatic.

From the sound of his footsteps, I discerned that he was heading to the coolers, near the juices. This is what saved me: Even at that moment, as I crouched on the floor, fighting with the matches, knowing that sooner or later I would have to stand and face him, I must have had some hint, some gut instinct, that ours was not a chance meeting, that anonymity and loneliness did not have to be my fate. In the hollow pathways of my psyche I must have said "yes" to notions of destiny and freedom and risk. I could not have explained it at the time as such. I was too panicked, too overwhelmed by angst seldom experienced by anyone older than fourteen. But in fairness to myself, it's the rare egg who can perceive life's imposed patterns, sanctions, gifts until long after the triggering event has passed. And so it was with me.

Rattled further by the vacuum-like swoosh of the cooler door slamming shut, I dropped the carton—matches scattered everywhere—and suddenly I was trapped in a frantic game of pick-up-sticks.

He reached the register sooner than I had expected and announced himself by clearing his throat.

"Be with you in a second," I said, trying to sound airy.

He leaned across the Formica counter, peered down, and asked, "Can I help?"

"No, no, no! I'm just, you know, straightening." I gripped the counter's edge and tried to stand with some modicum of gracefulness. As I rose to my feet he offered me his hand—I guess to be polite or steady me—but I did not accept, not trusting myself with the intimacy, regardless of how vague.

The next logical step would have been for me to say, "Will that be all for you today?" But I couldn't. My voice had fled along with my common sense. But he didn't seem to mind. He didn't fidget or huff or tell me to hurry. No glowering impatience. No superiority or disdain. He simply put his hands in his back pockets and said with humble clarity, "It's a nice day out."

I heard myself respond as if from afar, "Yes. Yes it is."

Those were our first words. To this day, in perfect order, I remember them. *Be with you in a second . . . Can I help? . . . No, no, no! I'm just, you know, straightening . . . It's a nice day out . . . Yes. Yes it is . . .* A meaningless exchange designed to hide the possibility that we were falling in love.

Our eyes briefly met and he flashed a gentle, wry smile that was tinged with what? Sadness? Regret? He looked down at his shoes and I out the plate glass window.

A car pulled up. Its driver got out and dropped two quarters in the newspaper machine. I compiled a split second mental list: Things I Know About Him. He spoke in a soft, halting coastal drawl. The whole of him—what I could see, face to fingertips—was finely boned yet his cheeks were graciously broad. As for his eyes, they were a haunting, wistful blue, nearly sapphire, and there was nothing unkind reflected there.

"Would you like your drink in a bag?" I asked, referring to the bottle of orange juice he'd set on the counter.

"I don't think so. You know, save the forest and all."

"That's good," I said, stupidly, and then with my heart fluttering like a tangled bird's I rang him up. He gave me exact change. As he pressed one dollar and twenty-six cents into my palm, I noticed the tattoo on his forearm. It was actually quite beautiful and I said so . . . *I like your tattoo* . . . the image of a dolphin riding white-capped waves, the words "Brothers Forever" etched in blue cursive script upon his cinnamon skin.

"I got it a long time ago."

"It's really . . . great." I looked over his head and tried to think of something fascinating to say. "I don't have any tattoos."

As soon as the sentence tripped my vocal cords I could have died of embarrassment. If the only conversation you can make borders on the insipid, I told myself, then keep your mouth shut.

"You're too pretty for tattoos. You don't need anything on your skin."

The compliment sent me spinning. I remembered my jewelry box doll—the one Daddy had given me—so perfect and appreciated in all her features—and then inexplicably, as the compliment sank in, I slipped off a shoe—one sensible shoe.

He turned two shades darker, however, and it became clear that he feared I had misconstrued his comment as a come-on. "I didn't mean that the way it sounded. It wasn't about being naked or anything. It's just—oh, man—it's just, you've got nice skin." He paused and rolled his eyes heavenward. "I'm sorry. I must sound like a jerk."

"No you don't. And thank you for the compliment."

"You're welcome." Again, he smiled, his eyes scanning my face, and I felt as though he were reading each hope, each fear of my hapless life. He stuck out his hand. It was scarred, callused. "My name is Nick. Nick Blue."

I placed my palm in his. "I'm Mattie."

We firmly shook—such an odd, old-fashioned gesture—and then fell silent again, as if we were too bashful to kick-start our future. But after several seconds I could bear the emptiness no longer. "I just moved here a few months ago," I said, "from Jacksonville."

"Really? That's the weirdest thing. I'm new in town, too."

"No way!"

"Yes!" he said incredulously, as if our timing had been dictated by the stars. "I moved up from the coast two days ago."

That's how it began, how we were suddenly engaged in something we couldn't control, nor did we want to, simply by indulging in that cornerstone of society called small talk.

People came and went all afternoon. When customers were in the store, he would disappear down an aisle, not to return until we were alone again. Each time I lost sight of him I feared that he had left and was gone forever, that the ebbing light of that cold day had stolen him from me.

I guess he must have felt a twinge of guilt, or at least uncertainty, about loitering (there was a sign posted, after all), because he kept buying things. Oreos, potato chips, trash bags, triple A batteries, a brownie, a can of beef ravioli, a car air freshener shaped like a tree. That was in the first two hours, alone. I lost track after the pop-up wipes and 40 weight motor oil. Come the end of my shift, I had to find him a box.

I decided I needed a fresh start . . . Yes, I know exactly what you mean . . .

That day, in the most unlikely place on the planet, surrounded by cigarettes and paper bags and shrink-wrapped honey buns, I began to discover a newfound confidence, a quiet off-the-cuff ease. How, you may ask, could a seemingly chance meeting between two strangers evoke such a change in me? How could I look at Nick Blue and decide that life was too interesting, too full of surprises, to remain bogged down in a thorny past? I believe the answer is deceptively simple: He saw in me what others had chosen to ignore. Goodness. Potential.

This is how I came to be more than a flicker in the world's peripheral vision. How I came to respect and value family. How I moved toward a deeper understanding of past wrongs. How I began to approach the future with both anticipation and forgiveness. *A stranger walked into a store . . .*

That night, long after we'd gotten a bite to eat at the diner down the street, we strolled along the shores of Lake Ella, and still I talked, on and on, exhausting him with my life story. My mother. My father. The Avon. The circus. Everything. I didn't know I had so many words inside me. By the oak where the children play, he turned to me, and held my hand, and pressed my palm against his heart.

Now, wandering through this fine mist of recollection and doubt, my memory stubbornly clings to the physical: his breath against my eyelids, his fingertips tracing my mouth, his arms pulling me tight, his lips finding first my cheek, then my lips.

But there was more to it than that. You knew it. You knew there had to be. With that kiss, we transcended the sum of our individual lives. We became more than human, more than we could have ever been alone. For a moment, we were gods, cast in a perfect state, gleaming eternally in the eyes of our imaginations, slipping this old earth, escaping for one unrepeatable instant the bruises and apathy of the times we lived in. I know it sounds fantastic, like a tale spun from ashes, a widow's cant, but what I say is true. The kiss plunged us into a sacred space. We were as one, afloat in a world of water and light and salt.

This kiss-induced sensation of full immersion in a salty body of water will not seem so unusual once you understand that Proteus Nicholas Blue was cut from the very skin of the sea.

I did not understand this myself, at first. But, of course, there was so much I didn't know.

Such as the push and pull water can exert on the soul, or that some people who are otherwise sane believe strongly in the following tenets — so strongly, in fact, that they view these beliefs as a sort of tide-born catechism:

Number one, tarpons are silver-skinned mermaids.

Number two, dolphins are the truest expression of a divine heart.

And number three, unnameable gods reveal their will in random splashes of sea spray.

Don't laugh. After all, are these beliefs any stranger than Moses parting the sea or Jesus turning water into wine or any of the numerous horrors predicted in Revelation? I think not.

But back to what I did not know.

I was caught totally by surprise by the idea that a person could be so affected by a place—by the scent of water—that his well-being was shattered if he ventured for too long beyond the ocean's reach.

I *love the sea. I love it so much. Sometimes I dream that I can breathe underwater. And then I teach you and we both swim away together, Mattie. I know it sounds crazy. But, baby, it's truer than true.*

This is where it gets tricky. Where I leave the world observed with my own two eyes and enter the realm religious folk refer to as faith. Because you see, to remember Nick fully, without reservation or meekness, I have to write about what I cannot possibly know, conjuring a world by connecting bits and pieces I've gathered here and there, coloring both supposition and fact with my own doubts, fears, wishes.

Other people's memories, I swallow them whole. A passing comment or a heartfelt recitation of the facts—it doesn't matter—I gobble them with equal greed, savoring each moment until there is no difference between my memories and theirs. If there is a gulf to cross between point A and B, I press on, guided by the full force of my imagination and intellect.

How do I know my version of Nick's life is accurate and pure? The same way saints and shamans know that what they saw was a vision versus a flight of fancy. They simply know it to be true. They believe. The fire in their bellies tells them it's so.

Yes, I am becoming religious. Ecumenical. My newfound zealotry should surprise no one. A wife's intuition is rivaled only by that of a widow's. Holy men have nothing on us. That being said, I must admit I do not choose this path willingly. Unwanted solitude and its accompanying pain have left me no choice. If I do not surround myself with memories—both stolen and otherwise—there is only absence.

It's a privilege, really, to explore Nick's life, to approach his days with wonder and awe, to slip inside his heart and become a faithful recorder. What divine irony that in the early days of my mourning, I have become my husband's attendant, his weaver of psalms.

Two days before Nick Blue took me in his arms and delivered a kiss so astonishingly sweet that even now—in the midst of my bewildered mourning—it makes me smile, he had quit the sea. Quit it for good. He had given to his baby brother, Demetrius, his nets, his culling iron, his muddy white crabbing boots, his wooden oyster tongs, his yellow rain slicker, his ice chests, his flounder gig, his compass which no oysterman would ever be without, his gloves, his hard hat with the halogen searchlight duct-taped to the front (his lucky flounder light, he called it), and even his lifetime supply of WD-40 which he used to keep the pulleys and gears of their small shrimp boat in some semblance of working order.

Having divested himself of the many tools and gadgets necessary in the life of a commercial fisherman, he decided there was no reason for him to even live on the island any longer. The island, named Lethe in honor of the mythological river of forgetfulness (when I asked Nick, "Forget what?" he said, "Anything you need to"), is an offshore bump in the sea just a few miles south of the North Florida mainland. Except in a dense fog, the island is easily discernible from the handful of fishing villages clustered along the winding, convoluted shore. Tourists and locals, alike, have been known to gaze out across Carrabelle Bay to the gentle rise of Lethe and whisper, "My God. Paradise!"

When Nick announced to his mother, who also lives on the island, that he was "packing it in," he did so in the room of her house where all major announcements were made: the kitchen. He stood with the refrigerator door open, staring into it as if it were an icebox chock full of genies, then slammed it shut and said, "Mama, I'm packing it in. Think it's best if I got a job on the hill. I done told Demetrius." The sleeves of his T-shirt were stretched out of shape, as all his T-shirt sleeves were, owing to the size of his arm muscles.

His mother paused from the business of cooking supper and tried unsuccessfully to harden her heart to what her son had just told her. Having placed on her butcher block a crock filled with Yukon Gold potatoes, she attempted to scoot past his words by concentrating on the task at hand: *Peel the potatoes. Don't forget to put the skins in the garden compost. Boil potatoes until tender. Puree with warm cream and butter. Season with salt and pepper and top with garlic chives which need to be snipped from the herb patch out back.*

In the same way people recite a mantra to help them slip into meditation, she ran through the progression of raw potato to mashed, but this time her old trick failed her and she got no further than *until tender* when the tears started to fall.

Nick planted his hands on his hips, pinned his gaze to a knot in one of the pine floor planks, and waited for his mother to compose herself. He did not wrap his arms around her because he knew a caring gesture would cause her to completely break down—something they both would regret. So he watched the floor until she cleared her throat. At that point he looked at her—most likely it was a gentle glance, for he loved his mother with a pathos-filled loyalty common between mothers and sons.

She pushed a wisp of hair off her forehead with the hand that held her potato peeler and said, "I don't want you to go. But I'll feel better if you're off that water."

As for Demetrius, who is two years Nick's junior and sports the smile of someone who is perpetually wonder-struck, he saw his brother off at the community dock where their skiff was moored. Nick and his brothers built the tomato red wooden boat in the summer of Nick's thirteenth year. I'm not sure who named the fourteen-foot flat-bottom runabout, but painted in yellow across its bow was the unlikely moniker *Poseidon*.

Nick and Demetrius avoided the verbal fencing of a long goodbye.

This was due in part to the fact that Demetrius didn't believe his brother could stay away for very long.

"My guess is I'll be seeing you sooner than later."

"No, Dem, you won't. I fed those wild cats this morning but you're going to have to do it from here on out."

"If you say so."

Nick started up the motor and began to idle away from the dock. Demetrius wildly waved and yelled, "Your stuff will be here when you get back."

"Take care of Mama," Nick hollered. Then he threw open the throttle and zipped across the bay.

The Ancients believed that if a person were to successfully leave the underworld and return to the land of the living, they had to drink from the River Lethe. In so doing, their memories would be wiped clean. They could then begin their lives anew, as if they were children—no history, no recollection of pain or mourning or bliss.

I believe that is what Nick was trying to do—cobble together a life that had utterly nothing to do with his past, with the core of who he truly was.

Once onshore, he unloaded his few belongings: a brown bag filled with various canned goods which his mother had hysterically removed from her own cupboard so "he wouldn't starve to death" and a duffel bag containing three pairs of jeans, five sleeve-misshapen T-shirts, seven pairs of undershorts, his razor, a horse conch shell, and a fading color photograph of his parents. He carefully set everything into the cab of his truck. I think he believed that if he was meticulous in the way he firmly wedged the sack between the dash and door, that perhaps an innate order would descend upon him and his new life, an order that had nothing to do with nature's cycles and the mythology of man.

He climbed into the Fordge—that's what he called his truck with its Ford cab and Dodge bed—and sat for a moment with the door open, staring out at Lethe and the bay, the only world he had ever known. I'm uncertain as to whether he shed a tear or two—he never told me—but I doubt it. He wasn't given to tears. I have seen him, though, so profoundly shaken that his hands whitened with sadness, preventing him from lifting a coffee cup to his trembling lips.

So I must ask, Were his hands white with grief as he gazed at the place that was the tap root of his soul? Did his lips tremble as he turned the key in the ignition? Did the faint wrinkles around his eyes—lines etched by three decades on the water—smooth into a merciless resignation as he shifted the truck into gear? Was the tightness in his chest nearly unbearable, so much so that for at least one clarion moment he considered getting back in that skiff and returning home? As his tires spun on the oyster shell path and as that wink of green and blue disappeared in his rearview mirror for what he thought was the final time, was my husband-to-be seized by a blind, slow panic?

Very simply, yes.

Let me make the enormity of his decision perfectly clear. Here was a man who had spent virtually every second of his life on or beside the water. And even though he made his living by taking from the sea, he did not do so indiscriminately or irresponsibly. In fact, if there was ever a man who approached the sea with a near religious reverence, it was Nick Blue.

Hanging above the door to his house were three stamped tin images he bought in a tourist shop in the Greek-settled village of Tarpon Springs, a Gulf Coast town about a hundred and fifty miles south of Lethe. An ear. An eye. A heart. He said the trinkets reminded him of how people on Lethe were supposed to live: listening and watching with honest, fair intentions. "If you don't sit down, shut up, and watch the sea, you won't know when the shrimp are spawning or what time of year the snook come into the harbor or even when the turtles nest. If you don't know this stuff, it's too easy to mess it all up," he told me.

In the short run, his ethics cost him money but as he would say, slipping into the regional dialect (something he did with amazing ease, considering that most of the time he spoke in rhythms mirroring his mother's easy-listening drawl), "At least I ain't stealing. Dem boys who take a coupla extra redfish here and dere? Who think legal limits don't apply to dem? De stealing from de own pockets. That bay out there, she just one big giant nursery. You don't treat her right, you got trouble on your hands."

A year before we met, he got into a fistfight with a recreational fisherman who hooked an undersized red but instead of releasing the fish tossed it on the beach to die. Nick's mother said her son strutted around Lethe showing off that black eye with all the pride of a peacock in full bloom.

I don't think Nick ever truly came to terms with the fact that as he farmed the warm shallow waters of the area's bays and marshes, inevitably there were unintended kills. He searched for a balance, though, between impact and stewardship. He installed a turtle excluder device—a thingamajig that enables a netted turtle to free itself—before the state required it. He and Demetrius were constantly rethinking the configuration of their nets to try to reduce by-catch. If, perchance, a pelican got caught in the net's webbing Nick would spend whatever time it took to free the bird, talking to it all the while. For his high school science project, he consulted a marine biologist from Florida State University and together they determined that to remove the meat-filled claw of the stone crab with the least amount of pain and trauma to the animal, the crabber should first fully extend the claw and then break it off cleanly at the joint. The fisheries commission was so impressed that its chairman, Mr. Carl A. Lykes, wrote Nick a letter on official stationery that was a wonder to touch with that textured surface and gold embossed seal, thanking him for his "fine work on behalf of Florida's natural resources."

The fact of the matter is, Nick was considered a conservationist even among overzealous marine patrol officers. Not that all marine patrol officers took themselves too seriously but a few would rather give a mullet fisherman a ticket than save a drowning man. Everybody said so. But that's not my point. My point is, here we have Nick Blue, a person who grew up believing that his primary duty as a fisherman was to nurture the sea, and inexplicably he's barreling down Highway 98 to seek a job with an independent contractor who cut down trees and sold them to St. Joseph Paper Company, the largest private landowner in the state.

On the surface of things, it made no sense. Even the circumstances of his birth suggest that Nick's destiny was tied to salt and water, not dirt and trees. Yes, from the very beginning, Nick Blue was a water baby.

It was March 22, 1967, half past ten in the evening, and Nick's father, George Blue, being a nighttime shrimper, wouldn't be back on the hill—as the locals called land—for another nine hours or so. As is often the case with North Florida's early spring, winter had made a sudden reappearance, threatening the azaleas' extravagant blossoms and prompting George Blue, who was trawling the bay for brownies and hoppers, to pause from his on-deck work and slip into the engine room to put an extra blanket over Lillian, his wife of fifteen years and whose job on the *Lillian B*, he reminded her each time she insisted on going out with him, was to sleep. To that end, he had built for her a bunk complete with a down-filled mattress and a light to read by.

The bunk, of course, offered a comfortable place to do things other than sleep, an advantage that I'm sure did not escape George Blue as he labored to router the yellow pine edges smooth and shellac its swirled grain against all possibility of splinters. In fact, being a man of amorous body and soul, he even constructed drawers beneath the bunk which latched shut to guard against them being flung open during rough seas and into which he placed various vials of sweet-smelling oils, crystal bottles filled with balm, and other feminine bric-a-brac which he deemed essential to unlocking his wife's ardor. A cobalt bottle of Evening in Paris cologne nestled in a padded, ribboned box. Gardenia-scented moisturizer and dusting powder. A satin vellum-colored negligee with matching slippers. A lidded basket containing hard sour candies—he would have preferred chocolates but rejected them as being too impractical (this was a shrimp boat, after all). A leatherbound book of poems by Mrs. Elizabeth Barrett Browning. And best of all, a silver-plate hairdressing set comprised of mirror, brush, and comb and onto which he had her initials engraved in a flourishing script: LAB, which stood for Lillian Athena Blue.

At thirty-two, Lillian was ten years her husband's junior, with a practical streak larger than the Gulf itself. She was charmed by George's amorous bent. She often told him, "George, dear, you were born into the wrong time. You're such a romantic. Nobody's a romantic anymore."

But her amusement wasn't enough to push her over the edge—she was damned and determined not to give in to her husband's lofty notions of physical love. It wasn't that she didn't enjoy sex—she liked it fine—she just didn't see the need to add any bells and whistles to it.

She was happy, though, with those drawers George built for her. "Perfect!" she said as he demonstrated how smoothly they slid in and out on their oak runners. "I've been needing a place to stash my socks."

However great the differences in how they viewed the negotiations of sexual love, perhaps George was onto something with his treasure chest of intended aphrodisiacs. Take as evidence the fact that the couple had been childless for the first thirteen years of their marriage and it wasn't until George built his little cubbyhole of a love nest that Lillian conceived. First came Zeke, followed in two years by the pint-sized fellow swimming in her belly on the night of March 22.

Lillian insists that all three of her children were conceived at sea, and I have no reason to doubt this. Of course she would know the exact date and time of her various conceptions. Blessed, that's what some folks would say she was, because underpinning her hard-nosed practicality was an abiding and even spooky intuition. The woman could discern her family and friends' fears and hopes with all the efficiency of a pediatrician capable of diagnosing measles at twenty yards out. And if perchance she was wrong, like the pediatrician, she prudently never admitted it.

On the face of things, it would seem neither her intuition nor her practicality was in working order when she insisted on going with George that night. After all, what would possess a woman who was eight months pregnant and counting to go out on a shrimp boat on an unpredictable spring evening?

To do her job. Sleep.

In its seventh month of *in vivo* existence, the baby suddenly became a tiny bundle of perpetual motion. At first Lillian joked that the child must be practicing for a career involving speed and stamina. "Maybe it's going to grow up to be a baker," she said to George one bleary-eyed morning over coffee.

"Baker?" George had no idea what baking and speed had in common but he rubbed her shoulders anyway. He gazed at the lovely hollow at the base of his wife's hairline and decided that if the baby's behavior meant anything it most likely involved athleticism.

Wistful notions about what profession the child might pursue soon withered as the baby's activity continued unabated. He behaved as if he were his own one-man conga line. It was enough to make even the most patient woman irritable, snappish, downright bitchy.

But she did her best to remain civil (with varying degrees of success) while simultaneously attempting to trick, cajole, and convince the child that floating could be just as much fun as nonstop *in utero* gymnastics. Since George shrimped at night she had the bed all to herself and, therefore, did not feel self-conscious as she tried to calm the baby by lying in various positions. Flat on her back, her arms extended. Flat on her back, patting her belly. Flat on her back, her arms akimbo. Flat on her back, singing "Fever!" (She loved Peggy Lee.) On her side. On her side with her feet pulled close to her fanny. On her side, her legs scissored. Flat on her back again, spread-eagled. One foot on the floor. One knee bent, the other prone. Both knees bent, rocking.

Nothing worked.

Predawn, she would hobble out of bed, go into her kitchen—her hands on either side of her belly as if it were an enormous bowl of Jell-O—and fix herself a cup of hot tea with lemon and tupelo honey. She would wander the house, sipping her tea and bargaining with her baby. "If you settle down, just for a little while, I'll feed you warm milk with vanilla and sugar all the days of your life."

Gentle negotiations, however, proved fruitless. On day fifteen of the sleepless siege, she resorted to damnations and threats, the brunt of which she aimed at George. He would walk into the kitchen, minding his own business, thinking he might rustle up a cookie or two, and Lillian would take aim and fire: "If this child doesn't give me some peace soon, I'm going to lose my mind. How in the hell does God expect me to bring a healthy child into this world if I can't get one wink of sleep! I heard you in there, snoring away! And me in the shape I'm in!"

The normally robust Lillian stopped deadheading her roses, began serving her husband TV dinners, forgot to brush her hair, and spent hours in the tub each night, hoping it would relax her and—more importantly—put an end to the child's ceaseless fidgeting.

Nothing doing. After a month and a half with no rest, she determined that the only thing she hadn't tried was lulling the unborn baby to sleep on the Gulf's gentle swells. Being on the water almost always put her to sleep, she reasoned, so perhaps it would have the same tranquilizing effect on her baby.

Lillian's plan was not well received. Her sister, Diana, who was three years older with two children of her own, told her it was far too dangerous and that, besides, if she would just hold on for a few more weeks the baby would be born and at that point sleep wouldn't even cross her mind.

Her brother-in-law, Dicky Crum, adjusted his toothpick to the side of his mouth and said, "Shrimp boat ain't no place for a pregnant lady."

Her husband looked into his wife's bloodshot eyes and said nothing because he recognized the ruthless determination of a woman who was at her wit's end, and in his book that was a frightening place for a wife to be.

Once George caved, everyone else soon followed. Diana offered to baby-sit Zeke. She had a two-year-old herself, a little black-eyed, blond-curled girl named Charis whose greatest joy in life was to bite Cousin Zeke and then scream as if she had been wronged. As for Dicky Crum, he wisely kept his mouth shut.

George was a big man. Six feet and one half inch. Biceps the size of hams thanks to twenty-three years spent hauling nets and wrestling crab traps. So hefting Lillian Blue, who weighed a pregnant one hundred and fifty pounds, onto the *Lillian B* was not a chore for George. In fact, it was a pleasure.

There he was, dressed in his rubber boots and a slightly moth-eaten woolen peacoat, doting on his wife, which was his greatest and rarest joy. In the chilly twilight, he cradled his big-bellied woman as if she were a swaddling child and barreled down the dock toward his shrimp boat. He didn't even have to buck up when he lifted her over the sides— he was that strong. He also didn't need to carry her—she was pregnant, not paralyzed—but he insisted on the grounds that she wasn't in her right mind and, therefore, there was no way he was going to allow her to waddle down the uneven and warped boards of the dock under her own steam.

She was right, of course, about what her baby needed. Her head had no sooner hit the pillow when the tidal wave in her womb that had been kicked up by that restless little creature began to ease. She put her hand on her belly and said, "It's about time."

Gratefully, she shut her eyes and summoned images of her and her child sharing vanilla and sugar milk each afternoon in the comforting warmth of her cluttered kitchen with its charming collection of ceramic chickens when the moment she had been longing for finally arrived: Like a woman floating through the depths of a cool, safe, bottomless well, she descended into a deep and dreamless sleep.

She had inserted her earplugs to muffle out the sound of the engine but it was narcotic, wonderful, needed, impenetrable sleep that prevented her from becoming cognizant of the chaos that soon descended all around her. When the aluminum coffeepot clattered across the hot plate, slammed into the cookie tin, and hit the floor, she did not wake. When her jadeite mug sailed off the small Formica table and shattered beside the bed, she did not wake. When the dime-store picture of the Lord Jesus Christ rattled on the wall as if an unseen hand had seen fit to shake it, she did not wake. Even when a lightning bolt struck so dangerously near that the air in the engine room turned acrid, still she did not wake.

Lillian Blue may have been privy to the kind of hypnotic sleep that with any luck clamps down upon the hopelessly overwhelmed, thus rendering her completely unaware, but I'm convinced that the child in her stomach—that nub of a human who had only recently lost his embryonic gills—knew exactly what was breaking loose over Apalachee Bay. I believe that as Nick Blue floated deep within the amniotic pool of his mother's womb, he heard the wind howl across the face of the sea. He felt the *Lillian B* roll and tilt as the bay's deceptive tranquillity erupted into a roller coaster of angry waves. He heard the thunder unfurl through both time and space and thought it was calling his name.

What an aching surprise that had to be—that sudden tugging urge to leave the domed shelter of his mother's belly. In the womb he had lived the life of a tiny god, his every need attended to by the vast machinery of his mother's body. He had not rested because his happiness would not allow it. In the dawning hours of his existence, he was frolicking. He may have been little more than a fetus, but he was already enamored with the sensation of dipping and spinning in a salty sea.

But as is the case with all mere mortals, a banishment from his state of grace was inevitable. Indeed, in the midst of his mother's contented snoring and as the *Lillian B* came perilously close to listing in the pounding waves, the child shuddered with the vague notion of paradise lost. He nudged his head against the widening eye of his mother's cervix. His bittersweet longing to stay put wavered as he became aware of a slight burning in his veins. Whatever was causing this slow singe, he wanted more of it. He needed to be able to open his little mouth and take in not water but this new thing that he craved. He worked his jaws, opening and closing, and his lungs began to expand, to push against the thin wall of his chest, in preparation for the nectar that was sure to come.

When the first birth pain struck, Lillian squeezed in her suddenly fisted hands the blanket that George had pulled up over her just thirty minutes before. She screamed for her husband but the wind which howled siren-like muffled her cries for help. Her firstborn, Zeke, had entered the world slowly, as if he didn't want anything to do with this earthly life. She was in labor for a full two days before the doctor, huffing and sweating, finally pulled the child out with forceps.

But this baby was different. There was no slow, inexorable march toward rapid contractions. They hit her with full-tilt fury, the pains relentlessly belting the wide circumference of her belly. She threw back her head, arched her neck, and pushed as hard as she could.

If she just had someone to help her, she thought. Just a little help.

George had no idea that there was a birth in progress on the *Lillian B.* And if he had known, there is little he could have done to help his wife, preoccupied as he was with preventing the boat from going down. The squall had blown in without warning, from the east—an uncommon but not unheard-of direction for a storm at that time of year. He had quickly pulled in and secured his nets and was attempting to set the anchor when the wind and water abruptly kicked the stern a good three feet into the air. George lost his footing and hurled like a pinball down the rain-slick deck. This giant of a man spun as if weightless, his legs snagging in a coil of rope and net, his head smashing into the rusting hardness of the iron winch. He shook off the blow and tried to sit up. Something warm streamed into his eye. He swiped at it and looked at his hand: blood. He pawed at his legs. His ankle, caught in the net's webbing, was grotesquely twisted.

The *Lillian B* slammed into the gullet of a wave and a wall of water cascaded over the sides. Blinded by the rush of water and driving rain, George helplessly clawed at the darkness, groping at his foot, pulling at the labyrinth of hemp and nylon. He remembered the knife in his back pocket. He reached for it, flipped open the blade, but was knocked backward again as the *Lillian B* heaved under the force of the surging tide. He landed belly down, the knife slicing a half moon into his thigh, the air popping from his lungs. Pain shot from his ankle, up through his groin, and he doubled over, crumpled in the grip of the storm.

Certain that he had been abandoned by God, George's mind filled with a blank whiteness, his sole comfort: the taste of his own blood as it flowed from his busted lip onto his tongue. The sound of the raging wind was deafening; he mistook it for his beating heart.

A clap of thunder boomed across the water, shaking the very ribs of the boat. It was at that moment, when he thought the *Lillian B* might come apart like so many matchsticks in the merciless sea, that he re-membered something: He was not alone. Lillian. Oh my God, yes. Lillian. Lillian. Her name crossed his battered lips and then he let loose with a scream so primal it must have sent the stars hidden in the firmament spinning.

George Blue was a Herculean beast, not a man, when he sat up on all fours and dragged himself to the wheelhouse, the tangled mass of rope and net trailing behind him like a lumbrous tail. Suddenly the world was a simple place, the darkness ablaze with his focus. He had to pull the *Lillian B* around. Had to face her into the wind and set that anchor. He would not allow his dear wife to die at sea. That was his fate, not hers.

Lillian's pain was the color of snow. The coldness of it blinded her. It burned through the layers of her skin even as it froze her contractions into a solid mass that began at her navel and radiated out.

Perhaps if she had been delivering this child in a hospital with doctors and nurses and her husband at her side so she could have screamed at the assemblage, she would have momentarily given up. No more strength, she might have said. I can't do it. I just can't. But there was no one to say that to, no one to fleetingly project her exhaustion onto while her body struggled toward the inevitable. No one to testify to her courage, pain, frustration. Not a single witness to her howling, dying animal agony. So after these words crashed across her tongue: "George

Blue, damned if I'll ever let you touch me again," she lifted herself up on her elbows, gritted her teeth, and pushed one last time.

The peculiar smell of her own insides filled the engine room as she felt her baby slide out. Grunting with the effort, she leaned forward and took the child in her arms. Pinch-faced and bloody, he bellowed as that first rush of oxygen flooded his hungry lungs. Lillian opened one of the drawers beneath the bunk and reached in for the pair of scissors she kept there, all the while managing to keep a grip on this little creature who was slippery as a fish.

She then proceeded to perform a task that would make most any man faint dead away: She cut her baby's umbilical cord—snipped right through it with one sure motion. If she'd been a less practical woman or one who suffered from a frail constitution, there may have been a hesitation mark or two. But that was not the case. She was all about the business of life. Whatever it took. However ugly it got. She didn't allow herself to feel a single bittersweet pang as she severed the cord that had connected her to this child these past eight and a half months. No. She simply did what was necessary and then tied it off. Next, she put the child to her breast, lay back against her pillow, and endured the after-birth—that purging of the placenta from her womb—with the quiet, practiced efficiency of a woman who understands that nature almost always takes its course.

Imagine George's utter shock when, after he had secured the *Lillian B* and the storm had begun to subside, he threw open the hatch to the engine room—blood still streaming down his face, his twisted ankle throbbing—to view a holy sight, indeed: his wife fast asleep, a baby boy suckling her breast. For a moment or two, he must have felt that it was all a dream. The storm and the gouge on his head and his wife's peaceful slumber as their son sucked away. Or perhaps he thought he was dead.

George did not put out his nets again that night. Rather, he busied himself with his true calling, with the one thing in life that gave him unmitigated happiness. He pampered his wife. He heated water, removed her clothes, and bathed her in the gardenia-scented bath oil that he had tucked into that drawer over two years before. He changed the sheets and fed her sweet warm tea with half-and-half. He soothed her skin—head to toe—with the gardenia body lotion. As she cuddled her baby, he combed the tangles from her black hair. And when she offered him his son—just as he did when Zeke was born—George Aristotle Blue cried.

In the wee hours of the morning, George tucked a pillow in the drawer, bundled his son in the silk negligee which his wife had never worn, and set the sleeping child sweetly on the pillow. The baby resembled a little prince, swaddled in silk, surrounded by scent bottles and the glint of silver. George eased into bed with his wife, who lightly rested her hand on the rising and falling chest of her newborn.

No longer in constant motion, the baby slept. Other than the steady, slow dance of his chest, the only thing moving was his eyes. They darted back and forth behind the paper-thin wafers of his closed lids. But what does a four-hour-old child dream about? Were his visions spun of ashes or earth? Womb or water? Did he possess a self-image—something visual, palpable, tactile? Or did he see sounds? Yes, this is what I want to know: In what language did my future husband dream?

In light of these ponderous questions I must admit I gain solace from recounting Nick's birth—from imagining how in the faint dawning light of March 23, 1967, as the Gulf lapped gently against the hull of the *Lillian B*, his mother looked for signs of herself in her child.

I close my eyes and see it all so clearly. A faint, prideful smile slips across her face as she marvels over his full head of hair—black ringlets just like her own father. I see him wrap his tiny hand around her finger, and I know that she welcomes his strong grip, believing as she does that it signals good, moral character. With more curiosity than disappointment, she notes that he has his father's long, black lashes and high forehead. And even though it is a bit difficult to tell—him being less than a day old and all—she gains comfort by her certainty that he has her nose, a thin blade of a nose that suggests good breeding.

Please, do not doubt me about these facts which I have gleaned and conjured. Do they harm you? Do they harm anyone? I think not. So give me this, the faint flutter of joy I gain from remembering a certain sweet moment: She touches the dimple at the center of his drool-damp chin, awestruck at his perfection, and whispers, "I love you."

The name, of course, was terribly odd. No one in their right mind calls a child Proteus. Lucky for Nick, his grandmother stubbornly refused to refer to him by anything other than his middle name (one that he shared with his fraternal grandfather). But the circumstances of Nick's birth, coupled with the fear the storm awakened in George, spurred Lillian toward Proteus as a kind of invisible talisman.

She knew her Greek mythology. Her uncle, John Pappas, was a professor of ancient studies at Florida State. When she was just a wisp of a girl, she would sit on her porch which overlooked a sweeping bend in the Ocklocknee River while Uncle John regaled her with tales of gods and goddesses, love and betrayal, retribution and triumph.

Lillian's favorite was Proteus, a sea god, the son of Poseidon, a dashing immortal who could shape-shift his way out of danger. She developed a mad crush on this mythic hero when she was twelve. She envisioned him as a golden-haired, wide-shouldered heartthrob whose only goal in life was to attend to her every need. Lying in the hammock, her uncle's voice fading into the dappled leaf-littered shadows, she would close her eyes and pretend that she and her young lover were in some sort of mysterious, sexually charged peril. In her mind's eye, she grew faint. Her beautiful slim hands trembled. She collapsed into Proteus' arms and—this is the part she loved the most even though it shamed her by its utter strangeness—he kissed her (on the lips, no less!), magically transforming them both into graceful, arch-necked swans who preened over each other before gliding across a nameless but hauntingly beautiful lake in the glow of a gentle sunset.

I suppose it could be argued that's what Nick was doing when he left Lethe—shape-shifting away from whatever nebulous dangers the sea might have in store for him. But I couldn't have known that the day he walked into the Suwannee Swifty. I could not have known that he was a man on the run, fleeing a place he loved because he feared for his life.

*S*ometimes *when I'm out there on that water all alone, when it's just me and my nets and that big starry sky, I get real lonesome. I mean all kinds of lonesome. You know, like the night might not end and I'll never see another human again and maybe I won't ever, ever get back to land. It's then that the singing starts. Beautiful faraway singing. Never been able to figure out where it's coming from but I'm telling you, Mattie, the songs are so pretty they bring tears to the eyes.*

*O*urs was not a slow love affair. Nor even a coy one. Pretense. Resistance. Feminine modesty. None of these things intersected the tight circle of our desire. We went at it as if it were our duty, as if the longing that began in the pit of our stomachs and then unleashed itself in unrepentant waves was the fruit of the righteous.

We observed one another's expressions of ecstasy with rapturous intent: the sudden gasp, the moan that slips through parted lips, the eyes that wander the body as if it were a canvas, the rounded hips that rise to meet a foreign hardness, the mouth that widens in surprise and then seeks a patch of flesh as the world falls away, the moist skin that pulses beneath a single fingertip.

Lucky for me our relationship started out with roaring intensity. I didn't have time to keep my arctic heart frozen. I was too busy, too downright blissful, enjoying the meltdown.

Now, this is not to say that Nick deflowered me. Until I fell in love with him, I was inhibited. Yes.

Frigid? Yes.

But dysfunctional? No.

In addition to my clandestine and embarrassingly hopeless infatuations with old men movie stars, I'd thawed out enough to have sex on three previous occasions. These encounters could not be considered "good" or even "enjoyable." Compared to what Nick and I had together, these earlier sexual experiences are most aptly described as being akin to a rather uncomfortable bodily function.

The first time was with Jeff Newberry in the front seat of his father's Jeep after a Fletcher High football game. It was an overcast night and we were parked on the hard-packed sands of Jacksonville Beach along with a hundred other teenage-driven cars. I really didn't want to have sex with him but saying "no" is sometimes amazingly difficult. My mother had taught me to be compliant. Polite. To not make waves. And while amiable agreeability is well suited to some situations, such as the classroom, in other arenas—say, the dark interior of a Jeep with a boy who's pulling down his pants—well-mannered compliance completely neutralizes all notions of chastity.

Let me go on record and say, Jeff was a lousy lover. Maybe it is this way with all seventeen-year-old boys, but to Jeff sex was all about himself. So much so that when I finally summoned a sense of humor about losing the tender cherry, I nicknamed him Master Bating.

I wish it had been different. I wish that much lauded "first time" had been with someone I cared about and that it made me feel beautiful, wanted, special. But given Master Bating's technique—or lack of it—it's a minor miracle that the very next day I didn't rush over to the Sisters of Mercy and sign up. There was no furtive searching of my soft hidden folds. Not even a rub or two. He simply spread open my legs and, without my expecting it, shoved himself inside me. As my flesh ripped, I screamed. In response, he clamped his hand, which smelled like a mustard-slathered relish dog, over my mouth. He then proceeded to thrust wildly, again and again, and I remember thinking, Whatever it is this guy's doing just might kill me. When he came, he grunted, shuddered all over as if wracked by his own personal earthquake, and then collapsed on top of me in a sweaty heap of dead weight.

And what did I do? I'm ashamed to admit it, but in my mind's eye I watched my mother shimmy for the stranger on the couch. As Master Bating pounded into me with no tenderness whatsoever, I stood just outside the orbit of her dance, a rising tide of nausea flooding my belly and then blossoming like a stain across my tongue. I looked into his face—his rigid jaw muscles, his unblinking eyes that were fixed on some point beyond my shoulder—and I began to feel as if I was rotting from the inside out. I wondered if that's how my mother felt all those years with all those men. Rotting.

It wasn't until Master Bating withdrew from me and yelled, "Shit!" because he saw the mix of semen and blood on his father's velour seat cover that I realized my face was frozen into a copycat expression of my mother's four-corner, cheerleader's smile. An involuntary but genetically mandated physical reaction? A woefully inept disguise intended to shield me from myself? Or maybe—like my mother—I was just trying to get along.

But Master Bating did not see it that way. "What's so funny, you idiot?" he yelled. "Look what you did! My dad's gonna kill me!"

That night when I returned home, my mother—dressed in leotards and a black midriff bra, her face fully made up and a cigarette dangling from her frosted lips—was lying on the floor performing sit-ups. Fitness had become very important to her. In fact, every morning she flipped on one of those cable exercise shows and watched the steel-bunned, fur-chested man exhort in an Eastern European accent, "You can do it. You can do it!" while she enjoyed the day's first smoke.

There I stood, between the hallway and the living room, wishing the pain between my legs would ease and watching my mother's valiant struggle to bend at the waist. I noticed how her teeth clamped down on the cigarette as if she might bite it in two and how her belly—despite her best efforts over the years—had grown soft and doughy, and the words just bubbled out. "Mother, I love you."

She kept her face pointed at the ceiling but her eyes darted toward me. The corner of her lips twitched as if she were preparing to say something. A space opened up in that room—a small silence that parted the air—and for a couple of seconds I thought she and I might actually have a chance—not at mother-daughter closeness—but at the type of honesty that passes between co-workers or fond acquaintances.

But it never happened. All too quickly that small slit of opportunity mended itself. Mother's eyes returned to their dead-ahead stare and she lifted her torso off the floor and touched an elbow to her bended knee.

I will spare you the details of my other two sexual encounters except to say they were with a man who was twelve years my senior and who was only slightly more attentive than Master Bating.

So I think you will agree that I was long overdue in finding a gentle, caring lover. But Nick—at least while we were courting—was also adventuresome. He enjoyed dangerous places. Such as under the twinkling holiday lights of a canopy oak in a public park in downtown Tallahassee at 3 A.M. The ladies' bathroom of a Mexican restaurant named Cabo's. The front lawn of the Capitol Building at dawn. And, of course, there was the checkout counter at the Suwannee Swifty. We got caught during that particular tryst by a seventy-some-year-old gentleman who'd come in to buy lotto tickets. At first I wasn't sure if he realized what he'd walked in on but as he slipped his five tickets into his wallet, he said, without looking up, "I was once young myself."

Nick preferred to make love with all the lights on. Either that or in the middle of the day. He would hold my face and say, "I want to see you. Everything about you. I want to see it all."

We had known each other less than twenty-four hours when we first slept together. I am not ashamed of this. In fact, in light of recent events, I am grateful about it. Grateful that we didn't waste the little amount of time we had together. Grateful that I found another human being to fully love, to hold nothing back from. Grateful that Nick was not only a generous lover but a kind soul. Grateful for his hands reaching toward me, for his arms circling my waist, for his small exhalation of breath each time I rested my head on his chest. Grateful that for two and a half years of my life, I had a partner, someone who upon waking would sleepily trace my lips with his finger and ask, "Sweetheart, what're we gonna do today?"

.   .   .

But I am getting ahead of myself. There is still uncharted territory to map. Barren hills to traverse. Hollow, wandering hours to account for. What did Nick see, feel, fear between the moment he climbed into the Fordge, blindly panicked, and the instant he entered the Suwannee Swifty and into my life?

Here are my answers. Guesses, at best. Perception and knowledge, they're not absolutes, you know. They waver in the light. Bold to dim. Stone to river. Yes, the whole ball of wax, it's ever-changing. You think you've got facts pinned down and then they wiggle away. But today, in my current state of mind, given my present circumstances, this is what happened to Nick. Exactly.

The faintly decaying aroma of fishnets lingered on his skin as the distance between himself and Lethe grew greater with every spin of his balding tires. The blind panic that had seized him upon his arrival on the mainland began to transform itself into something solid and cold and lethal, a rattlesnake winding itself around the double helix of his fear.

His instincts told him that if there were a cure it must have something to do with keeping the mind occupied. To that end, as he drove through Panacea, Medart, and on to Crawfordville, he tried to focus on the task at hand: finding a place to live. He would not think about Lethe or his mama or the feral cats that it would be up to his brother to feed. He would blot from his consciousness any and all notions of a piney island where sea turtles shoveled out oval depressions in the sand to lay their eggs and where dolphins came in so close to shore you could see the pigment in their eyes and where nighthawks darted through the twilight sky with such grace and precision that it was difficult not to be humbled by the very sight. He kept twisting the dial on the radio, the discordant jumble of music and commercials keeping him irritated which was a damn sight better than feeling lost.

Nick did have a plan, however. It was sketchy, far from ambitious, and deeply rooted in negative capability, but in times of confusion and despair people need to believe that they have a goal even if it's a flimsy one. His intent was to drive to Tallahassee, find a diner where a man could get a cup of coffee without feeling awkward, and search the newspaper's classified section. Apartments for Rent. That's where he would start. A small heading in infinitesimal print. The gateway to a new life. All he needed was a place to lay his head. Just a room. Maybe with a window. He would like that. Something to crack open and let a little air in.

He sped through Crawfordville, taking note of its many new businesses. Taco Bell. Subway Sandwich Shop. Discount Auto Parts. The IGA, though, was shut down. Couldn't compete with that new fancy Winn-Dixie where, it was rumored, you could buy pineapples—fresh and whole—just as if you were living in Waikiki. Who'd have ever guessed it. Crawfordville was becoming an ugly mess. Signs, signs, everywhere.

Gritting his teeth, he pressed on, north of Crawfordville and into the Apalachicola National Forest. He took a notion to sing, loudly, off-key. "Jimmy cracked corn and I don't care!" He laughed at his own self, amazed that the remnant of such a song was still floating in his brain, able to be called up at whim. He turned the radio knob and was surprised to find a tune he liked. He'd never heard this band before, didn't have a clue who they were. Maybe they'd say when it was over but probably not. Probably they'd go straight into a car commercial. But whoa! Look at that. Slow down. Take a closer look. A warped slab of plyboard. Hand-scrawled in green paint. Trailer 4 Rent.

"Well, there you go," he said and made a hard right onto a dirt road. He followed its curvy, potholed path for a good three quarters of a mile until it spilled into a grassy clearing—a couple of acres' worth—shaped like a rectangle. In the middle of the clearing sat a single-wide canary yellow trailer. Vintage 1960, that old tin can would have been unremarkable had it not been for the broad aqua stripe someone had painted with a good deal of precision around its midsection.

Nick, who was superstitious beyond what could be labeled reasonable, took the aqua stripe to be a sign. This was where he was supposed to be. In a trailer in the middle of the Apalachicola National Forest, surrounded by timber pines that grew tall and straight, their green bristle-like leaves rubbing against the ever-changing Florida sky, their shallow root systems lacing through the shifting sand.

All of it—the pines growing in regimental rows, the sap oozing into trails of frozen tears on the tree bark, the jays darting through the cool bright air, the dollar weeds stitching perkily through clumps of crabgrass and nettles, the ring-necked doves cooing from the highest branches, the thistle about to burst into lavender bloom—created a mirage of permanence, as if this was a substantive land instead of what it really was: an ancient ocean bed littered with fossilized oyster shells and prone to that peculiarly Florida phenomenon known as the sinkhole, the opening up of the earth that swallows houses whole.

Sinkholes, of course, are a more common occurrence in Central Florida, where overdevelopment has led to the limestone-banked aquifer being sucked dry in places—thus the caving in of what people had thought was stable earth. But sinkholes are not unheard of in North Florida. In fact the land here—the very earth where the canary yellow, aqua-striped trailer sat—was little more than a brittle birth caul veiling a maze of underground rivers and springs that flowed through limestone arteries in a cold, clear, sunless rush. Throughout Wakulla County, the underground rivers pooled to the surface, giant blue eyes blinking at the sun beneath gator-fringed lashes. But whether the rivers coursed through a cocoon of soft rock or the sandy brightness of exposed earth, they always, always meandered inexorably, doggedly south to the Gulf of Mexico.

The blue stripe. A sign. An omen. But of what? Nick stood in front of the trailer and took in his surroundings, ruminating. About thirty yards toward the eastern edge of the clearing rose a monument to other lives that had impacted this plot of ground. A solitary red brick chimney. Fuchsia and white camellia bushes bordered a spot where there had probably once been a porch. Wildly splayed Turk's caps and beauty berries created the outline of the former homestead, honoring the original footprint of the house as if the plants contained some kind of cellular memory, freely and wildly branching away from the now nonexistent structure, oddly resistant to encroaching upon its long-gone walls.

He wondered if the person who planted the camellias ever dreamed or intended that years after the house had ceased to exist and long after the gardener—whoever he or she was—had left this place, the bushes would still be here, tall and fat and blossoming with death-defying exuberance.

Maybe, Nick thought as he made his way over to where the house once stood, he could be happy here. Yes, he had simply reached another part of the sea, older and quieter and more seasoned than the Gulf that was but twenty miles away and fairly young, geologically speaking. That's how he should approach this place. It's what the blue stripe meant. He had, without even trying, stumbled upon an ancient remnant of long-receded waters. In effect, he was standing on what was once the ocean floor. That was all there was to it. He hadn't upset the balance of anything by leaving Lethe. Not at all.

As if he owned the place, he took big strides, his legs—which would have been lanky had they not been sculpted by physical labor—casting tremendous shadows. He stepped between the camellias and imagined himself gaining the pine stairs. He wiped his feet on a mat. One made out of thick grass. No, cypress, he decided. He gestured as if opening a door. It creaked open and his nostrils filled with the pleasant scent of mullet frying. Suddenly hungry, he took off his ball cap and walked inside the imaginary house.

Nick wandered through all the rooms. They were high-ceilinged, beadboarded, and full of light. The house was a simple shotgun affair with a large, eat-in kitchen off to the right at the rear. Each room had at least two double-hung windows and the lady of the house—a young woman from a nearby village such as Hosford or Sopchoppy—kept those windows sparkling clean. At least for the first few years of her marriage. But then the babies started coming. By the time child number three arrived she gave up on dustless windows and settled herself on the front porch where she snapped beans and watched her naked children play in the sprinkler. The groom, now, he was local born, a second- or third-generation mullet man, and he stretched his nets out in the back-yard on a rough-hewn cedar fence he and his brother had built. He didn't mind that as the years passed his wife's hips went wide and her once pretty face grew plump and toothless. He wasn't no Don Juan in old age himself. And when his missus died at fifty-three from cancer in the breast, he felt he'd lost all reason to live. He suffered the kind of grief that splits the heart in two.

Nick stood in the geographical center of where the house used to be and divined all of this. It just came to him and he knew that it was true because Nick was like that. Once he decided on something, there was very little chance he would change his mind.

But what Nick could not divine was who owned the trailer. The plyboard FOR RENT sign didn't include a phone number. After he stepped back out into the yard beyond the green and growing walls of the old homestead, he walked the trailer's circumference, checking the door and jalousies for a clue, a wedged business card, something, but came up empty. He noted, however, with great interest that a window in what was most likely the bedroom was shaped like a porthole. He stood in the sandy yard, staring at the window, slowly shaking his head in amazement. Just knock me over, he thought. Another sign.

He got in the Fordge and drove to the feed store that was a half mile back up on the main road. There, he bought a bag of boiled peanuts and an RC Cola. After he handed the grizzled old man behind the counter a five-dollar bill, he said, "Excuse me, sir, but would you know who owns the yellow trailer that's for rent?"

"He ain't here."

"Know where I can find him?"

The old man stared suspiciously at Nick through his bifocals. "Outta town."

Nick looked at the RC and the bag of peanuts as if he were suddenly laden with too much luggage. "Oh."

"You from around here?"

"No, sir. Lethe." In this part of Florida, if you lived ten miles down the road, you were not local. Nick set his RC on the counter and opened up the soggy bag. "That's where all my people are from." Nick offered the old man a peanut which he, unhesitant, accepted. "And you?"

"Born and raised right here in Crawfordville." He popped the peanut in his mouth, shell and all, and sucked on the salty juice. Then he cocked his head, licked his lips, and narrowed his washed-out gray eyes. "Lethe, eh? You ain't George Blue's son, are you?"

"Well, yes, sir. As a matter of fact, I am."

The old man grinned, peanut juice dribbled down his chin, and he chewed on the shell with his back grinders. "We used to go hunting together, your daddy and me! Goddamn, son, I miss him. I do."

"Thank you for that, sir."

"He was a good man. A flat-out crying shame, him dying the way he did. Wasn't a better shrimper than George Blue in the whole bunch. Don't make sense, it just don't. Don't ever tell my wife I said this, but sometimes the Lord God does things that bugs the bejesus out of me. And taking George Blue is one of 'em."

"Yes, sir," Nick said, and the uneasy fear that had stalked him these past few months and which ultimately pushed him to his decision to leave the island hit him with renewed, heart-pounding vigor.

The old man fiddled with the register, squinting through his glasses and trying three times before he found the secret combination that sent the cash drawer flying open. "Here you go." He reached into the nickel compartment and pulled out a key. "Jack Buford owns that trailer but he ain't gonna be back for a while. Went down to Miami to visit his new grandbaby. That mess south of here you can keep. But when your daughter has her first baby, well hell, I'd even go to Miami for that. You might know his girl. Louise Buford?"

"No, sir. Never had the pleasure."

"Well, whatever. Guess she's younger 'n you. Here's the key. Jack'll catch up with you about the rent when he gets back in town. In the meanwhile, you tell that mama of yours that Walter Strop said hello."

"Will do. Thank you, sir." Nick offered Mr. Strop his hand. They firmly shook. Mr. Strop had a helluva grip for a codger his age.

Upon returning to the trailer, Nick opened it up—all its jalousie windows and its sole door. If he could have, he would have peeled back the aluminum roof and let the sun bake away the stench of mildew. For a moment he worried about mosquitoes but then decided it was too early in the day and too cool for them to be bad and, besides, he'd rather deal with bloodsuckers than the smell.

The trailer was simply furnished. An old coming-apart-at-the-seams brown Naugahyde couch. A homemade surprisingly sturdy kitchen table. Two straight back chairs. A galley kitchen. A mattress tossed like a piece of white bread on the bedroom floor. A bathroom with a shower the size of a phone booth. The medicine cabinet mirror was shattered. He peered at himself and his face looked broken in the mirror's jigsaw reflection.

He walked from the front of the trailer to the rear three times in a row. Other than the mildew and the cracked mirror, the place was fairly clean. On his last lap he contemplated how strange it was that the first person he met in his new life was a man who knew his daddy. Maybe you could never escape yourself, he mused. Maybe we each have our own destinies and the people who are lucky are the ones whose fates have nothing to do with the past—ancient or otherwise. Walter Strop had it all wrong. It wasn't God that took George Blue. No, sir. It was the sea, plain and simple. It owned the Blues. Every last one of 'em. Wasn't any reason in the world for his daddy to have fallen into the nets. Folks shook their heads and muttered, accidents happen. But not to George Blue they didn't. No way. And there also wasn't good cause for the engine to have overheated the way it did. The Blues prided themselves on keeping everything in tip-top shape. But that engine, it damned near exploded. The blaze was seen for miles, lit up the whole night sky. To this day, people talk about being on the hill and seeing a fire far out to sea and nearly crying at the sheer beauty of it. Holy smokes, that was fifteen years ago. Seems like only yesterday, him and his mama and his two brothers shuffling out to their front porch to watch the sky burn and his mama saying under her breath, "George Blue, that'd better not be you."

Nick shut his eyes and rubbed them as if he could, with a mere gesture, wipe away his family's history. Then he thrust his hands deep into his front pockets, stared pensively at the dark paneled walls and dimly lit, depressing rooms, and thought, I can't stand it—the only thing worse than being on the run is being hemmed in.

So he grabbed one of the straight back cane chairs that had been tipped backward against the wall and dragged it outside. He crossed the yard, carrying the chair in one hand, over his shoulder. It was made of Florida pine and weighed nothing. He slipped through the camellia-flanked passageway and into the center of what for all intents and purposes was a room with beauty berry walls and a sky ceiling. He sat down in the chair and watched the sky. He observed how it grew nearly white as the sun reached its midday brightness and how as the afternoon progressed cirrus clouds began to move in from the north. A sign of a cold snap, he thought. If it got too cold Demetrius would stay in port. He would sit by the wood-burning stove and mend a net while his wife rocked their baby to sleep. And his mama would pull out her wool socks—the ones it was hardly ever cold enough to wear—and she'd slip them on and wrap up in a blanket while she watched an old movie on TV, sipping sherry and bitching to herself about how much she hated the cold. The fish would run deep. But the fingerlings would get caught in the swift winter tide, the extreme tide that exposed miles of seabed that were underwater the rest of the year. And the herons and gulls would put up with the cold because they knew about those low tides and the bounty they exposed: sardines, starfish, conch, whelk, anemone, crabs. But not ghost crabs. They wouldn't be back on the beach until April or, at the latest, May. But the sand would be scattered with shark eye shells. He was positive of that. They were a wintertime shell. Yes, everything has its season. It's funny. But he sure did like that. How everything returns. It's the design of things. Hands on a clock. Tick, tick, ticking. Moving on and on. Each little bit of life, even sea worms and coquina, trying like the dickens to find their way home.

·   ·   ·

When I was little, my great-aunt told me the boys in our family were baby dolphins. She said that before our mamas had us, we spent our time swimming in the Gulf of Mexico, eating mullet and chasing the tide. I said to her, "Why can't I remember that?"

And she said, " 'Cause once you became human, your dolphin memory withered away. Just like an old tomato."

I'm telling you, she reeled me in. Hook, line, and sinker. I believed every single word. I ran home and told my mama, "Mama, Mama! Aunt Betty says I'm a dolphin baby!" Man, oh man, did she get mad! Stomped down to my aunt's house and tore into the poor lady. Said if she ever again caught her filling my head with such nonsense she'd never let her see me. Don't know why she was so upset. I kinda liked the idea.

"But we haven't known each other long enough."

"What's long enough? Time doesn't have anything to do with what's in our hearts. I'm not afraid to say it, I'm mad for you, Mattie."

"But if I move in here with you without putting up any resistance of any kind, you might think I'm a pushover."

"Well, baby, we've been sleeping together since the day we met and you haven't put up any resistance. Why on earth would you start now?"

We possessed all the passion one expects in young lovers. And then some. Which is a good thing given the terrible turn the weather took. It got cold. Really cold. By North Florida standards, we were suffering. It was the winter that would not end. If it weren't for Nick, the world would have seemed hard and unforgiving. I might have packed it in, moved to Key West, and landed a waitressing job. In my view, people needed to sleep together just to stay warm.

Meteorologists far and wide blamed the severe weather on an unusually deep bend in the jet stream which allowed cold air from Canada to chase the snowbirds straight into the flatlands of America's subtropical paradise, leaving most of us natives pining for the advent of global warming.

But there were those who disagreed with the National Weather Service's explanation. Take, for instance, a professor of English literature at FSU—a certain Dr. Elkhart Callaway. He and his contrary opinion were showcased on the front page of the features section of the *Tallahassee Democrat*, complete with a color photo of the staid academic holding aloft a globe that had been painted glacial white, thus resembling a giant snowball.

Dr. Callaway, whom the article identified as one of the country's preeminent Henry James scholars (no mention was made of any climatological training), had developed the theory that the bad weather was the direct result of there being too many cows on the planet. Bovines, he asserted, suffered from chronic indigestion which wouldn't be a problem for anyone but the cows if it were not for the fact (his word) that their voluminous emissions dissipated airborne moisture and thus inhibited cloud formation. Without clouds, the professor concluded, there was nothing to prevent the arctic cold from blazing a trail all the way from the North Pole to the lower latitudes. Tallahassee to Key West, south through Cuba, deep into the rain forests of Central America, and onward to Antarctica. If we didn't do something about it soon, he said, we risked falling prey to another ice age. Global warming, he insisted, was nothing compared to a planet-wide freeze.

Astro Venus, whose address at the end of his letter to the editor indicated he was from a small hamlet east of Tallahassee named Chaires, responded to the professor's theory by calling it yet another World Bank conspiracy designed to further demoralize economically depressed indigenous peoples and that anyone with a grain of common sense knew that weather patterns were always disturbed at the dawn of a new millennium.

A man who pumped a tank's worth of gas each Tuesday and Friday morning into his black Chevy Suburban and who was a lobbyist for the citrus industry volunteered to me as he stood at the Suwannee Swifty counter shivering and waiting for his change that the magnetic lab at the university was to blame. "They're messing up everything," he said broodingly, offering no further explanation.

Nick may have been living the life of an inlander but he still approached the cold weather like a typical shrimper: with haunted resignation. On those frigid nights when frost silently whispered across the landscape, blanketing open meadows, windshields, and sidewalk weeds with a crystalline sheen, Nick would gaze out of the trailer bedroom's porthole window and watch the slow-moving moonlight cast stippled shadows across the dying grass.

"Have you ever seen moonbeams dance on the water?" he might ask.

"No. But I would like to."

"I wonder if Demetrius is oystering or if he's just laying low?" he would muse, his breath fogging that tiny, cold pane.

I would look up from my book. "Maybe he's shrimping."

"No. Not in this weather. Complete waste of time."

He would sigh and then lie down beside me on the new mattress and box spring he bought with his first week's pay and as his head hit the pillow he would worry that the freezing temperatures might kill the pelicans and I would say, "Baby, they're all right. They know how to take care of themselves," and he would look at me with the tenderness of a lover who understands that his partner has no idea what she's talking about but appreciates the effort anyway and then we would kiss and kiss and sometimes it would lead to something more serious and I would notice that his skin was beginning to smell like pine trees instead of sea salt and that would sadden me beyond all reason so I would concentrate more diligently on the details of our lovemaking, outlining his lips, eyelids, and cheekbones with my tongue and when we were finished I would try to match my breathing to his—beat for beat—and before long the dark, oppressive shadows that crowded the trailer with ghostly persistence would ease past our fingertips and we would sleep soundly, adrift in dreams that, come morning, would scatter amid the crisp refracted light of a new day.

· · ·

"He just walked out and you never saw him again?"

"That's right."

"Well, why not? I mean, why didn't you and your mama at least go to the circus, like he said? Maybe they would have gotten back together— seeing how he was doing what he wanted and all."

"He made it clear what he wanted the night he left. And it wasn't my mother and me."

"But he's your father. I bet anything we could find him. A circus guy can't be that difficult to locate."

"And if we did find him, then what? He doesn't deserve me, Nick. Not my presence, not my forgiveness, not even the hurt I feel when I think about him."

"If you had all the money in the world, Mattie, what would you do? I mean, for yourself. What big dream do you have?"

"Gee, Nick, I don't know. I don't think I have any big dreams. Maybe that's my problem."

"Oh come on. That's not so. Isn't there something you've always wanted to do or be but were afraid to try?"

"Well . . . yeah. Don't laugh—but—I've always wanted to go to college. I know it sounds stupid and that I'll probably never—"

"No, no. It doesn't sound stupid at all. You should go. We'll do that. We'll save up some money and get you enrolled up there in Tallahassee."

"We'll see. I'm not in any hurry. What about you? What's your secret dream?"

"I don't know, baby. I guess . . . I guess I've already lived it."

The fact that Nick adored being touched on his inner thighs and that sometimes he asked me to wear to bed a pair of lace crotchless panties which he gave me as our one-month anniversary present (the panties and a beautiful bracelet of interconnecting silver dolphins) and that after we made love he'd murmur over and over, "You are my life, my whole life," until he fell asleep in mid-chant needn't be elucidated upon any further.

But what I did find curious then and now is my husband's foot fetish.

One evening over dinner (I'd picked up burgers on the way home from work) he asked as he fiddled with a piece of shredded lettuce, "Where do you buy your shoes?"

"Wal-Mart. Target. Wherever they're cheap. Why?"

"I don't know. I was just thinking that they're always so, so . . ."

"Sensible?"

"Yeah. That's the word."

"Old lady shoes?"

"That, too."

I stared into my perky carton of French fries, uncertain as to how to feel about this line of questioning.

"Baby, now don't get mad at me, but what would you say if I asked you to wear shoes that were, you know, a little bit sexier?" And then he blushed at his own boldness.

I answered slowly, understanding that what I wore on my feet was for some reason important enough for him to risk ridicule and embarrassment. "Well. Sure. But I can't wear sexy shoes to work. I stand on my feet all day."

"No, no. Not at work. Just when we're alone or going to the movies or whatever." He leaned back in his chair, searching my face. His blue eyes went tender and he faintly grinned as if he were a little boy who was about to do something naughty and was happy about it.

"Come here." He stood, wiped his hands on his jeans, offered me his arm which I accepted, and guided us over to the couch.

"Sit down," he said softly. As I did, he knelt in front of me, slipped off my brown, rubber-soled clonkers, took my feet in his hands, kissed my ankles, and said, "Wait here."

He filled up a baking pan with warm water and sprinkled in bath salts someone had given me at work but I had never used since we didn't have a tub. He came back to the couch, carefully placed the pan on the floor, and slipped my feet into the water. I giggled as he began to slowly wash my feet.

"Relax. Just put your head back and let me do all the work."

He massaged each bumpy toe, each corn and callus, the soft thin tissue of my arches and the fatty pads of my heels. His fingers pushed hard and deep and sometimes gently. I heard myself moan and he ran his tongue along my toe tips.

We made love that night on the trailer floor and afterward he took me to bed, held my feet in his lap, and painted my toenails red.

Most every evening upon returning home, Nick and I would shower and change into fresh clothes, and before I started supper he would lead me by the hand into the ruins, as I took to calling the old homestead, and we'd sit within its living walls and watch the sky, our conversation intermittently interrupted while we paused to enjoy the silence.

Rarely did anything remarkable occur in the ruins. Except once. And if Nick were alive, he probably wouldn't even remember it. He made a simple observation. That's it. A comment about himself. A few sentences tied to a central theme. Nothing more. But the words he spoke that early evening have remained with me as though they were a string of worry beads worn smooth by time and touch.

We sat side by side in rickety aluminum lawn chairs, their webbing seriously frayed, the smell of distant chimneys sweetening the evening air, surrounded by the greenery of the ruins' walls. The sun was setting and the temperature was dropping in tandem to the pace of the dying day. In my mind's eye, I cast the sun into the role of an ennobled old man whose lot in life was to drag behind him a sack full of warmth as he continued ceaselessly along his circular journey. I imagined the bag breaking open and Nick and me being showered with heat and light. That would be lovely, I thought, to be drenched in all that light.

"Wonder what we'll be doing a year from now?" Nick asked.

"I don't know. Maybe I'll get enough nerve up to go to school. And maybe you'll find a job you like better."

He rubbed my cheek with the back of his hand. "Sometimes I feel lost, Mattie."

"I know. Me, too." I kissed his work- and weather-beaten knuckles. "I wish I could make everything right for us, that just by me snapping my fingers we'd both suddenly know what we were supposed to do with our lives."

"Do you regret moving in with me?"

"No! Not ever." Fearing that his question was a reflection of his own feelings, I asked, "Do you wish you hadn't asked me to? Do you want me to move out?"

"God, no, Mattie. You're the bright light in my life. It's just, you know, work and stuff."

"You sure?" I asked, picking up my beer.

"Yes. I am. You make me happy."

"You make me happy, too."

Nick leaned over and kissed me.

"You smell like soap," I whispered. "I like it."

He sat back in his chair, lightly held my hand, and we continued to watch the night. A bat flitted through the twilight sky. I kicked at a piece of broken glass that faintly twinkled in the sand. The land here was rubbled with bottle and pottery shards. More evidence, Nick contended, of former lives. After a heavy rain, he would walk around the property, picking up the fragments that had been revealed in the washed-away soil. He stored them in mason jars which he kept on the kitchen windowsill. I reached for the broken bit of glass. It was brown, probably from an old medicine or liquor bottle.

"How come you like the ruins so much?" I asked, fingering the shard's jagged edge.

"I don't know," he said. "I just do."

"But there must be some reason. I mean, when you're not working you're almost always out here. Which is fine. But I'm just curious. If it weren't for you, I don't think I'd spend any time in this place."

Nick scratched his arm where his tattoo stained his skin beneath his long-sleeved tee and flannel shirt. "Well, let me think about it for a second." He took a long swallow of beer, set the can between his feet, leaned forward, rested his forearms on his thighs, loosely clasped his hands, and gazed at the dirt. "It's a good place to think," he muttered. "I can sit out here and just let my mind wander."

"Do you think about anything in particular?"

"I guess so. I guess I think about home. Mostly."

"Really? I never think about home. I'm not even sure what that means."

"I'm sorry you had an unhappy time when you were a kid."

"It's okay. Things are better now." I dug my toe into the sand and tried to imagine what life had been like for the people who once lived here. I hoped that the house had been full of cheerful voices and that there had been pictures on the walls and jelly jars stuffed with wildflowers and a mirror at the entryway where people could catch a glimpse of themselves before hitching up the cart to go to town. "You think there's something about this old ghost of a house that makes you homesick?"

He swabbed his lips with his tongue and looked around at a house that existed only in our imaginations. "Beats me. All I know is this place feels right to me. I mean, I think that the people who lived here, I think they really loved one another. They built a life on this land together, one that they probably thought would last forever. And now," he snapped his fingers, "it's gone. Maybe by me coming out here every night, I'm sort of . . . sort of honoring them. Does that make any sense?"

I nodded, unable to speak. The wind blew, rustling the pine needles, sending a handful spiraling to the earth. Unmitigated kindness, I realized, nearly always moved me to tears.

Two days later, in the swampy no-man's-land called Tate's Hell, Nick looked on in a burst of surprised anguish as a co-worker—a boy, really—

tripped over his own feet and fell headfirst into the dark, shallow, moccasin-infested water, snapping his neck on impact. The men who watched it happen would say Baker Gregory Lee died because of his boots. Brand-new steel-toed jobs that were black and shiny and caused the boy to walk funny.

Bedeviled by the circumstances of life and death, Nick couldn't stop talking about the small moments of that day, as if in hindsight details that at first appeared ordinary actually possessed eerie significance, as if the most benign gestures had been omens warning of the impending disaster. If only we'd paid attention, Nick would say. If only we'd seen the signs.

Whether Nick exaggerated the particulars of that day, I do not know. I suspect not. His version of events was too clear and unvaried to have allowed much room for distortion. In fact, if there is any distortion in this, my faithful recording of the tragedy, I bear both the responsibility and consequence.

Upon arriving in the swamp that windy Tuesday morning, Baker announced to the assembled workers, "Look what was waiting for me when I got home last night." He held up a foot for all to admire. "Mama bought 'em for me. They are fine. I said to her, 'Mama, you shouldn't have spent the money.' You know, shoes like these, they ain't cheap."

Nick said the boy repeated this refrain, with various alterations and flourishes, on and off all morning. I inquired as to why the boy would be so impressed by a pair of shoes. Nick could answer this with some authority since he had known Baker for eighteen years. Not that he had run in his crowd, mind you. Baker was ten years younger. But the coast then and now is a small place. So Nick knew some things, including the fact that Baker had grown up in a hardscrabble fishing family and had spent most of his life either barefoot or in shrimper's boots. That being the case, Nick said Baker must have felt weighted down but mighty important as he strutted along in his gigantic lumberjack shoes—a child in a man's body—laughing delightedly, pointing at a bald eagle roosting in the bare crown of a cypress.

I met Baker once. Nick and I were at a pizza joint in Crawfordville

when he barreled in—all six foot two of him. Nick asked him to join us
and you would have thought that he'd just been offered money.

In the scheme of things, I only knew Baker for the time it takes for
three hungry people to eat two pizzas and share a pitcher of beer, but
that's long enough to glean some things.

He was just out of high school and as green as Nick when it came to
lumbering. But Nick possessed patience and forethought and a good
deal of guilt about cutting down trees, all of which slowed him down.
The Lee boy, on the other hand, didn't consider ramifications. Not of
his actions nor those of others. Please don't misunderstand. This wasn't
a negative trait. What I'm trying to say is that he was childlike in his joy,
in his ability to think that the here and now was a perfectly fine place
and tomorrow would be, too.

The night we met he kept making enthusiastic pronouncements
such as "I'm gonna save up and get me one of them monster trucks. I'll
give you two a ride in it anytime you want! It'll be bitchin'!"

Mindless, bull-in-a-china-shop enthusiasm, Nick called it. He said it
made Baker a delight to be around even though you had to keep a close
eye on him because he handled tools with such abandon that his co-
workers had a difficult time understanding how he could still have all
his fingers, don't even talk about his toes.

Let me set the stage. There are no real roads through Tate's Hell nor
any other telltale signals of civilization. Just dusty logging trails and
temporary railroad log bridges. From the air, the swamp looks as if it's
sutured together by blond, dusty ruts and thick wooden planks. Bear and
bobcat, coyote and fox, gator and snake, yellow fly and mosquito. The
swamp is their home. It's quiet, haunting, inhospitable.

If you asked Nick his opinion, he would tell you that the swamp was
a sacred space and people had no business mucking around in it. After
his first day lumbering in Tate's Hell, he came home thoroughly
spooked.

"Thought I saw a bobcat today. One second it was there, no more 'n
twenty feet in front of me. Next second, the big cat was gone. It was
damn strange. Made me think maybe I'd seen a ghost. I'm telling you,

Mattie, we shouldn't be in there," he grumbled. "Something bad is gonna happen. Just you wait and see."

At the time, I suspected Nick's unhappiness with logging the swamp had more to do with its closeness to Lethe than with any notions about what types of land—the sacred or profane—should be timbered.

From the trailer, the most direct route to Tate's Hell would have been the Crawfordville Highway south to 98 and then west through Carrabelle and on to the cutoff. But that would have taken Nick, every morning and every evening, past Lethe. Some of you might say, he could have sped right by, not turned his head, just kept his focus on the asphalt and potholes.

Impossible. Even if he had not looked at the glittering blue green water and the fog lifting from the island trees, his sheer proximity to Lethe would have awakened his bone-bred love for the place. The temptation to return home right then and there, to leave a job that required he sever a living thing from its earthly roots in order that we could all be supplied with toilet paper, would have been of monumental proportions, rendering mute the mere hint of resistance. So he drove a good fifty miles out of his way, traveling the inland route through the nearly deserted villages of Hosford and Sumatra.

Understand, other than grumbling occasionally about Tate's Hell, Nick never complained about his job. In fact, he hardly spoke of it at all. That's what gave him away. Silence, you see, is the great betrayer. So is idle chatter. And nearly all of Nick's chatter was about Lethe and the life he left behind.

For instance, we might be standing at the sink washing supper dishes and he would start rambling. "I wonder if Demetrius has fixed the net that needed mending. And the engine, been a while since it had a tune-up. He'd better take care of that. Not gonna be long before the weather's good enough to get back out there. You know what I'd do, Mattie, if I was still shrimping? I'd build me a new boat. One even prettier than the *Lillian B*. And I'd put your name on it. I sure would. Called my mama today. She said everything was fine. But I don't know. Maybe I should give Demetrius a holler."

And I would say, "Yes, why don't you?" And he would say because it wasn't his job to butt in.

"Do you think I'll meet your family one day?" I might ask, handing him a plate to dry, both fearing and anticipating the prospect of coming face-to-face with his sizable clan.

He would nod soberly and stare at the suds, but that was forever the extent of his response to my familial inquiries.

In the first few weeks after Nick walked into the Suwannee Swifty and swept me off my feet, his circumstances and the choices he'd made regarding his future didn't seem particularly odd to me. Nor did he seem to be taken aback that I was little more than an orphan adrift in her own insecurities. We were too busy making goo-goo eyes at each other to notice anything off-center. Which is how it should be. If biology and desire didn't momentarily blind us to weaknesses and inconsistencies, it's possible that none of us would ever fall in love. Blinding, hormone-driven joy is a biological necessity, one that time and routine whittle away like river water languidly polishing a rock.

And so the incongruity of his new life dawned on me slowly, revealing itself in wistful meanderings and sudden silences as well as in the usually overlooked minutiae of daily rituals. What time unearthed was this: Nick had grown up as if he *were* that dolphin-boy his aunt teased him about. During his years on Lethe he spent his days showered in sea spray, sand, and—if it was tonging season—oyster mud. Surrounded perpetually by sky and water, the world must have seemed dynamic, evolving, expansive.

What a shock to go from that wide-open universe to the enclosed sanctity of a forest—a world without horizons and only patches of sky and where hours are measured in shadows until the saws fall silent amid the sudden wasteland of a timbered acre.

And the shock strikes deeper if you're a person, like Nick, who possesses an artist's temperament. I believe I've heard the term before, a painter's sense of place. That's what Nick had, all right. He walked through the world perpetually painting a mental self-portrait, trying to get it right, trying to feel comfortable with a canvas that was ever-changing and sometimes cruel. When he moved inland, he tried like the devil to paint himself into a space filled with branch-laced skies and laser-straight rows of machine-planted pines. But all he ever came up with was himself and the sea.

Yes, it was the details of our lives that betrayed him. After a day spent logging, his skin was the color of earth and his black hair was powdered with sawdust. He'd take off his clothes outside—no matter the weather—and then parade naked as a babe through the trailer and into the bedroom, where he'd toss his workclothes into the laundry basket. Then he'd immediately take a shower, and if I was home, I'd scrub his back, and he'd stare at the dirt swirling down the drain as if he were watching pieces of his life being washed away. But it wasn't his life. It was pigment off the canvas, the hesitation marks of a painter who fears his work is not inspired. So he would stand silent and still under the showerhead, giving in to the water's ability to erase and erode, until not one speck of the forest remained on his weary skin.

I suppose what illuminated, more than anything, Nick's discontent with a landlocked life was his frequent, willful insistence on driving to the end of Bottoms Road—a place where land gives way to marsh and then liquefies further into a limpid swath of Gulf and sky and where nothing man-made mars the sparse beauty of this pared-down wilderness.

We'd sit in the cab of the Fordge, bundled up and colder than hell, gazing at a world unobstructed. Nick would eventually break the silence, saying something on the order of "I think it's important for people to just sit still and look out at nothing. I mean, always having buildings and condos and skyscrapers blocking your line of sight, it's not healthy. Probably why so many people wear glasses. You know, not a single person in my family wears glasses. Not a one. I bet more people are going blind today for that very reason—hardly any spaces left where you can just look out at emptiness—than ever before."

"Desert dwellers believe the same thing," I would say.

"Really? Huh. Well, this sure ain't no desert. But I get what you mean."

On the evening of the February full moon, we drove out to Bottoms Road so he could show me moonbeams on the water.

"It's beautiful," I said, watching the glimmering light. "You know what it looks like?" I turned to Nick. "Ghosts. Moon ghosts. They're out there dancing."

Nick jerked his head toward me and his eyes filmed over. He nodded and said, his voice choked, "I knew you would understand."

That night we made love in the Fordge cab amid a world that appeared to be born solely of motion, and when we were done he said, "I want to make love to you in the water."

"Right now?"

"No. Not right now." He wrapped an old blanket around my bare shoulders. "When it gets warmer."

I pulled the blanket close and gazed at the distant horizon, a wavering line of midnight blue against this full moon sky.

"Nick," I asked, "why did you hang around that day in the store?"

He pressed his face against my neck, ran the tip of his tongue along my collarbone.

"Because you were the prettiest girl I'd ever seen," he whispered.

"But did you like me?"

He stared at my face, not answering, and he was so solemn I regretted asking. I rested my head on his chest. He stroked my hair, kissed the top of my head. "No," he said, "I loved you."

"I loved you, too."

In the stillness that followed, a shadow of a night bird briefly darkened the water, a cloud eclipsed the moon, and an owl cried for its mate from a faraway stand of pines. I listened to the slow cadence of Nick's heartbeat and felt the even rhythm of his breath on my skin. Even though he was a big man, in this wilderness spun from rising tides and hidden fish and trilling birds his size seemed diminished, as if he were simply a part of the earth's wildness and not someone whose mortal purpose was to conquer it. I watched the moonbeam ghosts dance through the surf and wondered how he could have ever left such a beautiful place.

"Nick, why don't you move home? You seem—" I paused, searching for the right word. "I don't know. When we're out here you seem . . . complete." I pressed his callused, scarred fingers to my lips. "I know that once you start the truck and we head back to the trailer, we'll be leaving a part of you here. And I don't want to do that."

He rubbed his thumb across my cheekbone, my jaw, my neck. "Where I belong," he said, "and what would happen once I got there probably wouldn't make you very happy."

"I don't understand."

Nick reached behind him and retrieved my sweater. As he helped me slip it on, he said, "I don't think I can explain. And you probably wouldn't believe me even if I could."

I grabbed my jeans off the floorboard and shimmied into them. "Well, give me a hint."

"You know how many Blues have died at sea?"

"No," I said, arching my hips off the seat as I ungracefully zipped my pants and fumbled with the waist button. "Your father, that's the only one you've told me about."

Nick raked his fingers through his wild jumble of curls. "To tell you the truth, I don't know how many. There was my uncle. And my great-great-granddaddy. And a cousin down in Tarpon Springs." He paused, sighed heavily, looked at me, and said soberly, "The record isn't good."

"But, Nick, their deaths have nothing to do with you. Your chances of getting struck by lightning are probably greater than you dying at sea. And besides, wouldn't you be happier living in a place where you could honor them, the way you do those people from the ruins? They're not even real. You made them up."

Nick touched my hair and wound a strand around his finger. "That's different, Mattie." Then he sat up, his topheavy body straightening like an arrow, and whispered, "I'm sorry. I really am."

We didn't discuss it further that night, but the idea that he should return to Lethe did not go away. At least not in my mind. I didn't believe that Nick fled the island because others, years ago, had died. As a shrimper, he had participated too fully in the taking and giving of life to fear mortality. He understood better than most nature's disquieting para-dox. Something must die so that others can live. Animals for food. Trees for shelter. And—if you believe in such things—martyrs, saints, and holy men for the salvation of the masses. But maybe, just maybe, Nick had decided to tinker with the timing. Which would mean it wasn't death he was afraid of but fate. Yes, fate sent him running. Fate caused him to wake up now and again in a nightmare haze. Fate, with its steel-taloned ability to snuff out the future, sometimes chased him to just this side of crazy.

And this is where Nick's world intersects with Baker Lee's. They were both fishermen who'd walked away from the sea but fate came calling anyway. In Baker's case, destiny made itself known on a stun-ningly bright and cold day in the last week of March, a time of the year when the cypress was still bald but ready to leaf.

There he was, a two-hundred-pound man-boy pointing to the highest branch of just such a tree. He must have been a sight to behold. Him in his red plaid shirt and his new shiny shoes, laughing like an angel, his beefy thighs rubbing against one another as he heavily strode across the railroad tie bridge, paying no mind to the slatted, woefully uneven surface, clodhopping along and pointing at the eagle.

"Look look look!" he said.

Nick obliged Baker. He gazed at the eagle with its big white head and intelligent, predatory eyes and thought that yes, indeed, it was surely a majestic animal. He turned back to Baker and was about to tell him to walk slower and pipe down or he risked scaring away the bird, but the very moment Nick opened his mouth Baker tripped over his own gigan-tic, booted feet.

"Watch out!" Nick yelled and the eagle rose into the sky and with it wafted Baker's laughter. Nick said he would never forget the sound—Baker squealing with glee as he tumbled over the edge of the bridge.

I thank God for that laughter because it meant Baker had no idea he was about to die. He mistook his final seconds on earth as just one more high-spirited joke, that he was simply falling into the water like the clown at the dunking tank during the Carrabelle High School Fair. He believed with simpleminded purity that he'd climb out of the water and onto the shore sopping wet and cold, and everybody would get a good laugh and slap him on the back, and with any luck he'd get sent home where he would change into some warm clean clothes, and then he'd head down to Harry's Restaurant for a cup of coffee and a piece of pecan pie. He'd flirt with Becky Jean, the waitress, and he'd tell her all about how he tumbled into the muddy waters of Tate's Hell and for good measure he'd throw in a little white lie, just a little one. "I damn near fell on a big old bull gator. He floated right by me. This close." He would spread out his thick hands to illustrate a distance between his fingertips and his elbow. "I coulda touched him!" he'd say.

But, as you know, that is not what happened. He entered the shallow water with a thin splash and his fat ham-bone body—from his torso to his toes—slammed against the rippling surface. With his face, neck, and shoulders submerged, he floated but went nowhere. His oddly bent body was snagged on a stob or a log or only God knows what. His limp legs were splayed wide in the slow current, and his feet in those rounded, shiny boots looked like a couple of Suwannee cooters sunning themselves on a log.

One of the men on the crew rushed over to the company truck and called for help on the radio. Nick ran down the bank—cut up his arms on a stand of saw grass hidden in the bulrush—and then plunged into water that was thick as stone, five big steps, and from behind grabbed hold of Baker Lee, wrapped his arms around his chest, and pulled. But to no effect. The boy's head was stuck in the thick bottom muck. It's as if the belly of the swamp had swallowed him whole.

The next day I woke early, just past dawn, and watched my lover sleep. He had an erection (which wasn't unusual) and I wondered if sleep-time hard-ons plagued all men and how he could possibly sleep given his condition. Perhaps, I thought, Mother Nature has a sense of humor, after all. I rested my hand on his hair. His curls were damp with sweat. His skin smelled sweet and slightly sour, like an orange. I kissed his shoulder. He mumbled, scratched his nose with the back of his hand, and rolled onto his belly, never waking.

I eased out of bed, walked into the kitchen, and put on the coffee. As I stood at the sink rubbing the sleepers out of my eyes I slowly became aware of a new sensation—or, that is, the lack of a sensation. For the first time in months I wasn't cold. I opened the jalousie window over the sink, amazed that winter might have finally taken its leave. Air rushed in and I pushed my face into the warmth.

Determined to enjoy the change in the weather despite the horrendous events of the previous day, I headed outside, the morning's first cup of coffee in hand. The sun lacked the baking intensity of late summer but its heat was welcome, nevertheless. All manner of birds stitched through the cloudless sky, looking for food and mates and nesting materials. Creepers and wrens. Jays and titmice. Warblers and cardinals. They chirped and soared and scuttled through dead, dry leaves. A lizard sunned itself on the porch rail. A spider dangled from a mulberry limb via a gossamer thread and assiduously spun her web. Dragonflies gorged on gnats. Bees bobbed unsteadily in the wind, drunk on pollen. A mockingbird perched in a scrub pine outside our bedroom window and began to belt out its entire repertoire. I ventured into the clearing behind the trailer and watched a red-tailed hawk spiral with celestial precision on an invisible current of rising air. Overnight, without flourish or fanfare, the world had become a different place.

Mimicking the hawk, I lifted my arms and tried to imagine what it would feel like to fly.

"Hey, what're you doing?"

Embarrassed, I attempted to act as if I'd simply been fluffing my hair. I turned toward the trailer. Nick stood naked on the concrete steps, squinting. "It got warm," he said, confused.

"Look up there." I pointed at the hawk. Nick watched, his mouth tight.

"That's nice," he said without any enthusiasm and then skulked back inside.

Wearing nothing but his boxer shorts, Nick paced between the kitchen and living room, muttering lamentations and pulling his hair and picking at the corner of his lips and wringing his hands and overall behaving as if Baker Lee's death was a tragedy of such magnitude that its implications burgeoned far beyond the lowland banks of Tate's Hell.

"I knew something bad was gonna happen. Didn't I say something bad was gonna happen?" And, "What is wrong with this world? Baker wouldn't hurt a fly. Why did somebody as young and decent as him have to die!" And, "You just wait and see, Mattie, we haven't heard the end of this. More people are gonna get hurt in that swamp. More people might even die!"

I tried to offer bits of logic that would numb his pain but succeeded only in making myself sick at the inefficacy of my words. It's not your fault . . . You didn't have a thing to do with it . . . It was an accident, plain and simple . . . Baker wouldn't want you to be this upset . . . Some tragedies just can't be explained . . . Bad things happen and we simply have to get past them.

As I prattled on and on, ad nauseam, Nick squeezed his eyes shut and shook his head with the vigor of a wet dog, as if by shaking hard enough he could dislodge the awful images, as if they'd simply fall out of his ears or nose and disappear into the ether.

After about thirty minutes of catholic understanding and coddling, my patience wore thin. I began to clean the trailer—scrubbing sometimes calms my nerves—and as I rendered my sink spotless I continued to cluck sweet agreeables ("Yes, honey, I know. It's just a crying shame. Accidents like this never make any sense but at least you were there with him." Ugh!). I'm not making light of Nick's demonstrative anguish. But I will admit to turning my back and paying a great deal of attention to a speck of spilled tomato sauce after he beat on his chest and moaned, "Why wasn't it me!"

"Nick, honey, you're taking this too hard," I finally said.

"Too hard!" He stopped pacing. His eyes grew big like a cat's and his voice rose an octave. "How can you say that?"

"Just listen to yourself. You sound a little crazy."

"Well, excuse the poop out of me! Sorry for taking up your time. I guess I'll just go outside."

"Good idea."

I watched him exit the trailer. By the high tilt of his head and the stiffness of his gait, I could see that he was attempting to leave with some measure of dignity but that was extremely difficult since he was wearing nothing but his underwear and had just used the word "poop."

As the door slammed behind him I said, "Ah, shit." I tossed my cleaning rag on the counter. Why didn't I put my arms around him while he babbled? Why did I get angry when people grieved? Why did I think everyone should handle death and abandonment as if they were conditions that should be taken for granted and, therefore, paid scant attention to?

Because, came the answer, you're more like your mother than you dare admit.

I found him in the ruins. He was sitting in the lawn chair, his head back, his eyes closed. As I approached, carrying a grocery bag filled with a sheet, clothes, a bottle of white wine, plastic cups, and potato chips, he said, "Hey, baby."

"Hi, Nick." I put down the bag and kissed him. "I'm sorry for what I said in there. I just—well—I've never been good at grieving myself, so I don't know how to handle it when people I love do it so well."

"Forget it," he said, pulling me onto his lap. "You were right. I was feeling sorry for myself."

"At least you had a good reason," I said, kissing his eyelids.

"Mmmm."

"You know what?"

"What?"

"I think we ought to play all day long."

He slipped his hand inside my shirt. "What kind of play are we talking about?"

"It entails keeping our clothes on. Or, in your case, putting some on."

"Are you sure?" His hands moved up my rib cage.

"Yes. I am." I touched his face with my fingertips. Sadness clung to him like winter's dying remnant. I sensed this melancholia wasn't solely over Baker Lee. Perhaps it was also about himself—missing pieces, truths lying just beyond reach, fears that evade the intellect's ability to dissect and dispel. I pressed my hand against his cheek. "I brought you some clothes."

"Why?" He pretended to be preoccupied kissing my neck.

"Because we're going to have a picnic of sorts, and since I'm too white to be in this sun naked, I thought you might want to join me in putting on your shorts."

"I don't think any woman other than my mother has told me to put on my clothes," he said, sliding me off his lap and reaching into the bag.

"Have there been a lot of other women?"

"Not really."

"Why not?"

"There aren't a lot of women on Lethe I'm not related to." He pulled his T-shirt over his head.

"What about your mother?" I handed him a pair of shorts.

"What about her?"

"I don't know. Just tell me about her. For instance . . . what does she look like?"

He stepped into his shorts. "Pretty. Black hair. But hers isn't curly. It's straight with a few silver streaks. And her skin smells like nutmeg from all the cooking she does."

"Is she a good mother?"

He looked down at the ground and then at me. His eyes filmed over with tears. Nick was like that—he could cry at the drop of a hat. "Nobody could ask for better. She's a shin-kisser."

"A what?" I wrestled the sheet out of the bag.

"A shin-kisser. You know, the kind of mother who when you were little and skinned your knees the first thing she did was run over and kiss them. She called it kissing the owie away."

In my mind's eye, I saw Nick as a little black-haired tyke falling down on an oyster shell driveway and his beautiful mother running to him, picking him up, kissing his knees, dispelling both tears and pain. The image knocked me over. Flattened me as if I'd been hit with a stone. What wonderful gentleness I'd missed out on. A shin-kisser.

I snapped the sheet in the air and it settled on the sand like a giant white moth. "We should invite her over for supper," I said, working to keep my voice steady, ignoring for a moment that I couldn't cook worth squat.

"You're right, we should. But maybe we won't have to."

I looked at him, not understanding. "What do you mean?"

He turned a full circle, his eyes scanning the space around us as though he were peering into the rooms of the old house. "To tell you the truth, I'm not sure."

It was that afternoon on the first real, palpable day of spring, as we lolled on the sheet, drinking wine from paper cups and eating potato chips out of the bag, that the future began to take shape. We didn't immediately define it—we could not have written down our plans or discussed what we might be doing in six months in any terms that were concrete. But we could see and feel that something was happening; with very little effort on our part, we were being propelled forward and nothing could prevent the future from having its say.

Although I was ignorant of it then, I now know that destiny is continually reaching back in time, searching for what formed it, taking its shape, color, and consistency from the elemental winds of the past. Nick, I believe, would agree with me about this.

"I left home," he said, staring at some indistinguishable point amid the crabgrass, " 'cause I was scared. Scared that I was going to die if I stayed, that I'd get claimed just like my daddy and the others before him. And I'd been thinking lately that maybe that's why Baker had left the business—that fear had gotten hold of him, too. I was going to ask when it was just me and him, I was going to say, 'Baker, were you getting scared of that water? Is that why you're logging trees in Tate's Hell?' "

He sipped his wine and glanced at the crumbling chimney. "But it doesn't matter. All the old stories were bullshit. When it's your time, you're outta here. You can't outwit it."

I rested my hand on his knee. "I'm sorry, Nick, but I'm really not following you. What old stories? What's bullshit?"

He looked at me, sizing me up. "If I tell you, do you promise not to laugh or think I'm stupid?"

"Yeah."

"You swear to God?"

I crossed my heart, held up my hand, and agreed to the oath. "I swear."

"Okay then."

He took me by the shoulders and eased me toward him until my head was in his lap. He stroked my hair as he spoke and I watched his face.

"You know, I'm Greek," he said. "I mean, I'm American but my great-grandparents, they came over from Greece."

"Yes, I know that."

"Well, sometimes people who live in little villages or spend a lot of time alone at sea, they come up with these ideas, see, ways to explain things, and maybe it was just a story at first but somehow that story tends to become real to other people—the details get all jumbled up and confused and rearranged according to various people's needs—and before you know it everybody is taking the story on its face as fact. And sometimes as the years go by nothing real unusual or terrible happens so the story sort of gets forgotten. But the minute tragedy strikes—say someone dies at sea—the story is back, harder than ever, and even though you might say with the front of your brain, That's just a silly wives' tale, there's always that little marble of doubt rolling around in the back of your head, keeping you just an inch off-kilter."

I reached up and removed a windblown pine needle from his hair. "What kind of story are we talking about?"

"A crazy one."

"Like what?"

"Like some of us on my daddy's side of the family used to be dolphins. And if we're dolphins, we're free, see? But when we're men, we're not."

I sat up, faced him, and poured us each more wine. "This is what made you leave Lethe? This is what scared you?"

"No. This is the part that scares me. The legend says that sometimes the dolphins decide they want one of us back."

"I see. So somebody dies."

"You got it."

"Well, you know," I said, pulling out bits and pieces from my many hours of reading, "myths are just stories we create to make our pain go away. Ages ago someone in your family tried to make sense of a loved one's death and there you go, a legend was born." I picked at a dot of lint on the sheet. "You don't . . . believe this, do you?"

"No! Of course not."

He was lying and I knew it. His eyes were shifting in his head and his bottom lip twitched not once but twice. I was happy to find out that the man I shared a bed with couldn't lie worth beans.

"So this is the reason for the tattoo? And your mother, she doesn't believe the story and that's why she was so mad at your great-aunt when she started filling your head with nonsense about you being a dolphin-boy?"

"Yes, pretty much."

"What happens once one of you becomes a dolphin?"

"I guess we live happily ever after. My great-aunt believed in a city at the bottom of the ocean where the dolphins live."

All this was sounding vaguely familiar. I had read a book on animal myths several years back and it included a chapter on dolphins.

"This story isn't that strange," I said. "If I remember correctly, people living along the Amazon in Brazil believe that river dolphins come ashore and shape-shift into people. And that they live at the bottom of the river in a place called the Enchanted City."

"Why do the dolphins want to become people?"

"They don't stay human. They just show up at parties and dance. And sometimes have sex with humans. According to this book I read, they make extremely handsome people and fabulous lovers."

"But they like to dance?"

I nodded yes. "According to the legend."

Nick chewed thoughtfully on a potato chip. "So it's not just my family who's off their rockers. Other people believe in similar stories?"

"All over the world. If it's not dolphins, it's seals. And if it's not seals, it's crows. And if it's not crows, it's snakes. And don't even bring science into the mix."

Nick sipped his wine and then asked steadily, "What do you mean?"

"Evolution. Dolphins actually were at one time land mammals."

"That sounds more far-fetched than my story."

"But it's true. Scientific fact. They had feet and everything. And for some reason, they left the land and went to the sea and as part of that transition, their feet became fins. Maybe," I said, thinking I was about to say something terribly humorous, "you're the missing link."

Nick poker-faced me and then waved a gnat off his shoulder. "Where'd you learn about this stuff?"

"Books." I reached into the bag of chips and grabbed a handful. "It seems to me, if you left Lethe because you were scared of dying at sea, that's one thing. But if you left because you believed in the legend just a tiny, tiny bit? Well, that's a whole different reason for leaving."

"You think so?"

"Yes. I do."

Nick rested his chin on his hand and tapped his lips with his thumb. He stared down at the sheet, unblinking. "I'm unhappy here," he whispered.

"I know you are, baby."

"I mean, I tried. I really, really tried. But I don't fit in. I don't understand why people live in places that aren't surrounded by water.

Don't they feel shut in? Every day I wake up and stare at the ceiling and wonder what in the hell it is I think I'm doing. If it weren't for you, Mattie, I'd be completely lost."

"Maybe it's time for you to go home. We've talked about it before and you've always said no. But maybe you should give it some serious thought."

"Going home, man, that's a hard one to call." He stood up and his bountiful lips stretched into a grim line and he stared over the crown of the leafy walls. He breathed out hard and his eyes narrowed as if he were trying to get a better glimpse at his choices in life. But then, in a split second, everything about him changed. His face grew animated, his eyes widened, and he said, "Wow, will you look at that!"

"What?"

"Right there, on that Turk's cap bush. A monarch."

I scrambled to my feet and followed his gaze. A butterfly—its big burnt-orange wings veined in black, the edges stippled in white—sipped nectar from the red throat of an early blossom. "It's beautiful," I said.

Nick eased toward the butterfly. "Let's follow it. Wherever it goes."

"Really?"

"Yeah. Come on. This way, he's headed over there." Nick took off toward a patch of blue-eyed grass. He laughed as he ran. "Quick, Mattie, he's getting away!"

I ran through the field and at one point tripped and fell. He lifted me to my feet, pulled the weeds out of my hair, wiped the dirt off my knees and kissed them.

"Never before has anyone kissed my knees," I said.

"Then you're long overdue," and he kissed them again. "Do you see the butterfly?"

"Yes. It's behind you, maybe fifteen yards."

Nick stood and looked to where I pointed. "You okay?"

"I'm fine."

"Then hurry!" He took my hand and our wandering continued and I worried that we might get lost and he said, "Oh, no, baby, I know exactly where we are."

As we chased the butterfly—a creature destined by biology to be short-lived and perhaps whose extravagant beauty was in response to its numbered days—I could not have known Nick's sudden joy was prompted by a memory that kept him anchored to his past. Likewise, my interpretation of the events of that afternoon would take on new meaning only with the passage of time, as my own future inevitably ticked by, acquiring the patina of things remembered.

This was Nick's memory and what prompted his mood to swing from pensive to childlike: an island which in spring and fall is visited by thousands of migrating butterflies. Fritillaries. Zebra wings. Yellow sulphurs. Skippers. Satyrs. Dianas. Swallowtails. Hairstreaks. Monarchs and more.

But in the monarchs, with their bold colors and leviathan migratory route, Nick perceived nature's mystifying halo. Every spring, without fail, the monarchs journey from Mexico across the wide blue gap of the Gulf. Hundreds of miles and not one second of inertia. Not a single sip of nectar. Nothing but water and sky and their beating weightless wings until they make landfall at an island that offers both sustenance and rest, thus fulfilling a destiny that confounds science but which occurs without fail, in rhythm to the music of planets near and wide.

In the wake of Baker's death, on a day that belied nature's crueler side, Nick was engaged in something far greater than simply trailing the butterfly as it floated from plant to plant.

Home. He was journeying home.

There's nothing like it, Mattie. Nothing in the whole world. Even after all this time, I get so excited when I pull those nets and they're full of shrimp. Feel like God is smiling down on me. And that's a fact.

How can this be, you might ask. How can a man who was driven from his home by the specter of ghosts or death or some such nonsense experience a thoroughly devout change of heart?

I have a theory about that. Given his predilection for believing in signs and dreams, good luck and bad, fate and curse-mongering, Nick cast Baker Lee's death into a context he could understand: The horrible incident, occurring as it did on the day before true spring, was in actuality an omen beckoning Nick home.

In other words, he found the excuse he'd been quietly searching for to beeline it back to Lethe without having to explain to family and friends that his leaving had been a monumental mistake in the first place.

As for his concerns over fate and his family's morbid history at sea, I believe he managed to repackage them in the trappings of random inevitability. After all, no one could have predicted Baker's death. And if anyone had tried, they probably would have favored an accident involving heavy machinery or laser-sharpened power tools. Not his own big clumsy feet.

In my humble opinion, as Nick Blue chased that butterfly through the open field, he decided he had nothing to lose by returning home and everything to gain. In short, he'd be getting back his life even if the end was predestined. He had learned with clarion certainty what most of us take for granted: There's no avoiding death. But happiness. Now that's something you must chase after.

And I freely admit, I was proud to be by his side upon his return. Scared speechless. But proud. Because whether his departure and homecoming were driven out of superstition, or the earth's magnetic field, or the alignment of the planets, or simply life's unavoidable decisions and indecisions, Nick had traveled many miles in a very short time. His retreat from Lethe may have been marked by fear, but his return was deliberate, calm, accepting of whatever life had in store for him.

Let me make it perfectly clear that Lethe was not exactly what I expected. Oh, it was paradise, all right. But I don't think I really understood Nick when he spoke about taking the skiff to the hill or visitors coming over by ferry or residents passing laws to keep out mini-marts, grocery stores, liquor stores, restaurants, and any other sort of commerce you might think of. When he told me he had called his mother, I naturally thought they had spoken via an ordinary phone connected to the rest of the world in the accustomed fashion: with poles and wires.

Silly me, I assumed he took the boat to the mainland out of some sense of macho necessity. And that visitors cruised by ferry to the island because a short trip on the open water is good for the lungs. And that the lack of commerce not only kept the island pristine but that it presented no measurable inconvenience since you could simply get on the bridge and drive into Carrabelle.

Some of you are probably snickering right now because you knew that there was no bridge to Lethe. A few of you might have even known that as the rest of North America hurled into the high-speed digital morass called the new millennium, Lethe relied on shortwave radios, cell phones, and the mail boat which delivered news from the outside world twice a week. Good weather permitting.

The red skiff was docked on the Carrabelle River in between two shrimp boats, the *Nellie Mae* and the *Mayme Ellyn*. Overshadowed by the trawlers, the *Poseidon* resembled a bathtub toy as it gently bobbed in the wake kicked up by a passing speedboat. Nick took one look at his old wooden runabout and said, "Mattie, I do believe we've struck gold. Looks like Demetrius has come to town. Probably doing some grocery shopping."

"Where does he do that?"

"The IGA." Nick pointed down the road at an asphalt parking lot filled with trucks and grocery carts.

I must admit, I immediately found Carrabelle both charming and troubling. But troubling only because, along with the neighboring villages of Eastpoint and Panacea, it was one of Florida's last genuine fishing villages and seemed to be teetering toward the faceless, homogenized tourist resort abyss that much of the rest of the state had already tumbled into.

New condos were being constructed in front of aging shrimp docks. A trendy riverwalk was slated to be built on the very site where sponge boats once docked. Real estate offices and antique stores were sidled beside seafood processing plants and oyster middens.

Progress, however, had not yet besmirched Carrabelle's most enduring nod to local color, its police station. Touted as the world's smallest, it was located on the main drag, across the street from the river, in a phone booth. Or to be more precise, it *was* the phone booth. Tourists frequently stopped to have their pictures taken at the station, standing either outside the booth or holding the receiver to their ears and smiling broadly. Some even went so far as to purchase World's Smallest Police Station T-shirts at Burda's Pharmacy, an old-style drugstore where you could buy powdered toothpaste, red hots, moleskins for your corns, and even vintage one hundred percent polyester T-shirts of Donnie and Marie Osmond (the police station tees were a cotton blend).

Nick opened the Fordge's driver's side door, got out, and walked as far as the front bumper, the oyster shells crunching beneath his feet. I slid across the seat and joined him. I looked out at the Carrabelle River and at the riggings of the working boats and squinted against the sun's intense light. Nick put his arms around my waist and said, "Mattie, it's your last chance. If you've changed your mind, I'll understand."

This was the fifth time he'd asked if I was sure I wanted to move to Lethe. If I'd been a meeker woman (as I was a mere six months earlier), I might have become suspicious. As it was, I chalked it up to him being overly concerned that he'd pushed me into the decision. But nothing could have been further from the truth. I had repeatedly and carefully thought through my options and each time I found myself asking the same question: What did I gain from staying on the mainland? A job as a convenience store clerk? Days or even weeks without seeing him? Life alone in an efficiency apartment? A future duller than dirt?

I waved away a fly and said, "My mind's made up, Nick. I want to go with you. Unless you've changed *your* mind."

"Changed my mind!" He ran his hand down the length of my hair. "Oh, no, Mattie. More than anything, I want you with me." He pulled me close and whispered, "Thank you. You won't regret this." He glanced down the road, toward the IGA. "But we gotta work fast." He took off his blue denim shirt and threw it on the front seat of the Fordge. "Well," he said, "let's go see what kind of shape the *Poseidon* is in."

He headed toward the dock and I rushed to keep up. "Why don't we just take the bridge over?"

"What bridge?"

"You know, the bridge."

"Very funny," he said.

If there was a more colorful boat than the *Poseidon* along the Gulf coast, I would be hard pressed to believe it. The hull's exterior was tomato red, the interior safety yellow, and every seam was caulked and painted purple.

"I think this boat could use some polka dots," I said. "Maybe all over the inside."

Nick knelt down, surveying the skiff bow to stern. "That's not a bad idea." He stood and wiped his hands together as if he'd just finished a hard day's work. "She looks in pretty good shape. I'd best start loading her up."

He worked quickly, despite the fact that the dock seemed to be standing only because it was too worn out to fall down. Pilings leaned precariously. Many of the planks were so rotten they would bear no weight, others were springy, and still others were nonexistent. Everything was off-angle and uneven. But Nick navigated between the Fordge and skiff with the grace of a man who had learned the dock's crazy Braille ages ago and had come to implicitly trust it. A thin line of beaded sweat ran down his brow and the knobby track of his spine glistened.

I tried carrying a couple of boxes but succeeded only in impeding his progress so I stood to the side and stared into the green water and because it is my nature to be a second-guesser, I reconsidered my opti-

mism which I had pronounced just moments before. What in the blazes
was I going to do? How does one live on a bridgeless island? I supposed
that on the face of it, one could find it intriguing. High-spirited. Reck-
less. Romantic even. Just imagine—Nick and me and the surf and the
sand and the sun and all that water. But on the other hand, how would I
go shopping? Or to the library? Or the doctor? Yes, what about the
doctor? And don't even think about hurricanes!

"Come on, give me your hand," Nick said, breaking my train of
thought. "We gotta get outta here."

I looked quickly around, trying to keep in check the hard knot of
panic that had suddenly formed at the base of my skull. The dock. The
Fordge. The two shrimp boats with their gears and pulleys and massive
nets. Me about to live in a place surrounded by water and I didn't even
know how to swim. It was all so alien. So lacking in common sense. Too
outlandish. Too much. Too soon. But then there was Nick. Nick. Oh
God. I took a mental snapshot—the sun highlighting a faint blue tinge
in his stony black curls, him standing in the boat with his bare tattooed
arm extended toward me, looking into my face as if he didn't have a
doubt in the world about the two of us.

"Okay," I said. "Okay."

I stepped gingerly into the boat, praying that I would not fall overboard and drown or—worse—simply make a fool out of myself. I
squeezed into a tiny space between a box of books and a case of beer.

"Aren't we going to wait for your brother?"

Nick pulled the cord on the motor, a 20 horsepower Johnson.

"It's a family tradition," Nick said as he adjusted the throttle. "Whoever gets to the skiff first gets home first!"

"So, in essence, you're stealing the boat."

Nick looked over his shoulder as we idled away from the dock. He
thought he was getting away with something—I could see it in his
confident shoulders-back posture and his eyes' defiant shine.

"Nope. Just evening the score."

He guided us into the channel and I asked, "So that's how you get
groceries? You take the boat?"

"Unless you wanna swim."

I faced forward. There wasn't a single channel marker that didn't have a pelican or a cormorant sitting on it. I leaned over and stared down. As we traveled farther from the dock the water changed colors: green to aqua to prismed blue. I had never been in a boat before but I tried to look as if this were old hat to me. All I can say for my efforts is that at least I didn't get seasick. We rounded a bend in the river. Apalachee Bay and the Gulf of Mexico came into view. It was about eleven o'clock so the sun was high and brilliant. The sea sparkled, a colossal sapphire, and in the middle of it all, about three miles out, sat Lethe, the Island of Forgetfulness. Paradise.

Emotions tend to overtake me at the most inconvenient moments. And it was no different that day in the *Poseidon*. As Nick opened up the throttle and we sped toward Lethe, tears and salt spray burned my eyes. I was grateful that my back faced Nick so that he would not know I was crying. This sadness had little to do with him or our forward motion but was firmly planted in the life I was leaving behind, one that had largely been marked by shame. A mother who withheld her love for me but who divvied herself out to strangers with pathetic abandon. The fading visage of an alcoholic father who disappeared into the hot, dark Jacksonville night in search of what? Other women? Booze? The freedom afforded to those who abandon their children?

This may sound terribly selfish, but I think the most important person I was leaving behind was me, Matilda Fiona O'Rourke, a young woman who was so discomfited by her own intellect that she read books clandestinely and consciously altered her vocabulary so that her co-workers at the Suwannee Swifty wouldn't feel ill at ease.

At that moment, as Lethe loomed larger and larger, I closed my eyes and pushed my face into the breeze.

"Goodbye," I whispered, "and good riddance."

My hair blew wildly in the brisk wind. I probably resembled Medusa but did not care. I felt as if I were hurtling through the vast blankness of space, without direction or control.

Where would I land? Would this new earth be a place of beauty or a wasteland rubbled with hate and despair? What would I say when people asked me where I came from?

I opened my eyes and lightly dipped my fingers into the water. It was cold and clear and felt foreign against my skin.

Nowhere, I would say. I come from nowhere.

Nick called it the Lethe Marina but really it was simply a dock that wasn't in much better condition than the one in Carrabelle. It was located on the bay side of the island and jutted, snaggle-toothed, about thirty feet into the shallow water. Two other boats were moored there, a white schooner with aqua sails and a small Carolina Skiff. Seagulls stood, one-legged, all along the dock's handrails, which were covered in bird poop, as were the planks.

On land, a sandy clearing served as a parking lot. Two motor scooters, three bicycles, a metallic silver Galaxy, and a 1950-something Dodge pickup were parked facing the bay and all of them were rusting in the fine salt air.

"How did these cars get out here?" I asked as Nick hoisted a box onto the dock.

"Drove 'em over at low tide," he deadpanned.

"Really?"

I imagined a small flotilla of cars crossing the bay. It had to be an amazing sight. I started to ask if people routinely made the crossing via automobile but he was hurrying off the dock—three boxes stacked in his arms—grunting under the load.

He carried them to the Galaxy and stacked them in the backseat. Then he walked toward the dirt road, away from me and the bay, and stared into the distance.

I watched him in the bright midday light, so still and solemn, a solitary figure against the immense blue sky. I walked toward him, slowly, allowing him this moment, believing that like an astronaut re-entering the earth's atmosphere, he was reattaching himself to the place he loved.

In the days, weeks, and months to come, Nick would share this island with me, challenging me to understand it the way he did, urging me to become a more astute observer—a person who looked and listened with both body and soul, not simply ears and eyes.

To this day, I do not understand Lethe's complexities as fully as Nick did and probably never will. He had the gift. He was able to escape that division between man and nature. He once said to me, "I know what the Bible meant when it said God cast Adam and Eve out of paradise. God didn't send them anywhere; he took something away. Their animal eyes, all that under the surface stuff that lets us know we're part and parcel with the beasts and fish and snakes. He turned us into fools in our own land."

And it is true, I was a fool—or at least an immigrant—on Lethe. But from time to time, a quiet magic would settle over me and I would glimpse this world through Nick's eyes. Its fragile unpredictability that flourished in the midst of cycles asserting themselves with the resoluteness of stone. Sugar-white dunes ribbed as if the wind had fingers. Sea oats rustling in a language all their own. Pin oaks sculpted by gales into the shape of the southwesterly breeze—their branches resembling tattered flags frozen in time, pointing perpetually toward the mainland as if they were trying to warn or guide us. Shell-scattered shorelines building and receding in response to storms not yet spawned. Infinite vistas of open water that at high noon cannot be looked upon because of the blinding glint of the sun reflected off the Gulf's mirror-like surface.

Yes, this island, I would learn, was the physical embodiment of Nick's soul, the geography of dreams he could not mention, the gasp born in his bones at the sight of wonder.

"My God, it is beautiful," I whispered as I stood beside him and gazed across the dune line to the Gulf.

He put his arm around me, kissed the top of my head, and said, "Welcome home, baby."

"You, too, Nick. You, too."

The first time I saw Lillian Athena Blue she was standing in her backyard in her grape arbor, a pair of pruners in her gloved hand, yelling at a raccoon who was sitting atop the vines as if he were an ornament, eating her beautiful plump golden scuppernongs.

"I'm warning you, you beady-eyed bastard, if you don't stop eating all my grapes, the last thing you're gonna see will be the barrel of my Winchester!"

Nick squeezed my hand as we made our way down a pine straw path that curved through a garden redolent in shades of yellow, lavender, and green. Parsley and basil thrived among salvias and coneflowers. The garden smelled of many things, but most prominent was the scent of composted, fertile soil.

We had been on Lethe for all of fifteen minutes. I would have preferred getting settled in before meeting Nick's mother. But, as he pulled on a fresh shirt in the dock parking lot, he insisted that we go to her house first on the grounds that if anyone else caught wind of his return they would surely tell his mother and it was important to him that he be the one to break the news to her.

"Mama," he said, laughing, "you're making a bad first impression."

Lillian lowered her arms. Her back was to us. She did not move but her warning appeared to have some effect on the raccoon. He sat up on his haunches, cocked his head to the side as if he were considering the seriousness of her threat, and then scurried off the arbor and loped toward the bay where he disappeared into a thicket of wax myrtle.

It was only then that Lillian turned around, her black eyes wet with tears. She was no taller than me—five foot one, if that. Her silver-streaked ebony hair was pulled tightly off her face into a single tail at the nape of her neck. She was dressed in yellow shorts, a white button-down shirt, and a floral print chef's apron. Like Nick, she had gorgeous cocoa-colored skin, and the wrinkles that lined her face and framed her eyes barely put a dint in her austere, no-nonsense beauty. In fact, the wrinkles suited her. Without them she would have been unremarkably pretty. With them, Lillian Blue was handsomely imposing, which is quite an accomplishment when you're as petite as she.

But Lillian was also a woman who, as she gazed at the son who had spent the long winter off-island, appeared dumbstruck by his sudden appearance.

"Nick," she said, her voice trembling. "What are you doing here?"

He walked over to her and placed his hands on her shoulders. Nick's height and his beautiful curls and those sapphire eyes must have come from his father, I thought as I watched him hug her.

They stood for several seconds locked in this embrace, not speaking. The pruning shears slipped from her fingers and the dirt on her gloves left streaks on his back. He kissed her cheek, slipped off a glove, and held her hand.

"I've come back, Mama. For good."

She stared into his face and her eyes flashed with a hard, maternal light. "You sure?"

"Yes," he said. "I'm sure." He kissed her forehead and then held her once again by the shoulders. "Don't you worry."

She lifted the back of her hand to her lips and crossed her other arm in front of her. She looked toward the bay and back at Nick. "I've been so worried about you," she said. "No matter what happens, I'm so glad to have you home."

"It's all gonna be okay, Mama. I promise. Now no more crying. I've got somebody I want you to meet."

Nick waved me over. I stepped toward Lillian, my heart breaking, my fear of her careening.

She wiped a rogue tear off her cheek. "Oh my goodness, you must be Mattie." She placed both her hands on mine. "Nick has told me all about you!"

"He has?"

"Of course he has!" she said, smiling. "He said your pot roast is better than mine."

"Oh no, I'm sure it's not," I said quickly, fearing she felt insulted by her son bragging about my cooking and deeply confused since I could barely boil water without burning down the kitchen.

"I don't have any ego about food," she said, "so knock yourself out. But my garden. Now that's a different matter." She tucked her gloves into the pocket of her chef's apron. "Do you garden, Mattie?"

"I've never really had the opportunity. But I like flowers."

"Well, that's a start," she said, locking the blades of her pruning shears.

Nick said, "Be careful. Before you know it, she'll have you digging in the dirt until your eyes turn brown."

"That's okay. They'll match my thumbs."

"Really? Stick around long enough and we'll fix that." She touched her earlobe and looked at Nick. "How did you get here?"

Nick grinned. "Took the skiff."

"Now, Nick, when are you two boys going to stop that foolish game? I'll have you know, Lacey took that boat by herself. Demetrius is home with the baby!"

"Ooops," Nick said.

"Yes, ooops. Come on inside and I'll radio Vanessa. Maybe she's got room on the mail boat."

Lillian whisked past us and headed up the path. She took big, mannish strides and, as I hurried to keep up, my brain ground to a halt in the middle of trying to process what she meant by "radio" and "mail boat."

"Quick," she said, "before Vanessa leaves the hill. I ought to make you get in that boat and fetch Lacey. She's got a temper, you know."

Nick shook his head and stepped up his pace. "Why don't I just go and do that now?" he asked.

"Not yet, not yet," she said, waving her hand, and then she disappeared around a bend in the path but her voice trailed behind her. "How about some cold shrimp for lunch? That and a nice salad and some good sweet tea. Nicholas! Are you coming!"

.   .   .

This was the situation.

In the early days of the twentieth century not a single human soul lived on Lethe. The Indians were long dead, having succumbed to smallpox, bullets, and other European-born diseases. As for the Scotch-Irish and the English and the old French trappers, they didn't care a whit about that dot of green on the horizon. Sure, families occasionally took boats over from Carrabelle for day-long picnics. And it wasn't unheard of for a fisherman to pack his gear and spend a week—two at the most—camping on the beach and fishing from shore. But by most people's standards, the island was simply too remote to bother with; getting to Carrabelle in those days was difficult enough, never mind having to sail across a bay that was infamous for its sudden storms and hidden shoals. So despite Lethe's beauty, which was not in dispute, it remained uninhabited.

But when you've journeyed halfway around the globe in order to harvest sponges in foreign waters in a land populated by light-skinned people of European descent and black-skinned sons and daughters of former slaves, inconvenience and risk-taking are preambles to your existence.

The risk-taker in this case was Nick's great-great-grandfather, Nereus, a man who was slightly built but who had lungs bordering on gills. Which is an important attribute if you're a sponger. At least it was at the turn of the century when the only thing that sponge divers had as a lifeline to the surface was a hose snaking through the depths from the clutter aboard a patchwork boat.

Despite his legendary lung capacity, Nereus wasn't content. Sponging didn't fill up that hollow yearning perpetually squeezing his chest, causing his breathing to become labored even when he was standing still and upright on dry land. Destiny had tapped him for something greater. He just knew it. What that something was he hadn't a clue but he prepared himself as best he could.

He understood that to be successful in this new land he had to have command of its mother tongue. But life in Carrabelle offered the immigrants little chance at obtaining a formal education in English or any-thing else, so Nereus had been pulling together strings of words and their meanings on the fly, which—given his nebulous ambition—wasn't good enough. But it was a start.

Early one summer morning as the spongers were loading their gear into the boats, the mercantile owner's son, an eight-year-old towheaded boy named Eddie Paul, watched from shore, a hard sour candy lodged between his gum and cheek. The men on the sponge docks hoisted and hollered and laughed and cussed in a strange language so delicious that Eddie Paul felt as though he'd fallen under a spell. Just like when he pressed his ear to his bedroom door at night to try to hear each refrain of the dirty ditties his daddy sang after too much rum.

With his eyes, the boy followed one man in particular, a serious and thin fellow with a thick black mustache. The other men quieted down each time he spoke, which led Eddie to mistakenly think he was the man in charge.

Mustering his nerve, Eddie Paul took the lemon ball out of his mouth, dropped it into the breast pocket of his overalls so that he could finish it off later, zigzagged his way through the gaggle of men, stepped into the oval of Nereus' shadow as the sponger coiled a length of rope, spit into the water because that's what grown-ups did, wiped his mouth on the back of his hand, and said, "Hey, mister, you got any work a man can do?"

Nereus had dabbled in enough broken English that he was able to discern the boy's meaning. He laughed and repeated in Greek to the other men what Eddie had said. Smoothing his mustache with the thick pad of his callused thumb, he bent down and studied the boy's face. It was a defiant little white boy's face complete with a splattering of freckles.

A sponger hurried past with a load of baskets and said in Greek, "No good. He's got the blue."

Nereus nodded. People with blue eyes could not see the sponges underwater. It seemed everyone but the locals understood that. Never-theless, as the man and the child continued their staring match, it dawned on Nereus that what he was looking at wasn't simply a little boy. He was gazing head-on into the face of an opportunity.

"You," he pointed at Eddie and then at himself. "Me." He spread his palm flat and with his other hand ran his pointing finger back and forth as if following lines on a page.

"Teach you to read! Naaaah," Eddie said. "Crazy Greek!" He waved his arm in disgust, spit once more, and skulked away. But when the boats returned that night, Eddie was waiting for Nereus, pen, paper, and his first-grade primer in hand.

In exchange for the reading and English lessons, Nereus told Eddie stories about his homeland, shared with him fishing tips, clued him in on the finer points of poker, taught him how to say *yes, no, thank you, please,* and *go to hell* in Greek, and gave the boy's father one load of free sponges a month which Mr. Paul sold to a broker in New York City.

Being able to read, of course, opened up wide new worlds for Nereus—most specifically, the *terra firma* of U.S. citizenship and local real estate. At night, in a small, ramshackle room in the white clapboard Carrabelle boardinghouse, by the light of a single wax myrtle taper, he read periodical after periodical and came to understand the tenets of homesteading, squatter's rights, and the local resistance to living anywhere but on the mainland.

I wouldn't doubt it at all if a sly smile didn't slip across his weathered face as he sat in his cramped quarters, the candlelight throwing convulsive shadows across the room, acclimating himself to the notion that three miles offshore sat his destiny. According to family lore—often repeated in subsequent years with stout authority over platters of fried mullet and cheese grits—Nereus' thoughts ran as follows: *Yes, God has brought me here to settle that island. To become its patriarch. To harvest its abundant seas. This is not merely the desire of a humble sponger. It is my duty. Like Noah and his ark or Abraham and his altar.*

Nereus homesteaded the island in 1910 (squatter's rights were very much alive in those days) and in 1911, via mail, asked Theo Volcanus for his daughter's hand in marriage. He detailed his success in America. Not only did he own an island (no mention was made that he simply laid claim to it), he had saved enough of his earnings from sponging to build a thirty-foot shrimp trawler and had drawn up plans for a fifty-footer. He was highly respected in the community, and his facility with the language of his adopted land demanded that he serve as an *elaison* between the Greek and local populations. It is, he allowed, an important position.

The waters here are shallow and warm, he wrote. *Shrimp, flounder, snapper, grouper, and turtle are so plentiful that my nets routinely are full to overflowing. Only Greece, dear Greece, rivals this island I have named Lethe in her beauty and bounty. Your daughter will have not only a good life here, but a blessed one.*

He signed the letter, *Respectfully yours, Captain Nereus H. Blue, sole owner of the Isle of Lethe, United States of America.*

The letter was so convincing that Theo Volcanus booked passage not only for his daughter, but for himself, his two other daughters, his wife, and a distant male cousin who worked nets, according to Lillian Blue, like an artist. A sheer artist.

Being a gentleman of prudent wisdom, Nereus chose Lethe's highest point of elevation—which was thirteen feet above sea level and just about dead center in the oblong, eleven-mile island—as his homesite. He cleared the land himself and used the fallen trees as his framing materials. As a result, Lethe's first home was framed out of magnolia, pine, and a small amount of oak. The palm thatch roof, I am told, kept out the rain surprisingly well. He brought screening over from the mainland and enclosed the wraparound sleeping porch, which made the mosquito and no-see-um situation only slightly tolerable. Because of the elevation, the sea breezes almost continuously swept through the house, and the six-foot-high pine, metal-strapped rain cistern ensured that they had a constant supply of fresh water should the well run dry.

Nereus' success at sea and in land dealings carried over to his bed, much as he had hoped. He and his wife, Doris, raised eleven children. Eight daughters. Three sons. Some of the daughters eventually went to the hill, took husbands, bore babies, and settled in the coastal villages of Carrabelle, Apalachicola, Eastpoint, Panacea, and New Port. Nereus' oldest daughter married Eddie Paul, who was by then a retired captain in the U.S. Army. The couple moved to Detroit, Michigan, and was never heard from again. But the sons, they remained on Lethe and continued to fish and procreate with much the same ecumenical zeal as their father.

The original home was destroyed in 1928 when a hurricane flattened it, the island, and—according to old-timers—every tree as far as Crawfordville. Unfazed by the storm's destruction, the Blues rebuilt, this time ferrying the materials over from the hill. They constructed homes that weren't much different in style and intent from the original structures. Everything was designed to welcome in the breeze and keep out the water. Tin roofs replaced the thatch and the framing was pine and cypress milled upriver from Carrabelle.

You might think that being landowners, the Blues had it made, financially speaking. But that was not the case. Nereus Blue had laid claim to the island not for the purpose of investment and speculation but to establish a home for himself and his offspring, all of whom, he assumed, would be fishermen or the wives of fishermen. He knew full well that people who depend on the sea for their wages can—if they're smart and lucky—make a fair living. He also knew the rest of the story: Rarely does anyone get rich. Some folks go broke. Others remain or become frightfully poor. But the Blues were hardworking, tightly knit, and able to take care of themselves adequately, even happily, because luxury wasn't something they aspired to. Luxury would have not only seemed foreign, it would have been downright uncomfortable. So the Blues were not wealthy, monetarily speaking, but most of them fulfilled Nereus' desire that his descendants work, play, and procreate on Lethe. And they did so with the ease that comes to those who are gifted.

Despite the occasional feud or hurricane or accident at sea, Nereus Blue's plan unfolded remarkably smoothly. That is, until the mid-1970s, a time that the Blues refer to as "the troubles." George Blue—Nick's father—who was by then the family patriarch, watched helplessly as taxes skyrocketed in the same year that a red tide outbreak shut down fishing for three months. By the time the waters were reopened, many of

George's buyers had found cheaper sources for their seafood, primarily from Mexico and the western Gulf. It took him three years to rebuild his business. In the meantime, cash-strapped and disillusioned, he was left with two horrible choices. Claim bankruptcy and allow the government to seize his land. Or sell off some of the island and crawl out of debt.

There was little doubt as to what path he had to take. With a steady-eyed determination that is common in this family, he broke up what Nereus Blue had called his legacy. For the first time since 1910, people other than members of the Blue clan began to populate Lethe.

Lillian said her husband was never again the same and that he might have gotten over the pain inflicted by being forced to sell the land had it not been for the battles he fought with an endless regiment of bureau-crats, lawyers, and developers. "They pummeled him," she said. "Right down to nothing. To them it was sport."

But they didn't win every skirmish. Much to the consternation of his opponents, George sold the western end of Lethe to the Nature Conser-vancy. Another fifty acres, however, went to the Mander Corporation, a shell set up by a bank of attorneys for a client they would not name.

"Those city people, they stole his soul," Lillian told me one after-noon over tea. "Two years after we lost the land, George was dead," she continued as if his horrible accident at sea was the result of the ruthless, calculating blood lust of a real estate deal.

So Lethe was not untouched. The Blues had neighbors to whom they weren't related and rarely spoke to, not out of snobbery or hard feelings, but because nearly all of the newcomers were part-timers who feared the Blue clan, whom they inexplicably referred to as "crackers." They feared their knowledge, and their readiness to take on the sea, and their refusal to give up on a way of life that was sometimes harsh and offered only minimal financial rewards. But what frightened the new-comers more than anything was the Blues' refusal to simply head inland and get "real" jobs. An honorable, independent life tied to the sea was not valued or understood by the newcomers. They felt threatened by it. What they preferred and what they could grasp was conformity. After all, if Lethe would only give itself over to condos and hotels, the Blues could become porters and maintenance men and yard boys. So when the newcomers were on-island, they tended to stay inside their massive, well-appointed, multistoried, columned homes, which would have been much more appropriate on a golf course than a barrier island where everything, including the land itself, was temporary.

Virtually every time Nick passed by one particularly garish home—three stories, five thousand square feet, stuccoed brick with columns, and a pesticide-soaked, meticulously landscaped yard—he would sadly shake his head and say, "Those fools don't understand where they're living."

But it must be said that even though poor George Blue had felt himself mortally wounded by the loss of part of the island, in actuality, the Blues had done remarkably well. They no longer could single-handedly control development on the island but they still managed to maintain an authoritative hand in most of its issues. Also, George had shrewdly held on to Gulf to bay frontage, so for all intents and purposes, the Gulf of Mexico was in their front yard and the bay their back yard. Nick's mother, who shared her residence with her aged in-laws, Rhea and Charon, lived in the 1928 house on three acres. Nick's cottage sat on two, as did most of the other houses owned by family members. Because George had retained the land adjoining the parcels he sold to the Conservancy and which they turned into a refuge for the endangered piping plover, the Blues essentially had the west half of the island all to themselves. In truth, they freely came and went on the Conservancy's land as if they still owned it. And though property taxes continued to rise, they owned free and clear the ground and the houses that sat on it. So they managed.

When the ins and outs of Lethe's dominion and geography became clear to me, I did not mourn the fact that Nick's family no longer owned the whole kit and caboodle. Not at all. In fact, I had only one thought. Lucky me.

. . .

In a hole dug in the sand in an area beyond Lillian's garden near the soft, sandy shore of the bay, embers at their core glowed red-hot and their coal black surfaces slowly withered to ash.

A rectangular piece of corrugated metal straddled the pit and a burlap bag blanketed the entire contraption. Every now and again one of the men—specifically, a stocky, bald forty-ish man wearing nothing but baggy red swim shorts and green rubber flip-flops—sprayed the burlap with water which sizzled and hissed before billowing into the air in a cloud of pearl white smoke. As the smoke rose so too did the musky scent of roasting oysters—their ugly sharp shells hidden from view beneath the burlap—as they were forced open by the stinging heat.

Up at the house people ate. On the large screened-in bayside porch decorated with gray salt-crusted nets, gale-battered wind chimes, flowering tropical plants, and seashells vacated long ago by a sundry assortment of gastropods, bivalves, and mollusks, dark-eyed amply hipped women shuttled from the kitchen platter upon platter of steamed shrimp, boiled Panacea blue crabs, and fried mullet.

Half-naked children ran gleefully from the garden to the porch and through the house, chasing one another with crabs, frogs, earthworms, and grasshoppers, until Lillian, whom the children referred to as Nana Blue, put a stop to it.

Nick's older brother's son, a quiet fourteen-year-old named Lucas, sat in a straight back chair in a corner, his guitar resting on his rail-thin thighs, finger-picking tune after tune. As he played he kept his somber gaze fixed on his guitar. When people applauded or shouted their appreciation, his face briefly radiated with a self-conscious, embarrassed grin. In the coming weeks, I would understand that music allowed Lucas to deny the demands of a tender, painful past. His mother died in a car accident when he was nine. Two years later his father, Zeke Blue, ran away to only God knows where, leaving him to be raised by his Aunt Beth and her partner, Maya. But that afternoon, residual effects of his fractured home life were nearly impossible to discern.

The women sang. The children danced. The feral cats paced outside and meowed for scraps. The men roasted more oysters and drank more beer. The old people tapped their feet and wiped tears from their eyes and every once in a while one of them reached for my hand and whispered, "Thank you for bringing him home."

All of these things occurred on my first night on Lethe. Word gets out fast on a small island and it was no different with news of Nick's return. Unbidden, the family made the pilgrimage to Lillian's house—some by foot, others by car, and a few by boat—to celebrate generously, in the only fashion they knew how—with food and drink and music and the good-natured gossip they called storytelling.

These were coastal people and the stereotype was true. They smiled too much and talked too loud. Most of them weren't terribly interested in culture as that word was defined in urban centers. A painting by Jackson Pollock or Jasper Johns would simply prove puzzling. The women might cast a glance at the painting and then at their children, wondering if their offspring had the sort of talent that people in the big cities went for. Most of the men might stare at the canvas, readjust their baseball caps, rub the backs of their necks with sunburned hands, and then honestly admit, "Sorry. It don't do a thing for me."

But the stereotype and these people's absence of cosmopolitan airs obfuscate who they truly were. Their boisterousness was not born out of stupidity or dull-wittedness but from a down-to-the-core love of life. They were seized by joy, curiosity, and a brand of wide-eyed wonder that was only occasionally tarnished by the bitter skepticism born from un-fulfilled aspirations. If they didn't know Jasper Johns from Cy Twombly, that was okay because what other people pursued with good intentions was all right by them. They didn't want to judge or be judged, especially not by standards set by strangers who knew little if anything about their lives and livelihoods. They read books and listened to music and didn't really care much for that mess on the mainland. They worked hard and made time for family and understood where it was they lived. And how many of us can say that? How many of us truly grasp the nuances and troubles of the ground or concrete beneath our feet?

If there was anyone who was ignorant that night at that table it was me. I didn't even know how to pop open a crab, a detail which didn't escape Rhea Blue's all-encompassing, cataract-fogged gaze. She caught me staring dumbfounded and disgusted at the plateful of crabs someone had set in front of me.

"Nick, I cannot believe you brought home a girl who doesn't know how to pick crab. Will you please help the poor child before she starves to death," Rhea said, aiming a screwdriver at me which she was using to eviscerate her pile of crabs.

Nick walked me through what seemed to come naturally to everyone else. In an attempt to save me from further embarrassment, he whispered, which only made things worse.

"You got some secret technique, Nick?" one of the men asked.

"Jimmy, hush!" his short-haired, pinch-faced wife said and then she started laughing.

"You can pretty much eat everything except for these things, the gills," Nick said, ignoring them. "They'll make you sicker than sick. Besides, you won't want to eat 'em. They taste like mud."

"Dead man's fingers," one of the kids piped up, waving the grayish white tissue through the air until her mama ordered in a staccato lilt, "Jessie May, put that thing down this very second."

"Here we go, this is what you're after," Nick said, exposing the crab's flaky white meat.

"I just eat it right here?" I asked.

"Well, yeah. Unless you want to take it inside."

"I mean, I eat it right out of the shell?" I looked around. Evidently I was the evening's entertainment. People quickly diverted their eyes and tried to appear engrossed in their supper. I noticed that most of them were eating as they picked and then tossing the shells into a pile in the middle of the table, but Nick's aunts were exhibiting what I interpreted to be both restraint and good manners. They fastidiously picked crab after crab, not eating until their bowls were full of meat.

"You won't regret it," Nick said.

Knowing I had no choice, I took the dive. I pushed aside the gills, dug in with my fingers, and popped the meat in my mouth, a meat that tasted oddly delicious even though it barely had any flavor at all.

A cheer broke out across the table. Nick kissed my forehead. I did the only thing a person could do after being challenged and prompted through this coastal rite of passage. I reached for another crab.

As night fell, lanterns and candles were lit. Some people switched from beer to coffee, others iced tea. The children grew cranky, the husbands loaded, and the wives fed up. As is prudent in such situations, people slowly began to drift home.

Going home—wherever that was, we'd been at Lillian's since our arrival that morning—sounded like a fine idea to me but Nick was reluctant to leave before the final guest was out the door. I wasn't accustomed to being around so many people—all of whom talked at once, often about individuals and events I had no frame of reference for. They went on for a while about Diana, Lillian's older sister who had died of ovarian cancer a year ago.

"It just ate her up something awful. That beautiful head of hair of hers fell out, every single strand. Chemo, you know."

"But she was still an attractive woman, hair or no hair—cancer didn't steal that from her."

"Lord God, she loved her lipstick! She'd be sick as a dog—up-chucking and everything—and she'd say to whoever was around, 'Hand me my lipstick, I think I could use some.'"

"Is Charis still out there in Hollywood?"

"Yes. Can you imagine!"

"Is she an actress?"

"She wishes! She's a costume design assistant or something like that. She helped with that movie, what was it called?"

"*Pulp Fiction.*"

"Couldn't watch it, myself."

"The language!"

"She never comes home."

"Now that's not true, she came to the funeral."

"Well, big deal."

"She only writes at Christmas. Then it's just a card and her signature. L-U-V, Charis—with a heart underneath it. And no mention on that card—front or back—of Jesus."

"Dicky Crum, he still shrimps but he took to the bottle after he lost Diana. Living over in Panacea."

"Bless his heart."

"Nick, you ought to go see him. It would do him good."

"Uh-huh."

I sat largely in silence, trying to be unobtrusive, speaking only when spoken to. When Nick suggested we go for a walk, I was beyond grateful.

As we headed off the porch, Lillian said lightly, "Don't you two lovebirds stay gone too long."

Rhea, her voice cracked with age, snapped, "Lillian, leave them alone. If I were them I would have left hours ago!"

We walked around the east side of the house, down a pine straw path lined with night-blooming jasmine that spilled into Lillian's front yard, a wild, eccentric, and unruly garden completely unlike the manicured paths out back. Coontic palms, sea oats, palmettos, lantana, plume-topped grasses, and nodding sunflowers.

The tiny clusters of orange and yellow lantana were so pretty I was compelled to touch them. I pinched off a flower head, expecting a sweet, perhaps even citrusy aroma. "Yuck. That smells horrible."

"Stinkweed," Nick said, smiling. "Fools people every time."

I dropped the flower and rubbed my hand on my pant leg. "Your family is real nice, Nick."

"Sorry for all the people. I was hoping for a quieter homecoming. Is this all too much for you? Do you regret coming with me?"

"Yes. It is a bit much. And, no, I don't regret it. Not for one second."

He kissed me. I pulled on his lower lip with my mouth, keeping him near. "You do that for very long and we won't make it back to the party."

"Sounds like a plan."

"Yeah, for ticking off Mama." He squeezed my hand and led me deeper into the garden. A crescent moon rose in the east while lavender streaks of fading light dappled the western sky. We came upon a weathered cypress bench and an old iron bell hung by a chain looped over an arched limb of a camphor tree. A hemp rope snaked from the bell, its end coiled in the sand.

"What's this?" I asked.

"Nereus' bell."

"Who?"

"My great-great-granddaddy. They say the bell washed ashore in the twenty-eight hurricane. He took it to be a sign. Said it meant we were supposed to stay on Lethe and rebuild and that if the family was ever in danger again, the bell would warn us."

"Wow," I said and reached for the rope, wanting to give it just one good clang.

"No no, don't! You ring that thing and you'll have everybody out here."

"Oops."

"Anyway. I don't know that it was ever used to warn anybody of anything. Mama always rang it when she wanted us to come in from the beach."

"That's nice. It's like a family heirloom."

"Yeah. I guess." He guided me over to the bench and we sat down. "Except every few years the thing gets so corroded from being out here in the salt air that we have to take it to Tallahassee where this fella puts it in an acid bath. And then we repaint it and after a while, you got to wonder how long the bell can last. Seems to me that eventually time will take its toll and that the acid will eat away what's left. Then old Nereus' bell will be just another family legend."

"Well, that's okay, too."

"Yep. I suppose so."

I rested my head against Nick's shoulder. The surf sighed endlessly. The twilight sky faded to purple. My cheek grew warm against the soft cotton of his shirt.

"You don't get nights like this on the hill."

"I wonder why?"

"Water. It changes everything."

He stroked my hair. Laughter filtered out from the back porch but was then whipped landward by the breeze.

"The stars are coming out," I said.

"That means the shrimpers are, too." He stood and, with his hands shoved into his back pockets, walked toward the sea.

I followed him to the base of the dune line and it was then that I saw them. The running lights of the shrimp boats seemed flung across the night, inshore and beyond, and there was no difference between the light that sparked the water and that which gleamed in the heavens. I slipped my hand into the crook of Nick's arm, and it dawned on me that one evening very soon I would venture onto the porch of the house Nick and I would share, and I would gaze upon the Gulf, and the only thing visible would be the incandescent glow of shrimp trawlers on the horizon, and I would know that Nick was out there amid that soft glare, his nets trailing through the water, the waves slapping the sides of his boat. And maybe, just maybe, he would pause from his work long enough to look up at the stars and think of me. And if not that, then perhaps some ancient yearning would tug at his heart, prompting him to make his way to the bow where he would lean into the darkness, straining to hear one more time those distant mythical sirens he had told me about. How did he put it?

I looked at him but he was scanning the horizon with a purity of focus I was unwilling to interrupt. So once more I cast my gaze beyond the dunes and finally it came back to me . . .

Some nights when I'm out there on that water all alone, when it's just me and my nets and that big starry sky, I get real lonesome. It's then that the singing starts. Beautiful faraway singing.

The party had thinned out by the time we returned. Demetrius, Nick, and Lucas were the only males still around. Sizing up the situation, Demetrius said, "Looks like we are seriously outnumbered," and he slapped his brother's shoulder.

"What's new?" Lucas said with a shy smile, looking up from his guitar.

"Come on, you two, let's go down to the bay," Nick said. He kissed the back of my hand. "Don't let her get away," he said to Beth.

"I don't think you've got to worry about that."

And thus I was left to fend for myself among the women. We were gathered around the pine porch table which had been cleared of most of its clutter, and I feared I had probably committed a terrible *faux pas* by not contributing to the cleanup, but I didn't have much of a chance to chew on that because Rhea, who was sitting across from me, said, "Men! They just can't keep up. Let me tell you something. What did you say your name was?"

"Mattie, ma'am."

"Well, Mattie, I'm going to tell you a few things." She leaned back in her chair and gripped the arms as if she might take off. "I didn't always look like this. I was pretty once. You can ask any old-timer 'round here and they will tell you Rhea Volcanus was a looker in her day. But big deal. Look at me now." She threw up her hands in disgust. "Young people these days, they think beauty lasts. But it doesn't. And it won't buy you supper. Not even a cup of coffee. So if you haven't got one already, you'd best begin building up a steel-eyed character."

Beth started laughing and Lillian moaned. "Rhea, please!"

But Rhea simply blazed ahead, telling me about how osteoporosis had whittled away at her bones so thoroughly that she was now two inches shorter than when she was a girl flirting with the soldiers and painting stocking seams on her legs from her ankles to her thighs while working at the PX at Camp Gordon Johnson during the war. And despite the inconvenience and pain associated with her medical condition, she suffered far more from chronic virtuousness than bone disease. Her piety, she said, prevented her from indulging in smoking or drinking, but it evidently left room for cussing because every so often she would disappear to check on Charon, whom she repeatedly referred to as "the old goat," "the jackass," and "the senile old bastard."

"You may be wondering where my husband is. Or if I even have one.

Well, I do, but you're not going to meet the old goat tonight. He's laid up in bed with a cold." And then she whispered conspiratorially, "I'm feeding him hot toddies. It's the only thing that keeps the jackass quiet."

Beth said, "Charon is not a jackass."

"I don't think so, either," chimed in Maya.

"Hmpf! You live with the damned old bastard for fifty years and then say that!"

"She doesn't mean it," Maya said to me.

Lacey Blue, Demetrius' wife, walked out of the house with Gabriel, their six-month-old boy, on her hip and an unlit cigarette dangling from her freshly painted Dracula-red lips. She patted the baby's back, trying to burp him, a clean diaper draped across her shoulder. "Rhea, are you scaring Nick's girlfriend?" she asked and the cigarette bobbed between her clenched teeth. Despite bearing the baby in her arms, she looked like a brawler.

"No, I'm not scaring her." Rhea glared at me. "Am I!"

"No, ma'am. Not at all."

Rhea struggled up from the chair and, leaning on her cane, said, "Best go check on the old bastard."

Lillian sighed as if her mother-in-law was simply too much for her and then followed her inside. Lacey was preoccupied with her baby so after I performed the obligatory "Oh my, how cute he is," I settled into a conversation with Beth and Maya.

With muscled thighs and calves, and shoulders broad-beamed and tan, it was easy to believe Beth when she said she had spent her entire life hauling nets. She was Nick's cousin and they were the same age and shared the same black hair and cocoa skin and I would soon learn that they loved each other not only like brother and sister but with a warrior-like bond that I would see again and again between fishermen.

Like Nick, Beth had left Lethe for a few years, thinking she'd be gone for good. In Tallahassee she pursued her other passion—literature—and earned a master's in English lit, specializing in contemporary women's novels, which, she said, many of her colleagues found puzzling because they considered anything written post-1900 to be frivolous unless it was penned by a man. When she and Maya met, she was teaching at a local high school and volunteering two nights a weeks at the Refuge House, a shelter for battered women in Tallahassee.

"Maya tried to play hard to get," Beth said, a mischievous grin tilting across her face.

"I did not!" Maya protested. "I was trying to be professional."

Maya hailed from Lakeland, a small Bible Belt town in Central Florida. Physically speaking, she was Beth's geographical opposite. Small-boned and blond, intense green eyes, and pale like me, Maya had spent five years as director of the Refuge House. But after dealing that long with, as she put it, "bubba judges" who thought battered women had "asked for it," she decided a change was in order. She was seriously contemplating law school when Beth made a suggestion that, on its surface, seemed ludicrous.

"Before I knew it, Beth was trying to convince me that our mission in life was not to save the world or go to law school or whatever, but was to move to Lethe and shrimp," Maya said as if she found the idea as absurd as the first time she heard it.

"I thought Beth had lost her mind. But I agreed to try it for twelve months. That was . . . let's see now . . . four years ago this August."

As I listened to their story, I tried to see myself owning a shrimp boat, and piloting it through calm and stormy seas, and working a quagmire of pulleys and gears, and keeping the engine oiled and running, and I thought, There is no way. Not in a million years.

Beth walked over to the ice chest and opened it. "My God, it's empty!"

"Well, we can't have that!" Maya said and the two of them left me alone with Lacey as they walked out to their Ford pickup to get a six-pack and a liter of Coke from the cooler they kept in their truck bed.

Lacey was bouncing her beautiful black-eyed boy on her knee and talking baby talk.

"Rhea and Lillian have been gone for a while. Do you think everything is okay?" I asked.

"Beats me. They're probably trying to force some food down

Charon." She made a face at her baby. "Don't know if you caught on or not, but those two," she said, jerking her head toward the door where Beth and Maya had exited, "are, you know, AC/DC."

"Well, I guess since it's not infectious, none of us have anything to worry about."

"I'm not worried," she said defensively. "I just thought you might like to know."

She fiddled with her baby's diaper, her face set in a scowl. My first impulse was to pursue her obvious bias against Maya and Beth but then thought better of it. This wasn't my home and I didn't know Lacey well enough to walk down a path that could lead to an argument. Not on my first night on Lethe, anyhow.

"Lacey," I said, trying to mend the fence, "I'm really sorry that we left you stranded on the hill today. I had no idea."

She shrugged her shoulders. "Hey, it wasn't the first time. I'm used to it." She shook her keys in front of Gabriel. The baby reached for them and gurgled delightedly.

Lacey was younger than me but her face was old, as if life had gotten in a few early, mean kicks. Her dyed blond hair was permed into tight, frizzy curls. Her teased bangs extended a good four inches from her scalp and resembled a giant insect. She was small—maybe all of five feet—which only added to the incongruity of her sky-high bangs. The whole creation was kept in place by a heavy application of hair spray. It was a dangerous hairdo, capable of inflicting bodily harm. I remembered what a mess my hair was in after the boat ride from the hill and then thought that hers probably didn't move one iota in the breeze, it being more like a helmet than a head of hair.

She cooed at Gabriel. "Do you want those keys? Yes, Gaby wants Mama's keys."

"Tell me something," I said. "Why doesn't everybody just wait until low tide and then drive over to Carrabelle? Seems easier than taking the boat."

"Drive over?" She smoothed the peach fuzz on her baby's head. "What do you mean, drive over?"

"Nick told me that people drive their cars between here and Car-rabelle at low tide."

"Let me clue you in on a little secret."

Rhea and Lillian came out of the house, bickering about whether Charon needed to see a doctor. Rhea walked over to us and held her hands out to the baby, who bounced on his knees, squealing and drooling.

"Do you want to go see Big-a-Mama? Okay. Go on. Go to Big-a-Mama," Lacey said, handing him over to his great-grandmother, whose shriveled and bent body did not add up to being tagged "big."

Rhea shuffled off, telling Gabriel what a handsome boy he was and that she suspected it was time for a diaper change and nighty-night. Lillian zipped into the kitchen and began rummaging through her refrigerator.

Lacey reached for a pack of cigarettes on the table and then tossed them back down. "I'm trying to quit. The baby and all."

She pulled a pack of gum out of her purse, offered me a stick which I refused, and then helped herself. As she unwrapped the foil wrapper she said, "The first rule of surviving out here is to not believe a single word Dem or Nick say.

"Miss Lillian." Lacey leaned back and yelled into the kitchen where Lillian was bent over putting a covered dish in the refrigerator. The only part of her that was visible was her rear end. "Nick had her believing people drive over here at low tide!" Lacey crowed.

Lillian closed the fridge door. Her eyes narrowed and her lips folded in on themselves as she tried unsuccessfully not to laugh. She and Lacey were utterly amused at my expense. I felt the blood rush to my face but I managed a halfhearted chuckle in an attempt to hide my embarrass-ment.

"Those boys!" Lillian said, walking out to the porch and taking a seat across from me. "Last year they had one of the people down on the east end convinced that oysters were harvested by dynamiting them!"

Beth opened the screen door and held it open for Maya. "Who's dynamiting oysters now?" she asked, stomping her sandy bare feet on the slatted porch boards.

Lacey told her about the low-tide cars and Beth said, "Don't feel bad about it, Mattie. When I was little he had me believing that flounders came ashore at night and ate little girls whole!"

"Well, not just that," Maya said in her soft southern accent as she and Beth loaded the ice chest with the drinks. "When I moved to the island, he and Demetrius told me never to go outside without a stick because of the wolves."

"The wolves!" Lacey screamed and her voice cascaded into a guffaw. "I saw you with that big stick and thought you were scared of the snakes!"

That sent everyone into laughing fits. Lillian slapped the table and then held her sides. Maya's face turned beet red. Tears streamed over Beth's cheeks. Rhea came back out, having put the baby to bed, and she took one look at us and started laughing, too, even though she didn't have the slightest idea why we were all so tickled. It was as though we'd been infected with a disease—the measles, for instance—that manifested itself in uncontrollable fits of laughter.

As our giggling slowly subsided and with the same ease with which this day gave way to night, the women began to share stories. They bantered in a feminine shorthand that was at once familiar and comforting, meandering from one subject to another with a logic that would have confounded the men had any of them been present.

They began with politics.

"None of 'em are any damn good. Not a single one," Rhea said.

"That guy that ran for governor last election was the worst," said Beth. "He thought women should be down on the farm milking cows and pumping out babies."

"Yeah, and he'll probably run again in four years and this time he'll probably win," Lillian said.

"God, I hope not," said Beth, shaking her head in dismay.

The ladies could not reach a consensus regarding whether some cousin named Lauralyn who lived in Carrabelle should start her own business or not.

"She's empty-headed," Rhea said. "She can barely make out a grocery list without asking for help."

"All she wants to do is start a junk store. Anybody can do that. Maybe if she's got something to do besides watch soaps all day she won't be so empty-headed," countered Beth.

"Antiques," Maya corrected her. "It's not a junk store. It's an antique store."

"Antiques, my butt," said Lacey. "She'll be in there trying to sell people dirty sheets."

"Yes," said Lillian, "and some of them will buy 'em."

"Probably," said Lacey and then she grumbled incomprehensibly before saying, "Men! They're such big babies!"

"Yep. God knew what he was doing when he gave them wienies instead of uteruses," Beth said, even though she had no childbearing experience of her own.

"That's the damned truth," said Rhea. And then she went off about the time she and the "old goat" toured Paris thirty years ago and she had to embarrass herself by walking into the American Embassy and asking for a list of doctors because Charon was scared he'd get sick and didn't want "just any Frenchy looking at his bare bum."

"I bet there wasn't a single man here today who's ever had a prostate exam," said Lillian.

"Yeah," said Beth, " 'cause they're chicken. Imagine if they had to put their feet in the stirrups every twelve months."

"Well, if that was the case, speculums would be made out of something other than cold steel."

"Forget speculums. They couldn't even handle getting cramps once a month!"

"Ugh! I get terrible cramps," Lacey said. "So bad that sometimes I can't even get out of bed. I'm hoping it'll be different since I've had the baby."

"Don't count on it," said Rhea.

Lillian, who said she was happy not to have to worry about such things anymore, recommended hot baths with Epsom salts and a tall tumbler filled to the top with sherry.

"Sherry! That's hard core, Miss Lillian," Beth said.

"Forget sherry," carped Rhea. "Just go for the goddamned Wild Turkey."

"I thought you never drank," Beth said.

"It's not drinking if it's for medicinal purposes," shot back Rhea.

Maya stepped in, trying to sound like the voice of reason. "Valerian root stops cramps before they even start. Some people call it nature's Valium," she said expertly. "And also, the dirty sock pill because it stinks to high heaven."

"It couldn't smell any worse than Demetrius when he's been wearing the same pair of underwear for five days," said Lacey, rolling her eyes.

"Is that what that stench was?" Beth joked.

Then Rhea said that it must be close to twenty years ago when a friend of hers over in Spring Creek, Eloise Boyd, taught fifth grade for a good ten years or so, went absolutely wacky once menopause got hold of her. "There were days she barely knew her name. One of her neighbors saw her standing naked as a jaybird in front of her picture window and called the sheriff. Eloise explained to Sheriff Crum that she was having hot flashes something awful and would he like a glass of tea. The sheriff said no to the tea but he did go mullet fishing with her husband later that day and had a private man-to-man. Well, to make a long story short, her husband took her to a fancy doctor up in Tallahassee, some jackass know-it-all who wasn't even from around here, and he told Eloise she was sick in the head. Said she needed shock therapy."

"Shock therapy!" Lacey shouted indignantly. "She didn't go through with it, did she?"

"Yes, ma'am, she did. Didn't have any choice. Her damned husband agreed with the doctor and that was that." Rhea slapped her hands together to emphasize her point.

Lacey was floored. "But how could they do such a thing? She wasn't mental! Just hormonal!"

Lillian looked over her half-frame glasses which she had put on sometime earlier in the evening (evidently Nick wasn't entirely correct when he claimed that no one in his family wore glasses). "Dear," she said, "not that long ago they were still saying that cramps were in our imagination."

"That's right," said Beth. "I remember reading something when I was real young—one of those teen magazines, I think—and sure, it said right there in print that some of us suffer . . . let me get this right . . . I think they called it menstrual hysteria."

"Menstrual hysteria!" Lacey spit the words. "Jerks." She nervously twisted an empty cigarette pack into a paper corkscrew. "When did they wise up?"

"When women started becoming doctors," Beth said.

"Amen!" chimed in Rhea.

"And they gave us a name for our troubles. PMS," said Maya.

"The old goat would probably say that I suffered from pre-, during, and post-menstrual whatever," Rhea observed bleakly.

Maya clinked her beer against Beth's and said, "Ladies, I propose a toast. To PMS!"

"Here, here! To PMS!"

"To bad moods and chocolate!"

"To sore breasts and swollen bellies!"

"To being so mean you get the bed all to yourself," Rhea said sweetly.

"To being unbearably horny!" Lacey shouted but as soon as it was out of her mouth she looked stunned by her indiscretion and shot Rhea and Lillian a quick look. "Sorry," she said.

"Don't be sorry on my account," Lillian said.

"Or mine either," Rhea agreed.

And then as if to prove she was not a prude, Lillian lifted her coffee cup and offered her own toast: "Here's to hot flashes and good sex, neither of which I have anymore!"

"Yes! Yes!" We all joined in, giggling and clinking cups, cans, and glasses.

Maya worried that we might wake up Gabriel and the two older women answered for Lacey that once that child was down it was for the night.

A string of bells hanging from the handle of the screen door clanged as the door swung open.

"Sounds like we've been missing the party," Nick said and his eyes settled on me. Demetrius and Lucas shuffled in behind him.

"Just girl talk," said Beth. "You wouldn't be interested."

"Nick, you look like you've gained a little weight," Rhea said.

"It's Mattie's good cooking." He cracked his knuckles, which was his version of a nervous tic. He walked over and kissed my cheek. I quickly glanced at his mother, fearing that such an open display was inappropriate.

She sipped her coffee and it seemed to me she was making a point of not looking at us. She set down her cup, straightened her napkin and fork, and said, "Nick says that Mattie is a wonderful cook. He prefers her pot roast over mine."

I stared at my nails and made a mental note to tell him to never say anything like that to his mother again.

Maya said politely, "That's nice. Mattie, you'll have to fix it for us sometime."

Nick put his hands on my shoulders and squeezed. He cleared his throat. "Will everybody please stay put for a few minutes? I have a, uhh, an announcement to make." And then before anyone could respond, he, Demetrius, and Lucas hightailed it into the kitchen, boxing one another on the shoulders as they went.

The women turned to me, looking for an explanation.

"I don't know what he's up to," I said.

"I hope it's not anything that's going to make me cry," grumbled Rhea.

"You old softy," chided Beth and then she said, "It's probably some bull about how he and Dem are gonna start retailing shrimp."

"Not if I have anything to do with it," said Lacey. "Which I do."

"Quit bitching," Demetrius said gaily as he came out of the kitchen.

He and Lucas were each balancing a tray of glasses. "It ain't anything like that."

Nick followed with two bottles of red wine. He looked stricken.

Lillian said, "My God, boys, I think most of us have had enough to drink."

"You won't think that in a minute," Nick said, which caused us to break into giggles yet again.

"Beth, can I have some wine? Pleeease?" asked Lucas.

"Yeah. Try this rare vintage called Coca-Cola," she said, passing him the plastic liter.

With exaggerated movements and a goofy smile, Demetrius served us each a glass of wine. Nick wavered in the shadows, obviously on edge. I thought, He's either drunk or sick. He stepped up to the table, wiped his palms on his jeans, and breathed out hard. Then he backed away and started to pace.

"What's this about, Nick?" his mother asked.

"I'm getting there, Mama. Just give me a second." He turned his back to us and stared out at the scrub. When he faced forward again, he reached for my hand. He spoke my name and his voice cracked. "Mattie, I know we haven't hung out together all that long. What's it been—six, seven months? But I just have to say, well, you're the best thing that's ever happened to me. I'm telling you this in front of my family 'cause I don't ever want it said that I didn't know what I was getting into. I do. I really do."

He paused, searched my face, then said inexplicably, "I'm just gonna shoot my wad right here." He knelt down and someone gasped. He reached for my hands and sandwiched them between his. "You would make me the happiest man in all the world if you would agree to be my wife."

"Oh my God, he's proposing!" squealed Maya.

"Yea!" yelled Beth, who clapped him on the back, nearly knocking out of him what little breath he had left.

Faintly, I heard Rhea say, "Lillian, he's just like his father."

As I often do when I'm overwhelmed, I double-checked the facts to make sure I heard correctly. "You want me to marry you?"

He nodded "yes."

A small voice deep inside me whispered, "Remember this." His earnest, faintly lined face. His gaze jumbled with fear and love. The night crickets chirping in the palmettos and palms. The dog barking far down the road. Lillian's wind chimes clanging wildly. A cat mewing on the back steps. Beyond the dunes, the surf rolling on and on, a constant tidal hum.

"Okay . . . Okay."

Nick kissed me smack full on the lips and Beth started whooping. The family cheered and Demetrius furiously clapped his hands as if he'd just won a trip for two on a game show.

"I told you she'd say yes," he chortled.

"Yeah, we both did!" Lucas joined in.

"I love you," Nick whispered.

"I love you, too."

Nick got off his knees and raised his glass. "To Mattie," he said.

"No. To us," I insisted.

"To Nick and Mattie," everyone yelled, and we clinked glasses and drank wine and Maya let Lucas have one sip of hers and he scrunched his face and said, "That tastes terrible!" He wiped his tongue on his shirtsleeve. People rose from the table and gathered in close, wishing us well and offering advice.

"Don't spend too much on the wedding. You'll need that money later."

"Honesty, that's the key ingredient—"

"Put off as long as you can having babies—"

"Help with the cleaning and cooking, Nick. Don't make her do it all."

"Mattie, do not let him get by with leaving the toilet seat up or he'll do it for the rest of your lives."

It was Rhea's advice, though, that I remember as being most important and true, without triviality or complaint. "No matter how difficult things get, young lady—and you, too, Nick—don't ever, ever forget what it was about each other that caused you to fall in love in the first place." Then she pecked my cheek.

"Yes, ma'am," I said.

Lillian hugged me and held my face in her bony hands. Without wanting to and without warning, I burst into tears.

"There, there. It's all going to be okay," she whispered, and I saw that her eyes, too, glistened. "I hope you'll both be very happy." Then she turned and embraced her son.

Demetrius gave me a brotherly pat on the back, saying something to the effect of, "Welcome to the family, sister." Then he jumped up and hugged Nick, who was by then surrounded by family.

That is how, with my engagement only minutes old, I found myself sitting alone, outside their circle. I sipped my wine and watched my soon-to-be in-laws. Nick was hugging his mother, who was saying, "At least I've got you and Demetrius. That other brother of yours is no good. I don't understand how he could turn out to be so rotten. He's not welcome here anymore."

Lacey was fussing at Demetrius about painting the baby's room and Rhea was saying to Beth and Maya, "Fifty years of marriage and the damn fool doesn't even know who I am!" Maya, for some reason, kept rubbing Nick's back.

Perhaps I should have inserted myself into the circle but I couldn't bring myself to do it. Despite the fact that I was the person Nick proposed to, this moment was not about us. It was about his homecoming and family ties cut, bound, and renewed. I looked at the table jumbled with glasses and cans and half-full bags of potato chips and I thought, If I don't get out of here I'm going to faint.

No one noticed as I stood and slipped into the house. They were caught up in the tangle of their own lives and for that I did not blame them.

There were no lights on inside but the outdoor candles cast dancing shadows across the living room, randomly illuminating the furnishings and creating the illusion that the house was in motion. I slowly made my way past a couch, a rocker, two overstuffed side chairs, and then down a long dark hallway. The laughter from outside drifted through the wide-flung doors but dissipated into the shadows before it could overtake me.

I followed the hallway to its end where it emptied into a Florida room. I stepped inside, closed the door, and flipped on a light. On the north wall a bank of windows provided a stately view of the garden and beyond to the bay. I pulled shut the curtains, sat on the rattan couch, and closed my eyes.

My mind drifted, the events of the day scattering hither thither and then slamming into one another, casualties of my misfiring synapses. Amid the careening fragments, though, a chant quietly unfurled. *You're getting married. You're getting married. You're getting married.*

Good God, I thought, I have absolutely no idea how to be a wife. I never really knew one. I mean, not intimately. I needed a role model. Maybe Lady Macbeth. Or Ma Baxter. Or, and I started to giggle, how about Carol Brady? It's not as though my mother had an opportunity to set an example for me. Maybe it would come down to this: I would fail miserably as a wife. Or maybe marriage would fundamentally alter me, robbing from me what little sense of self I had. Maybe I would become lonelier and lonelier and Nick would slowly come to rue the day we met and his eyes would gradually darken into a dull, dead gray because as the years rolled on he would realize that he was gazing upon a wife whom he no longer loved. I was completely sick. Not physically. But deep down in the darkness of my heart, in that place that science has not yet been able to name.

How, in less than twenty-four hours, I lamented, did I go from being a checkout girl at the Suwannee Swifty to the fiancée of a blue-eyed shrimper on an island overrun by his relatives—an island that, given my aptitude for boats and swimming and tidal charts, was a million miles from nowhere with no way off and no one to turn to?

I opened my eyes and looked around at the room. The west wall was lined with bookcases. Someone in this house, I deduced brilliantly as I walked over to examine the books, must be a reader.

Seashells served as bookends. A small hand-painted, weather-beaten sign was propped at an angle on one of the shelves. In childish print, it warned, *No Smokin At'all Under The Thatch!* There were bronzed baby shoes and plaster casts of tiny hands, books on nature, politics, religion, and war. A tattered collection of the Hardy Boys was lined up beside *The Mind of the Dolphin*. Cookbooks and gardening books, romance novels and good, sound literature by the likes of Proust, Wolfe, and Hurston. On a shelf by itself, underneath a charred piece of wood, was a copy of *The Old Man and the Sea*. I took it down and thumbed through it. Its pages were yellow and thin. Someone had underlined various passages in pencil with a steady, purposeful hand.

Everything about him was old except his eyes and they were the same color as the sea and were cheerful and undefeated.

And on another page:

Why did they make birds so delicate and fine as those sea swallows when the ocean can be so cruel?

Next a fragment about the great fish:

. . . his determination to kill him never relaxed in his sorrow for him.

I quickly flipped through the pages. There were no notes in the margins. Just marked passages carefully chosen and meticulously, even lovingly underlined. A sentence here. A paragraph there. The annotations weren't the work of a student forced to study. I felt certain that someone of their own accord had been moved to glean meaning from the fisherman's struggle with the creature he called his brother.

I closed the book and held it to my chest, knowing that I would return to this room and Hemingway's old man, and I would follow the trail forged by whoever had cared about the book enough to try to gather its words into a map marked by fine, penciled lines.

Absentmindedly, I smoothed the dust jacket's tattered creases. That was always a comfort to me, the simple act of running my hand over the face of a book. I'd done so for as long as I could remember, standing in libraries, and study halls, and schoolrooms, and kitchens. It wasn't a deliberate act. More like an unconscious ritual of devotion. A priest presses his lips against the worn cold leather of a Bible and I caress the covers of novels I love. I placed the book on the shelf exactly as I'd found it, anchoring it with the charred wood.

My head was no longer spinning and I knew I needed to rejoin the party and would have to develop a strategy—like the wives I'd watched earlier—for urging Nick home before dawn, but as I started toward the door something caught my eye: a pine table in the corner cluttered with framed photos. I walked over to it, hoping to find pictures of Nick.

At the rear of the table sat a primitive wooden cross into which someone had burned a vining leaf motif. Interspersed among the photographs were votive candles, their wicks black from use. Paper images of various saints were anchored beneath some of the frames. This was more than a family photo collection. It was an altar.

One by one, I studied the photographs. They were filled with proud faces frozen into an emulsified flatness by the shutter's click if not for eternity then at least for a very long time. Most were snapshots, some candid, others posed. But there were also school pictures and wedding portraits and military-issued eight-by-tens. People I could not name stared out at me, their visages cast into a purgatory of gray tones. The newer photographs were garishly colorful like a Technicolor movie. Those with age on them were fading, but the disintegrating dyes lent the images an air of importance that they might not have otherwise possessed, a patina driven by time.

Pinned down inside a plain black frame was a shot of three wildly grinning bare-chested boys cradling their catch—a fish so large not a single one of them would have been able to hold it on his own. Its bill was long, narrow, lethal. But its torpedo-shaped body suggested an athlete's grace. It was a beautiful creature, really, all silver with streaks of violet and a dorsal fin that reminded me of a Chinese fan. What a shame to kill something so lovely, I thought. So mighty and lovely.

And then I was gripped by a strange fear that these grinning boys, each so full of himself, hadn't said a prayer over this fish before they took a blade to it and scaled its silvery skin, and chopped away at its body, and tossed its head and tail and fins and guts into the water as if they had never been of any importance whatsoever, and filleted its white flesh into shapes that would give no hint as to the animal's living glory.

No, I thought as I pressed my thumb along the creamy bulge of the fish's belly, they were not inclined to pray over the body of this dead fish. But maybe they admired the struggle it put up. At least that.

I decided the boy on the right must be Zeke, the oldest brother, the one who'd abandoned Lucas. And beside him, in the middle, was Nick.

Wiry and tattoo-free, Nick was probably all of fourteen in this picture. His gaze was open and clear and he held the fish so close to his body that he and the animal were most likely skin to scale. And then I noticed Nick's hands. They were wrapped crossways around the midsection of the fish, in the same manner that one holds something precious—a butterfly, a small gold trinket, a lucky marble, a leaf turned red by the wind.

Demetrius stood to the left of Nick, holding on to the fish's tail fin as if he were presenting a banner and looking at his big brother as if to say, "Boy, ain't we something!"

Zeke sported a heavy build and a cruel body. His bulky muscles were taut and prominently veined. He was smiling but that did nothing to diminish the cold hard edge in his blue eyes. What was that edge? Arrogance? Meanness? Fear? Or maybe just bravado? He had a high forehead and wavy black hair and a chipped front tooth which reduced what would have been a drop-dead gorgeous smile into a clownish smirk. He gripped the fish's head near where it had been hooked. One hand was stuffed halfway inside the fish's gill and a thin trail of blood ran down his arm. I hope I never meet you, I thought.

I set aside the photo and moved on to the others. Lillian was a beautiful bride in a lace veil and princess sleeves. Her long hair flowed over one satin-covered breast and she carried a bouquet of callas.

George Blue was a handsome, roughneck sort of man with an Elvis grin and even though I couldn't prove it by these pictures, I'd bet money that he walked with a swagger. His tuxedo, complete with tails and pleated cummerbund, was just a smidge too small but I doubted that there was an off-the-rack jacket in the world able to accommodate those broad shoulders.

Of the three brothers, it was Nick who most closely took after his father. Nick wasn't as heavy as George, but they both had big, well-defined upper bodies and their features were so similar, even down to the almond slant of their light eyes, that I felt sure that after George's accident Lillian must have, from time to time, looked into the face of her middle son and felt death's nagging tug.

As I perused photo after photo, I began to feel like a voyeur, deliciously stealing glances into a world as foreign to me as Hong Kong or Timbuktu. An old shirtless man in baggy dungarees mending a net. Children frolicking beside oyster middens taller than they were. Women in long skirts and floppy hats facing the open Gulf, fishing reels in hand. A Victorian studio portrait of a man looking decidedly uncomfortable beside a stuffed gator. Men going to war. Boys casting for mullet. Girls posing coyly beside dune buggies. Planes landing on the beach and trucks pulling seine nets from the sea. Children and adults, alike, crawling beak to tail over an enormous beached whale. Gap-toothed toddlers and radiant brides and stooped-over grandparents leaning on canes. Faces evolving from youth into old age as the camera tracked them through christenings of babies and boats, celebrations of weddings and births, indulgences of Christmas and Halloween and Easter and the Fourth of July and baby's first birthday and lordy lordy look who's forty, the luxuries of reflective lone walks along the beach, and the sorrowful rituals enacted out of duty by a family gathered around a flower-laden plot for the dead.

One day I would walk into this room and there on this very table among all the others would be a photograph of Nick and me. Perhaps one of us on our wedding day. And even further into the future, I'd come in looking for a book and I would pause to linger over photos of our children. And just as I can see Lillian growing old in these pictures, I would be able to step back from my life for a moment and observe in what ways my own family had grown and changed. Whenever I felt I had lost my way, that my compass had gone awry, I would come into this place and study these images and begin to regain my footing.

I stood in the room that night and made myself that promise.

Then I flipped off the light and closed the door, grateful that finally, finally I was a part of something.

I returned to the celebration as quietly as I exited. This was not a difficult feat given the turn the party had taken. They'd pulled out a boom box and were playing Greek folk music. The family—other than Lacey, who had evidently gone home—looked on, laughing and clapping in time to the exotic rhythms, as Beth and Nick danced. Beth's dedication to the dance overrode her clumsiness. Nick, however, was graceful. Divine. His eyes closed, his face raised to the stars, he twirled and dipped and shimmied. There wasn't a single drop of self-consciousness as he gyrated across the porch. He seemed possessed. But gloriously so. I sat beside Lillian, floored.

"Are you okay?" she asked.

"Yes, ma'am, I'm fine. I was just looking at pictures," I said, continuing to watch Nick.

"In the Florida room?"

"Yes."

"Good." She patted my hand and I felt myself strangely moved by the gesture. "That child has always loved this music. He can't sit still when he hears it. Never could."

He and Beth were performing an inept but rigorous belly dance. "I've never seen him this way."

"That's because you've never seen him at home."

She watched her son and tapped her foot and lightly hummed but she clasped and unclasped her hands, over and over, as if stumbling through a hesitant prayer.

.   .   .

Proteus Nicholas Blue and Matilda Fiona O'Rourke were married exactly seven months to the day after meeting one another. The date was July 19, 1996. It was a Wednesday (a Wednesday evening, to be exact) and the weather was good. Clear and warm with only a few high clouds.

They took their vows aboard a thirty-foot, full-masted schooner named (unfortunately) *The Dixie Belle* with only their closest family and friends in attendance.

At 6:30 P.M. they sailed out of Apalachicola and anchored two miles offshore in the middle of Apalachee Bay, where a snaggletoothed old man named Captain Johnny conducted the ceremony, timing it to run in tandem with the sunset, which officially occurred at eight seventeen.

Captain Johnny spoke in a coastal patois that was completely understood by everyone present except for the bride, who, by all accounts, looked splendid.

She was well aware that the women had taken a poll among themselves, as females tend to do, and had agreed that though the bride did not wear conventional wedding attire, her dress was lovely in and of itself.

The bride, however, had her own thoughts and concerns about what she was wearing. She consciously avoided spilling champagne, cake, or cocktail sauce on herself because the dress was a rayon and silk blend and, therefore, would require dry-cleaning should she ever soil it. The fact that the dress was sleeveless was a big plus because there was less fabric that could inadvertently find its way into the smoked fish dip or the bowl of whipped cream (cream which had been dyed pink with the aid of two tablespoons of grenadine). It troubled her that the neckline was such that it revealed her prominent collarbones but did nothing for her modest cleavage. And finally, the dress, which fell very prettily over her slim torso, was the color of bone china and was scattered all about with a pattern of faint lavender flowers that even the mother of the groom could not identify.

And speaking of the mother of the groom, she had been kind enough to take the bride-to-be to Governor's Square Mall in Tallahassee three days before the wedding. Took her there herself—piloted the skiff, drove the truck, bought the lunch, everything—and dragged the poor girl to store after store until finally they found a dress they could both agree on. The groom's mother paid for it out of her own pocket. A hundred and twenty bucks. Plus there were the shoes, the faux pearls, the tube of Coral Mist lipstick, the waterproof long-lash mascara, the Ivory Rose foundation, the manicure, the pedicure, and the snipping off of those annoying split ends.

The bride, utterly ill-equipped to deal with the have-to-haves of a wedding, would have done none of this for herself, you see. But the mother of the groom insisted. "You cannot get married feeling like a frump," she said.

The bride quietly agreed and at the end of the day as they scooted back across the bay toward Lethe, the skiff loaded with packages, the bride thanked her future mother-in-law. She thanked her quickly, without flourish or tears, because if she'd gone on and on, trying to elucidate the depth of her gratitude, she was afraid she would crack open and her insides, which were teeming with fragile and ill-conceived secrets, would suddenly be exposed and, therefore, vulnerable to all sorts of judgment-making and nit-picking. And that was more than she could stand. She couldn't let these words pluck the strings of her vocal cords: "No one has ever been this nice to me. And by no one, I mean my mother. She wanted to be nice—I really think so—but something held her back. So thank you. Thank you so much."

No. She couldn't say that. She could barely even allow herself the thought. So in lieu of spill-the-beans honesty, amid the din of the motor, she yelled, "Thanks, Lillian. I mean it."

But the wind whipped away the words, so unless the older woman could read lips, she never got the gist of what was being shouted.

The groom, it must be said, had it much easier. A new pair of jeans, one of those modified Nehru linen shirts that required no tie (nor could it accommodate one), a matching set of clean sneakers, a haircut courtesy of Beth who evidently was a virtual jack-of-all-trades, a thoughtful brother who gave him an unopened package of underwear, a shower, and that was that.

The bride was mildly irritated that after she and her mother-in-law-in-waiting had spent countless hours poring over the minute details of the wedding (should ice cream be floated atop the fruit punch or offered separately, for instance), the groom's only responsibility was get to *The Dixie Belle* on time.

You may find my detached recitation of the outer trappings of our wedding odd but I assure you it is due solely to the fact that very often sanctified rituals are far less interesting than the flaming hoops couples jump through before finally reaching the point where a ceremony is deemed necessary. And because the rules and parameters for getting married were laid down ages ago by politicians and holy men who had their own self-serving agendas, weddings have far less to do with the love, hate, trust, and mistrust of the couple involved than with the expectations of their community. So in that sense, a wedding is a wedding is a wedding.

Granted, there are differences in the details. Not everyone gets married on a boat, for example. And not every best man (Demetrius, in this instance) jumps overboard after a can of Budweiser which inspires four other drunken souls to jump in after him, all of whom end up being rescued by the bride, the groom, and an oysterman heading back to port in his homemade flatbottom full of freshly tonged bivalves. And I suppose there aren't even that many weddings that have no bridesmaids and two maids of honor, in this case, Beth and Maya, who wore identical green vests which they purchased at Goodwill and that had felt cutouts of martini glasses sewn on the pockets. (I found it touching that rather than carrying flowers they brandished New Year's Eve noisemakers which they rattled with abandon.) And I suspect it's rather rare when the person officiating over the ceremony asks, "Who gives this woman's hand in marriage?" for the entire boatload of people to shout, "We do!"

Yes, in some of its particulars our wedding was unique. I'll admit that. But at its core it was as traditional as the other countless weddings held that day in churches and homes and on hillsides across America.

After all, you can get married on the moon in zebra-striped space suits but when push comes to shove you still have to say, "I do."

I think we should all feel very fortunate that in our society virgin brides are as rare as ivory-billed woodpeckers.

Simply surviving the logistical and familial demands of getting married is enough to make any sane couple pine to elope. But throw virginity into the mix and you've got all the trappings of a medieval practical joke.

This isn't to say that wedding nights, even for the well seasoned, should be devoid of anticipation, expensive lingerie, and champagne. But bold-faced ignorance regarding the delicate negotiations we call lovemaking has the potential for souring the erotic into the ridiculous.

And don't overlook the notion of a level playing field. I would think that for virgin brides the phrase "Come to Papa" should evoke illegal connotations. But such is the dynamic if the only person in the wedding night bed with a sexual clue is the groom.

In some respects, I believe it can safely be said that post-feminist sex mirrors the advantages of a free marketplace over its state-run cousin. Think about it. During those bleak decades when men maintained a patriarchal monopoly on sexual experience, they had absolutely no incentive to become better lovers. The poor wives suffered through the motions as their husbands selfishly muddled along. Collectively, men were like AT&T in the days before deregulation—they had all the power and money yet nobody thought they were doing a particularly good or inventive job.

Nevertheless, it is, I believe, fair to ask what in the world sexually active couples have to look forward to on their wedding night? It certainly crossed my mind. After all, what could possibly make nuptial lovemaking more memorable than all that prenuptial coupling (especially when so much of it, as I recall, took place in public venues)?

As it turned out, for Nick and me the answer was simple. In lieu of chaste purity and in the absence of the excitement and fear and fumbling which I am told often accompanies having sex for the first time, we simply threw at one another everything we had.

First, we got a room at the Mariner Inn, a rambling Victorian hotel in the heart of Apalachicola's historic district and a favorite spot among honeymooners. Why it is a favored destination I do not know since its polished wood surfaces and rod and ball ornamentation are designed to hide the fact that the hotel's interior walls are paper thin.

Our room was located on the second floor and overlooked the water but the oddly curved Apalachee Bay Bridge hogged the vista, providing us with a great view of the slab of roadway that connected Apalachicola with Eastpoint. We also could catch glimpses of the hotel's patrons as they stepped off the veranda, arm in arm, joking or fussing with one another or chastising their children.

Understand that Nick at his core was a man of chivalry and tradition so even though he'd had far too many beers to carry me through the threshold, he did it anyway, grunting and staggering, and nearly ramming my head through the flimsy wall before making it over to the bed, where he apologetically and unceremoniously plopped me and then collapsed onto my chest.

After our giggling subsided, the very next sound we heard was the person in the adjoining room passing gas and then a child's voice screaming exultantly, "Daddy farted!"

I looked at Nick, whose face began to open like a blossom as the hotel's lack of privacy began to sink in.

"What are we going to do?" I asked.

He thought for a moment, his head angled toward the ceiling as a female voice announced: "I'm gonna take a bath."

A door slammed. Pipes in the walls shuddered and groaned. Water rushed through a tub spigot. Nick lightly brushed my forehead with his fingers. "I'm going to make love to my wife. That's what we're gonna do," he said.

And so we did. But to get back to my original point, the tension of being sexually inexperienced did not factor into our wedding night lovemaking. What was at play was a desire to please, to own and be owned, to give and take with guiltless abandon.

But I'd be dishonest if I did not admit that the night was made sweeter by the tinge of exhibitionism that hung in the air of the natty corner room and slipped under the door and drifted through the walls and burned the ears of our fellow lodgers.

It needs a woman's touch.

That's what Lillian confided to me sitting on her back porch that first day on Lethe.

She was talking about Nick's house. Our house. And she was right. Beyond a good cleaning, it needed some sort of ornamentation. Something that would say, This may look like a storage shed for tools and shrimping paraphernalia but people actually cook meals and make love here.

That's the optimistic version. The more honest observation is that I had a lot of work to do.

If a stranger had entered Nick's house and searched for clues regarding its owner, they most likely would have been struck by his lack of possessions (withstanding tools, of course). For instance, he owned one plate, one fork, one knife, and two coffee mugs which bore a suspicious resemblance to those at the diner in Carrabelle. There was a decent gas range but only a single pan. "That's all you need to fry an egg," he explained.

I suppose all he needed to sleep, then, was one set of sheets. Bathing only required one towel so why have two cluttering up the place? He did have three weather-beaten wooden rocking chairs which he moved in and out of the house, depending on where he felt like sitting.

"Why three?" I asked.

"People visit."

As I pointed out, his domestic sense of asceticism did not extend to his tool collection (multiples of everything, including five pairs of pliers, all of them identical as far as I could tell) or his backyard (a small mountain range of junk rising out of a sea of stinging nettles).

All that being said, I have to admit that despite my initial surprise that his days on Lethe before meeting me were lived somewhat monkishly, I loved the house. I interpreted its simplicity and lack of clutter as a green light for me to do with the place whatever I pleased. Money would determine the timeline but that was all right by me. Slowly, as our bank account and luck would allow, I would warm up the bare wood floors with a few strategically placed throw rugs. I'd pick out a line of vintage dinnerware I liked and would try to buy a plate here, a butter dish there for a few dollars at garage sales and antique stores. The blank walls cried out for art. That too, though, would take time. Better to save up and buy one fabulous piece than junk up the place with crap, I told myself. I wandered through the empty rooms considering and reconsidering what types of couches, chairs, chest of drawers would eventually find their home here. I kept telling myself, Keep it simple. Stick to clean, basic lines or you risk overwhelming the house.

Our board-on-board wood frame cottage did have one rather startling attribute. It was capped with a beautiful sapphire blue roof. Nick was proud of that roof. After a windstorm in the late eighties tore off the old one, he put the blue one on, relishing the fact that it was the only roof of that color on Lethe. He worried endlessly that someone on the island would copycat him, as he put it, and each time a new house started going up he would ask the work crew, "What about the shingles? What're you gonna put up there?"

My favorite feature of the house was not its blue roof but that it had more windows than walls. They were handmade pocket windows that slid noisily aside, disappearing behind the wall board, leaving the house wonderfully exposed to the elements. With those broad water views fore and aft, I sometimes imagined that I was a wealthy woman cruising the world on an ocean liner.

It wasn't a very large ocean liner but with fifteen hundred square feet and at least that much screened porch it was more than adequate for the two of us. The walls were railroad board, the floors heart pine, and everything was crooked due in large part to the sandy foundation on which the house sat. The kitchen was on the west end and the bedroom on the east. In between was what a real estate agent might call a great room but that term suggests towering ceilings and tacky chandeliers. What we had was a very sizable living area with a big black wood-burning stove stuck in the corner.

From nearly any vantage point in the cottage I could glimpse the Gulf to the south and the thatched roof of the beachfront chickee which sat at the foot of the dunes. George Blue had hired Seminole Indians from South Florida to build the traditional Seminole structure, which amounted to a raised platform with a palm frond roof. When storms tore away at the roof, the family simply replaced the missing thatch or hired people knowledgeable in chickee-building (I was told that an aging group of hippies who lived in the woods surrounding Sopchoppy were reliable). The chickee was the perfect place to sit and stare out at the water without fear of getting sunburned, as well as an ideal perch for storm watching.

The views were equally inspiring to the north. Beyond the rubble of the backyard, the bay whispered quietly and the trees on the far shore changed colors with the mood of the sun. Our ten-foot dock (it had originally been thirty feet but through the years storms had whittled it down to a stub) sat high and dry at low tide but it was a perfect roosting spot for pelicans and gulls. As for human use, Dem and Nick liked to drink beer out there and I enjoyed its sunset views.

Lillian's house could be seen from our back porch. An acre's worth of scrub pine, blanketflower, and prickly pear separated us and though I was at first alarmed by my mother-in-law's close proximity, in most cases the snake-inhabited acre proved to be distance enough.

As for the landscaping, the front of the house, much like Lillian's, was planted with native species that required virtually no care. Sea oat, cabbage palm, coontie palm, yaupon, confederate jasmine, palmetto, and dollar weed (which Lillian told me to learn to love because there was no getting rid of them).

Lillian, of course, was the gardener who had been inspired to go native and salt-tolerant on our Gulf-facing yards. She had meticulously planned, first plotting everything out on graph paper and then arranging and rearranging in her mind until the various elements came together so seamlessly that the gardens appeared utterly unforced, as if nature's inspired hand had been given free reign to paint its own unruly portrait.

Despite the success of these native plots, there were those who did not appreciate their wildness, their exuberance, their unflagging willingness to give refuge and sustenance to lizards, snakes, beach mice, and birds. In fact, newcomers had been known to ride their bikes down the sandy road past Lillian's front yard and fret loud enough that their words filtered onto Lillian's front porch where she sat with a glass of sweet iced tea, gazing at the sea oats swaying to and fro in the breeze. "When is she going to do something with that yard?"

But Lillian, like all great gardeners, was undeterred by the drivel that fell from the lips of the uninformed. She was evangelical in her mission, trying to inspire her own children to take up the hoe and till. But they weren't interested. Nick's imagination was sparked by water, not earth. She had given Nick a front yard that he needn't lift a finger to care for, but the backyard—she had decided—was his to plant. That was the battleground, the line in the sand, the place where his latent gardening abilities would spring forth. Or so she hoped.

Nick must have at various intervals attempted to get something to grow back there but as Lillian forever reminded us, the first step in creating a successful garden was soil improvement. Her little Garden of Eden owed its vitality to the many loads of mushroom compost the boys hauled over from the hill. But her staunch belief that her children would one day be able to coax scented geraniums, purple salvias, homestead verbena, and possibly even rugosa roses from the enriched earth was forever challenged by Nick's hearty expanse of stickers, nettles, and junk piles.

My first night in the house was the evening Nick proposed. We walked in and I took one look at the crab traps and ropes and toolboxes and fishing rods and anchors and nets and buckets and white rubber boots strewn from end to end—the house smelled like decaying fish—

and I thought, Gee, that trailer in Crawfordville looks pretty good right now.

"Dem must be storing stuff in here," Nick said lamely. "I'll clean it out, honey. I promise."

"It's okay," I lied. Then we both went about the business of opening windows and doors in an effort to air out the place.

You might think since our engagement was just hours old that we indulged in wild, passionate love that night but you would be wrong. We made the bed with clean sheets that his mother had blessedly given us on our way out her door. We lay down and Nick held me and he sighed so contentedly that no one could have doubted his relief at being home. He started snoring before I had the chance to say, "Sweet dreams."

Exhausted, I watched the darkness and listened to the surf. I was the kind of tired that makes your leg bones ache from the inside out and prevents sleep from coming on easily. I tried to count sheep but got irritated because they wouldn't stand still. Then I fantasied that Nick and I were making love and that did the trick. I drifted off and dreamed of dolphins.

They were just offshore, a large pod, and they lingered in the shallow waters, watching me with tourmaline eyes. I stood alone on the white sand beach, a sentinel witnessing their gathering. Day turned to night and the wind grew cold and I held at my side a broken strand of pearls. Slowly, endlessly, one luminescent bead at a time, the pearls fell from my fingers and the foaming waves that rushed over my feet and legs carried them away.

I had done all this before. There was nothing odd about my solitary presence on the beach. I had stood in that very spot with the wind combing my hair and the pearls falling from my hands and the dolphins remaining so close in that someone less attuned to their habits might fear they were trying to beach themselves.

Whatever was happening was about them and me. And in the dream I did not question it. I acted out of longing, theirs and mine, standing still and silent, and all the while they swam parallel to the shore, singing my name.

I became a fishmonger.

If Nick had shrimped the night before, come morning I would feed the feral cats (Rhea and Lillian insisted they were related to Athens, Nereus' pet feline who would allow no one to touch her but Nereus himself) and then head down to the dock where I would board our new Carolina Skiff. The family decided that because of our sheer numbers we could no longer rely exclusively on the *Poseidon*. In reference to what my hair looked like after a ride across the bay, I dubbed the boat *Medusa* and that name stuck. Just past dawn, the air was cool and often thick with fog or sea mist. The world appeared soft, slightly out of focus, and as I prepared the *Medusa* for her quick trip I would find myself wishing that I were a painter. I would start up the boat without any help and bounce across the bay and upriver—feeling freer than I ever had in my entire life, paying no regard to the fact that if perchance the boat should sink, my inability to swim meant that I was nothing more than lead in the water—and I would tie up at the shrimp docks and wait for Nick and Demetrius. I would do these things just as if I belonged here, just as if I truly were an independent young woman who had chosen to live a life that demanded I acquire a local's knowledge of shifting shoals and hidden oyster bars, and that my body become attuned to the hollowness of the air when the barometric pressure quickly drops, a sure sign of stormy weather.

It was in those hours, as the sun settled more evenly across the Carrabelle River and as pelicans made their way out to sea to feed, their wings creaking as though they were attached to rusty hinges, and as my husband and brother-in-law headed back to the hill in their thirty-foot trawler named *The Lucky Miss B*, that I would take a legal pad out of the backpack I carried with me and begin to scribble. Just notes. Nothing special.

August 20, 1996
Shrimp dock, Carrabelle
Early morning

Lillian pinched the blossoms off her basil yesterday. She explained to me that this was called deadheading and that it promoted new growth and prevented the plant from going to seed. I didn't ask, but evidently once a plant goes to seed its life cycle is pretty well spent.

She is trying to make a gardener out of me but I have to admit to being slightly intimidated by her. Or maybe I'm scared of mothers in general. Also, at the moment I don't have time to garden. My priority is putting my new home in order. I'm thinking lace curtains—they'll let the light in and look pretty without being fussy. So that backyard garden is just going to have to wait.

August 27, 1996
Same place, same time

Nick has been helping me to learn the names of the various shells on our beach. Every day we try to take a walk during the outgoing tide. Without even knowing it, he has become my teacher, my guide through a world that, I am learning, is as harsh as it is forgiving. Death and life commingle here as easily as water and ice.

This is a direct quote from yesterday's walk: "My blood thins during low tide." He claims he's energized by the waxing moon and worn down by the waning. I hope one day to be that blessed, to be so connected to this world of blue that its mysteries push and pull on me.

I might not yet be as tied to this place as Nick is, but I'm already able to identify a wide variety of shells. At a glimpse, I can tell the difference between, say, a Florida Crown Conch, a True Tulip, and a Channeled Whelk (need to work on the Lightning Whelk, though). I still get confused between the Angel Wing and the False Angel Wing. And also, the Moon Shell and the Shark Eye still give me trouble. I have a sizable collection of Lettered Olives but am beginning to feel guilty about it.

It's fair to say that what I was doing was compiling a journal, logging the events of my daily affairs and trying to pin to memory words and objects and deeds. But at the time, I simply saw my scribbling as something to do while I waited for the boat.

Each morning as the trawler rounded the bend, I would put away my writing and smooth my hair and take a deep breath in an attempt to slow my heart rate, which seemed to pick up at the mere sight of my husband. This was a curious phenomenon, my speeding heart, and I took it to be a sign of true and lasting love, and sometimes I would worry about what it might mean if that flush of excitement ever withered.

Nick piloted *The Lucky Miss B* and Demetrius acted as his deckhand. I was fascinated with how my big-framed husband could so delicately and precisely guide the trawler to within a hairsbreadth of the dock. Perhaps he approached the piloting and docking of the shrimp boat in the same way he approached his crazy tendency to suddenly rise up and dance. In both arenas, he adopted an unmistakable grace, a natural understanding of navigating a given object through a physical world.

Once they were docked, Nick would help me aboard and kiss me "hello." After a night on the bay, his skin smelled of sweat and salt. It was a smell that I would come to love. Even crave.

Working quickly, Nick and Demetrius would secure the *Miss B* and then load the bed of the Fordge with iced coolers filled with their night's haul. Once that chore was completed, we would walk over to Harry's for breakfast, where Nick always ordered a stack of pancakes, cheese grits, two strips of bacon, a small orange juice, and coffee. I usually ordered cereal. Dem was incapable of ever making up his mind so Irene, our waitress, brought him whatever she thought he looked like he needed.

"You look like you need a Delmonico," she might say on Tuesday, but come Wednesday she'd shake her head and her bottle-blond bun would tremble and he'd get nothing but biscuits with gravy.

After we ate, Nick and I would say our goo-goo-eyed goodbyes and he and Demetrius would take the *Poseidon* back to Lethe and sleep until mid-afternoon. I would climb into that ugly, beat-up, no power steering Fordge and drive from Carrabelle east to Panacea where under the oaks and wisteria stood a lavender cinder block building of not much size. The hand-painted sign by the road was of a mermaid. *My-Way Seafood*, it said, *Come see what kind of fresh seafood the Mermaids have!*

Miss Lucy ran the business with the help of her two sons. Petite and blond with sharp green eyes, she was in her mid-forties and her reputation for offering fresh, clean seafood at honest prices extended far beyond this coastal hamlet, attracting people from as far away as Georgia and Alabama.

It was to Miss Lucy, and Miss Lucy only, that I sold our shrimp. I made that call and Nick backed me one hundred percent. She offered us fair prices and never insulted our product. And besides, we could talk about things. Nearly every morning, standing on My-Way's porch, as we weighed shrimp and made sure that Nick and Demetrius had separated out the jumbos from the mediums (at this time of year that meant the brownies from the hoppers, the brownies being the big guys and the species, oddly enough, *without* a brown spot on their tails) we solved the world's problems.

"If they would make me president for just one day, I could clean up Washington and Russia, too," she was fond of saying.

Seafood was a mystery to some of the folks who stopped into My-Way, but they could count on Miss Lucy to give them instructions and advice free of condescension, ridicule, or error.

"How many people did you say you needed to feed?" I heard her ask a well-appointed woman on her way to St. George Island for the weekend and who, it was obvious, had never dreamed in all her days that she would be asked to "step inside the cooler and pick out your fish."

"Well, I believe there will be five of us," the woman said, casting an uneasy glance at the bin of grouper piled up whole on the ice. Trying to hide her lack of knowledge regarding the ins and outs of buying fresh, whole-form seafood, she pointed with a tremulous hand at a grouper that would by day's end be bait in a crab trap and attempted to say confidently, "I think this one will do."

"No, ma'am, I can't sell you that old boy. He's got cataracts. But this fellow over here, he was swimming this morning. See that clear eye? Fresh as can be. And he's just the right size for five people. I do believe you'll be serving up a gracious plenty."

Before long, Miss Lucy and I discovered we shared a common interest; we were both avid readers. On slow days we could be found on My-Way's porch talking about books and arguing over endings and plot twists and agreeing wholeheartedly that our favorite novel of all time was *To Kill a Mockingbird*. In fact, she named her two dogs, a couple of mutts she rescued from the pound, Atticus and Scout.

After I finished my business at My-Way, sometimes I would go into Tallahassee and do some shopping and stop at the library (there was plenty of time to read on Lethe), and once back in Carrabelle I might pop into the IGA and rent a few videos. I enjoyed the time spent rambling down the highway in that old rattletrap truck. It gave me all sorts of time to think.

It was while driving down the road that I decided I needed a pot rack in the kitchen. Perhaps one made out of pecky cypress. Nick could do that for me.

And I liked the wall cabinets Beth and Maya had in their kitchen. The cabinets' glass doors made the whole room look larger and more inviting. All Nick would have to replace were the doors themselves. He needed a woodworking project. Maybe if he fixed up the place he'd be less willing to leave his dirty clothes strewn from end to end.

And in the bathroom, I could hide the ugly plumbing beneath the sink if I bought some nice fabric. Nothing too elaborate but with a rich texture. I could probably borrow Lillian's sewing machine and, barring that, well heck, I could hem the thing by hand. We were only talking about a couple of yards of fabric and I could hang it with a length of dowel. Nick wouldn't have to do anything at all. He'd come home one day and go into the bathroom and there it would be, a nicer place to pee. He might not even notice that the plumbing was no longer hideously on display, or that I'd hemmed the curtain using hidden stitches and measured the fabric so precisely that it fell in soft, graceful folds, or that I'd attached the dowel up under the lip of the cabinet just the way he would have done had I asked for his help (which I would not do). No. He probably wouldn't notice any of this. But he would sense that something had changed and he'd understand that I had been nest-making and he would come into the kitchen where I might be trying my hand at a goat cheese soufflé when all he really hankered after was a hamburger and he'd kiss me and say, "The bathroom looks nice, honey."

And I would turn away and hide my smile because for some reason I never wanted him to know when I was pleased right down to my toes.

These are just a few of the thoughts that kept me company during my fishmongering journeys. I felt very independent, driving into town to sell our shrimp. And even though many of my meanderings had to do with wifely duties, I was not ashamed of them. I wanted to be a good partner and live in a nice house that bore no resemblance to a storage shed and spend my free time discovering new things about myself, my husband, and the world at large.

Not all of my travels were directly related to performing a task. I took to driving down dirt roads just to see where they would lead me. I struck up acquaintances with the man who had a vegetable stand in Medart and the cashier at Earl's Home Center and the antique dealer in Carrabelle who used to be married to a shrimper herself.

Around every bend, down every dirt road, and deep into the marsh the voices of the people and animals who'd long called this place home slowly began to make themselves known to me. People offered up their pasts freely, sharing the family tales and neighborly gossip as if the knack for spinning their lives into narratives that others could latch onto was in their genes. I loved their stories.

I loved knowing that there was an Italian woman in St. Marks who was a trained opera singer but who married a mullet fisherman when he was overseas in the army. Her two sons sang like angels, people told me. Country and western, swing, and rock 'n' roll.

I loved knowing that tourists used to come from far and wide to Panacea to take the waters at the spring on land that was now overgrown and neglected and that in the spring's heyday Saturday night dances were held complete with a piano player who had to compete with the wind to be heard and that more than half a century later townspeople were trying to raise funds to restore Panacea Mineral Springs.

And that before the forest was opened up to logging people sat on their front porches at night and listened to the wild yowl of the Florida panther.

And that a man named Yancey was the area's last real honest to God hermit and that when he passed people mourned not only for him but for a way of life snuffed out by progress.

Yes, simply put, these piney woods and salt marshes were full of stories and secrets. I felt certain, given enough time, I would begin to understand.

September 2, 1996
Kitchen table
Sixish

I brought a cookbook from the antique store in Carrabelle. It's Greek to Me—that's the title. Thought I could start making Nick some good Greek food. Rhea knows a lot of the old recipes but Lillian prefers coastal Cracker cuisine and steamed veggies. Anyway, I tried to make the simplest recipe in the book: Kota Soupa Avgolemona, which translated means Chicken Egg–Lemon Soup. I don't know what went wrong. By the time I was done mangling it, what should have been fragrant and delicious turned out to be akin to rancid egg-drop broth. Everything curdled. Poor Nick. He didn't want to hurt my feelings. I could see that he was spooning the stuff way back in his mouth and swallowing immediately to get past the God-awful taste. But I was afraid the soup would make him sick so I took away our plates and fixed us a couple of peanut butter and jellies.

.   .   .

September 4, 1996
Lethe (Gulfside)
Late afternoon

Senility has its advantages.

That's the conclusion I've come to after watching Nick's grandfather, Charon Blue, negotiate through his latter years by pleasing himself to the exclusion of all others, ignoring his family's minimal conventions regarding social and familial responsibility, chasing from sunup to sundown all manner of beached sea life, and in good weather months wearing nothing but a pair of baggy, green checkered, faded shorts. I am told that during cold snaps, Rhea somehow manages to get him into an overcoat. How is beyond me.

I guess now is as good a time as any to face up to the fact that nearly everyone in this family refers to Charon as Big Daddy. I, myself, referred to him as such just yesterday. The children, young and old, call Rhea Big-a-Mama. I don't know what the "a" is for but, nevertheless, there it is. Maybe it's just me, but I find these nicknames vastly entertaining. Somebody might say, "Well, what's Big-a-Mama going to think?" or "In his prime, Big Daddy was the best flounder man you ever did see," and I'm suddenly overcome with a strange sensation that I've just been dropped onto the set of Cat on a Hot Tin Roof. *I'm Elizabeth Taylor to Nick's Paul Newman and I'm skittering around Big Daddy's plantation like a frustrated butterfly. Yes, I'm a sex-deprived southern belle dressed in a white full-skirted, low-necked, wide-belted, waist-cinched number pleading with Brick for a little love. I wonder what Nick would say if he knew how my mind drifts into such silliness nearly every time the family is all together? But then again, maybe I'd be surprised as to where his mind is meandering, as well.*

Everyone had a theory as to what was "wrong" with Charon Blue.

Beth and Maya insisted Alzheimer's was the culprit.

"I'm telling you," Maya would say in her thin Southern voice, "Big

Daddy needs to see a doctor. There are drugs that will help slow the progression of the disease."

"He seems to be holding his own," Beth would say lamely. "And even if Big Daddy doesn't know his own name, there's no getting him off this island."

Staying true to his superstitious core, Nick rejected Beth and Maya's science-based theory in favor of the notion—long held by seafaring souls across the globe—that all water and no land can drive a person mad.

"It happens to sailors all the time. They just go crazy and begin believing they're one of *them*," Nick observed on a stormy afternoon in our front yard, jabbing his head toward the Gulf.

"One of who?" I asked.

"I don't know," he said, irritated. "A sea critter."

Lillian was much more pragmatic.

"It happened when the county commission shut down his ferry. Big Daddy simply didn't know what to do with himself after that. And don't overlook that fall he took. I think it was his second to last trip ferrying passengers and he slipped in Coke someone had spilled and hit his head so hard he had a goose egg the size of a heart cockle. The swelling didn't go down for a good week. You mark my word. Hitting his head like that was the last straw."

"Nonsense!" That was Rhea's response every time she heard her daughter-in-law's theory. "The senile old bastard is as sharp as he ever was. He's just stubborn. That's all."

She'd slam down the bottom of her cane with one good thrust to drive home her point. And then she'd work her lips back and forth and in and out because the subject of her husband's odd behavior nearly always sent her into a tizzy.

Sometimes it takes an outsider to point out the obvious but if they do, it is at their own risk since truth—no matter its source—is quite often viewed with disdain, as if it's no better than a rotten peach, especially if people have already made up their minds to the contrary. So I kept my theory about Charon Blue to myself.

I share it now only because my thoughts on the matter relate to Nick.

You see, had my husband been fortunate enough to live into his mid-eighties, I am positive he would have behaved much like his grandfather, disappearing into his bliss, tracking the comings and goings of starfish and sea urchins with the single-mindedness of a blue tick heeler.

For all intents and purposes, it appeared as if Rhea's beloved senile old bastard was mute. But he was far from silent. His guttural outbursts which at first glance seemed to occur at random were completely incomprehensible. Rhea, in her endearing attempt to save face by behaving as though she were an expert on all subjects, insisted she could translate his various mutterings but I never saw any evidence to support her claim and no one ever pushed her on it.

This is not to say his outbursts had no meaning. It's just that, like the hidden mechanisms of a clock or the secret yearnings of the human heart, they were beyond us. In his old age, Charon gave himself over fully and completely to an outmoded way of life, one driven by self-styled sanctity and ritual.

Every five days, without fail, at 5 A.M., he stood beneath the biggest pine in our backyard (the tree was a marvel, really, so large that if I wrapped my arms around its trunk, my fingertips would not touch), and he talked to God, or perhaps, gods. And though I'm uncertain about the plurality of his deity(ies), I do not doubt that he was trying to communicate with something more powerful than himself.

I came to look forward to his predawn homilies, setting my alarm so that I would be sure to wake, and then pattering out to my back porch with a cup of hot tea, and watching clandestinely as he preached to the moon and stars.

His ceremony went something like this: He began at his thighs, progressed to his belly, chest, and hollow cheeks—in that order—beating them with his open palms, four times each, expelling the air from his lungs and humming simultaneously. The result was a primal chant both frightening and beautifully awesome. It was as though he were speaking in Surround Sound for his noise was loud and clear and it echoed off the bay's flat surface and rang brightly through the air.

The ritual ended the same way every time. With his chant building to a frenzied pitch, he would raise his fists to the heavens and violently shake them. I could never discern whether he was cursing the gods or praising them. But whichever the case, he finished by kneeling and kissing the earth, just as the Pope used to do when he could still bend over. And that was that. He'd walk off either toward the bay or Gulf and not be seen again until it was time to eat.

I came to think of Charon as a latter-day, paganistic John the Baptist, wandering Lethe's wilderness, searching for something to save. No longer able to sail the seas, he roamed the island's shorelines on the lookout for beached sea creatures that hadn't yet given up the ghost. More often than not, as he obsessively returned to the water fistfuls of starfish that had been swept too far upshore on the incoming tide, someone would come along right behind him, scooping up the ones he'd missed so that later, once the starfish were dead and dry and brittle as glass, they could be displayed, trophy-style, on beach house windowsills.

If Charon Blue noticed what these "beachcombers" were doing, he never let on. He simply continued his work. Starfish, sea urchins, sea pansies, jellyfish, sand dollars, baby sharks, conch shells. Everything he could find went back into the Gulf of Mexico.

Our first meeting was, all in all, rather monumental in the sense that he and I communicated. I am certain of this.

I had walked down to the bay for no other reason than to gaze at the water when behind me someone or something grunted. Fearing both wild boar (there were none on the island) and escaped convicts (none of those either), my fight or flight response immediately kicked in. I spun around, thinking in that split second that I needed to find a good-sized rock to throw and damning myself for leaving my pocketbook Mace on the kitchen counter even though everybody said there was virtually no crime on Lethe. But then again anyone with any sense knew that women could never be too careful. Our mothers, even mine, had taught us that certain types of men were predators and, therefore, we were cursed to go through life in perpetual danger. Yes, all of that in a single second.

But at the sight of what stood no more than three feet in front of me, I stopped dead cold. Imagine it: a wide-shouldered, tanned-to-leather, blazing blue-eyed, white-haired and -bearded, almost naked, lanky old man clutching a horseshoe crab in one hand and a sea whip in the other.

He raised his arms chest high, shook the crab and whip, and growled.

I had heard enough about Charon Big Daddy Blue to know whom I was looking at, and despite his studied fierceness, there was something exquisitely engaging about him. Something familiar and dear. Something tapping at the foggy window of my memory. A blurred form I couldn't quite make out. His old, weather-beaten flaccid skin was scaly and his knuckles were lumpy with scar tissue and his white Einstein hair looked as if it had never seen a comb. Most puzzling of all was that I found the old coot faintly attractive.

We stood on sand dappled with raccoon tracks and the calligraphy of auger shells. No sounds passed between us. Not a grunt. Not a syllable. Not even a peep. Nor did we take our eyes off one another. We sized each other up the way animals do, nonverbally, testing the silent air.

I'm not sure how long this standoff went on. I guess long enough for me to feel damned foolish. I was just about to throw in the towel and divert my eyes when the fog lifted: Charon Blue was the future. He was Nick's spit and image fifty years down the road. My face softened and, I swear to you, I think his did, too.

I wondered if when Charon looked at his grandson he saw visages of himself as a young man, healthy and strong and full of longing to understand that deep sea which we allegedly crawled out of at the beginning of human time, claiming ourselves to be in God's image. Did he long to be that young man again? Did he long to whisper into Nick's ear all that he had learned? Did his silence break his heart or did it set him free?

Quickly, I scanned the bare-white curve of beach and spied a crown conch that had been tossed into the saw grass by the surf. The conch was alive but trapped in the maze of snail-covered reeds. I picked up the shell, held it aloft, and shook it, grunting as boldly as I could. Then I set it in the gently lapping water where the monopedal mollusk slowly made its way offshore. Maybe, I thought, no one has been speaking Charon Blue's language.

The old man's eyes narrowed and his full lips settled into a purplish thin line. He lowered his arms, raised his head in what I took to be a sign of respect, and nodded. Just one quick bob of the head. Then he turned and ambled away, the dead horseshoe crab and neon yellow sea whip hanging from his hands like morphed appendages.

W*hen I look in your eyes, I see infinity. I'm not very good at love talk. But you bring it out in me. You make me want to tell you everything I know. Everything I feel. Come here, come to me, Mattie, so we can* . . .

N*o* one knows what caused her to do it. Some people said it was the weather, that she always got a little crazy in the heat. Others blamed it on the lunar eclipse, saying it can twist a person's mind and make them act in ways they never thought possible. But still others chalked it up to her weak character. Imagine. Leaving behind a baby and a husband and running off to the hill with a man she barely knew. She didn't even have the decency to slip the child into a clean undershirt before she left. No. She just pinned a note to the one he'd slept in, the sour one that stank from the bananas he had thrown up after breakfast.

Dear Dem, she wrote, *I hope you will not hold my leaving against me. I can't explain all my reasons. There's not enough time in the world. Let's just say I can't see myself on this island forever.*

I want you to know Chuck is a good man (please don't say otherwise). Just 'cause he can't stand a crying baby doesn't mean he's a bad person.

To be perfectly honest, I really can't listen to too much more of Gaby's hollering either. Don't get me wrong. I love my baby. Fight to the death for him, in fact. As you know, I even gave up cigarettes for him. But I know you. As hard as my leaving might be, if I took little Gaby and raised him on the hill you would never forgive me.

I feel sure he'll have a good life. His grandmother loves him and so does Big-a-Mama. Also, Beth and Maya, even though they are queers, will be good influences on him as they both have big hearts.

You will always have a part of mine. I hope there will be no hard feelings. I'd like to believe that if chance ever caused us to run into each other that we would be able to say "hello."

Good luck, Dem, and all that. Believe me, this has nothing to do with you. Your wife, Lacey Blue.

Her postscript was particularly poignant: P.S. *The baby burped up his breakfast so if he's fussy that's why.*

Lacey could not have known the train of events her departure would set in motion. Demetrius was so beside himself with grief that he didn't leave his house for three whole weeks, nor would he accept visitors. He didn't even bother to go to work so Nick went out every night alone, without a deckhand, yet still he continued to pay his brother. Every Saturday, Nick and I walked down to Dem's house and knocked on the door but nobody answered. Nick would press his face against the screen door and peer inside. Dem was in there, all right. He and the baby looked fine but Dem behaved as if he didn't know we were standing on his stoop, spying, calling his name.

The family held a meeting on Lillian's back porch. Rhea voted that we go over to the hill and "kick that good-for-nothing girl's scrawny ass."

"Rhea, what good would that possibly do?" Lillian asked and then continued on before the older woman could proffer a response. "Maybe all of us should march down there and demand that he talk to us. And if he won't, well then, maybe we should take him to a doctor. Nick, you think you're strong enough to control him if he fights us?"

Nick planted his hands on his hips, which is what he always did when he was concentrating, and he said, "Mama, I'm not forcing him to do anything."

Beth rubbed the back of her neck. "Yeah, but we can't just do nothing."

"What we can do," Nick said, "is give him some time. If we go running in there now, making demands like we're a bunch of know-it-alls, well, it's just not right."

Lillian looked at her shoes, trying to hide the sudden tears that filmed her eyes. Rhea worked her lips but kept quiet. Beth and Maya stared in silence at one another and then Beth said, "I'm with Nick."

When Demetrius finally stepped back into the world, he did so a different man. His ever-present smile was gone, replaced by the stern glare of the defeated. It was as if Lacey had packed his easygoing spirit in newspaper and tucked it among the dishes and glasses she hauled over to the hill, leaving him empty except for the despair. His left eyelid ever so slightly drooped as though loss or sadness were pulling on it, weighting it down. He quit shrimping and became a full-time oyster-man. Nick tried to talk him out of it, explaining what Demetrius already knew: Between pollution and red tide blooms and bureaucratic squabbling in Tallahassee, the oyster beds were closed nearly more than they were open. But during his self-imposed isolation, Dem had become hardheaded. He would oyster by day and care for his son by night and no one, including Big-a-Mama, could talk him out of it.

Without Demetrius as a partner, it meant Nick and I got the total share of revenues from our shrimping business. But it also meant that Nick had to work twice as hard and in conditions that were made more dangerous simply because he was alone. I begged him to hire someone or to take me on as his deckhand, but he refused, staunchly insisting that Demetrius would come around.

"You don't want me on that boat, do you?" I had asked, challenging whatever latent chauvinism might be lingering in that long-boned body of his.

"No, not that boat. I sure don't."

Two days later I was standing in our kitchen slicing a fat Cherokee tomato that came from Lillian's garden (she was fascinated with heirloom vegetables and was in a seed exchange club, which is how she acquired most of her nearly-lost-and-forgotten varieties) when Nick, who was sitting at the table reading the *Carrabelle News*, looked up and said, "That's it!"

"What's it?" I asked, guiding the blade through the deeply lobed fruit (sliced tomatoes served with a Grecian meat roll was on the menu that night and it proved to be yet another cooking disaster—the roll fell apart so that it was actually little more than Grecian ground meat and tasted faintly like mud pie).

"What we need is a new boat. A bigger one. Maybe fifty foot."

"What on earth for?" I wiped my hands on a dishcloth and faced him.

"Number one, more money. Number two," he set aside the paper and looked out the window, "Demetrius never saw a new boat he didn't want to be on."

I hated the sound of my own voice as I said, "Nick, how much money are we talking about? I'm pretty sure new trawlers don't come cheap."

"I don't know." Nick cricked his head side to side and his curls trembled. He scooted back his chair, walked over to the refrigerator, threw open the door, and peered in. "But we'll find out."

Remember Captain Johnny, the man who married us aboard *The Dixie Belle*, the man who spoke with a patois so thick I needed an interpreter at my own wedding? As it turns out, he was also a craftsman of the first order. Flat-bottom oyster boats, sailing runabouts, shrimp trawlers, chifforobes, chest of drawers. He could do it all. But only if he dreamed about it first. That's what he said.

"It comes to me in dreams."

Nick translated his fanciful claim because even though I'd lived on Lethe for four months and counting, I still could not understand the captain's lyrical language.

I think I may have been a bride savant because the ink had barely dried on our license when it dawned on me that convincing each other of the soundness of an unreasonable plan is what marriage is all about. Thus, Nick and I spent hours discussing the pros and cons of a new boat. We made lists. We added long columns of numbers. We began talking bad about *The Lucky Miss B*.

"She's giving out."

"She's barely seaworthy."

"She looks like hell."

We knew the decision was made when we began referring to her in the past tense.

"She wasn't built for the kinds of rigs we're using today."

"She could withstand some weather, though, I tell you that."

"She hauled more shrimp in her lifetime than most people could eat in theirs."

"She was a good boat."

"Yep."

Life is full of temporary, unnamed rituals. They soothe us for a while, bridging the gap between a need and its fulfillment. And then we go on.

That's how it was with Nick and Captain Johnny. Every afternoon before Nick headed to work, he would stop by the captain's small wood frame whitewashed house which was located at the end of a dirt road in Carrabelle, and they would deal with each other using a choreography they both instinctually understood and accepted.

Nick would make it no further than the third, termite-wobbly front porch step before Captain Johnny would open his front door just wide enough to poke his head out.

"Well?" Nick would readjust his ball cap.

Captain Johnny would nod soberly. "Not yet." He'd run his deeply freckled hand over his head which was bald except for three silver strands and he'd mutter, "Maybe tonight."

Then he'd withdraw back into the house as if he were a turtle and the clapboard structure his shell. The door would slam with a whoosh of air, vacuum-sealing the old man inside.

But before Nick could throw the Fordge into reverse and ease out onto the dirt road, Captain Johnny would crack open his front jalousie window and yell, "You tell Miss Lillian the captain said hello."

Anyone in Carrabelle or on Lethe who paid the least bit of attention to the romantic yearnings of their fellow citizens was well aware that Captain Johnny had a fifty-year crush on Nick's mother. If you ran upon the captain after he'd been in the rum for a few days, he'd tell you, "I fell in love with her long before George Blue did. That ain't to say nothing bad about Mr. Blue. Just that it was me who loved her first."

The torch he carried for Lillian, of course, was never to be requited, partly because she insisted she was married to George Blue for life, whether he was dead or alive.

But it wasn't simply pious, long-suffering fidelity that prevented her from returning the captain's amorous gazes. Firstly, the captain wasn't exactly what you'd call a good catch, him with his rum and cigarettes and those teeth that were kicked out years ago in barroom brawls, leaving a trail of ivory pegs from New Orleans to Tarpon Springs (more recently, several remaining teeth had fallen out all on their own due to neglect).

Secondly, Lillian liked her life just the way it was. She may have been the outsider at one time, having married into the Blues, but now she was the thread that bound the clan together.

The good captain had been a bachelor his entire life. But his marital status had less to do with Lillian than with his own proclivities. "Never met a woman I truly liked who wasn't married," he explained simply.

He also, it should be noted, claimed to be a man of God.

And that leads me back to his carpentry. When he was twenty-five years old, sitting in the back room of Mr. Odum's general store in Carrabelle, Florida, he pulled a knife on Josiah Packer during a poker game. Captain Johnny accused Josiah Packer of cheating.

"You beady-eyed son of a bitch. You got a whole fuckin' deck of cards up them dirty sleeves of your'n."

According to town legend, Josiah sucked air between his teeth, downed a shot of whiskey, wiped his mouth on those dirty sleeves of his'n, and said, "Prove it, you no-good, wide-mouthed Cracker."

In those days, by his own admission, Captain Johnny was a mean drunk. "It was the liquor that made me do it."

That's how he explained how he came to flip open the switchblade he kept hidden in his right boot, and how he happened to slice a chunk of skin the size of a robin's egg out of Josiah Packer's cheek, and how just for good mean pleasure he impaled Josiah to the pine-top table—a crucifixion of sorts—plunging the knife into the ponderous network of bones and sinews of Josiah's left hand and out through the thin rubbery flesh of his palm and beyond—another two inches beyond—straight into the heart of that table.

But meanness and drunkenness combined do not explain why he picked up off the sawdust floor that robin's egg, living-warmth chunk of human flesh or why he put it to his lips and paused to smell and enjoy its saltiness or why he popped it into his mouth and chewed heartily—as if the flesh were full of gristle—or why he swallowed it with a grin on his face.

And all the while Josiah watched, screaming in both pain and at what he could look forward to if he lived—a hideous hole in his face right below the high blade of his cheekbone.

When the judge asked why he hadn't stopped at simply cutting poor Josiah, Captain Johnny responded without a hint of remorse, "I was hungry."

Josiah Packer survived the assault and his wound earned him the nickname "Dimple." He put a trailer on land right across the road from the captain's house to prove to the town and his assailant that he did not fear the man who had disfigured him, who had eaten of his flesh.

The brawl earned Captain Johnny three years in the state pen over in Marianna. That's where he first heard the Gospels.

I initially found this hard to believe, the Gospels part, I mean. Even the smallest North Florida village had at least two, maybe three, churches. Plus, come summer, there were tent revivals and traveling preachers and even missionaries. If for no other reason, people went to church just to get out of their own tiny fish-stinking houses for an afternoon or a windless evening.

Using Nick as my interpreter, I questioned Captain Johnny closely on this issue, but he stuck to his story, claiming that he grew up wild on the outskirts of Tate's Hell and there wasn't a preacher man in the whole world crazy enough to spout the Word in, as he put it, "that Godforsaken snake house of a swamp."

But again, we find ourselves on the topic of Captain Johnny's carpentry skills. "Follow me, and I will make you fishers of men." That's what the prison chaplain told him Jesus said to Simon called Peter and Andrew, his brother, just as they were casting a net into the Sea of Galilee.

Captain Johnny swears that upon hearing those words, his body was flooded by the Holy Spirit and he felt no need to sin ever again. He made a pact with God, using Matthew, Chapter Four, Verse Eighteen as his guide.

I'm no Bible student but I think he misinterpreted the intent of the verse. Nevertheless, it inspired him to promise God that he would, by the sweat of his brow and the labor of his very own hands, build boats according to God's will in order that there might be more fishermen on earth as there are, he always hastily added, in heaven.

While still in prison he completed a correspondence course in theology. "God's Word will set you free!" proclaimed the matchbox advertisement. He sent the World Missionary Bible College ten dollars which he earned by brokering cigarettes on the inside and they sent him a diploma that bestowed on him the title of Pastor.

Being an ordained man of the cloth, he could preside over marriages and funerals alike. Given his past history, not too many people asked him to do either but the Blues believed in giving people a second chance. Besides, he was desperately poor and, other than smoking and drinking, he hadn't sinned in twenty-some-odd years as far as anyone could tell. And as for boatbuilding, even Josiah Packer would tell you that there was something special about the way Captain Johnny used his hands. Just something special.

It was a warm, breezy Thursday afternoon toward the end of September and there were no signs anywhere that something unusual, even momentous, was about to happen.

My teapot was on the palm tree tile trivet, which is where I always kept it. The lunch dishes were in the drainer, air drying. My sun catchers—the tiny crystal hummingbird and faceted crescent moon that I'd hung with twine at my Gulf-facing kitchen window—cast prisms of afternoon light across the old pine floor, just as they were intended to do. In the backyard, Nick's junk piles seethed with the day's heat, and the only plant that wasn't a weed—a root beer plant—drooped beneath the sun's fierceness as it did every afternoon unless it was raining.

A front was due in that night from the west. Small craft warnings were already posted from Mobile to Cedar Key so Nick stayed in port. The beach, though, is at its most beautiful a few hours before and after a storm, so Nick and I decided to take a long sunset walk, maybe to the end of the Conservancy's land and back.

I was a sight, lathered up in sunscreen and covered in a long-sleeved madras shirt and cotton skirt. I swept my hair off my neck, secured it with a rubber band, and planted my floppy straw hat firmly on my head. My getup, which was inspired by my pale skin's ability to burn in no time, was in stark contrast to Nick's attire. He wore oversized khaki shorts, that was it, and he was deeply tanned.

Holding hands, we walked across the sand dunes, pausing at the crest of the tallest peak. I shaded my eyes and searched the horizon. "Do you ever get bored with it? Do you ever think, God, I'm sick of all this water. Give me some dirt and a mule or a swath of pavement?"

"No. 'Cause she's never the same."

"If you flew straight ahead, due south, where would you land?"

Nick cocked his head sideways and thought it over. "Well, let's see. I think you'd scoot right past the Keys and probably end up in Cuba. That or the Yucatán. But I'm pretty sure we're well to the east of anything in Mexico. Yep," he slapped a mosquito off his shoulder, "we'd be knocking on Fidel's front door."

A flock of skimmers glided by, their bright red, black-tipped bills piercing the sea. "When you're out there do you ever get the urge to just keep going?"

He looked at me as if he were surprised at the question. He brushed a wisp of hair out of my eyes and then ran his hands down my shoulders and settled them on my waist. "Sometimes. But you're here. So I always come back."

I kissed him and he softly moaned and I tried to push away the sadness that his words awoke in me, a sadness that gently nudged me as if it were a human hand tapping on my bones.

We wandered down to the beach and walked westward, into the sunset, and he asked if I was happy and I said you know I am and he said he was the luckiest man in all the world to be married to a girl like me and I tried to think of something suitably syrupy to say in return and was coming up blank when we both stopped dead in our tracks.

"Look!" Nick said. He pointed at his toes. A silver-dollar-sized sea turtle frantically tried to traverse the Mount Everest of Nick's foot in an effort to get to the water.

"No, look," I said and spread my arm out to indicate the broader view.

"Holy mother of Jesus!"

Hundreds of baby turtles were on the move. Most were headed seaward but a few, possibly confused by the sun's brightness, struggled inland across the sand. I ran over to one that was headed in the wrong direction, scooped it up, and ferried it to the water. I began to panic as I realized that the ghost crab holes which studded the beach end to end were acting as giant booby traps. The turtles were falling into the sandy depressions at the openings of the tunnels and burning precious energy trying to free themselves, energy that they would need simply to survive the night.

Frantic, Nick and I ran hither-thither, looking like two Charon wanna-be's, trying to save the booby-trapped and direction-challenged newborns. In one ghost crab hole, alone, I found five struggling turtles. I rescued all but one; by the time I reached for it, the hatchling on the bottom was dead.

Down the beach, a heron feasted, eating turtles faster than we could save them, and a small battalion of gulls standing at the shore's edge appeared ready to move in. Nick looked at me, his face streaked with tears. "It's no use. We can't possibly get to them all."

"Stay here," I yelled. "I'll go get help!"

I ran as quickly as I could through the sand, over the soft dunes, and into Lillian's yard. I wildly clanged the bell, over and over. She ran onto her porch, a book in her hand. "What's the matter, Mattie?"

"Sea turtles! Lots of 'em!" I said, out of breath, pulling on the rope. "Trying to save 'em!"

"Big-a-Mama!" Lillian called.

The old woman wobbled out with the help of her cane. She looked terribly frail—not like the blustery Rhea I was learning to love—but when Lillian explained what was happening, she perked up and that ornery gleam sparked once more in her cataract eyes. "You two go. I'll do my best with the bell and steer everyone over there."

It was quite a sight. The Blues young and old, crazy and sane, running around the beach, ant-like, trying to give a proper send-off to these baby turtles, a fraction of whom would survive long enough to ever return to these shores. But some of them would. At least a few would reach adulthood, safely navigating through the Gulf's warm waters, some traveling as far south as the aqua seas of Guatemala and Costa

Rica. And whether it was an ancient magnetic stone hidden in the rain forest or Charon's pagan gods or an astounding feat of instinct, something strange and wonderful, something as old as the earth, would stir inside their prehistoric bodies, compelling them to turn their sights northward and journey home to Lethe, where they would lay their eggs on its white sandy shores, and the cycle would remain intact if only by a tremulous thread.

As I worked, I kept wiping away my tears. I could not believe how fortunate I was to bear witness to a small part of their journey, to their determination, to their ancient instinctual memory that propelled them achingly forward to the sea.

But the true miracle occurred when that first wave rolled over them. Understand, these creatures were only seconds old and their odyssey across that sand was not easy, quick, or without danger. But something happened to them at the first touch of water. It was as if their genetic code was unleashed by baptism; they were no longer land-based creatures struggling across a foreign, hostile environment.

No. In the water they were winged and they were light and they were perfect. And to not have felt blessed at observing their maiden passage, to have not felt a connection to an unwritable purpose and plan, would have been inhuman.

That night we celebrated. The storm didn't blow in until well past midnight and other than for Demetrius' noticeable absence, nothing marred our gathering. Nick and Lucas built a bonfire out of driftwood, and in the glow of the flames, the family told stories.

With a light blanket thrown across her lap, Rhea talked about how in the old days wooden makeshift lookout towers were erected on the beaches up and down the coast. Someone would stand watch in the tower, waiting for the huge schools of mullet to come inshore, and when they did, the sentinel would ring a bell, and the coastal folk would hurry down to the beach with their nets and harvest the fish, and the poor honest people would be joyful because they knew then that for the next few nights no one would go hungry.

Lillian reminisced about the time she first laid eyes on George. She was with a group of her friends on old Carrabelle Beach, standing beside a jalopy someone had driven onto the sand. In the distance, walking toward her, was a wide-shouldered, nearly naked young man.

"He'd been oystering and had on nothing but a pair of shorts. As he came closer, I could see that he was covered in oyster mud and he was so handsome with that black hair and cocky smirk and I said to myself, Oh my Lord, I think I'm gonna die! It was love at first sight. Oyster mud and all!"

Beth got tears in her eyes at the story but managed to whisper, "George Blue was a good man."

Nick didn't say a word, and I saw him blinking back not tears but the threat of them. I squeezed his hand to let him know everything was all right. His mother did likewise, giving him a quick pat on the knee.

Maya commented on Demetrius' absence and Rhea said, "The poor boy is taking care of that baby all by himself."

And Nick said, "I'd like to take care of that no-good wife of his. She needs her neck wrung."

Maya asked, "Do we know if they're in Carrabelle?"

Nick shook his head. "I don't think so. I've asked around. No one has seen 'em."

"Well, it's spilled milk at this point," Lillian said. "We've just got to concentrate on your brother. And that poor little baby."

Nick tossed aside a shell he'd been fumbling with and Beth said, "Remember when we were having that picnic over at Otter Lake and somebody got a bee in their mouth?"

"Who was that?"

"Damned if I know."

"Didn't they think it was a boiled peanut? Picked it right up and popped it in?"

"Fool musta been drunk whoever it was."

The family went on and on like that, swapping tales they'd heard before but laughing just as hard as the first time. And when the stories turned sad, the hurt on their faces and in their eyes was genuine, palpable.

We stayed on the beach until nearly midnight. Rhea couldn't keep up. She fell asleep right there on the sand and Beth eased the old woman's head with its bountiful crop of tightly permed curls onto her lap.

I did not feel as self-conscious that night as I had on previous family occasions. I found myself laughing more easily and even took part in the storytelling, sharing with them the tale of my father running away to join the circus. As the words crossed over my tongue and took flight in the evening air, I felt released, as if my public acknowledgment of my past eased the burden, inviting anyone who paid attention to help shoulder the weight.

Most everything about that night seemed right and good, including the sight of Charon far down the beach. Moonlight glowed on his shoulders and the surf rushed over his ankles and a cry rose from somewhere deep in his soul and the breeze lifted it from his old parched lips and carried it out over the Gulf where it hung on the wind's invisible current before echoing back to shore and disappearing among the infinite grains of sand.

While we chattered beside a bonfire on an empty beach, Captain Johnny dreamed of a ship carved out of hand-sawn yellow pine, white oak, and bald cypress.

His rum-sodden body had hurled itself into the kind of sleep that is coma-like in its completeness, yet his dream glowed with the hard light one associates with life.

Horrified, he saw himself lying naked in the leaf litter under the old magnolia in his backyard. His legs were spread wide and where his privates were supposed to be there was nothing but smooth, hairless skin. As if he were more woman than man, the skin between his legs parted and he heard a holy voice curse the old man's sins and then command that for all his days he must give birth in sorrow and pain. Captain Johnny screamed so violently that the magnolia blossoms shuddered against its echo and then the ship was born of his own loins.

As it left the captain's body, the world became a sea composed solely of fire. The flames raced through Captain Johnny's body, converting muscle and tendon and bone and blood to a trail of ash. He suffered. Oh how he suffered! But his pain was exquisite and pure and, in the end, mitigated by pride. Yes, it was a fine whale of a ship with a belly big enough to store an ocean's worth of shrimp or two of every creature on earth and nowhere in it—not in its keel or ribs or deck or bow or stern or wheelhouse—could a nail be found.

He heard his own ragged voice raging through the dream's unreasonable twists and turns: *It was nails they used to crucify Jesus.*

Feeling light, as if he were nothing more than the breath that rises on a sigh, he floated out of the ship and up through the depths of the sea and into Mr. Odum's store. Damned if Josiah Packer wasn't sidled up to the poker table, looking young and lean and full of hidden cards, and Captain Johnny felt the hunger all over again.

It flew upon him the way sex flies on certain men, with an unyielding fury that blinds a fella to his kinder potentialities. He knew he couldn't stop himself. He knew it had to happen.

Josiah grimaced, his face contorting into a mask barely human, as the captain nailed Josiah—palms up, heels down—to the table, all the while mumbling, *forgive me, forgive me.*

When he was done, even as Josiah lay dying, the hunger did not abate and it was then that Captain Johnny knew he was not forgiven and never would be forgiven.

His own voice woke him from the dream. It was a long, hopeless yowl that glazed the shadows flickering on the wind and his cypress-paneled walls.

He got out of bed, stumbled onto the back porch, and peed off the steps into the rain that was just beginning to fall. His hands were shaking and he knew in this instance his tremors weren't caused by rum.

Stumbling on his uneven porch boards, he made his way back inside, put on a pot of coffee, and tried to erase Josiah Packer's terrible face from his mind. On his supper table, white paper napkins were stuffed into a red plastic holder shaped like a tulip. He set one of the napkins in front of him, reached for a pencil that had fallen on the floor three days prior, and began to sketch. By morning, one napkin at a time, he had a set of finished plans for our boat.

Captain Johnny told Nick and me all of this while sitting at our kitchen table the very next day, the three of us drinking sweet iced tea chased with boiled peanuts.

In an orderly progression, with the calm, intense countenance that afflicts the obsessed, he showed us the drawings and diagrams, napkin by napkin. His plans included a decent galley by trawler standards and a nook of a bed large enough for two people to squeeze into.

"It's a lot like your daddy's boat. He added some extras to help make Miss Lillian comfortable and I thought you'd be wanting to do the same for your missus."

Nick didn't say a word, just nodded soberly, but I discerned a glint of recognition in his eyes, as though for a moment his father's fierce love for his mother felt as real to him as it did when George Blue walked the earth.

The captain went on for the next hour, explaining every cranny, every inspired notch, every commonsense and far-flung notion he held about boatbuilding. Because the terms were foreign to me, I understood even less than usual. Garber board, stern post, shaft log, stop water, cut water. He went on and on.

After about a ten-minute lecture concerning the keel, he reconsidered his design. He picked up the napkin, studied the drawing of the ship's spine from one angle and then another before saying, "Nuh-uh. Dat ain't it. Ma'am, you got any clean white paper?"

I set a pad in front of him and he resketched three of his diagrams, revising and perfecting the boat's joinery, fine-tuning its design for maximum ballast and strength.

Throughout the captain's meandering presentation, Nick listened closely, shuffling from one diagram to the next, occasionally rubbing his forehead or reaching under the table to pat my knee.

When Captain Johnny had spent all his words and could finally say nothing more, Nick put his elbows on the table, rested his head in his hands, and cleared his throat.

Captain Johnny sat straight and sober, his eyes drifting over the many pieces of paper, looking almost as if he were a proper gentleman who'd never tasted human flesh.

I looked at the trail of rings left by my glass of iced tea, wiped the table clean with my palm, and rubbed my hands on my jeans.

We were waiting for Nick to speak, to pass judgment on the merits of the captain's plan, to perhaps offer a suggestion or two. But he was certainly taking his sweet time. He remained locked in a pose that suggested only one thing: a desire to think in private, without interruption or aid.

Still, I wondered if I should try to help things along by uttering polite, harmless niceties such as "You certainly did do a lot of work, Captain," or "You are quite the sketch artist," but I decided against either phrase, opting to let Nick's silence carry us for as long as he saw fit.

A fly, which had been making the rounds through my kitchen (coffeepot, cutting board, yellow ware crock) and which I couldn't shoo or smash for fear of interrupting Nick's intensely solitary thought process, lit on my arm. I discreetly waved it away. As the pest flew out my double doors and onto the porch, Nick leaned back in his chair, looked at Captain Johnny without malice or strain, and very softly broke the silence, asking just one question. "No nails?"

Captain Johnny aimed his spirit-filled gaze out the front window, past my sun-catcher prisms, and said flatly, "I done give 'em all away."

Nick nodded as if he completely understood, as if the captain's response was full of substance and weight and altogether reasonable. Then my husband looked at me and asked earnestly, "Mattie, what do you think?"

I rested my hand on his, fully aware that for him the boat was already a reality. In his silence he had made it real. The curve of the hull and the way the seams of this nailless wonder would lock together, and the winches and towlines and trawl boards and rigging, and the smell of diesel and the roar of a perfectly tuned engine, and the gurgling purr that would rattle amid the seagulls' sharp cries as he idled away from the dock and into the channel in his new trawler for the first time. All of these things existed. They tumbled through his brain, pushing him rapidly forward to that crossroads in our reasoning where discussions of pros and cons are irrelevant, where thoughtful decision-making is as dangerous as a pothole on a freeway, where desire and compulsion run over any and all voices that attempt to whisper, "Let's take a day to think about this."

Yes, we both knew that we were going to fling rationality to the wind and pay an old drunk—a vision-seeing ex-con—to build a nailless boat based on plans that came to him in his dreams.

Given all that, it's still a mystery to me why I looked over the heads of the two men in that kitchen, tapped my fingers on my pine-top table, and murmured, "I don't know, Nick. I'm just not sure."

November 17, 1996
Evening

I'm sitting on my front porch writing by the light of a candle. I don't want to flip on the lamp—it'll draw bugs and, also, I can see the lights of the trawlers better in the dark.

Nick is out there among them. From my vantage point, he and The Lucky Miss B *are just one more distant glow in the crowd. It's a funny thing, how that old ugly ship and my sweetie are turned into starlight.*

The shrimp have been running real strong. So much so that at the end of every week we've been able to make a payment on the new boat. By the time the trawler is in the water, I want her paid for, free and clear. I hate owing anybody money. That's something I've learned about myself. It surprises me, my conservative attitude regarding finances, but I suspect I'll thank myself for it one day.

I wish Nick didn't feel compelled to help the captain every afternoon. I know he's right. The boat will be finished sooner and we're saving money by him helping (that, alone, should make me happy), but we barely see each other. It's odd, I've never before physically ached just because I wasn't around somebody. Maybe I ought to start going with him. Maybe I could be useful.

Lillian says the new boat has less to do with Dem and more to do with Nick wanting to follow in his father's footsteps. He worshiped the ground his daddy walked on—those are her words, not mine. But I bet she's right. Nick wants a boat as fine as the one his father died on. He wants to make his father proud.

The migrating butterflies didn't arrive in their usual numbers this fall. Everybody says so. Chalk it up to last year's hard winter, I guess. Spring's numbers were down, too, according to Beth and Maya. Maybe we'll have a mild winter. The ghost crabs haven't left the beach yet. Rhea says that's a sure sign of a cold snap, when the ghost crabs disappear.

Lillian stood on my porch in a pink matching shorts set, her exasperation with my lack of gardening skills evident, her silver hoop earrings glinting in the hard afternoon sun, and said, "I'm going to get you some mushroom compost for this lousy excuse of a backyard and we're going to turn it into something."

I shook my head and pointed at Nick's junk piles seething in the Indian summer heat. "I can't plant anything until the mess is gone and Nick is working too hard for me to nag him about it. He already told me he didn't want me touching anything back there. He says some of that stuff is worth money."

"Hah!" Lillian folded her arms in front of her and tapped her tiny, sandal-shod foot. "That's what men always say when they don't want to clean something up."

I looked at her little defiant face and thin-lipped smile, trying to determine if she knew what she was talking about. "Really?"

She daintily pushed a strand of graying hair off her temple. "Trust me on this one, Mattie." With her face grave, her fingers still touching her hair, she turned to me and said, "If we don't do it, it will never get done."

In the face of bald truth, sometimes the best response is silence. So I just stood there, staring at my husband's beloved hills of rusted radiators, mufflers, screens, buckets, paint rollers, hubcaps, and who knows what.

"We'll start tomorrow," Lillian said.

I evenly measured my words as I assumed one would when entering into a conspiracy. "Should I mention this to Nick?"

She arched her perfectly plucked eyebrows at me. "Well, honey, you're his wife. That's up to you."

Conspiracy or not, when Lillian set her mind to something, there was little hope of dissuading her. I wonder if this particular characteristic irritated George Blue unto death or whether he found it endearing. At any rate, I believe her sons—and most likely her husband, too—had decided that their lives would be happier if they just learned to cope with Lillian's stubborn determination. The ride downstream may be harrowing but it's better than going against the current, which some-times can kill you. So that's what I did. I surrendered to Lillian's back-yard demands and everyone, including Nick, seemed to take my un-qualified capitulation for granted.

The next day, right after Nick left for Carrabelle, we began. Lillian arrived at my house dressed in pastel blue coveralls, spouting motiva-tional slogans such as "Let's get to it! Go! Go! Go! Nothing like tackling a big job to make you feel alive!"

And so commenced my gardening odyssey. Every day after running shrimp over to My-Way, I would come home and put on my work clothes: jeans, an old torn T-shirt, and leather gloves. After the coast was clear, meaning Lillian and Rhea watched for Nick's departure, the two women would arrive at my back porch, Gaby in tow. We set up the baby's playpen under the pines so we could keep a close eye on him as the three of us picked through Nick's various piles of rubble, deciding for ourselves what should be kept and what should be tossed.

This may sound as if it were boring, backbreaking labor but actually it was rather challenging. It seems that snakes love junk piles and so do cockroaches and mice. The sight of a black racer slithering away like a ribbon sent me running toward the house more than once.

If none of us could identify what an object was or what it could possibly be used for, we threw it into one of two chaff piles — that which could be burned and that which would have to be hauled away. If we could discern a usable purpose for something, it went into the keeper pile.

Not all of our decisions were easy or quick. Take the metal fragment that was shaped like a crookneck squash. Lillian held it aloft as if she were presenting a diamond tiara, fodder for our admiration. "What do you think?"

"Beats me," I said.

Rhea poked it with her index finger as if its ungiving surface would tell her something. "Hmpf!"

"Looks like chaff to me," Lillian announced and she started to toss it into the haul-away pile.

"No no no no!" Rhea yelled. "It's a muffler!" she said triumphantly. "I'll bet my bottom dollar!"

"Big-a-Mama, this is not a muffler. Unless it fits a moped. And since my son doesn't own and has never owned a moped, I seriously doubt it."

Rhea shook her arthritis-swollen finger in her daughter-in-law's face. "I'm telling you, it is so a muffler!"

"It's too small!" Lillian insisted.

"Everything is smaller these days. Mark my word, one day one of us is gonna need this muffler and we're not gonna have it because of your hard head and then who's gonna go to the hill and buy a new one? Hmm?"

I could count on at least one or two of these tête-à-têtes a day. To settle matters, Lillian would behave as if she were giving in to Rhea, throwing up her arms and tossing the object in question into whatever category Rhea deemed appropriate. But when the old woman wasn't looking, Lillian would switch everything around. The result was that by the end of the day, none of the piles made any sense, and I was fairly certain that once Nick had time to putter again he would ask me where the moped muffler was and I'd say what moped muffler and he'd say you know that thing that looks like a squash and I would be forced to claim that I had no earthly idea what he was talking about.

At the end of two weeks, three sizable junk middens graced my backyard. Rhea and I were completely confused as to which was the keeper pile but Lillian claimed to know, deeming it to be the far right heap.

Rhea looked at me and said, "She has no idea what she's doing."

My lowly status as the newest member of the family prevented me from commenting but if the truth be known, I agreed completely with Rhea, suspecting that Lillian had spent her entire life forging ahead, bullheaded, with such confidence that she inspired terror and witless agreement in all who knew her.

"Once the other two piles are gone, what's left is still going to be an eyesore," Lillian announced. "Mattie, you're going to have to get a storage shed. That's all there is to it. Besides, you'll need someplace to store your gardening tools."

Lillian floated her storage shed idea at the end of a very long, hot afternoon during which Gaby had fussed nonstop at the top of his lungs. Having exhausted himself with his own fury, he was finally sleeping soundly in the playpen, his blue rabbit rattle clutched tightly in his spit-glistening fist. I was prostrate on the ground, giving absolutely no regard to the red bugs and ants. Rhea, who had dirt smudged on her nose, collapsed into a chair and mumbled something to the effect that she didn't believe she would ever walk again. Lillian—forever in motion— paced back and forth, surveying our work with all the intensity of a field general inspecting her troops.

"But, Miss Lillian, we don't have any gardening tools."

"Don't worry. You will," Rhea grumbled. Then she glared at Lillian, her face scrunched with disgust. Her tone of voice left no doubt that she thought her daughter-in-law had lost her marbles. "A storage shed! How do you plan to do that? Somebody would have to build it. And all our men are dead, working, or crazy!"

Lillian, taking her work gloves off one finger at a time, employing the snippy movements of a gentle lady settling down for tea, said, "That's true, Big-a-Mama. That's very true. So, we'll just have to build it ourselves."

"I've never built anything," I said, hoping to quickly nip her idea in the bud.

"Neither have I," Lillian intoned, elongating every vowel, which made her sound horribly condescending. "But, ladies, we're talking about a *shed*. How difficult can it be?" She looked out at the bay, pushed back her shoulders, and took a deep breath as if summoning the ancient Greek Furies. "Look. Men have been building skyscrapers for years. I think we can manage a little bitty storage shed."

"Were you this crazy when my son married you?" Rhea growled.

"Just about," Lillian said, and then she walked down to the chaff piles and yelled, "I think we can start burning some of this tomorrow. The ashes will be good for the garden!"

Fortune smiles down in ways great and small, and in the case of the shed construction, we were graced with a really big grin in the form of Beth and Maya, who volunteered their help after I threw myself upon them, pleading for mercy.

Because they, like Nick, worked at night, our construction hours were limited to afternoons. They would show up in their big red pickup with their hair wrapped in neon yellow bandannas, tools swinging from their belts.

"Good afternoon, ladies," Maya would always say.

"Good afternoon," we would always respond like good pupils.

Beth would clap her hands. "Let's get to work. Daylight is burning!"

I have no idea how Beth came to be so proficient with power tools but I'm grateful for it. She taught us how to use drills and change their bits, how to operate table saws without slicing off our fingers, how to swing hammers without battering our thumbs.

Rhea was too old to do any hard labor but she could measure wood and cut two-by-fours and watch Gaby at the same time. I was pretty handy with a measuring tape myself, and before long, Lillian and I were hefting sheets of plywood and setting them in place and banging nails (yes, nails, Captain Johnny) just as if we knew what we were doing. I learned quickly that what one hand might not be able to do, two probably could, and if not, then three or four positively could get the job done.

Maya and Beth proved to be a formidable team. They each had their strengths and they played on them. Maya delegated jobs and barked orders with such authority that none of us, even Lillian, questioned her. And Beth, besides her innate talent with tools, was especially gifted when it came to fixing our screwups.

It took us a solid month of afternoons to complete the shed and in that time my scrawny arms actually developed muscles, which was a turn-on for Nick, so in that sense, the construction project presented an unforeseen bonus. Also, my fingernails broke off and my palms developed first blisters and then calluses. At night, after my shower, I would look at myself in our bathroom's full-length mirror which was nailed to the back of the door and marvel at my body's transformation from lithe and weak to lean and hard.

I liked this new me. I liked being stronger and knowing that if push came to shove, I could make my own patio furniture or bookcases or benches or just about whatever else came to mind. I wouldn't have to think of ways to trick Nick into building anything for me ever again. Freedom through carpentry, that was my new motto.

During this phase of our life together, Nick displayed both prudence and good sense by steering clear of the backyard project.

This was as close as he came to interfering: Woefully silent, he would stand on the back porch and stare out at the junk middens. As he watched the middens grow in size and as their rhyme and reason descended into chaos, I feel fairly confident that he knew he was losing any chance of being in control of the gears and gadgets and springs and anvils that make a man feel as if he is fulfilling God's purpose. Without a ready supply of junk, how could a man, for instance, cure a sudden and amazingly infrequent desire to tune up the lawn mower? Without cigar boxes filled with sundry pieces of smelted and tooled metal, how could he ever bring to life those greasy little diagrams that are tattooed onto men's brains at conception?

The answer, I'm sure he realized with blunt finality, was that he wouldn't. Not for the time being, anyway. His only choice was to wait for the tide to change, to seize that unpredictable moment when he was no longer outnumbered by women who were on a mission. Thusly, he kept his head down, working on the boat by day, shrimping by night, and gaining solace from the simple dictum that given enough time, all seasons pass.

As for the shed, every day during its construction and for months thereafter, he would wander out to this board-and-batten cube of a structure and scratch his head in unadulterated amazement. Even though his shed was being built by his wife, mother, grandmother, and female cousin and her equally female lover—a turn of events that most likely left him feeling slightly emasculated—he had to admit we were doing a damn fine job.

I'm sure the ransacking of his junk piles and the construction of the shed were not easy for him. But Nick had a good heart. That's why, when we found the time to lie down and take a nap together, he would hold me tight and tell me I was precious and I would say that he was, too, and we'd murmur that we were proud of each other, and then we'd drift asleep, comfortable in the mistaken and impossibly romantic notion that in our sleep, as in our waking hours, we shared the same dreams.

· · ·

I had barely begun to implement my freedom through carpentry motto—the building of the shed was as far as I'd gotten—when Lillian temporarily put my nebulous plans on hold by reminding me as I drove the last roof nail into the shed's final blue shingle that the reason we had gone through hell for the past several weeks was so I would be able to plant a garden.

Two men with gleaming butt cracks and no teeth delivered the mushroom compost via boat. They hauled away the junk we could not burn, leaving behind what amounted to a steaming mountain of horse shit.

At this juncture in my gardening saga, Rhea disappeared. That is to say, at eighty-some years of age she had done all the gardening in her life she intended to do, so after casting a weary eye on the fine white butt of one of the delivery men, she announced, "That's it for me. If you need any advice about your tomatoes, ask Lillian. I'm through."

It would be a vast understatement to say that spreading the mushroom compost was a nasty chore, but Lillian insisted it had to be done. Under her tutelage (she made me do all the labor, contending that the only way I would learn what gardening was truly about was if I went at it using my own sweat and not hers), I cleared a thirty-five-by-fifty-foot swath, hoeing dollar weeds, tick weeds, sticker burrs, and stinging nettles. I tilled the sand and added compost and created raised beds with pressure-treated two-by-fours left over from the shed construction. I got sunburned and I groaned and I cursed and I cried.

On one of the rare afternoons when I was alone, when Lillian wasn't standing over me barking "suggestions" that I first thought of as orders and eventually veiled threats, I tripped over a rake, twisted my ankle, and landed head down in the compost. Shit was in my eyes, up my nose, in my mouth.

This is it. No more. I've had enough. I tried to stand but the compost was similiar to a bog in that each time I attempted to extricate myself I only succeeded in sinking farther down. Finally, like a pig in mud, I rolled down the dunghill and onto the oyster shell driveway where I lay, face up, staring at a mountainous cloud and its refracted light, cursing the day I allowed Lillian to tell me how to run my life.

If she wanted my backyard to be a garden then she could damn well do it herself. Who was going to take care of me if I got sick from ingesting compost? No telling what kind of microbes are in this stinking stuff. Probably hepatitis. And rare equine viruses that can cross over into humans. A plague of sorts. Jesus, maybe even rabies. Maybe I should go to the clinic in Carrabelle and get checked by that physician's assistant. What's her name? Something-or-other Singh? She's from India, that's all I know. And she's so small boned I bet her arm could be snapped in two. Crack crack. What if I died? Would Nick ever recover? Would he get married again, maybe real soon because he couldn't bear living alone? That's all right. Hell, I'd be dead and wouldn't even know. Imagine, all of this because I fell face down into a compost hill, a gift from my mother-in-law. Ha—there's karma for you! What would my gravestone say? *Here lies Mattie Fiona Blue. She died from eating shit.*

And then I started to laugh. The whole situation struck me as hilarious. Me falling into a compost heap, me trying to be a gardener, me lying there in the oyster shells feeling sorry for myself. I must have been quite a sight. The madwoman of Lethe covered in horse manure and laughing herself into tears. Breathless, I sat up and, as if I were a child with meager coordination, utilized all fours to get on my feet, my laughter slowing into halting guffaws. As I brushed myself off I realized that Charon was in the field that separated our two houses. He studied me, his blue eyes as quizzical and fierce as the sun. My appearance and behavior probably frightened the poor old geezer. I waved and shouted "hello." He didn't respond but he kept me in his sights as I walked up to the house.

Adjacent to my back porch was a privacy deck which led directly to the shower. I had always thought that this was a rather odd setup but in my current condition it made perfect sense. I entered the privacy deck and, hidden from view, took off my compost-sodden clothes, leaving them in a reeking heap. I tried the shower's exterior jalousie door and was grateful that Nick had left it unlocked. In the hottest water my skin could tolerate, I showered, scrubbing myself raw with Ivory soap and a loofah.

When Nick got home I would tell him about my day, about how I looked pitiful, lying there in the compost, and about how I swore my gardening days were finished, and I would describe how I resorted to rolling down the dung heap to escape its clutches, and we would howl with laughter, and he would say through his giggles, "I'm sorry, honey."

After my shower, I slipped into fresh clothes, gulped down cold water right out of the pitcher, slammed shut the fridge door, and headed back to work. But I took a gentler tact.

I surveyed my seedlings which I was growing in containers of all conceivable shapes, sizes, and materials on the back porch. I had never started anything from seed before but Lillian had insisted, saying that it would save money and teach me about the "whole shebang." I didn't ask her to elucidate what she meant by shebang, but she made a solemn pledge that if my seedlings failed, she would personally dig up flowers and vegetables from her garden and plant them in mine.

In gardening terms, Lillian was light-years ahead of me. She had spent the long winter months while Nick was off-island poring over seed catalogues—something she predicted I would get hooked on, as well—and to get me started she gave me "cold weather" seeds from her own stash. Broccoli, romaine, spinach, cauliflower, green onions. She also gave me summer seeds—squash, tomatoes, sunflowers—which she said would flourish as long as the weather cooperated. "If the weather turns on us, just act as if your living room is a greenhouse," she said. She claimed that Lethe rarely had any freezing temperatures until January at the earliest (the previous winter was a freak of nature, she insisted) and that with proper care, I should be able to keep things going until at least February and if I was industrious, maybe beyond. I didn't exactly know what she meant by "industrious" but I feared it had something to do with smudge pots and agricultural fabric and staying up all night in a dust-bowl attempt to save crops so that people worldwide would not go hungry.

Despite my sarcasm, I have to admit, it was sort of thrilling, making things grow. What a wonderful surprise, the first sight of those surprisingly sturdy green stems poking up through the soilless mix and their tender nearly transparent leaves budding overnight, two at a time! I couldn't leave my baby plants alone. Instead of allowing nature to take its course, I would stir the soil, trying to wake the dormant seed. I would talk to them, hoping to give them the encouragement they needed to rise from their slumber and begin the process of sending out tap roots and petals. And once the miracle occurred, I could be found slipping off the seed husks that often clung to the leaves long after the plant had germinated.

I might not admit it to Lillian, but I felt sure that I would grow old gardening. I would become one of those ladies who take tea in the garden and who wear heavy black shoes and broad-brimmed straw hats and learn the Latin names of salt-tolerant ground covers so that they can impress their friends, who all belong to the Carrabelle Yaupon Society. I might begin pronouncing basil as though it had a short *a* rather than a long one. Who knows, before it was all over, I might begin grafting fruit trees and creating new hybrids. Or perhaps I would become a respected rosarian and one day Jackson and Perkins would see fit to name a rose after me. The Mattie Blue—a mysterious azure-tinged hybrid tea—the first blue rose known to humankind.

I was unclear as to the reasons. Perhaps it was all the time I was spending digging in the dirt or the ingestion of fresh, fertile, pungent compost, but by and by gardening had awakened in me a hunger similar to the one Captain Johnny was stricken with, except my hunger was without violence. My hunger spawned dreams of tomatoes ripening on the vine, and squash blossoms displaying their golden throats to the delight of bees, and snap beans sizzling in a teaspoon of sweet butter, and morning glories climbing my white trellis and shocking the eye with the intensity of their deep purple blooms, and rose blossoms opening so slowly they brought to mind the long gentle touch of a lover.

So I put up with my bossy mother-in-law, listening closely to her advice; she wasn't a carpenter but she was a damned good gardener. When she said that herbs didn't need any fertilizer, just a dash of bonemeal, and that roses were a good choice on the island because they thrived in the ionized air (as long as they were in wind-protected locations), I believed her.

She suggested that I create shaded sitting areas and that I incorporate the kitchen and vegetable gardens into the overall scheme so that we would achieve an effect of fluidity and balance. As for specific plants—perennials versus annuals, native versus exotic, climbers versus tidy bush specimens—she lent me horticultural magazines and flower catalogues, encouraging me to develop a feel for my garden's latent potential.

One early evening, as the bay began to darken in time to the fading light, Lillian and I sat in my backyard in lawn chairs placed where I planned to eventually put in a patio, and we drank sherry out of crystal cordial glasses that she had received as a wedding present thirty-three years earlier, and our conversation flowed easily, as it does between people who have seen one another at their worst and decided not to allow their failings and foibles to obstruct a possible friendship.

She told me that, if I hadn't figured it out already, Nick was allergic to feather pillows. "He got that from his father. The man couldn't walk to within ten feet of a feather pillow without sneezing. You don't have feather pillows in there, do you?"

"No, ma'am. Ours are foam-filled."

Lillian nodded her approval.

"Is Nick a lot like his father?" I asked. "I mean, besides the allergies?"

Lillian sipped her sherry and then licked the residue off her lips. She was wearing those silver hoop earrings and a white cotton shift which looked lovely against her brown skin. She traced the rim of her glass with a delicate finger, thinking over my question, and I wondered how she kept her hands looking so soft, considering the sizable amount of time she spent gardening.

"Nicholas is a lot like both of us," she finally said. "If I had to parcel it out, I'd say he's got his father's love for the water. But any grain of common sense he might have, that's from me. George Blue was many things. Practical wasn't one of them. But romantic! Oh my Lord, was he romantic!" Then she tilted her head at me and asked, bemused, "Is Nick? I mean, is my son a good lover?"

I could have died right there from embarrassment. It would have been different if Beth or Maya had asked, but his mother! I glanced at her. Her eyes shone with good natured curiosity. This old bat wasn't going to let me off the hook. I cleared my throat and said steadily, trying not to give too much away, "He's very romantic, too."

"Good." She patted my knee. "That means I raised him right." She sighed and looked out to the bay. A hyphenated line of pelicans cruised inches above the water's surface and a dolphin swam slowly eastward, its undulating movements tied to the rhythm of its breathing.

"People looked up to him. They sure did," she said wistfully, keeping her gaze bayward. "And a respected shrimper, Mattie. Nobody better. Not to this very day. The man could fix anything—toasters to diesel engines. But like I said, practical," she rolled her eyes, "he was not."

A smile slipped across her face and I tried to imagine what that must be like, afloat in so many memories. But I couldn't do it. I hadn't lived long enough. "Do you miss him?"

"Oh yes. Of course I do." She fiddled with an earring and then flicked imaginary dirt off her shirt. She and Rhea, I thought, battle so much because they're just alike, hard-shelled softies.

"It's been eighteen years. And the hurt is there all the time. Some days it's like a trinket I carry in my pocket. I can touch it and look at it and then put it away and go on with my day. Barely even know I'm hurting except that my hand keeps reaching into that pocket, fumbling with the memories in a distracted sort of way. But there are other times, my God, when the pain just knocks me down. I mean, flat out." She tilted her face skyward and narrowed her eyes. "Can't figure out why."

"I'm sorry," I said.

The sound of my voice surprised her. She jerked her head toward me. "It's not your fault, sweetie," she said and took a drink.

I tried to change the subject by yammering stupidly about how hard Nick was working—I thought that was the polite thing to do—but Lillian wasn't done.

"Sometimes, the pain is so real that I think if I try hard enough I'll be able to will him back. I know that must sound crazy to you. But the terrible fact of the matter is, I love that feeling. I'm awestruck by it. Like when you wake up really early and you see the sun cresting over the Gulf and you think for a moment, Anything is possible. And then you go put on the coffee and you start to make it real strong the way he liked it and then you remember that it's just you. So you stand there in the near darkness wanting to cry, knowing that when he died all of those grand possibilities died with him."

She looked at me, her face suddenly defiant, nearly angry, but a moment later she shrugged her shoulders as if to say, What're you gonna do, you can't win for trying. Then she poured us each more sherry and I saw that her hands were trembling. "Do you ever visit your mother's grave?"

I shook my head "no." "Not since the funeral."

"Where is she buried, Mattie?"

"Jacksonville Beach. On Penmen Road." I looked around at the tilled raised beds that were just about ready for planting. "It's a pretty cemetery," I heard myself say. "Lots of oaks. She's buried under a crepe myrtle."

"White?"

"Uh-uh. Fuchsia."

"Ahh!" Lillian nodded as if she understood the significance.

"It's kinda funny. I never thought about it before. But pink was her favorite color."

"She must like it, then, when it's in bloom."

A picture flashed in my mind of my own garden come spring. It would be wildly colorful. And fragrant. And birds would flock to it and sing. "You think she knows?"

Lillian reached over and held my hand. "Sure she does."

I took a small sip. The liquor was oddly sweet and smoky and I liked the way it coated my tongue. "This is my first time drinking sherry."

"Really?"

"Never had the opportunity before, I guess."

"Well then, this is an occasion. Doctors say this stuff is good for the heart. But I say, it's even better for the soul." She merrily topped off our glasses and I found myself stifling a giggle at the notion that I was getting slightly looped with my mother in law.

Lillian drew in her lips and made a sucking noise before saying, "It's a thinking woman's drink. All those early suffragists—even the ones who claimed to be prohibitionists—were sherry drinkers. I bet Miss Elizabeth Cady Stanton drank more sherry in her lifetime than she did water."

"How do you know?"

"Just a theory."

Lillian went back to fiddling with that earring. With her free hand she held her cordial glass at a jaunty angle, as if she were mesmerized by her own deep thoughts. "You know," she continued on, "I'm usually not one to run around giving advice. And I know you are most likely sick to death of me interfering in your garden."

"No, I welcome your input," I said, only half-lying. I welcomed *and* resented it.

"Well, let me just share this with you then." She looked at me as if she were peeking over her half-frame glasses even though she was not wearing them. "Mattie, gardens are amazing places. They satisfy you deep inside. When you make things grow and give order to the world, you feel good about things. But gardens can also stymie the bejesus out of you and you'll find yourself wanting to pull everything up and start over. I've had my moments over in my garden, I mean to tell you. I'm glad my son chose you to be my daughter-in-law. You make him happy.

I can tell. And that's why I'm going to say this to you straight out and I don't mean anything bad by it." She leaned into me and said with a mother's urgency, "You can discover yourself in a garden, Mattie. If you want to."

A rogue lump mushroomed in my throat, blocking any possibility of a response. I wanted to hug her and run from her. I wanted to say, "My own mother never talked to me that kindly. Not that there was anything wrong with her. No, not at all. She was just confused. Sad. Not like you. You're not anything like her, not one teeny bit."

But amid those conciliatory and unspoken words, others designed to stopper my tears rose and fell, all of them having to do with Lillian minding her own business.

These thoughts and emotions shaped my silence, giving weight and form to the aching knot in my throat. But Lillian understood, or at least accepted my mute, near hysterical behavior. She pressed the back of her hand against my cheek and our eyes met and I could hold back those rising tears no longer and as I cried over both the barren weed patch of my childhood and dreams buried deep inside me as if they were dormant seeds just beginning to wake from their long, cold sleep, she whispered, "I'm here if you need me."

Lillian thoroughly cleaned her house four times a year, top to bottom, and recommended that I do the same. But somehow this recommendation turned itself inside out and I found myself scrubbing Lillian's dirty corners instead of my own.

We were tackling her Florida room, dusting furniture, blinds, shelves, photos, and knickknacks when the subject of her deceased husband came up again. She set down her dust cloth, picked up the charred piece of wood that was poised atop the tattered copy of *The Old Man and the Sea*, and said, "This is all that's left of George's boat. Can you imagine? I found it in the surf about a week after he died." She ran her hand over the wood and then looked up at me. "You must think I'm silly, keeping it like it was a relic or something."

"Oh no! In your shoes, I would do exactly the same thing."

Our eyes locked. Scared that she might think I was pandering and still slightly intimidated by her, I glanced away. "You know, I think you would," she said softly. She set the burnt remnant of George's boat back on the shelf and retrieved *The Old Man and the Sea*. She gazed at its cover and appeared to be thinking. Finally she said, "Mattie, I'd like you to have this. It used to belong to Rhea but she gave it to me not long after I married George and now I'm giving it to you. It's marked up a little bit—Big-a-Mama and I tend to write in our books—but I hope that won't bother you any." She handed me the novel and pressed my hands against it.

"Lillian, are you sure?"

"Of course I'm sure. The women in our family tend to be readers and Nick said you were, too. And besides, when you're the wife of a shrimper, something has to keep you company. It might as well be a book."

"I'll take really good care of it."

She flashed me a faint smile, picked up her dusting rag, and went back to work. "Just be sure that when the time comes you pass it along to the right person."

"Yes, ma'am." I hugged the novel to my chest and felt wildly honored to have been included in the chain.

"Those photos could use a good dusting," she said as she wiped down a bronzed baby shoe.

I set the novel on the couch and started in on the photos. I picked up the picture of her sons holding the fish and as I wiped it clean I innocently inquired about her firstborn. "What about Zeke? What's he like? Nobody ever talks about him."

She paused, slowly set down the baby shoe, and turned to me. A mixture of hurt and confusion clouded her normally calm face.

I thought that perhaps she hadn't heard me correctly so to try to clarify my question I held the photo out to her but her eyes stayed on me. "And nobody ever will," she said. Then she grabbed the broom and sternly, almost frantically, swept her spotless floor.

"She blames herself."

"But you and Demetrius turned out good."

"Doesn't matter. Zeke didn't."

"What's wrong with him?"

"Who knows? He was getting into fistfights and suspended from school for as long as I can remember. Beth says it's all about Daddy, that Zeke went wild after he died. But I think he was always trouble. And anyway, Daddy dying didn't give him the right to drink himself into oblivion and beat his wife and then abandon his child. That's something more. That's like—I don't know—bad seed."

"Still, his behavior is not your mother's fault. Sounds like he was determined to be a screwup from the get-go."

"He's worse than that, Mattie. I've seen him do some really bad things—stuff I don't want to talk about. We should all be glad he's not around. And as for Mama, just don't bring it up anymore. When he left Lucas, that was the final straw. Zeke's name hasn't crossed her lips since. Don't think it ever will."

I would have never done it, had I been on my own. But marriage, fishmongering, carpentry, and gardening conspired to fundamentally alter the way I thought of myself.

The basic assumption that we won't fail—I guess that's what confidence is—had escaped me until I moved to Lethe and began to meet with the kind of success that most people take for granted. For instance, I learned that most women were not like my mother and that among people of the same sex one could find enduring and trustworthy friends. For me, that was a huge discovery and to this day I regret that it was one that escaped me until I journeyed into womanhood.

But there were other less ground-shaking yet nevertheless important triumphs. I became more adept at bird identification. Much to my own amazement, I found myself hopping into the *Medusa* and zipping over to the hill without so much as a second thought. With unerring accuracy, I did the bookkeeping for our business. I made an outdoor bench out of driftwood and oak. My garden—though sparse—began to produce and we ate lettuces and broccoli and beans that I planted from seed with my own two hands, and I learned that Nick occasionally got moody but that if I gave him a bowl of ice cream and read passages to him from *The Old Man and the Sea* he would recover and we could continue on with our life as lovers and friends. Cooking continued to be a challenge for me, but I was determined to keep trying. I didn't really have much choice—we had to eat and Nick was a fairly good sport about my lack of culinary skills.

These successes, earned in their own time and in their own way as if each one possessed a distinct personality with unique needs and special charms, may sound trivial. But they are not. They are what allowed, even compelled me to say yes when, during a late autumn storm that kept Nick in port, having just finished making love, he leaned up on one elbow, traced my lips with his finger, and asked, "If I did more of the housework, would you be willing to go to school? We've talked about it before and we're bringing in money pretty steadily and it's what we said you would do. Remember, back there in the trailer?"

That's how I came to be so busy that even drinking a cup of tea in the early morning seemed like a luxury. I kept the garden going on my own, but Nick sometimes had to run our shrimp to My-Way himself. He and Captain Johnny were making great progress on the boat, or so I was told, and with Nick out of the house I was able to excel in my studies. I found that I was more mature than my classmates, most of whom were a good five years or so younger than me, and while I did not purposefully avoid making friends, I wasn't in school to socialize. I attended class and did my homework and handed in my assignments and took it all very seriously. But my life, its core and future, I realized was on Lethe.

I did not major in literature, as might be assumed. Lillian's pragmatism had begun to rub off on me. That's my explanation for how I came to major in accounting. I learned about flow charts and tax laws and profit and loss statements. I realized that Nick and I should incorporate.

And the same was true for Beth and Lillian and even Demetrius. We bought a laptop computer and an ink-jet printer—it was the first computer on Lethe—so that I could produce decent-looking reports and term papers (I couldn't get on the Internet because there were no phone lines but the computer's mere presence on the island prompted Rhea to mutter that we were all going to hell in a handbasket). Eventually, I would recommend that the family pool its resources and create one corporation and that we share in the profits equally. This idea was not well received at first but school helped to harden my head and strengthen my resolve. They finally gave in to me and we formed Blue Seas, Incorporated.

We voted in Lillian as our president. Lucas was a budding artist and after we begged and browbeat the poor boy, he finally agreed to create a logo for us. And a fine one it was—two leaping dolphins whose figures formed a heart and below them in the water pranced a chorus line of dancing shrimp.

All that reading I had done through most of my life did not fail me. I was able to test out of several of my core subjects—English primarily—and those that I did take were made far easier since I had already read many of the books.

Despite Nick's optimism regarding our finances, most of our expendable income was being sunk into the boat, so school put us immediately in debt. And for me, debt equaled guilt. Every time I balanced the books and saw so clearly in those carefully scribed figures how much my education was costing, I would tumble into a dark mood and would have to rely on Nick to dig me out.

"Just like with the boat, we're in this together. We're growing, Mattie, you and me." He would gather my hair in his hands, lift it off my neck, and stroke the pale skin at the crown of my spine, trying to comfort me.

But perhaps I paint too rosy a picture. Going to school meant that the time Nick and I had together was whittled down even further. If I had foreseen what lay ahead, I would have never stolen the hours from us. I would have stayed beside him every second of every day. I would have cherished each exhaled breath, each sigh, each utterance no matter how banal.

These thoughts stalk me from time to time, pulling me out of the fragile comfort of this narrative and away from life, even though I know that monitoring his every move would not have been living. No. It was better the way it was—each of us pursuing our individual notions of bliss rather than spending our days and nights shapelessly waiting for death.

"Nick told me about the family legend. He said it's why he left Lethe last winter."

"Nonsense. He left Lethe for the same reason all sons leave their homes."

"Why's that?"

"To see what's out there."

"So . . . you don't believe in the legend?"

"I don't believe in anything, Mattie. After George died, that was it."

"But you believed in it until then?"

"Listen to me, accidents happen. That's all there is to it. The only thing that superstitious rattletrap will get you is trouble. People start believing in that baloney and they forget things."

"Like what?"

"Like the engine needed to be overhauled six months ago. Or they stop paying attention for one instant—that's all it takes on a shrimp boat—and the next thing they know, they've fallen into the nets."

"And that's what happened to George? Just one mistake and it was over?

"Yes."

January 3, 1997
My kitchen table, early morning
It's cold and the tide is out. There hardly seems to be any water left in the bay.

I've been reading up on astronomy thanks to the book Lillian gave me for Christmas. I was surprised but not disappointed that she gave me something unrelated to gardening. Now, in addition to being able to name birds and shells and plant life, I'm learning about the stars.

Get a load of this: Delphinus is a star that can be seen in the northern hemisphere in late summer. The name is Greek and means "the Dolphin." According to the book, the Ancient Greeks also referred to Delphinus as the "sacred Fish"! As the story goes, a dolphin helped Poseidon find Amphitrite—a gorgeous mermaid. He took her to be his bride and they lived in his golden palace at the bottom of the sea. (Just like the river dolphins' Enchanted City in the Amazon. It's amazing how all this stuff is linked together—myth and religion—spanning continents and the ages.) But back to Delphinus—to reward the dolphin for helping him find his bride, Poseidon placed him among the stars.

I spent much of my first winter on Lethe consumed with homework. Not wanting to be in school forever, I took a heavy load and Nick did not seem to mind. In fact, I would look up from a textbook to find him watching me, a crooked smile burnishing his bony face. Sometimes that's where it ended; my attention would shift back to the text and I would silently attempt to memorize an accounting formula while Nick went on with his day. But on other occasions, he would slip off my socks and rub my toes and heels, and my gaze would trail off the page even as his hands would slowly wander beyond the hard geography of my feet.

Winter's chill kept Nick in port more often than during the rest of the year, and on the few cold and blustery nights Nick stayed home or when the tide was too low for me to make it across the bay and to school, *The Old Man and the Sea* became a haven for us. We would pile pillows on the floor in front of the wood-burning stove and draw the blankets up to our chins and drink red wine and I would read to him. *He was an old man who fished alone in a skiff in the Gulf Stream . . .*

That is how the novel began and where Nick and I set out together on our shared journey through a book that I had read half a dozen times but was new territory for Nick.

As my small voice filled up that large room with words that brought to life the humble existence of an old fisherman who perceived in his daily struggles a glint of the true nature of God—a warm, tarnished glow that was both fearsome and unavoidable—I would pause occasionally to look at Nick and find that his eyes were closed and his lips slightly curved. "Are you sleeping?"

"No. I was imagining the fish, the flying ones."

"I was seeing the sun draw diamonds on the water."

"His hands hurt but they'll be okay. Just so long as he keeps dipping them in the salt water."

"I was thinking about the lions, how beautiful they must be."

As I read on, it became apparent that Rhea and Lillian's finely mapped passages (I could not discern one woman's delicate annotations from the other's) weren't haphazardly chosen. They all, in one way or another, elucidated the connection Santiago felt for the sea. Maybe the two women had been trying to unravel their own husbands' attraction to the water and everything that swam in it. Maybe they thought that if they understood Santiago they would become better partners or that the old man's odyssey would teach them something about the Blue legend, something that was preventing them from believing. Or maybe they were trying to grasp how one man who respected a fish's will to live so completely that he called it his brother could then take its life. After all, hadn't one of them (but which one?—I was too shy to ask) underlined with a heavier hand "Do not think about sin"?

Because we read the novel in fits and starts it took us far longer than that slim volume would normally require. But our hopscotch reading schedule did not lessen the novel's impact. The passages I read one night would linger in our minds for several more, and normally I would backtrack in my reading in order to refresh us on points of plot and mood.

We finished the book on a Sunday night. Gale warnings had been posted from Apalachicola south to Cedar Key. Our old pocket windows groaned and stuttered and the cold rain fell in sheets, blocking out the moon and stars. Sometimes I had to raise my voice to be heard above the wind. To read of the warm sun and the Gulf Stream and the cumulus sky while a winter storm raged all around was to make me pine for summer.

We were near the novel's end when the electricity went out. Nick lit three green candles and I followed the book's typeset lines with my index finger and the words flickered from dark to light in tandem with the flames. As I read, Nick wept. Santiago's struggle, his wisdom, his miscalculations, his reverence for the great fish, his guilt at having taken its life, and then for that life to be wasted on the glutinous frenzy of sharks—all of these things resonated in Nick. He knew about them. Every time he hauled in his nets he experienced the same glory and guilt.

I held his hand to my face and like a person who travels a very far distance on foot, I uttered one word and then another until finally we reached our destination and the old man was once again dreaming of his lions. I closed the novel and set it aside and Nick said, "Sorry for blubbering," and I kissed his cheeks that were wet from his tears, and I rubbed his arm and though he was wearing a sweater, I knew that below my fingertips, beneath the wool cabling, embedded in the very cells of his skin was that tattoo. *Brothers Forever*. Yes. It was starting to make sense, the connection this family felt to the sea. That's why the family myth, that grand embroidered fairy tale of being part dolphin—how else to explain their need, their absolute hunger to be part and parcel of the sea? Just like Santiago, Nick saw himself not as an observer but as a necessary participant in the grand scheme. *Do not think about sin.* That's what Santiago had said. But in the give-and-take between life and death, there lies tragedy. Forget about the sin. What does one do with the pain? Perhaps that was the conundrum, the unanswerable question, that from time to time darkened the blue of my husband's eyes. Yes, pain spurred people to spin tales of dolphins and enchanted cities and animals who become stars and humans who become sea creatures. Divine pain born out of a longing to transcend nature's bounds.

As I held him tight, he said, "Maybe the new boat is all wrong, Mattie. Maybe all of us are wrong. My daddy and my great-granddaddy and the whole fishing bunch of us. Maybe the only life that's fair is Santiago's. One small boat, one man, one harpoon, one great fish."

"But he's not real, baby," I said, rocking us both back and forth. "Believe me, he's not."

Those nebulous, tear-producing reservations Nick held about the way in which man fished the seas in the soon-to-be late great twentieth century were quickly quashed by the day-to-day practicalities of life. As we were all thick in the midst of the global economy and owing Big Brother (taxes, insurance, electricity, retirement), self-sufficiency in the old-fashioned sense wasn't feasible. There was a world to feed and a world to pay. Cuba circa 1930 in a village named Cabanas where running water and lightbulbs were considered indulgences of the rich was a long-gone nether region, a dusty hamlet existing in the shadows of memory and imagination. So by the time the spring of 1997 was upon us, as our boat was ready for launching and as the butterflies arrived in pastel clouds, ruffling the sky in flurries of pink and yellow and the deepest blue, Nick's primal doubt piqued by Hemingway's Santiago had drifted into the murky depths of his subconscious.

And life went on.

Lillian took personal responsibility for the well-being of the short-lived butterflies whose numbers far outpaced those of the previous year, turning our end of the island into an oasis planted to overflowing with flowers to their liking. Indian paintbrush. Passionflower. Penta. Lantana. Borage. Gay feather. Coreopsis. Coneflower. All hideaways for clusters of pearly eggs and silken chrysalises, some meeting the nutritional needs of the mid-stage caterpillars as they chomped their way into butterfly-hood.

I spied on Lillian one morning from the clandestine vantage point of my shed window. I had gone in to retrieve a trowel in order to plant a flat of parsley I had started from seed during the winter when I saw her standing in the meadow between her garden and the bay, a smug satisfaction brightening her black eyes as the butterflies (she would say *her* butterflies) flitted from flower to flower. In her pert little mint green shorts set and straw hat and brushed-to-a-sheen black hair caught in a plain white ribbon at the nape of her neck, she had the air of a one-person welcoming committee content with a job well done.

Nick and Captain Johnny had worked hard all winter and by the time the butterflies arrived we were making plans to trailer the boat from its birthplace beneath the oaks to the shallow saltwater bay that would be its home. As soon as word got out that the *Mattie Fiona* was to be a nailless boat, folks started stopping by Captain Johnny's to watch the construction and offer advice and encouragement no matter what they were actually thinking. After taking their leave, most headed straight to Paradise Shores Realty where Mr. Abe Cutler acted as the town bookie, taking bets and figuring the odds as to whether she'd ever float.

I suppose it was both gambling and the town's natural bent toward goodwill that account for the launching's impressive turnout. It was high tide on a Saturday morning and I mean, everyone was there. Schoolteachers, schoolchildren, the staff from Burda's Pharmacy, women of all ages and sizes and economic strata, bankers, the town librarian, the antique dealer, the seafood wholesalers, their workers, mullet fishermen, crabbers, oystermen, shrimpers, Harry from Harry's Restaurant, the waitresses, the town's preachers—all ten of them—glad-handing real estate agents including Mr. Cutler who dressed for the occasion (black shiny shoes, baby blue polyester pants, white belt and a stiff shirt to match, plus a Panama hat), bartenders, bar owners, politicians, city police, county sheriff, marine patrol, Josiah Packer, folks from the marina and the IGA and the hardware store, county workers, city workers, county prisoners on work detail. I'm sure I'm leaving some people out but you get the idea.

When it comes to boatbuilding, nothing is cheap or easy. We met our goal of not owing Captain Johnny a dime by the time she was ready for her maiden voyage. But there are end costs that are huge. Radar, for instance, and don't even blink when talking about engines or the price will go up. Trying to pinch pennies, we went in search of a used engine. But as it turned out, the pennies pinched us: seven grand, eight grand, ten grand. I wasn't prepared for so many zeroes and by the end of the day I would wander home feeling pummeled.

In the evenings, I would sit at our kitchen table with a glass of wine and my calculator, crunching figures that never came out in our favor, and if Nick was home he would pace from one end of the room to the other, rubbing his neck with his scarred hand. All of that came to an end, however, when Lillian showed up one afternoon with a check for thirty thousand dollars.

"Mama, where'd you get this money?" Nick's eyes swelled in his head and the edges of his lips paled which is what they always did when he was under sudden pressure.

"Investments," she said smartly. "After your father died, I invested the life insurance settlement. I've done fine, financially speaking—I won't miss this money so don't worry about me. I want you to take this check and buy what you need for the boat."

Nick was speechless. He held the check with his open palms as if it were too precious to sully with fingerprints. I glanced at it myself, not trusting what I had just heard. But there it was in Lillian's perfect penmanship, made out to both of us, every number and letter perfectly slanted and spaced and sweetly feminine. I counted. Yes, those were four zeroes after that three.

"Now, I want you both to listen. There's a string attached to this money."

I looked at Nick who was still in shock. I slipped my hand into the crook of his arm. "Honey, do you need to sit down?"

He looked up from the check, humility striking the angles and valleys of his face as if it were sunshine. "Anything, Mama. Whatever you ask."

With the finely faceted authority that only mothers possess, she said,

"Don't either one of you fool around with any used stuff. I want you to buy new and go for quality. No skimping. It's too important." Then her motivation chased her emotions to the surface, causing her face to go stiff as she muttered, "And you know why."

Nick bear-hugged his mother. I kissed her cheek. "Thank you so much, Lillian," I said.

"Thank you isn't enough, Mama. It's just not," Nick whispered.

So the *Mattie Fiona* was solidly outfitted and everything on her was new from bow to stern. She didn't have any rigging yet, for logistical reasons that would have to wait until after she was launched, but other than that she was ready to go. Nick and Captain Johnny may have notched and sawed and pegged her together, but I helped paint her. She was white with yellow trim. I had wanted to paint the wheelhouse blue but Captain Johnny wouldn't let me.

"Bad luck," he clipped, his pale hazel eyes squinting against any possible elaboration.

The day of the launching, Rhea stayed home and baby-sat Gabriel. Charon patrolled his shoreline, as usual, and Demetrius went to work. We had invited him to join us. Indeed, Nick begged. But with his childlike joy on hiatus, Demetrius wandered through his days and nights depriving himself of the minor flourishes which most of us have decided make life bearable. I am not casting aspersions. I am simply reporting. And therefore, to be balanced and fair I must say that much to his credit, he also exhibited a noteworthy, even priestly, devotion to his baby. Besides, the new boat was the talk of the town—I don't think he wanted to risk running into Lacey.

But the rest of the core group showed up to help in any way they could. Lillian, Beth, Maya, Lucas. If all went well, once Pigott's House Movers got her in the water, we would take her out into the bay, enjoy a celebratory lunch, and be back in port by sunset.

By the looks of the crowd, you would have thought we were the royal family. People stood on their tiptoes and craned their necks to get a good look at our boat as she traveled down Highway 98 courtesy of the house-moving equipment. She was an awesome sight, perched as she was in the truck's wide, long bed, police cars escorting her fore and aft, people clapping as she came into view. Fathers hoisted their children onto their shoulders. Teenagers flirted. The gamblers in the crowd worried and muttered to each other. Two city policemen took it upon themselves to instruct Captain Johnny and Nick on how to get her into the water even though the folks from Pigott's were doing fine without any advice from us. Someone near the rear of the crowd shouted, "You think she's gonna float?"

Nick shouted back, "I've got money on it," which caused most of the folks to titter with laughter but sent Mr. Cutler into a red-faced silence because no one was supposed to admit to the taking or placing of bets. Since it was our boat and our launching, the crowd had been kind enough to make room for us at the dock next to the launching site. Nick, Captain Johnny, and Beth headed over to the ramp as Elmer Pigott slowly began to back the *Mattie Fiona* into the river.

"I sure hope she floats," Lillian whispered.

"Me, too."

Nick and Beth were yelling instructions at one another. They were sweating and serious and appeared on the verge of panic. But Elmer Pigott ignored both the panic and the advice as he continued to painstakingly guide her into the water.

"Maybe this nailless thing wasn't such a good idea."

"I'm afraid you're right."

I grabbed hold of Lillian's hand as they eased her in. The crowd fell silent. It was as if the entire world was holding its collective breath. This was better than New Year's Eve. Ten. Nine. Eight. Seven. Six. Five. Four. Three. Two. One. Like velvet on glass, the *Mattie Fiona* made a soft, muffled sound as she entered the water. After much shouting and head-scratching, the supports were removed and Elmer Pigott threw his rig in drive and gave the boat her chance. Yes. Without a doubt, the *Mattie Fiona* was floating. She was light and buoyant and rested high in the water. A cheer went up. Even those who'd bet against us seemed to be taking their losses in stride, clapping, whooping, hollering. Nick and Captain Johnny hugged each other. I heard Nick say, "Go with us."

Captain Johnny shot an ardent glance in Lillian's direction, put his hand on Nick's shoulder, and spoke but his words were incomprehensible to me. Nick shook his hand, hugged him once more, and then the old man made his way, sopping wet, back to shore. Nick and Beth boarded her and waved to the crowd. Nick looked so proud, so happy — a man with a big new boat, now that was something. He ducked into the wheelhouse and with a single push of a button, started up the diesel engine. A second cheer ruffled through the crowd and people hugged and kissed, including Lillian, Maya, Lucas, and me. Nick idled the boat over to the dock, tied her up, and came ashore. He kissed me in front of God and everybody. Beth handed him a bottle of champagne which he presented to me.

"She's your namesake, Mattie. You do the christening."

In the movies it looks easy. But it took me three tries — banging that bottle against the bow — before the glass shattered and we were sprayed with bubbly.

Nick helped each of us board and as we headed into the channel Beth and Maya threw yellow and red roses from Lillian's garden into the water. Lillian opened another bottle of champagne and poured it into paper cups. Lucas worked harder than was necessary distributing the drinks. He got a can of Coke for himself. I looked at the crowd, searching for Captain Johnny, but did not see him. For a split second there was a shift among the onlookers as a group of men made their way to the real estate office to settle their bets and I thought I saw Lacey, standing alone, hair on end, knotted and lost. But when I looked again, she was gone. It's good Dem stayed home, I thought. He wasn't ready to see her, under any circumstances.

As we headed into the bay a cluster of white butterflies flew rapidly by, landward bound. I watched until they disappeared into the bright light. Nick sounded the horn just to show off.

"Congratulations, sweetheart," I said.

My husband's eyes were brilliant and there was no sadness about him. He tipped my face to his. "This is a good thing, isn't it, Mattie?"

"Oh, yes, baby, it's a very good thing."

Nick strutted around the *Mattie Fiona* as if he were Alexander the Great and the trawler was his conquered world. In intimate detail, he spoke of the struggle and triumph behind every perfectly fitted plank, peg, and notch (this is only a minor exaggeration on my part).

Beth was fascinated—she was a natural-born carpenter, after all—but the rest of us, it must be said, glazed over from time to time. Still, I had never seen Nick this proud or animated. He owned a brand-new trawler that was a marvel of craftsmanship and he aimed to enjoy every single inch of it. "Look! Look at this!" he said, slamming shut the wheelhouse door.

Dumb, we looked at each other and back at Nick. "The door!" he explained as if we were morons. "It's a perfect fit. No air. No light. Tight as a bug in a rug."

Lillian gazed at her son and a wry tenderness slipped across her face. I knew her well enough to recognize when she was drowning in memories. George Blue, he was there, right there. She could almost touch him. He was alive, even flourishing, in Nick's enthusiasm and the boldness of those cheekbones and the Byzantine slant of his eyes and the prideful joy he displayed at owning a boat that was the envy of the shrimping fleet. The vulnerability that imbues our hopes and dreams with that golden thread called humanity filled up the space between mother and son, connecting them to the man who revolved like a wisp of air at the center of their imaginations. So many reflections: the father the son the husband the lover the loss the life.

When we boarded the *Mattie Fiona*, Lillian had whispered, "Sixteen years." Until seeing her look at her son with so much wistful love and pain-tinged grace, I did not realize the meaning of her breathless words. But I should have known. And I should have been more sensitive. This was her first time on a shrimp boat since George Blue's death. My God, here was a woman who made love at sea, who gave birth at sea, whose husband died at sea, yet his death had put her at arm's length—an in-house exile of sorts—from a way of life that she had at one time taken for granted.

As Nick chattered about the barber's chair he'd bought from Debbie the antique dealer and installed in the wheelhouse as his captain's chair, Lillian quietly broke away and descended the stairs that led to the engine room. Thinking she might want some company and while Nick was still deep into his story (he bargained her down and "got a deal, a real decent deal"), I followed Lillian's path into the belly of the ship.

I swung open the door and was just about to say, "Lillian, is everything okay?" but the words never made it across my lips. Perhaps it was her demeanor, so wide-eyed and tentative. Or the way her hands fluttered along the various surfaces, sometimes lingering, sometimes not. She felt the mattress, testing for firmness. She chipped at the rolled edge of the cot's wood trim with her thumbnail. She tried the drawers which were empty. She looked confused by their emptiness, as if she didn't understand where George's lovely gifts had gone. The vellum-colored negligee. The box of hard sour candies. The Evening in Paris perfume. Mrs. Elizabeth Barrett Browning's love sonnets. The silver-plate hand mirror. And what about her socks? She rubbed her cheek with the back of her hand, then sat on the cot, brought her knees up to her chin, wrapped her arms around her legs, rested her head on her brown knobby knees, and closed her eyes.

I stood motionless, ashamed, as if I had stumbled into a moment so private that my witnessing of it bordered on sin.

Slowly, as quietly as I could manage, I made my way up the steps and into the light.

We had just finished eating lunch—cold chicken, potato salad, and pound cake—when they arrived. Lucas was the first to see them. He was fishing off the front of the boat, his line lazily drifting through the sun-prismed water, when he shouted, "Dolphins! Starboard bow!"

It was a pod of six bottle-nosed, including a mother and her youngster, and they cut gracefully through the water, intrigued by our presence, and unthreatened. They blew air out of their blowholes. They clicked and squeaked. They lolled on the waves, watching us out of one eye and then the other. There was no doubt about it—they were check-ing us out, perhaps even showing off. One of the larger dolphins dived out of sight, then resurfaced and swam briefly at an angle, revealing a spotted white belly.

"See that!" Nick pointed with his free arm—the other was draped over my shoulders. "She's an old female."

"How do you know?"

"The spots. All these dolphins are different, Mattie, just like you and me. Take a look at that one over there. See how light he is compared to his brother?"

"How do you know it's his brother?"

Nick shrugged. "I just do."

Beth looked at her cousin sharply and then broke into a wide grin. "They're so beautiful!"

"That baby is just as sweet as it can be. Look at the way he stays right by his mother," Maya gushed.

"These bottle-nosed like to ride the bow waves. Sometimes they follow me all the way out, surfing the wake."

"A friend of mine, Sean Hankins," Lucas said, "was floating on his back off Carrabelle Beach and a bottle-nosed came up and nudged him back to shore."

"Really?" I asked.

"He swore it was so. Mrs. Nichols said the dolphin must of thought that Sean was sick and was trying to get him some help."

"Maybe Sean was in danger and didn't know it," Nick said. "Coulda been a shark in the area."

A dolphin breached the water, revealing its full length as it arced through the air—a silver ribbon unfurling—and upon reentry slapped the water with its caudal fin. As if we were tourists at Sea World every-one except for Nick squealed and clapped and bounced on the balls of our bare feet.

"Wow!" I said, completely happy, thrilled down to the calluses pad-ding my sunburned toes. I looked at my husband and started to say, "This is tremendous!" but I skidded to a halt right at the edge of the sudden gulf that had opened between us. Nick stood stone-still, his beautiful face framed in wind-tossed curls, his body dark and imposing against the vacant sky, watching the dolphins swim in lazy, curious circles around the *Mattie Fiona*.

"Nick?" I asked. "Nick?"

He didn't respond. Invisible and unexpected, a fissure had cut a jagged path through the life we shared, and he wasn't with me. I mean, physically he was on the boat. But mentally and in every other way he was with them. He was in the water, swimming around the *Mattie Fiona*, gazing with a bemused air of superiority at the two-legged, hair-headed, landlocked mammals.

For the first time since Nick told me about the family legend that had once haunted him off Lethe and away from the sea, I was afraid.

This was the beginning. This is when I began to understand how very powerful myth can be, how it can nestle itself among the sinews and ligaments of our subconscious until it doesn't matter if the story is illogical and empirically unsound. Against our better judgment, we find ourselves in the grips of ritual, giving thanks, breaking bread, drinking wine, singing praises, offering sacrifice. And all the while we are surprised—so, so surprised—that without any hard-fought effort on our part the myth has become bone.

It happened at the IGA. It was a Sunday in early spring and most of the family had taken the day off because we planned to celebrate Nick and Demetrius' birthdays together. They were both born in March (Demetrius on the sixth and Nick on the twenty-second) so we chose to combine the celebrations at mid-month.

Lillian watched Gaby as the three of us—Nick, Dem, and I—headed over to Carrabelle in the *Poseidon* to buy food and drink for the party. It was just like in the old days except that Demetrius, who had just turned twenty-eight to Nick's big three-oh, was prematurely stooped over and crotchety.

Nick and I were filling up our cart with chips and dips and beer and cookies when my husband paused and said, "Will you look at that—he's reading labels!"

Sure enough, Dem was at the other end of the aisle, studying a can of green beans, his finger following the tiny type, his lips moving inaudibly as he read.

"Something has got to give," Nick said. "He behaves as if he's ready for the grave."

"Hey, Dem," I called. "Let's go see if the cake is ready. I think you'll like it. I had them decorate it special."

Without looking up from his label reading, he said, "You go on. Gaby, he's hard to buy for."

Nick and I looked at each other, our lips stretching into mirror images of thin grim lines. Neither of us could think of what to do. Dem seemed determined to be serious the rest of his life.

"Come on. He'll catch up," I grumbled. I rounded the corner and started down the next aisle. Nick followed, pushing the cart. But I suddenly stopped in my tracks and Nick, who was paying more attention to the cereal than he was to me, rammed me with the cart.

"Sorry," he said.

"Shhhh!"

"This isn't the library," he whispered, sounding like a little boy with hurt feelings.

"It's her!"

"Who?"

"Her," I said, jerking my head. "Lacey!"

Nick's jaw dropped. "Where?"

I turned around. The aisle was empty. "Well, she was there," I muttered. "Come on!"

We left the cart in the cereal aisle and skulked past boxes of sanitary napkins, baby diapers, soft drinks.

"I just saw her!" Nick whispered by the canned soup. He pointed in the direction of produce. We tiptoed and stuck our heads around the corner. The stock boy paid us no heed. There she was, her hair teased big as Texas, looking at Dem, who was staring at a box of frozen corn, unaware of her presence. Dem tossed the corn in his cart and headed away from her, toward the frozen dinners. But she trailed him.

"Oh my God, she's following him!"

"We gotta warn him," Nick said.

Thinking we could head Dem off by the magazines, we started down the fish-and-tackle aisle. We made the turn but it was too late. Right there, in the deli section amid its disgusting displays of headcheese, salami, and bologna, she made her play.

"Hello, Dem," she said—she wasn't carrying anything, not a basket, a bag of apples, nothing. "I've, I've been looking for you."

Dem's hands dropped to his side. It had been nearly a year since he'd seen her, since she'd left him and the baby. He blinked as if he wasn't trusting his eyes. He backed up, bumping into a center display of pies and cakes. He was crumbling. He wasn't going to make it. This was all too much for him, I just knew it. But then he surprised the hell out of me. He stopped blinking and his posture improved. He stepped forward and said, "Really? Gee, Lacey, seems to me you know where I live—*we* live."

"I can't go back there. You know that." She spit out the words as if they were bullets.

Demetrius stared, his face impassive, his eyes black and cold. The power base between him and her subtly shifted as the pain he had been carrying around like a sack of stones all these months began to mature, evolve. He wasn't letting her in. I could see it. And so could she, so she tried again.

"Your family, they don't like me."

"Lacey, it's nothing personal. They just don't take to women who abandon their babies."

"I didn't abandon him!" She pulled on her hair which was a particularly odd gesture since it already stood on end. "I, I, I just made a mistake. I just needed some time."

Dem breathed out as if he'd taken a blow. He shut his eyes, rubbed his forehead, and swallowed hard.

"We can be a family again, Dem. Just move to the hill. I know you're oystering now. There's no reason to be on Lethe. It'll be easier with you here. Just the three of us."

Dem stared at the floor for a good five seconds. Then he looked up and asked quietly, "When did he leave you?"

Her mouth twitched at the corners. She glared at the deli case. "Two weeks ago."

I reached for Nick's hand and held it, my heart breaking. What if Dem were so desperate and blind that he took her back and moved to the hill? How do you rebuild trust? How do you have a life? You can't. I wanted to protect him. I wanted to yell, "No, Dem, don't! Don't believe a word she says!" I turned to Nick. "Do something!" I whispered.

Nick didn't respond, and I knew he would not intervene, and even though it stank, I also knew he was right.

Lacey fidgeted with her purse and pulled out a pack of Virginia Slims. The cigarettes slipped through her fingers. Dem picked them up and lit one for her. "Whether I like it or not, you're Gaby's mother," he said and tossed the match on the floor. "No matter what went on between us, you and him are another matter. I won't drive a wedge in that. So—" He paused and shifted his weight as if he feared losing his footing. His eyes drifted up to the ugly, fluorescent-lit ceiling of the IGA. His broad, sad face folded in on itself, pinched in concentration as the solution to his troubles rushed at him like specks of sand in a storm, grain by grain, until he felt firmly rooted. He leveled his eyes and when he spoke it was in slow, even tones as if he were a man who after months of stumbling finally perceived exactly where he stood in the world.

"This is how it's gonna be. You can visit him. Twice a week. On Lethe. Maybe, if you get your life together, we'll work out a schedule and he can visit you on the hill. We'll have to see how it goes. But as far as you and I are concerned, we're finished. We have a child together. That's important. Beyond that, you're not getting into my life again."

Lacey weighed his words. She listened starkly, as if Dem were a judge handing down a sentence. She touched the tip of her tongue to her upper lip. Her eyes darted about, she looked nearly mad, a frantic crested bird. "Okay, Dem. Whatever you want. Okay."

She walked away, passed Nick and me without so much as a nod, and slammed the automatic door with her fist before it fully opened.

Nick walked over to his baby brother and put a hand on his shoulder. "You okay, man?"

"Yeah," Dem said. "Actually . . . I am."

March 22, 1997

Morning

The Carrabelle docks

God, I'm glad to be relaxing! If I don't graduate at warp speed, fine. At least I'll be sane. I'm so used to studying night and day that taking only six hours is like being on vacation. Still, I feel a little guilty but Nick keeps saying, "Let up on yourself." I guess he's right but it's hard.

Dinner tonight: mushroom risotto, something special for Nick's birthday. Parmesan Reggiano. White wine (lots of it). Four kinds of mushrooms (could only find two). Arborio rice. I wonder if Nick has ever had such rice? I wonder if it tastes terribly different than Uncle Ben's?

My latest cooking mishap: the stuffed squash from two nights ago—salted bricks.

I bet Lillian wonders why I have never invited her over for supper. I'm too ashamed to tell her I can't cook worth squat and too prideful to ask for help. Maybe cooking is one of those things like juggling. Either you have the talent for it or you don't. But I'm not ready to throw in the towel just yet. I'd like to become a gourmet baker one day. Or someone who knows all about wines. An educated palate, that's what they call it.

I can't decide when to give him his present—this morning or tonight over supper? I'm leaning toward supper. It'll be more romantic. He's not a jewelry wearer but this is different. A small silver medal of a dolphin strung on a leather cord. When I saw it in the window of that shop in Apalachicola, I just knew he had to have it.

This is what I wrote on his card (I'm including it here just in case he's not a card-keeper): My dearest Nick, You are my wings, my light. You make me whole. All my love, Your wife, Mattie.

I know that's not the most original writing in the world, but it's really how I feel. Besides, it's for Nick, not the Nobel committee.

Ap`ril 2, 1997`
Front porch. Evening

It was soooo hot today. And not a stitch of air. Seems like summer has arrived early.

In Jax Beach, the wind sometimes howled for days. Nor'easters they called them. One of the girls I went to school with—what was her name? Deidre. Yes, that was it. I always liked that name. She lived right on the beach and her mother insisted on putting their laundry on the clothesline and Deidre would come to school in clothes so stiff with dried salt spray I'm positive they would stand up on their own. She always looked as if someone had gone hog-wild with the spray starch. She said her mother liked how quickly the wind dried the clothes and how it made them smell. I bet because of that, Deidre is living someplace landlocked where the only salt to be found is in the grocery store.

I sure hope my tomatoes make it. I tucked basil in around them. An article in one of Lillian's horticultural magazines recommended planting vegetables together that are good eating combinations. Tomatoes and basil. Squash and thyme. Okra and onions. I think my garden is actually going to look like something this year. The oxeye daisies are already popping as are the rudbeckia. In the meadow, both the coreopsis and sprawling rosemary are thriving. Last year, I got started too late. That's all there is to it. But at least I laid the foundation. I sure did. I think I'll try to grow poppies. I love their big fat colorful faces. Lillian says it's too hot here. She said go for nasturtiums and put them in early as to beat the heat. But maybe I'll prove her wrong. I'll plant poppies and nasturtiums and they'll thrive if I'm at all lucky and my mother-in-law will grow green with envy and maybe even ask how I accomplished such a gardening feat.

. . .

April 10, 1997
A full moon midnight
Back porch

My garden appears gilded in liquid silver. I wonder if the plants feel it, all that soft, sweet light.

It's funny, the pull this place—Lethe and the coast—exerts on you if you let it. On my last few trips into Tallahassee I was lost. I mean, lost in my heart. The concrete and asphalt felt foreign beneath my feet and I found myself wanting to know who in the world ever came up with the notion of pavement.

It has come to this: Cities don't make sense to me anymore. Once we latch onto those larger cycles, the ones we fool ourselves into thinking we're not a part of—like Lillian's butterflies and Nick's dolphins and my growing fascination with the ever changing topography of the shoreline—I see no way of going back. Yes, I was once a city girl. But now I am wild. I'm salvia and sea oat. I'm beach juniper and sand oak. I'm someone who is starting to plan her days around the comings and goings of the tide. Imagine that!

April 20, 1997
Night
Aboard the *Mattie Fiona*

I am sick to death of doing homework (so much for an easy semester, trig is killing me!) and it's a little rough out so I can't sleep.

Maybe I should have stayed home tonight. But the weather report sounded as if it were going to be clear. At least half the time they don't know what they're talking about. We're rolling pretty good. I'm glad I've got aboard a hefty stash of Dramamine. But I must admit, being out here in stormy weather is kind of exciting. I like the sound the wind makes as it whips across the Gulf. It sounds like forever.

Nick's plan to get Dem shrimping again once the new boat was ready didn't work out. Obviously. But at least he lets me go with him now even if it's only two or three times a week. Just like George Blue told Lillian, Nick insists my job onboard is to sleep. Especially in bad weather. I guess he doesn't think I'm truly a fishing kind of gal. He claims he has never had on a life jacket, even during gales. His motto about trouble out here is you never leave the boat—you let the boat leave you. Still, he doesn't let me go anywhere on the Mattie Fiona without my life jacket close at hand. When I pop up on deck, the first thing he says is "Mattie, where's your life jacket?" It's endearing—in an irritating kind of way—but I suppose he's right since I can barely tread water much less swim.

He hasn't seen the holes yet. At least if he has he hasn't let on. Maybe I should tell him. Actually I should have asked before I did it. But I couldn't give him the chance to say no. Thank goodness I learned how to use a power drill. It's an ingenious solution. Now when things on deck get a little too quiet, instead of worrying myself sick or clambering on deck with that unwieldy jacket, I can just peek through the holes and look for his yellow slicker. As long as I can see that bright patch of color flash by, I know he hasn't fallen overboard.

The corporation now officially owns The Lucky Miss B. We're leasing her to one of the Register boys. The extra money will come in handy. The plan is to lease her until Lucas is old enough to go out on his own (if that's what he decides to do). I'm thinking he might surprise us and become a concert musician or maybe a schoolteacher.

My husband doesn't realize he's like the hands on a clock: predictable, predictable, predictable. I love that about him. For instance, if I put capers in something, he'll say, "This is delicious, honey," and he'll eat around them. And I'll say, "You don't like capers? You should have told me." And he'll say, "Oh no, I like them. I'm eating them." But when I go to clean up there they are, a pile of tiny olive green fruits dotting the plate. And, you know, capers are expensive.

Also, every time he sees a caterpillar, this is what he says: "Boy, that guy's got 'don't mess with me' written all over him."

If I were a gambler, I would wage money that toward morning, he'll *come down and get in bed and kiss me awake and ask if I'm still taking "those pills" as he calls them and when I say yes he'll want to know why and I'll say because I'm not sure if I'm ready for a child and he'll say "Mattie, ah Mattie, let's make a baby" and I'll say "Soon, I promise" and then, despite the fact that my uterus will not yet yield itself to another, we'll make love on this tiny cot in the middle of a churning sea.*

May 15, 1997
Late afternoon
Back porch

Nick is cleaning up after spending the day working on my new kitchen cabinets. They're just what I've been wanting: pine with glass fronts. I tried to make them myself but cabinets are beyond my skill level. Actually, they are beyond Nick's, too. Thank goodness for Beth!

Nick gave me a book yesterday. Peterson's Field Guide. *Every bird in the eastern U.S. is represented with detailed drawings plus migratory, behavior, mating, and habitat information. They're all there—the clown-faced Atlantic puffin (how I'd love to see one of those!), and our very own piping plover, and all manner of heron and warbler and swift. So now, in addition to being a gardening nut, I'm becoming a bird nut. I think I saw an indigo bunting today. It was in the pittosporum in the front yard. According to the book, we're located in the bird's breeding range. I suspect it was simply passing through, going north for the summer. Lethe is amazing that way. It's a stopover for all sorts of creatures in their journey to someplace else. I'm going to make birdhouses and feeding stands out of Nick's wood scraps. And he promised me that next winter he would put up a gourd pole for the purple martins. Lillian has one on her property with eight gourds. I call it her purple martin condo which makes her laugh. Beth and Maya have two poles, six gourds each. They say that martins consume many times their body weight in insects—no-see-ums, mosquitoes, what-have-you.*

·   ·   ·

June 1, 1997
Midnight
Aboard the *Mattie Fiona*
  I stopped taking my pills today.

A family member. That is what I had become, among other things. Perhaps one should be tested or otherwise qualified for this position. At least, prepared. As you know, I was plopped (with very little training) into the heart of a sprawling family and, considering what could have gone wrong, I fared fairly well. That's because the Blues (thankfully) valued happiness over principle.

For instance, no one seemed to find it inappropriate that Nick and I embarked upon a sexual affair nearly from the moment we laid eyes on each other. There were no lifted eyebrows or disapproving glances when, out of the yonder, he brought me home. No one said, "Shouldn't you two slow down and think about this marriage thing?"

They eased my path into their world simply through the power of steadfast acceptance. I will always consider myself fortunate that the platitudes which sustain, confine, and turn much of society into a judgmental brood of unhappy hypocrites seemed, for the most part, to have escaped the Blues.

And that is how I account for the matter-of-fact way in which we all pitched in to raise Gaby. Lacey was gone. Kaput! A puff of air that occasionally wafted by demanding our notice. An unreliable wife and mother. A person who pinned judgments on others with scant attention to her own foibles. By her callous actions she had nearly mortally wounded poor Dem and had sentenced her child to a motherless existence. Fine, we would raise Gabriel George Aristotle Blue ourselves. Lacey would be allowed to know and love her son if she chose to do so. But the chances of that ever happening looked slim since after that fateful day at the IGA we never heard from her again.

Lacey's choice not to be a member of our family did not prevent us from fulfilling our charter as Gaby's guardians through life. We did not dwell on the mother's absence. Rather, we celebrated the child.

Gabriel was a happy baby. And very well loved by aunts and uncles and grandmothers and cousins, not to mention his devoted father, who marked down in Gaby's Journal his first crawl, his first word ("Go! Go!"—I suspect this wasn't truly a word but sound play; however, it seemed dispiriting of me to point this out), and his first glorious wobble of a step which occurred on Christmas Day at his grandmother's house in front of the entire family, even Charon, who was watching but pretending not to be.

Not a day went by when we didn't coo at the child and make silly faces and tickle his toes which made him laugh (in his case, a sound very similar to a churlish song) and cover him in slobber via Bronx cheer kisses which we enthusiastically delivered upon his healthy fat brown belly.

And when the time came for him to be told about his mother, we would do so with an eye toward diplomacy and an artful rewriting of history. We would say that she was a generous person who worried about the feral cats each winter and fortified their food with vitamins to try to keep them healthy, and that her hands were lovely (*so small-boned*, we would say), and that she had a marvelous, full-throated singing voice. *She used to sing you to sleep. You have her lips, you know, heart-shaped and perfect. She loved to cook, made a wonderful blackberry cobbler. And love you—oh my, how that girl loved you!*

She would become for him a tragic figure, a point of light in his imagination, someone who desperately adored him but to whom life had been unspeakably cruel, so cruel that the details of her downfall would waver just beyond our capacity for speech, forever shrouded behind a scrim of well-intentioned secrets and lies.

Because of us, he would go through life remembering what every child should experience and accept as his birthright: a pair of maternal hands that had joyfully diapered him and sweetly massaged his chubby legs and fed him sugar water when he was feverish and had swabbed his sore gums with a touch of bourbon when he was teething. Yes, through our stories, he would know these hands.

And now and again, often when he least expected it, those same mythic hands would reach out of that place in his soul reserved for mourning his spectral mother, and they would caress him. In these moments—so unpredictable in their timing, so shocking in their clarity—he would grasp with a certainty that surpasses all understanding that no matter where she was on this earth, he was loved.

Then, of course, there is Lucas. Dear, sweet Lucas, bereft of his biological parents, a child about to hit puberty with maddening fury (as all boys do, Rhea claims. "No boy I know ever went into puberty gently. Not a one! They're not like girls—some of them actually remain human while they're teenagers.").

Yes, Lucas, a sensitive, artistic-spirited child whose mother died in a head-on collision with a logging truck on Highway 98 while her nine-year-old son played a game of pickup basketball at the Carrabelle courts and whose hard-drinking, short-tempered father abandoned the child when he was eleven.

Family members cannot hide or even color the truth to an eleven-year-old—it's not like a baby whose memory of a parent, if there's one at all, drifts into the ether even before the bones have hardened, allowing for the aforementioned revision of history. Eleven-year-olds—they know. They remember even when they don't want to.

I suppose it's one of nature's safety mechanisms—like shock or fever—but despite the sting of awful truth, young people cope with their knowledge concerning wayward parents in imaginative, sometimes soul-saving ways, and with any luck the talents and gifts they pick up along the way will see them through those dark nights when the truth insists on its due.

Lucas, a self-taught musician who fingerpicks bluegrass tunes with such proficiency one wonders if artists truly are born under a special covenant with their own muse and light. Lucas, a boy who without any prodding graduated from finger paints and crayons to oils on canvas (self-portraits composed of cubes and curves and harsh, furious colors). Lucas, a student who taxies himself over to the hill in a flat-bottom runabout five days a week (as long as the weather holds) during the school year to attend Carrabelle High. Lucas, a child who loves the water with a zeal equal to that of his relatives and who every summer shrimps with his various aunts and uncles. Lucas, the very beloved blood relation of Beth Blue and simply the beloved of Maya Botero—two women who, if they could, would give the child the moon, the stars, the sky, the wind, and the very air they breathe. Lucas, the wavering sweet soul who, after sensing the betrayal and loss I felt concerning my own parents, shared a note he keeps safety-pinned to the pocket of his father's denim jacket—the jacket being the only physical manifestation (other than Lucas' own life and his grandmother's collection of family photos) that the man ever existed.

It was a Saturday afternoon and I was at Beth and Maya's. We were going to attempt to make pita bread, which requires a very hot oven and much patience. We had gotten just past the kneading stage and the three of us were fairly covered in flour when Beth and Maya began questioning me about my childhood. Lucas was on the front porch, which is straight off the kitchen/living room, absentmindedly picking a few high-tenored strains on his guitar and listening to our chatter.

"But don't you want to know where your father is? I mean, is he still alive? What did he end up doing with his life? Maybe you have half brothers and sisters," Maya said, flour dotting her nose.

Her words angered me, she was prying too deeply, so I tried to skirt past the issue by answering, "I don't know. I, I just don't know."

Lucas walked inside and nonchalantly said, "Mattie, I want to show you something."

Beth and Maya exchanged glances and then we all followed him down the hall into his bedroom. Its walls were thumbtacked with posters of whales, dolphins, and the planets. A black light cast violet hues on a stack of drawings. An FSU football schedule was taped to his door. With a somber face and deliberate slow movements he opened his closet door, pushed aside some shirts, and took out the jacket. As if he were handling something of value—his mother's wedding gown or the shroud of Turin—he laid it on his bed, smoothing the rough fabric, adjusting the worn collar, fussing with its tarnished trail of brass buttons.

"My father left this for me," he said, pointing. "You can read it."

He did not unpin the note but I caught in his voice not a stitch of bitterness or anger or disgust. Only pride. I wiped my flour-dusted hand on my shirt and held down the whiskey-stained paper with the tip of my index finger: *I want you to grow up and be a man. Do what you're told but don't take guff off nobody.*

That was the extent of his parting shot. No "Dear Lucas." No "Love, Daddy." No mention of where he was going or if he ever planned to return. *Nobody,* however, was underlined three times. The writing was crude and blocky but the fact that the benign, no-brainer message was written on a flimsy paper napkin from the Driftwood Bar ("Where the beer is cold and the music's hot") may account for the poor penmanship.

Quickly, I reread the note, thinking there must be more to it, some word that signaled Zeke's true intentions, and then my own father's voice drifted out of what I thought was a buried past. "Make sure your mama brings you to see me next time we roll into town." And that tinny music box song filled my ears. The box with its perfect dance-on-command ballerina. Where did it go? When did I lose it? Where in the hell was my father? Who did he think he was, leaving my mother, forcing her to raise me all on her own? How dare he! As the hurt and pain, both ancient and humbling, boiled through my veins I did something I refused to do the night my father left. I put my arms around Lucas, and I cried.

"It's okay, Mattie, I swear." The fifteen-year-old child stroked my hair with a father's tenderness. "Don't be sad. He'll be back one day."

And so he was.

I picked a brilliant June afternoon to try my hand at making focaccia.

My herb garden was flourishing. Especially, for some reason, my rosemary, which is what led me to my choice of breads.

Standing barefoot in my kitchen with my wooden spoon held like a scepter, I scanned the recipe, imagining my beautiful, yet-to-be-baked whole wheat and unbleached white flour creation: Greek olives, garlic, and rosemary tossed artfully atop a perfectly kneaded, raised, and rolled rustic flat bread. Next, a sprinkling of sea salt—two dollars plus change for a few ounces at the store and me living by what amounted to a briny pond! The final glory: the entire work of art divinely coated in golden drops of extra virgin olive oil (imported, of course).

That is how I spent much of my time in those days, dreaming of perfectly prepared dishes intended to make my husband swoon and my in-laws whisper in amazement at what a fine cook I was. It was this sort of creative obsession—culinary madness, you might call it—that inspired and dogged all great cooks. At least, that is what I told myself as I muddled through one minor gastronomic disaster after another. Fried chicken bloody at the bone. Apple pie with a crust reminiscent of baked dirt. Dumplings the consistency of semi-dried glue. Vegetable soup so spicy-hot Nick's eyes teared (the poor soul ate a bowlful, anyway, and paid dearly for it later that night).

However, the focaccia recipe wasn't all that complicated. I needed simply to slow down and follow the directions, one line at a time.

Have all my ingredients measured and at hand.

Don't even start if I don't have the proper equipment (Is a mixer required? What about a special baking sheet, something I might have to mail-order but would not because of the expense?).

Be patient!

Be meticulous!

You can't substitute if you don't know what you're doing.

Isn't Julia Child's credo (after Eat, drink, and be merry) Measure precisely?

Before the first pan is coated or the flour is retrieved from the cupboard, read the recipe over from start to finish as many times as needed—no one knows but you that the measurements and ingredients dance together in a blurred and meaningless, clubfooted high step.

See it in your mind.

Preheat the oven.

If something is supposed to be chilled before it's added, underline that instruction in the recipe.

Do not get out that bird book. You might get so engrossed you'll forget all about the bread until the horrible smell of burning crust fills the air.

Watch it like a hawk.

But do not keep opening and closing the oven door, because you don't want to disturb the dough with drafts.

And whatever you do, if the bread comes out rock hard or explodes in the oven (remember the soufflé?), toss it in the trash before anyone finds you out.

I was nothing if not determined. I would prepare a fragrant, tasty focaccia that would be a perfect complement to the oyster chowder, which Nick would marvel over because of its champagne base.

Yeast, salt, warm water, olive oil, sugar. That part was easy. But because turning flour and fat into dough requires a deft, experienced touch, I would struggle and fumble through the next few steps. I knew that starting out.

Add flour in two or three batches. Turn dough onto lightly floured surface. Knead for several minutes (*several*, a terribly vague instruction). DO NOT ADD TOO MUCH FLOUR, only enough to keep dough from sticking (obviously, recipe writers need to take courses in specificity). Place smooth, shiny dough in lightly oiled bowl, turn to coat, put in draft-free place—covered—for thirty to forty minutes or until dough has doubled in size.

As you can see, bread baking is an inexact art. Without a chef standing over me to point out that fleeting magical moment when the dough was sufficiently kneaded (and thus the gluten pounded to the point that somehow the entire mess would hold together and might actually taste like something), I had to fully rely on my own innate sense of right and wrong, intuition and common sense. After all, what gentle touch or tug would give me a perfectly textured, gorgeous-smelling, great-tasting loaf of bread versus an oven-baked brick? I was learning that like life, baking was an exercise in trial and error with tremendous doses of self-flagellation, doubt, and willfulness thrown in.

And also like my life at the time, I believed I was on the right track with this focaccia. I may have added a wee too much flour as I was kneading, but the ball of dough I ended up with was both pliant and substantial. I liked the feel of it resting in my palm. If I were to squash it (which I would not do) there would be no splintering into countless dry and floury dough-thorns. Rather, it would hold together, bulging but not breaking, its character and bulk intact.

Had I finally stumbled upon the hallmark of a well-formed dough? In the dual world of firm yet flexible could one eke out a metaphor for the seasoned human soul? After innumerable failures, at long last, did I hold perfection in my hands?

I wasn't sure. But I slipped the belly-ball of dough into the oiled bowl anyway, covered it with a clean dishcloth, set it on my kitchen counter, and noted the time. Two thirty-three. Nick would be waking soon. If he slept for another hour the focaccia would be in the oven. How pleasant for him, to rise to the scent of baking bread. I put on a pot of coffee before pouring myself a glass of sweet iced tea. I picked up the book I'd started the previous night. It was by a Florida author, a young woman. Beth told me she actually lived nearby—I think on the barrier island to our east. The book was about a little girl whose mother, in the face of the father's death, was given to horrible rages that were fueled by alcohol. The little girl was scrappy, wise, and profoundly damaged. A part of me was actually afraid to get to the novel's end because I feared the child might not survive. But I am an obsessed reader, even brave, when my nose is stuck in a book.

So there I was, at my kitchen table, my dough rising, my husband sleeping, my eyes following those lovely but terrifying lines down the page, when my world was disrupted by the mail lady honking her horn.

Mail was delivered on Tuesdays and Fridays. Vanessa made the trek over in nearly any kind of weather in an old Chris Craft with a home-made cabin. Once she was on the island, she made her rounds in a rattletrap buttercup yellow Dodge pickup that was missing its front fender, its driver's side headlight, and all mirrors of any kind.

If she had a package for me, I wished she had left it on the porch or just knocked rather than risk waking Nick with that annoying horn. But I would not say this to her. She was an extremely nice woman with a ready smile, generous with her advice (home remedies for most any malady, including a sour disposition). Besides, it wasn't wise to tick off your postal delivery person. They had—even if they did not realize it—an awesome power over their customers. A delayed bill here, a lost letter there, and before you know it the entire island is thrown into pandemonium.

Barefoot, I ventured into the blazing sunlight. Vanessa stuck her head out of the truck window and said, "Sorry to make you come out into this awful heat."

"That's all right. It's nice to see you."

"How've you been?"

"Good. And you?"

"Not bad." She shoved at me an envelope with a form attached. "Certified letter. You have to sign." A white handkerchief circled her forehead. I suppose it mopped up the sweat before it could roll into her brown eyes. Vanessa was from Puerto Rico. She settled in Carrabelle about twelve years ago. Why, I do not know. But after Miss Shriver passed (she had been Lethe's mail lady for thirty years), Vanessa took her place. Not long after becoming our mail lady, she married Bud Crawford, Carrabelle's city attorney. People on Lethe feared she would quit her job, having settled down with a respectable, powerful city employee and all. But Vanessa, evidently, was independent to the core. She continued to deliver our mail because nobody else wanted the job and because, she insisted, it was an honorable hobby.

"We could sure use some rain," she said as I studied the envelope. Holland and Knight, Attorneys at Law. Jacksonville, Florida. "If we don't get some soon, we're going to have the red tide again. The scientists don't believe it"—my hand shook as I signed the postal form—"but if that bay doesn't get some fresh water falling into it, we're going to have trouble."

"Yes, I'm sure you're right," I said. Vanessa expertly tore off her half of the receipt and handed back the letter. "You take good care, Miss Mattie."

"You, too, Vanessa."

I went into the house. Dots floated in front of my eyes as they adjusted to the dim light. I sat at my table and stared at the envelope. What could a law firm possibly want with me? And why did the mere sight of the letter awaken in me a sense of doom? Maybe it was the formality with which it was addressed. Ms. Matilda Fiona O'Rourke Blue. Too official, too all-encompassing. I reached for a knife, slid it under the paper flap, and slashed it open.

Dear Ms. Blue, the letter began. *As executor of your deceased father's estate it is my duty to inform you . . .*

I read the letter slowly, as if waiting for a block of ice to melt on a very cold day. Counselor Andrea Louisa Smith did not elucidate the details of my father's death. Only that it occurred May 1, 1997, at 10:42 P.M. at the Shady Oaks Nursing Home in Green Cove Springs. *A staff person was in attendance.*

Green Cove Springs? That was a small town just a few miles south of Jacksonville. Please don't tell me he didn't get any farther than Green Cove. *Mr. O'Rourke named you as his sole beneficiary. After funeral costs, nursing home care, a few miscellaneous outstanding bills (seems your father was quite the magazine fan!), estate taxes, and attorney's fees, his net worth totals ten thousand four dollars and twelve cents. We cannot release the funds until the enclosed paperwork has been signed, notarized, and returned to us. Please accept our sincerest condolences.*

The space behind my eyes throbbed. Bile gathered in my throat and my stomach lurched with an urgent need to empty itself. In my mind's eye I watched myself scream. But reality was far different. I remained silent and tried to steady my hands and lips as I read the letter once more. The words on the page did not change, nor did they answer questions. They only created them. How did the attorney find me? Had my father kept tabs on me? Did Mother for all those years know of his whereabouts but kept it from me? Maybe she wouldn't let him see me. Maybe there had been something inherently deviant about him. Or maybe he was victimized by time, circumstance, and the inescapable ironies of fate. Maybe he never joined the circus. How very laughable that notion suddenly seemed. Of course he didn't join the stupid circus. He probably spent his days and nights within walking distance of his ex-wife and daughter. How did he die? *It is our understanding that you and your father were estranged. Nevertheless* . . . I neatly refolded the letter, slipped it and its attached documents into the envelope, walked to the trash can, and tossed it in.

Estranged, indeed. How about abandoned? How about the notion that I was better off without a father? He never wanted me. He never loved me. I sure don't want any of his stinking money. Forget, Mattie, forget this ever happened.

I checked on my dough. To my surprise, it had risen nicely. It looked fertile, so round and plumb and nearly moist. I dusted my large wooden cutting board with flour and turned out the dough. I reached for my rolling pin and then thought better of it. I needed to use my hands. I needed to feel the dough's give-and-take, its sticky resistance, and finally its compliant surrender to the heel of my palm and the tap, tap, tapping of my fingertips as I tried to create smooth, even edges.

This time, I would be a success. The bread would be the proper consistency. Its coarse, airy texture would be a marvel. Nick would ask for another piece. His eyes would widen in tender surprise—his wife had finally whipped something up that was palatable—and he would say, "Sweetie, this is really good."

I was wholly focused on shaping the focaccia when Nick walked in wearing nothing but the T-shirt he had slept in. He pressed himself against me—his chest to my back—and kissed my neck, then my cheek. He smelled sour with sleep and sweat.

"What're you doing?"

"Making bread."

"Mmmm."

"The coffee is ready."

"Thanks, honey."

"You're welcome."

I kept my face averted, stayed on task, concentrated on the dough. It was soft and slightly sticky, a block of clay beneath my hands.

We carry the past with us.

Yearbooks. Scrapbooks. Textbooks. Novels. Biographies. Encyclopedias. (What is a library if not a repository for all things past?) Snapshots. Gossip. Rumors. Songs. Quilts. Obituaries. Oral histories. Movies. Memory. Blood. Bone. Teeth. Hair. Skin. The curve of a lip. The color of an eye. Secrets hidden and revealed within the double helix of our DNA.

Life before Nick—I tucked it into an imaginary silk pocket, filled it with sand—an irreducible element, lean and barren. From time to time I would tear at the silk until finally I had created the smallest of holes. It was then that my unhappy past began to drift away, one finite grain at a time.

But the letter changed all that even as I tried mightily to pretend as if I had never received it. The focaccia, by God, turned out beautifully so I attempted to bask in that success. But if my mind were to be turned permanently away from that gleaming white, finely textured piece of legal stationery and its crisp rows of horrible words lined up like a brigade of mocking crows I would need to do more than rest on the laurels of my immediate past. I needed full immersion in the inconsequential tasks that when lumped together make up a life. I weeded my garden daily. I worked ahead in my classes. I cleaned the shower with a toothbrush (the grout, I felt, could be brighter). I made three birdhouses, attempted an apple strudel (failure), and composed a list of ways in which I could improve myself:

1. Read the ancients. Start with Plato and work forward.
2. Buy classical music. Liszt, Mozart. Perhaps Mahler.
3. Get in at least thirty minutes of acrobic exercise a day.
4. Learn to swim.
5. Become a more artful lover (Massage? Kama Sutra? Adult movies?).
6. Work on your astronomy. Reread that book. Learn to identify *all* the constellations.
7. Know your place in the world—stars, geography, ideas (What do I believe in?).
8. Spend more time with Rhea—she won't be around forever.
9. Turn off the TV.
10. Become politically involved. Write letters. Compile lists of congressmen and representatives.
11. Learn to express your opinions calmly yet forcefully. Be serene.
12. Be more diligent in all things: life list of birds, shell identification, cooking, studying, bookkeeping, listening, making love, housekeeping.
13. Learn a foreign language.
14. Devote yourself to a charitable cause.
15. Iron your clothes (spray starch?).
16. Read less fiction. Bone up on the great world wars.

A week had passed since I'd received the letter and I was pretty well exhausted. Nevertheless, on one of the rare evenings that Nick took the night off, I couldn't sleep. Five A.M. found me in the living room, spreading newspaper on the floor and opening paint cans. The window trim needed a fresh coat. It had begun to look gray and dull and irritated me every time I walked by. I dusted and taped and prepared the surfaces by roughening them with sandpaper. I was just about to fill in some holes with white putty when Nick wandered into the living room, naked and lovely, put his arms around me, and whispered, "Baby, put on some clothes. We're going to Green Cove."

Whatever strength I had been marshaling those seven long days seeped out of me just as if I'd opened a vein. As he stroked my hair and took the putty knife out of my hand I realized I understood nothing. Not the world. Not myself. Not the kindness of my husband. So I let myself be held, all of me: my fears, my questions, my anger, my love for a father who didn't deserve my affection. "How did you know?"

Nick rubbed my face. "I saw the letter. I was going to let you tell me. But, Mattie, you're not doing real good so I'm going to take care of you. We're going to get some answers. Together."

He led me into our bedroom, and as if I were a child, he took off my T-shirt and shorts, helped me slip into a fresh clean jumper, and held my hand until I was ready to go.

The Shady Oaks Nursing Home was located on a treed knoll overlooking the St. Johns River. As if I'd actually known my father, I found myself saying to Nick, "At least he was in a pretty spot. I wonder if his room had a river view."

The floors of the Shady Oaks were covered in industrial green linoleum and were in dire need of a good scrubbing. The ceilings were low and stained. An anemic plastic potted palm near the entrance was gray with dust. A spider lazily spun a web amid its stiff fronds. Nick approached the receptionist's desk but I held back. "We're here to speak to the director, ma'am," he said.

"Do you have an appointment?"

The receptionist looked as though she were straight out of high school and wanted to be anywhere other than the Shady Oaks. Her huge glasses swallowed her thin face and she kept working her lips over the ridges of her braces.

"No ma'am," Nick explained in a tone of voice I had never heard him use—polite, cold, hard, like marble. "But we drove three hours to get here. My wife's father died in your custody. We're looking for answers. We won't take up much of your time. But, ma'am, my wife is beside herself. We won't leave—we can't leave—until someone sees us."

Mrs. Katrina Smidley, the director, had two faces. The one she was born with and the one she painted on every morning. But the painted-on face was a poor fit. It was too small, stopping about half an inch from her hairline, curving away from the knobby ridges of her ears, and meandering well above the downward slope of her jaw and double chin. As a result, her real face—fat and paler than the one created out of a thick film of foundation—appeared as a glowing outline around the circles of rouge, the heavy black cyeliner, and those red lipstick-flecked tobacco-stained teeth.

"We weren't aware Mr. O'Rourke had a daughter," she said, scanning the attorney's letter, which Nick had, days earlier, fished out of the trash.

"We just want to know about him," Nick said. "Whatever you can tell us, we'd appreciate it."

Mrs. Smidley's faces shook like jelly as she scooted back her chair, nakedly staring at Nick and me, sizing us up, determining if we were trouble or simply annoying. She set aside the letter and clasped her pudgy hands in front of her. Her Home Shopping Network diamonds gleamed in the fluorescent light. Her nails were the exact shade of her lips and I thought my mother would appreciate such painstaking color coordination. She tapped her knuckles once on her desk. "I'll see what I can do." Then she spoke into her intercom. "Sally, bring in Mr. O'Rourke's file. Would you please?"

Sally was the spit and image of Mrs. Smidley, only younger. Her nails and lips were bright pink, chosen, I suppose, in deference to her pink pumps that her plump feet were squeezed into. She labored under her weight and the sides of her face—the portions which had escaped makeup—seemed so soft as to be blurred. She set the file on Mrs. Smidley's desk without a word, making eye contact with no one, and I felt a tinge of sorrow for her because she was actually quite pretty and I hoped other people saw that in her, too.

"Thank you, Sally," Mrs. Smidley said, flipping open the folder. "Let's see here," she said, all business, and then commenced to delivering just the facts. "Seamus Patrick O'Rourke was sixty-two years old at the time of his death. He had been a resident of Shady Oaks for three months. He was admitted in very poor health, having been transferred here from the county hospital with liver and kidney problems." She elongated the last word of each sentence as if to drive home the point that Seamus O'Rourke's death was not only ordinary but utterly unremarkable. She continued to browse through the folder as she said, "We tend not to accept people as ill as your father but the county insisted they'd done everything they could for him." She looked at me, unblinking. "He had, it would appear, nowhere else to go."

Bitch, I thought.

"Sixty-two?" Nick asked, not believing someone that age could be that sick.

"Alcohol tends to age a person," she said with a tight smile.

I managed to find my voice, which cracked as I asked, "What about the circus?"

"Circus?"

"He, he said the night he left that he was going to join the circus." I looked at Nick, feeling as if I were speaking gibberish, hoping he would make this woman understand. I shifted in my seat. He reached for my shoulder. I didn't want to be here.

Mrs. Smidley shuffled through my father's folder. "No. It doesn't say anything here about the circus. Last employment. Let's see . . . ah, yes, here it is. Mayport Pest Control. Imagine that, they spray my home." Her raccoon eyes darted from side to side as she read. "Term of employment, fifteen years." She looked up. "I don't imagine that spraying all those chemicals for all those years did much for his health. But," she said brightly, "at least he had insurance."

Nick squeezed my hand. "Mattie, this doesn't mean anything. Whatever's written on that piece of paper doesn't account for what he might have done before that. And you know, people lie about things."

"Not about this. His pension and retirement fund helped pay for his care." She closed the folder. "Is there anything else I can do for you, Mrs. Blue?"

I stared at a photo on her desk. It was of a baby boy dressed in navy shorts and blazer, holding a ball, grinning. In bold gold letters across the top of the white plastic frame were the words *Ask me about my grandchild!*

"Do his records mention any family?" Nick asked.

"Not at all. As I said, we were under the impression that he had none."

Nick rubbed his hand over his hair and down the back of his neck. He sat forward. "Did he have any friends here? Someone who might know anything about him?"

"I'm afraid not. His roommate died two weeks before he did. We hadn't put anyone else in with him yet. So in effect, during the final days of his life he had a private room for the price of a double." She paused, balanced her elbows on her desk, and brought her hands together—fingertip to fingertip—so that they formed a fleshy pyramid. "I do hope you understand how very sick your father was when he came to us. And that he got superior care while in our custody. As all our residents do." She smiled indulgently, as though we were three-year-olds to whom she'd just offered cookies. "I'm very sorry but I've told you all I can. Maybe his employer would know something more."

Nick sat back in his chair and huffed as he looked over Mrs. Smidley's head and out the window to the river. I followed his gaze. A snowy egret flew from its roost in one of the oaks and landed near the shore.

"Let's go, honey," I said, gathering my purse and feeling humiliated. "We've taken up enough of her time."

Nick cocked his head to the side. "What about belongings? I'm sure he didn't come here empty-handed."

"Well, I, I don't know."

"Can you check?"

Mrs. Smidley's patience was wearing thin. Her garnet mouth turned in on itself, forming a tiny bright fist. She stepped out of her office and spoke to her secretary softly enough that we couldn't hear. Then she stood in the doorway, and said, "Sally will check on that for you. If you'd like to take a seat out there."

As we filed past her she said in a practiced, saccharine voice, her eyes targeted at the nameplate on her door, "I'm so sorry for your loss, Mrs. Blue."

After fifteen minutes of watching the clock on the wall behind Sally, who was popping lemon drops and chasing them with Diet Coke, I said to Nick, "That's it. This was a mistake."

"Do you know what's taking so long?" Nick asked.

"I don't have a clue," Sally answered, and then she inexplicably laughed.

"Well, can you find out?"

"I'll try," she said as if she couldn't hold out much hope. Slowly, she punched in an extension number with her pencil. "Any progress on—ummm—Mr. O'Rourke's stuff? Yeah. Uh-uh. Okay." She put down the phone. "Lester's on his way."

Lester, it turns out, was an orderly who, with his shuffling gait and cauliflower ears, looked like an old punch-drunk boxer. "Here's Mr. O'Rourke's shoe box," he said, beaming, offering it to Sally, who jerked her head toward us, indicating it was ours. "Oh, it's this young lady's!" Lester turned to me. "Well, here you go, missy. Everything he came in with. It's all right here." He patted the box lid. "Lucky you showed up today. We was gonna toss it out this afternoon. You know, nobody claiming it and all."

"Thank you, Lester," I said, smoothing my hand over the box.

Nick pecked my cheek and brushed my hair off my shoulder. "You okay?"

"I'm fine," I said, surprising myself at how defensive I sounded.

"You want to see what's in it?"

"Not now."

He put his hands over mine. He was trying to make this easy for me but I was drowning all on my own. Lester shuffled off. Sally took a call. Nick leaned in close and asked softly, "You want to go over to where he worked? They could probably tell you lots of things. Or," he looked around, trying to think of what to say, "we could pick up flowers and visit his grave. Whatever you want, honey. It's your call."

I stared at the box. I wanted to be a good daughter, full of grief and brimming with knowledge about how a child behaves in the face of their parent's death. But I was at a loss. The rituals and sanctities that pass naturally between fathers and daughters both in life and death were foreign to me, lost in some vague memory of Swan Lake and air thick with Jim Beam and white eyelet curtains heavy with dust. I could not rewrite that past. I could not make my childhood into something it was not. No flowers on a grave. No meeting buddies from work. No seeking out his landlord for anecdotes that might shed light on who he had become. Because none of that would turn him into the man he should have been.

"Nick, I think I just want to go home."

I sat on my living room floor, contemplating the shoe box, summoning the nerve to sift through its contents, fearing that once I removed the lid I would be faced with objects that would humanize Seamus Patrick O'Rourke, reminding myself that I had spent most of my life convincing myself that the man who sired me was subhuman.

Nick came in from the kitchen and handed me a glass of wine. He sat down beside me, drew my hair into his hand, and kissed my neck. "You want me to take it out to the shed? Or maybe set it in the closet? You don't have to go through it right now, baby. In fact, you don't have to deal with it at all if it's going to upset you."

I looked at my husband and tried to find the right answer. "No. I think I've got to do this."

"You sure?"

"I think so." I picked up the box and read its label. "Ladies. Size six. Nikes. Probably a nurse's or something."

"Probably."

I tapped the lid, bought a little time. Nick reached for the box. "Let's do this later, Mattie."

"No! I'm fine. I swear." Quickly, I removed the lid, a musty scent wafted over us, and my anger and sadness hardened as I stared at my father's meager belongings.

A Timex waterproof watch with a stainless steel band, its face crystal cracked, the time frozen at 3:32. A swirly green marble. A tattered Boy Scout badge. A black-handled screwdriver. A rusting tape measure. A Budweiser cap. An inkless felt tip pen. An empty wallet. An expired MasterCard. A Masonic ring. Five magazine subscription cards (*Sports Illustrated, Gun and Ammo, True Detective, Time, TV Guide*). A movie stub (*Die Hard*). A dog-eared, spine-broken, beer-stained paperback copy of *The Great Gatsby*.

"There's nothing here," I said. "It's just junk. Trash. They gave us his trash." I picked up the book. "This was probably somebody else's. Probably his old geezer roommate's from the nursing home."

Nick took the book from me and thumbed through it. He held it spine up and fanned the brittle, yellowed pages. A photograph spiraled out and landed silently in his lap. "Hmm," he said, studying it.

"What? What is it?"

"I think it's you, baby."

He offered it to me. I hesitated, fearing the image would be of some other daughter or girlfriend or wife. Nick placed the creased and torn photograph in my hand and closed my fingers over it. I held it to my chest, closed my eyes, and tried to summon some backbone. Finally, I opened first one eye and then the other.

"Oh my." I felt a tear roll down my cheek. I wanted to pull the image off the photo's flat surface, to animate it—no, to turn it into flesh and blood. There we were: my mother, my father, and me, standing on the front porch of our Jacksonville Beach house. My mother glowed, fresh and pretty, as if she was happy with herself and her little white porch and her petunias growing in that terra-cotta pot. My father had one arm around her shoulders and held me in the other. Jesus, he was a handsome devil. Piercing blue eyes. Light red hair, just like mine. Prominent bones and a free, easy smile. He was leaning into my mother. It was a gesture of adoration, as if he couldn't get close enough, and his hand draped down her shoulder and lingered along the top curve of her breast. I must have been no older than two or three. I had little stick legs and my butt rested easily in the crook of his tattooed arm (an anchor and something else, perhaps a name, maybe my mother's name—I had forgotten that my father was tattooed but sitting there looking at the photo I had to ask myself if that buried memory contributed to my instant attraction to Nick). I was waving at the camera, looking stunned and pleased in the way that only children can.

Why had that moment ended? What dreams, what secrets, what sweet yearnings and aspirations did my parents nurture at the moment the shutter clicked? And when did they lose them? Was their happiness destroyed by some external force, cruel and enigmatic? Or did the hopeful young couple in the photo never have a chance from the outset? Did their desires exceed their potential? Did mine?

Nick took my face in his hands and kissed me. "He never forgot about you, Mattie. This proves it."

I laid myself down, resting in my husband's embrace. The copy of *The Great Gatsby* was my father's. Without any evidence, I made this decision. Yes, even in his small meaningless life, as he watched whatever grandeur he had dreamed for himself wither, and while he spent his days on earth spraying pesticides into the dark corners of strangers' homes, and while his manhood became a premature gnarly mess between his feeble legs, and while he pickled his brain with bourbon and beer, and while his guilt at abandoning his only child assailed his consciousness, he was perhaps seeing a glint of himself in Gatsby's rise and fall, in his own desire for an unattainable state of grace. Maybe he had been haunted by a hunger to be a better man, by wanderlust, by dreaming beyond his means. Maybe he'd gone off in search of the kind of absolute love that only poets believe in. I touched Nick's lips. "Don't you ever leave me."

I asked Lillian if I could place the photo alongside those in her collection. I thought it fitting that the only surviving picture of my parents be displayed alongside those of the family I had married into. One day a visitor might happen into that room full of books and images and point at that snapshot in particular, and ask, "Who are these people?" and Lillian would be able to say, "Mattie's parents. Aren't they a handsome couple?"

As for my inheritance, since Seamus O'Rourke had been, for whatever reason, unable or unwilling to perform his duties as a father, I certainly didn't want his money. So I signed the papers the attorney had sent me and donated the entire sum to the Refuge House, the domestic abuse shelter where Maya had once been the director.

Nick had been right—I needed answers. And though the ones I finally came up with were sketchy at best, they eased the burden of the past, paving the way for my passive acceptance of a fractured childhood. I was pleased that my father had at least been decent enough to keep a picture of his family close at hand. But that single sentimental gesture didn't change the fact of my abandonment. Nor did it allow me to forgive him—at least not in a whitewashed, universal, religious sense. But knowing he had remembered Mother and me, that he had carted around our photo and maybe had imagined that our lives were better without him—that alone was worth something.

Mattie, baby, I think about you all the time—what your hair smells like, what you taste like, how pretty you look sound asleep with the morning light scattered across your face, how your breasts . . .

. . .

August 25, 1997
10:34
Aboard the *Mattie Fiona*

Wouldn't it be wonderful if at the moment of conception, we felt the world change? I mean, I know it does change. Each new life is another thread in the web, but there's no Aha! the moment it all begins. We just keep muddling along, completely ignorant until our periods stop or our bellies grow big. And even then we have to take a test to believe it. Oblivious conception—that's another of nature's little mistakes.

Here's my theory. You start out in this life assuming you are the center of the universe. Then after any number of rough tumbles you figure out that's not necessarily so. But the hard edge of adulthood becomes blurred when you fall in love. Lessons learned seem like nothing more than the excess musings of a cynic, and thus the way is paved for you and your lover to blithely spin within a universe of two. But the cosmos shifts again, the orbit forever altered—necessarily so—if and when a baby arrives on the scene.

And this is where I run into trouble. For the longest time the possibility of a baby seemed to me to be as distant as the moon. But that's not true for Nick. The way he sees it, we already have a baby. It's in him and it's in me and it's just waiting to be born. I know his is a horribly antiquated and insufferably romantic point of view. But that's Nick for you. I certainly wouldn't expect him to believe in, for instance, pure science.

So why am I rambling on? Because I'm scared. Because I sense the orbit is changing. Because lately, I've been imagining myself holding our child and whispering all manner of sweet gobbledygook and sometimes she reaches up and touches my face. At that moment I feel as though I'd give up anything for her to exist someplace other than in my imagination. I mean, I want her so much that my temples pound against the fear that she will never be born, that some sardonic act of fate or nature will prevent her from ever being anything more than—to borrow an old-fashioned expression—a spark in her father's eye. In those moments, I grit my teeth, take an aspirin, and wait for the yearning to pass.

*I haven't been off my pills all that long. Dr. Singh (she's not a full
doctor yet—I don't know if she'll ever be one, but she's the closest
thing we've got) says sometimes it takes a while for the body to readjust itself. "Be patient," she says. Still, a part of me worries that
because I grew up in an unhappy house my cervix has shut down,
making me the victim in a game of sadistic poetic justice. Yes, if I
were a cartoon, attached to my womb would be a ramshackle wooden
sign: Closed for Business.*

That summer, the *Mattie Fiona* became our second home. We were a
team—much like Maya and Beth—shrimping by starlight and sleeping
by day. Sometimes Nick would even expand my job description beyond
that of sleeping passenger and allow me to help out on board. He'd haul
in the nets and empty the catch—mainly shrimp and scattering crabs—
and then stick the culling iron in my hand. "Go for it, Mattie," he'd say,
and then he'd slap me on the back as if I were a pal.

Culling shrimp was not a difficult job. It did not require great skill or
intellect, simply the ability to overcome my fear of the pincer-armed
blue crabs—but the fact that he asked me to help at all pleased me far
beyond any reasonable measure. In fact, as fate would have it, on the
nights I stayed home, I missed the water and the freshness of the air and
the gentle movement of celestial bodies across the vast black sky. But
more than any of that, I missed watching Nick at ease in his element.
Him shirtless in his yellow slicker coveralls. Him with his wild tangle of
curls wet with sea spray and sweat. Him with his hopeful grin each time
he hauled in his nets.

He loved this life and I knew why. It was freedom and something
more. To make a living as a shrimper you had to be smart. You had to
know the geography of the waters you harvested with the same intimacy
of a farmer who has walked and tilled the same field for fifty years. The
cyclical, omniscient moon. The shifting, mercurial tides. The intrica-
cies woven—hidden and revealed—within each season. The hills and
dales, gullies and cliffs of the seabed. The temperaments and tempta-

tions of the wind. Shrimpers had to understand these fits of nature both intellectually and instinctively. They had to see themselves not only as part of the grand scheme, but as essential to it. *Brothers Forever*. Ostensibly, Nick was on the bay night after night searching for shrimp. But really, he was seeking himself, clarifying his place in the world, reaffirming his connection to the wild.

Toward the end of August on a warm, windless night, under a crescent moon, I slept in the wheelhouse—the engine room was too warm—while Nick guided us through the night. I was dreaming I was alone on the beach, gathering heart cockles, when Nick pulled me out of my sleep. "Mattie, Mattie!" He shook my shoulders. "Wake up!"

"Huh? What?" I leaned up on my elbows and rubbed the sleep out of my eyes. "Is something wrong?"

"No, honey. Just a storm. A fast mover. Jesse Gray radioed that he nearly got caught in it. We'll hole up in the cove till it passes. But come on, I want you to hear this. Hurry—before the storm!" He grabbed my hand, pulled me to my feet, and hustled me onto the deck.

I looked around, bleary, feeling as though I were floating in space. I grabbed hold of the side of the wheelhouse and tried to get my bearings. The engine was off, the anchor set, the nets in. The world was deadly quiet.

Nick looked at me, triumphant.

"What?" I whispered.

He walked to the bow and leaned into the night. He motioned at me to join him and then closed his eyes.

"What is going on?"

"Shhh! There! Right there! Hear it?" His eyes remained closed and a sweet, crooked smile spread across his face. "They're singing!"

"Who's singing?"

"You know, them!"

Ah—so those mysterious sirens were at it again. I never believed Nick about the singing—not when he first told me, not as I stood on the deck of the *Mattie Fiona*. A fertile imagination tilled by hours of isolation, a quirk in my husband's nature to be thought of with fond, slightly

patronizing affection. To humor him, I tilted my head and tried to hone
in but all I found was silence—a sure sign that a storm was on its way.
The Gulf lapped gently against the hull but the slurping sound it made
could not be mistaken for seductive sirens singing near or far.

Lightning flashed across the western sky, illuminating an impressive
cloud bank. Before long, the wind and rain would overtake us and we
would have to seek shelter in the wheelhouse. I looked at Nick. He
appeared beatific, transported, listening to voices angelic, voices beyond my scope. Perhaps, I thought fancifully, he was able to plug into
the music of the spheres. Or the strains of his own far-flung heart. Or
the secret musings of a restless sea. How lucky, how very lucky for him.
I pressed my fingers against his cheek. He appeared so sure, so very
definite, that I held my breath and tried once more. A high lonesome
cry unfurled across the sky. A seagull? A tern flying ahead of the storm?

"Maybe I do," I whispered. "Yes, yes. I think so."

The sweltering latter days of August and early September mark the
height of hurricane season. Everybody said so. The local TV anchor-
woman whose job, evidently, was to alarm the populace at every turn no
matter the nature of the event—mundane or tragic ("The Big Bend
region is hurricane country, its residents at the mercy of these killer
storms.")—Calinda at the IGA ("Been quiet so far but it ain't gonna last.
Water's too hot for it to last."), Debbie at Traders Antiques ("This is the
kinda year you gotta watch out for. Right when we let our guards down,
wham. Funny, but it always seems to work that way. And these North-
erners who've come down here—they don't have a clue."). Even Miss
Lucy over at My-Way ("Auntie Mae says her preserves have gone bad—
sure sign of a storm.").

Nick, being a cautious and responsible shrimper, normally paid
close attention to the vagaries of the weather but during hurricane
season he became an unusually ardent fan of the Weather Channel. He
kept the TV tuned to it, favored some meteorologists over others, grew
horribly excited when a red screen flashed on, and had hair-pulling fits

over a new hire, a scared blonde whose intelligence seemed to be snuffed out by a massive dose of stage fright and who didn't know Cleveland from Miami and who once identified the State of Florida as the Republic of Texas.

Every afternoon Nick watched the Tropical Report which came on precisely at ten minutes to the hour, every hour. Some people keep track of baseball statistics or can recite the major battles of the Civil War and who the generals were and how many casualties were suffered by each side. Nick knew the names of the major hurricanes of this century and where they made landfall. He knew that Hurricane Andrew which hit South Florida in 1992 left one hundred and sixty thousand people homeless and nearly one and a half million without electricity. Dade County, alone, he could lecture, suffered thirty billion dollars in property damage. He could tell you that in 1900 a hurricane killed six thousand Galveston residents and the 1928 'cane (that which destroyed Nereus' house) first hit Lake Okeechobee, claiming nearly two thousand. He likened the movements of a hurricane to that of a pebble in a stream—the big storms had no motility of their own but were at the mercy of the currents to guide them from one place to the next.

Yes, indeed, in the same way that a stockbroker could read an annual report or a geologist the seismic hen-scratching on a graph, Nick could look at a weather map and divine the future.

As the Tropical Report hurled along, the weatherman shifting from the Atlantic to the Pacific, Nick would prognosticate about what routes the various storms might take, creating scenarios that could lead even a sane person to muse that each named storm was the cycloptic eye of God with its own willful mind and Old Testament agenda.

On a Friday afternoon in early September, as I sat on the couch going over my schedule for the new semester and while Nick drank his first cup of coffee, he flipped on the Weather Channel and a satellite picture of the southern Atlantic flashed across the screen. With false enthusiasm, the weatherman said, "Just look at that! It's a virtual rumba line of tropical waves stretching all the way from the west coast of Africa to the Lesser Antilles. Oh yes, it's that time of year, folks!"

"You mark my word," Nick said. "One of those suckers is gonna hit us." Then, without explanation, coffee in hand, he shuffled outside.

When the high buzz of his table saw sliced through the thick summer air, I went seeking answers. I walked out to the shed, where he was measuring a piece of plywood. He wore safety goggles and earplugs and looked slightly frog-like. He took a pencil from behind his ear and marked the board.

"What're you doing?"

He didn't hear me so I walked over and tapped him on the shoulder. He jumped, saw it was me, and took out his earplugs.

"What're you doing?"

"Making new hurricane shutters. The old ones are warped." He reinserted his earplugs, placed the plywood on his worktable, and sawed it into a rectangle large enough to cover a window.

Morbid warnings crossing the lips of others did not affect me. But if Nick was concerned, by God, I would join in. So after he went to work that night (I elected to stay home and battle the mealybugs which were sucking the life out of my roses), I walked over to Lillian's and told her I needed to know how to get ready for a hurricane.

My mother-in-law was in her backyard weeding her tomato patch and Rhea was sitting in an Adirondack shelling beans. "Well, the first thing you need to do," Lillian said, standing up and brushing herself clean before Rhea cut her off.

"Hurricane! There's no hurricane coming. At least not for a while." Rhea glared at the bay. Charon was wading up to his waist. He looked apocryphal—his wild white hair aglow in the light of the setting sun. "Old man, get out of that water!"

"How do you know?" I asked. "Everybody I talk to is sort of storm crazy. Even Nick."

"Have you been on the beach lately? Flat as a G.D. pancake."

"Lillian, what is she talking about?"

"I don't know." Lillian removed her gardening gloves and whacked them against her purple martin pole, sending loose dirt flying.

"The sand! On the beach. It builds up before a storm. The bunkers help keep back the water."

Lillian waved away Rhea's silly notion.

"Don't wave that hand at me! Chaaaarrrooon!"

Charon continued to wade. In fact, he ventured farther out, probably propelled by his wife's screeching. Rhea brushed off a mosquito that had lit on her arm. "That's it!" she said and took herself and the beans inside.

Lillian and I followed. "It's best to just keep the supplies on hand year-round," Lillian said. "You didn't prepare last year?"

"No, I didn't really think about it."

"Yes, I suppose you did have other things on your mind. But listen to me, we have bad weather in the winter, too. And if a storm does hit, you'll have more than enough to do without worrying whether or not you have a sufficient supply of batteries on hand."

She led me into her pantry and pulled an old steamer trunk out of the corner. She fiddled with the lid but couldn't lift it so I did. "You can rummage through here. If I've got several of anything just help yourself."

I refused Lillian's offer of procuring extras from her emergency stash but I did get a good idea of what I should stock up on. I thanked her, wondered how in the world I got along last hurricane season without a single battery in the house, and said good night to Charon, who had come in from the bay and who was seated at the kitchen table, sopping wet, eating a bowl of chowder as Rhea fussed over him.

"You take care of Rhea, Charon," I said as I opened the door.

"Hah!" Rhea retorted, placing a basket of bread in front of him.

I walked home along the bay, wondering if there was any truth to Rhea's folk wisdom about the beach building up before a storm but rejected it as being merely the bent raving of someone who'd spent all her days on an isolated island.

Once home, I fixed a glass of iced tea and, instead of dealing with the mealybugs, curled up on the couch and studied *The Audubon Soci-*

ety Field Guide to the Atlantic and Gulf Coasts. Discomfited does not begin to describe how I felt as I read up on sharks and discovered that of the nine species discussed, seven thrived in the shallow inshore waters of the Gulf.

And then there was this: "The Alphabet Cone Shell, like cone shells everywhere, can stab grasping fingers with a poisonous barb at the tip of its proboscis (protruding mouthpart). Any cone shell should be handled with extreme caution, if at all." I looked at my collection of cone shells which I kept in a clear glass jar filled with water on the coffee table (the water brings out their color) and was amazed that for over a year I had been in peril and not known it.

Near midnight, as the Latin names of invertebrates began to grate on my nerves, I set aside the book and started composing a hurricane to-do list. As always when I was home and Nick was shrimping, I had on the VHF radio. This was what most shrimpers' wives did. It allowed us to listen in on the shrimping fleet, kept us convinced our men and sons were safe. Of course, there were those who used the VHF as if it were their private phone line, and it was no different that night. Seems Mary Lou was in quite a state. "Honey baby, I just can't stand it when you're out there. This big old bed seems awfully empty. Over," she caterwauled.

Honey baby didn't answer. "He's probably mortified," I said to no one as I wrote, *bottled water.* If a storm struck, we'd probably be without electricity for days and Nick would have to stay home (*why* he would stay in port, I didn't know, but my fantasy required it).

I envisioned our predicament—the two of us roughing it in a subtropical post-disaster paradise complete with chilled wine and fuzzy close-ups. I was Uma Thurman to his Johnny Depp. I managed to have on just enough makeup to look fresh, natural, radiant. I continued to jot down supplies even while I thought of the two of us grilling Gruyère cheese sandwiches under the light of the moon. Where in the world would I get Gruyère cheese? Certainly not on the coast, but I added it to my list anyway and then: *canned goods (garbanzo beans, tuna, pickles, Vienna sausages), saltines, can opener, extra flashlight, coolers (not to be*

kept aboard the boat!), batteries (the bargain pack), ice, charcoal. Medi-
cines? Candles?

That's as far as I got. I was bone tired—my intermittent nights on the
boat with Nick had left me feeling completely confused as to when to
sleep and when to wake. I tossed the list onto the coffee table. I missed
Nick horribly. I thought about calling him on the radio and telling him
good night but thought better of it. I wasn't going to be like those nitwits
on the hill, making a fool out of myself in front of the whole world.
"Honey baby, I miss you so bad"—gads, it was enough to turn your
stomach. I shut off the lights and stretched out on the couch. I closed
my eyes and in the darkness of my imagination, a hurricane formed.
From the vantage point of my mind's eye, I gazed at an awesome aerial
view just like the ones they show on the weather. I'd never been in a
hurricane before and while I knew it wasn't appropriate to wish for
natural disasters, I admit I was curious, even slightly enamored by the
notion of nature taking over so fully.

But I wouldn't want to stay on the island. No. We would evacuate.
We would board up the house and hope for the best. I would tote with
me a carrying case full of supplies and minor comforts (hand lotion,
chocolates, talcum powder) and then we'd take the *Mattie Fiona*
upriver and ride her out. It would be a grand adventure that would
spawn stories as naturally as hurricanes spawn tornadoes. The wind
would howl and the candlelight would flicker and Nick and I would
make love as the storm washed the world clean. Yes, clean. And so
much darkness. Everything blowing like crazy—the tree limbs and the
signposts and the flowers. Canvas awnings. Sheet metal siding. Garbage
cans flying as if they had wings. Where do the birds go? What about the
birds? No idea. All the little creatures. So many noises, something rat-
tling on the windowpane, thunder shaking paper walls, furious wind as
strange as Nick's sirens so sweet like a lullaby.

Sleep took me fully. I did not dream. If the dog down the street
bayed because he sensed something on the island was out of order, I did
not hear him. If there was a knock on my unlocked doors, it went
unheeded. Therefore, when my walnut side table that I'd purchased

from Traders Antiques clattered to the floor and when someone shouted, "Goddamn son of a bitch!" and when that same someone landed on top of me, having tripped on the rug, I was understandably startled. My first sleep-sodden impulse was that the hurricane must be tearing apart the room and then I remembered that there was no hurricane and that caused me to come to in a terrified rush, screaming and throwing off whoever had fallen on top of me.

I've always hated the Hollywood-inspired notion of the hysterical woman. But that's exactly how I behaved as I leapt off the couch, stumbled on my overturned table, and reached for the wall switch. I gasped for air as I choked on my own breath. Should I flee or throw something? I flipped on the light. Maybe I could heft that side chair. Hit him square in the head.

The intruder was splayed on the floor, his legs crumpled, his jaws slack. He was squinting and covering his eyes as if I'd just turned on the sun. I grabbed the horse conch I had fetchingly placed just so on the top shelf of my bookcase only the day before—the shell being the closest weapon I could find—but I didn't take my eyes off the enemy. I wrapped my hands around the knobs of the weapon, ignoring how very brittle it was, and thinking that whoever had just broken into my house seemed horribly vulnerable, sunken and hollow-eyed, a fuckup to use one of Beth's expressions.

"Don't move!" I said, jabbing the conch shell as if I were about to eviscerate him.

He wiped his nose on the back of his hand. "Be careful. You might hurt yourself." Then he closed one eye and asked, "Where's my God-damn brother?"

"Your brother?" If I aimed at his heart, maybe I could stab him with the tapered end of the shell. No, his eye. Less resistance.

"Yeah, my fuckin' brother." He glared at me accusingly, then buried his head in his hands, and without warning began to sob. "I just came to see my baby brother. Didn't mean to scare nobody."

I bit back my impulse to scold him over the use of a double negative even as the fog which had obscured the situation lifted.

"Zeke?"

He nodded and mumbled incoherently. I could barely believe it. This emaciated, fallen-apart man was the teenager in the photograph with Nick and Dem. He'd been that smirking big kid with the chipped front tooth and the ready-to-rumble demeanor. The one with his hand stuck inside the fish as if he were claiming the animal by violating it. That's right—the no-good who'd beat his wife and abandoned his son and hurt his mother so desperately she couldn't speak his name. But the man sprawled on the floor possessed no bravado and just a thin veil of meanness. He was stone drunk, bone thin, and unshaven. His long black hair was pulled into a ponytail and his jeans and T-shirt were filthy. If I had been an older woman I would have said, "My God, son, you look pitiful."

I set the conch shell back on the shelf. "I'm Mattie. Nick and I— well—I'm his wife." I paused, waiting for a response, but all he did was gaze at his surroundings as if he couldn't figure out how he happened to be on the floor in his brother's house.

"Come on," I said, offering him my hand which he refused. "I'll put us on some coffee."

He followed me into the kitchen and settled himself at the table. As I filled the pot with cold water, I watched him out of the corner of my eye. He kept tipping back his chair, jiggling his leg, flicking his left wrist with his right index finger. I hadn't been around any drug addicts in my life but I didn't need a degree in pharmacology to know that this guy was strung out.

"Where'd you say Nick was?"

"Working." I leaned against the counter, waited for the coffee to brew.

He smirked and then jerked his neck from side to side as though he were working out a kink. "Fuck. Still shrimping. What a waste."

"Well, you know, it's a living."

He shrugged his shoulders and tapped on the table. I poured the coffee. "You want anything in yours?"

"Nope."

I set the coffee in front of him and peeked at the inside of his arms. Sure enough, a red trail of needle marks punctuated the wobbly lines of his veins. "What're you looking at?" he snapped.

"Nothing," I said, backing off, thinking that maybe I ought to get on that radio and call somebody.

"So—Nick got himself married." His fingers danced along the cup's rim.

"Yes. Just over a year now." I poured cream into my coffee and stirred, tried to make conversation. "What brings you to Lethe, Zeke?"

He looked at me as though trying to discern if my question was a challenge and then, with shaking hands, lifted the coffee cup to his lips.

I attempted to keep my tone light even as Nick's admonitions about his brother rolled through my mind. "You plan to stay a while?"

"Nah. Just passing through." He shot me a grin that really wasn't all that friendly. His eyes were the same color as Nick's but the resemblance ended there.

"What about your son?"

He ran his hand over his head and then rubbed the back of his neck—a gesture I'd watched Nick do a thousand times. "Like I said, I'm just passing through."

"Lucas is a . . . he's a real good boy." I wiped down the counter, let the words settle, and then pressed my luck. "He'd love to see you. I think, I think he misses you, Zeke."

He pushed away his coffee. "No he doesn't. He misses somebody else." He scratched the side of his face and then started flicking his wrist again. "When do you think Nick'll be back?"

"Morning."

"That's no good. I can't wait."

"Would you like me to go get your mother?"

Before he could answer he started coughing. His shoulders bowed, his back curved into a question mark, and his entire body shook. He looked like an old man. I suddenly feared he had TB or AIDS. I put my hand on his back and was shocked at how loose his skeleton felt as it rattled beneath my palm. Slowly, his hacking subsided. He jerked away. "Nah, nah, don't get nobody. Just let me use your bathroom." He scooted back his chair and stood unsteadily. I didn't need to point the way—he'd spent more time in this house than I had.

I walked into the living room and over to the radio. I could call Dem. Lucas had started back to school a couple of weeks ago, so if Beth and Maya were shrimping he would be spending the night with his uncle. They could be here in a flash. I sat down and started to make the call but a scrap of wisdom stopped me. No son should see his father in Zeke's condition. Better, I thought, the fantasy. Better to try to keep Zeke around and nurse him back to health, and once he was steady and on his feet we'd help him patch up the relationship with Lucas. Yes, I decided, that's the proper course of action. I heard the toilet flush and hurried back into the kitchen.

He's so thin, surely he needs some food, I thought. I opened the fridge door. I could fry up some bacon and eggs. That would do him good. And I'd invite him to sleep on the couch, and I'd lock myself in my room just in case he was weird, and I'd take him with me to the dock in the morning—he'd be better for the food and sleep, and Nick and I would take care of him. Everything on the QT until he stabilized.

As Zeke walked into the kitchen he cleared his throat. I looked up from the fridge and smiled. "How about some breakfast?"

"No, lady, I gotta go." He lurched toward the door.

"You're welcome to sleep here. At least hang out long enough to see Nick."

"Nah. I said I gotta go!"

"Really, Zeke. We would love for you to stay here with us for a while."

"What's your problem, lady, can't you hear?" he yelled. He kicked open the door. Afraid, I backed up, bumping into the counter. Zeke hesitated, put his hands on his hips, looked over my head, and fumed. He seemed to be measuring his words, not for my sake but his. He hit the door frame with his fist and then said, "So. Uhh. The boy. He's okay?"

"Lucas. He's wonderful." I crossed my arms in front of me and tried not to hate him. "You should be proud."

Zeke did not speak but a flash of recognition, of connection, of ties bound and cut—these impulses passed like shadows across his gaunt features. It was the answer he wanted to hear, expected to hear. It's what allowed him to nod once and then step into the night, pretending he was guiltless.

I latched the door behind him, sick to my stomach, knowing that I had to keep a horrible secret. I would tell no one of Zeke's brief presence on the island. This visit had been an aberration. He was not the man his family remembered, even when they remembered him at what they thought was his worst. I cut on the outside lights, locked all the doors, and then headed into the bathroom. Maybe he's terribly ill, I thought. Maybe I should contact the sheriff. Just in case. But what good would that do? He'd be in jail overnight—if that—and then once word got out that he'd drifted on and off the island in the middle of the night, two innocent people would be wounded: Lillian and Lucas. But Zeke would still be out there, using people up, his conscience unpiqued, damned and determined to barrel along, making a mess of his life and everyone else's. But Lillian, she wouldn't see it that way. She blames herself for her son's faults and failures. She sure does. She carries around his guilt as if it were a sack of ashes. I sat down on the toilet, started to pee, and then caught sight of the vanity sink and the little curtain I had installed to hide the plumbing. It was pushed aside and my purse was pulled out, its contents spilled on the floor. I'd cashed a check that morning for a hundred dollars—grocery money and more. Jesus Christ, I thought, I should have known. When I finished my business, I searched my wallet. It was as empty as on the day I bought it.

If a family member can't steal from you, who can? I mused wryly as I walked back into the kitchen and poured myself a glass of wine. Feeling certain that he was already off the island—he'd gotten what he came for—I wandered out to the back porch, settled down into my old pine rocker, and watched the sky. If he had asked for the money, I would have given it to him. But he couldn't have known that. And he was too strung out to take a chance on me saying no. What a sad, lost soul. What a waste. He was gone for good—or at least until the next time he was desperate to score—blundering through the world without once considering the ramifications of his actions. Now I knew why Zeke's name never crossed his mother's lips. The whole idea of what he had become was too painful, the load of atoning for her firstborn's sins too great.

I rested my head against the chair and drew imaginary lines between the stars, connecting the constellations, following the paths laid down by the Ancients. First I found the sailor's best friend: the North Star. Then the two Dippers. Pegasus. Hercules. Andromeda. A sky full of diamonds, a Milky Way of endless swirls, of pixilated light. I searched for Delphinus but couldn't find it. My mind drifted as if its thoughts and half thoughts were nothing more than stardust scattered by the breeze. I fell asleep and dreamed of sea oats, of my hair lying tangled upon the sand, of my husband's naked back. I touched his spine and his smattering of dark freckles turned into moons, planets, white-hot suns—a galaxy luminous and bright spinning upon his skin. I slept deeply and when I awoke, the stars had moved across the sky and the world seemed completely different, the celestial map altered by the beat of its unknowable purpose. But my gloominess over the evening's visitation had not lifted. So in solidarity with Lillian and Lucas and their unspoken grief, I said to the heavens what Lillian could not. "Zeke," I whispered. "Zeke."

Later that morning, much to my surprise, I discovered that secrets weren't something I easily harbored, not from my husband anyway.

It had been my full intention to stoically burden only myself with Zeke's predawn visit. Spare the family. If possible, erase the details from my mind. Refrain from even confiding about it in my journal lest someone's prying eyes ever saw fit to wander over my private ramblings.

As soon as I saw the *Mattie Fiona* round the bend, my heart quickened. This is what it means to be a woman, I thought. Indeed, this is what it means to be a wife. Cheerful, misleading, conniving in the face of bad news. Isn't that what women had done for years? Selectively fed information to their husbands and relatives all in the name of the family good? In essence, performing a sleight of hand, creating an illusion of a fair and just world so that those she cared for could march on in blissful ignorance? Yes, I thought, smoothing my white linen shirt. Exactly.

Nick eased the boat into the slip, gently nudging the dock.

"Hi, baby!"

"Hi, sweetheart! How'd it go?"

"Oh . . . fair."

I helped tie up the boat. He shut off the engine, stepped onto the deck, kissed my lips, and before the spit had a chance to dry I spilled the beans. Every last pinto, even down to the needle marks on his brother's arms. The words gushed out of me, an unstoppable torrent. I felt as though I were confessing and, as I did, the proverbial weight of the world lifted off my shoulders.

Nick, completely unaware that my babbling was a mistake, listened intently, his anger gathering like a storm. His eyes darkened and his knuckles went white. "Son of a bitch!" he said. "He didn't hurt you, did he?"

"No, honey. I wasn't going to tell anybody, but . . ."

Nick hugged me. "No. You're right to tell me. But Mama and Lucas can't know."

"That's what I thought." And I suddenly felt so smart once more, being in cahoots with my friend and lover, the two of us bearing the secret against the ravages of time, which in this case was a few days.

Three to be exact. That's how long it took for cousins and in-laws and aunts and uncles and sundry other relatives living on the hill to know what was supposed to never be spoken of and for me to discover something else about family life—at least this family's life. Secrets were like rare jewels, objects to be held to the light, admired, conspiratorially shared and envied, and then put away until the next occasion.

"Have you heard?"

"Yes!"

"Who told you?"

"Just the other day, I ran into Dem . . ."

"The man should be horsewhipped."

"Disowned and horsewhipped."

"Listen, nobody else should know about this."

"Don't worry—I won't tell a soul. Not a single solitary soul."

"I really shouldn't be telling you this but . . ."

"Poor Lillian. It would just kill her if she knew."

"There ought to be a law!"

"And Lucas! What about Lucas! He thinks so highly of that no-good excuse of a human being."

"We can never breathe a word of this to him. That's all there is to it. Not to Lucas, not to Lillian, not to anyone."

"No. No. Of course not."

"Not a word. Not even a hint of a word."

"The secret is safe with me."

"My lips are sealed."

"Did you hear who showed up on Lethe last week in the middle of the night?"

A broken heart is an amazing object, chock full of paradoxes. Empty. Hard. Splintered. Brimming with the frothy pain of sudden vacancy yet repelled by its own barren desolation, yearning for a stranger to come along and paste the pieces back together. Unsuspecting of name, appearance, politics, the heart does not care if the stranger is a particularly moral or kind person. To be filled again with that heady spirit we call love—that's all it craves.

Demetrius Plato Blue (how odd the middle name strikes me, given the fact that Dem both instinctually and willfully rejects most notions proffered by the rational mind) was a young man in his mid-twenties. He was older than me—if by but a few years—but I considered myself older in female years and that gave me room to pass judgment upon his behavior as if I were his big, wiser sister who'd learned a few things during her soirees around the block.

This is the way I saw it. Lacey had rendered Dem senile before his time. Which was a shame, really. He had been so genuinely goofy, so starstruck happy, so oblivious to life's disappointments before she reached into his chest and ripped out his aorta and all that was attached to it.

That his blind devotion to happiness survived intact for as long as it did is a marvel, really. I mean, his life had not been untainted by tragedy. There was his father's premature death, his oldest brother's rejection of even the slightest familial decency, and sundry other garden variety missteps, mishaps, and miscalculations (the drowning death of a childhood friend, the early demise of his hound dog, Pickles—et cetera, et cetera).

Such occurrences are likely to take the blush off some roses—but not Dem. He had sailed through it all—the bad and the good—never giving himself over fully to anyone or anything until he met Lacey.

The attraction was beyond me. She was not particularly pretty, not with that teased peroxide blond hair and the vastly annoying smoking habit and her judgmentalism of all things outside the sawed-off container of her own flesh. In the brief time I knew her she was constantly bossing and belittling poor Dem. "He can't even match up his own socks! And if he manages to, he usually has one of them on inside out. He's really pretty stupid," she would say gleefully and then chortle like an old crow. There is the possibility that she was amazing in bed but I'm not willing to go there.

I guess it can fairly be stated that one of life's cruelest ironies is, psychologically speaking, we're all freaks of nature. A willful heart can outfox even the brightest mind on nearly any given day of the week. I believe the family was fully cognizant of this decidedly human quirk as they chewed over the details of Dem's attraction to Lacey and his subsequent breakdown.

Behind his back some family members mused that perhaps he enjoyed being humiliated and controlled by her. But I didn't agree—there was nothing in his upbringing to support this sort of mental and moral failure as far as I could tell. (For instance, the likely culprit to instill in him such a warped view of love would be his mother. But she was neither mean nor controlling. By all accounts she meted out praise and discipline with an even, loving hand.)

In the absence of any clear evidence suggesting he liked being mistreated, I developed a different theory: Dem didn't enjoy Lacey's company much at all but by the time he discovered that ripe piece of information, it was too late. He was already hitched. And the Blues are nothing if not loyal to the idea of marriage. Except for very rare exceptions (Zeke, for example) people stayed married in this family forever. In the coffee shop and in the grocery line and at the bank people on the hill whispered about Lillian's refusal to remarry. *She'd be so much happier. She was young when George died. Any man on this coast would have considered himself lucky to be her husband. She's out there holed up with her in-laws. What's wrong with her? Even at her age now, she could find a new husband and kiss that bunch goodbye.* What's wrong with her is that she married once, for life, and George's death didn't change that.

And so I came to this: Given the hardtack approach with which his family approached marriage and given the fact that most everyone Dem knew on the island (i.e., relatives) seemed happy enough in their various stages of matrimony (yes, even Rhea, the old curmudgeon, who after all these years was still on fire for Charon), his broken heart could be attributed to one thing and one thing only. Embarrassment. Demetrius Plato Blue was absolutely dying of it.

Did he return her furtive glance right there in the front office of the Carrabelle Medical Clinic, with its dingy green carpet and its wood product paneled walls and its cartoon-like posters encouraging patients to vaccinate their children, stop smoking, and lose weight? I think so.

And I also believe, in fact feel certain, that she made the first move. Her initial intentions might not have been focused on Dem at all, but on the child. She probably saw a serious, reasonably handsome guy sitting in the medical office, his baby on his knee, and she was just so taken. Her heart filled up at the very sight of this obviously wounded man behaving in such a genuinely tender fashion with his child. And the next thing she knew, she was leaning across the space separating her from her destiny, talking baby talk.

Surely, Dem answered politely to her inquiries as to his son's age and disposition. And then, as always, like a calling card announcing his fragile state of mind and manhood, without any regard to the possibility that here was a young woman he might possibly fall in love with one day, he probably said something such as (swallowing his words, hurtling headlong into the next bleak second) "His mother left us. So it's just me and him."

This is the way I have decided it happened and whether the details are accurate or not doesn't really affect how I view this incident in my brother-in-law's life since I've already made up my mind:

She lets the baby wrap his slobbery hand around her finger. "How long are you two on your own?" she asks brightly.

Dem, confused by her question, looks at her quizzically and as he does, he notices how her light brown hair curves around the wide oval of her face, and that her green eyes are speckled with bits of brown, and that the tip of her nose is turned up ever so slightly as if it were just begging to be kissed. "Forever."

"Oh." And she blushes, both because of her error and because here she is, sitting on the floor beside a single man, playing with his baby. And to think, the only reason she had stopped into the clinic at all was to let Sami Singh know she couldn't go to the movies in Tallahassee until Sunday.

My, how Dem's heart must have shivered as it sensed it was about to be put back together. And how endearingly sweet he must have looked as he stood in front of his bathroom mirror later that day and watched himself say her name. "Kelly. Kelly." And how light he must have felt, how fully surprised, when during their first meal together sitting in a booth overlooking the marsh at Julia Mae's Seafood Restaurant he said something—he can't even remember what it was—which she found witty and he heard her giggle, a laugh pure and sweet and free of recriminations. And how all those many months of desperate shame withered into the safe and unnavigable distance the first time he softly touched his lips to hers and heard her whisper. A breath of air lifted on angel wings, that's what he thought. "Dem, oh, Dem."

The first time any of us caught wind of this new phase in Dem's life was Labor Day weekend. As usual, the family gathered at Lillian's house, bearing food and drink, children and friends in tow. A good dozen of us were milling about and gabbing on the back porch when Lucas breathlessly threw open the screen door and announced in the conspiratorially charged tone of someone who is about to reveal the most tantalizing of secrets, "It's Dem. He's walking down the road right now. With a girl!"

As if we were lemmings or the in-concert appendages of a giant amoeba, we moved in a single cilia-like motion to the west side of the porch, gawking in amazement.

"Oh my God!"

"I thought something was going on!"

"And you didn't tell?"

"I wasn't sure."

"She's pretty."

"Looks don't mean squat. Is she nice? That's the question. After the last one, I think he may have a thing for jackasses."

"Give her a chance."

"Yeah."

"I just hope she makes him happy. He can't afford to have another broken heart. I think it'd just kill him."

"Maybe she's nothing more than a friend. Y'all are acting like they're already engaged."

"He wouldn't be bringing her around if it weren't serious."

"At least her hair ain't teased all the way up to heaven."

"Look, she's talking to Gaby. How sweet!"

"Her little shorts set looks real nice. Pressed and everything."

"Ooo, ooo, ooo, here they come!"

"Quick, everybody, act normal!"

It had to happen. There was simply too much foreshadowing for it not to. The rumba line of tropical storms. Nick's sudden insistence on making new hurricane shutters. My wifely and very practical decision to stock up on emergency supplies. Rhea's moody wisdom regarding the beach's shifting sands. That bizarre, unsettling visit from Zeke (people and animals grow agitated, behaving in ways otherwise unthinkable when they sense an impending natural battle). Who knows, maybe even Dem's newfound love was a result of the world rearranging itself in preparation for the big blow.

Three weeks after Lillian's Labor Day party, tropical storm Cerberus (the naming committee obviously barked at a very tall tree to come up with that one, Cerberus being the mythological three-headed, dragon-tailed dog who guards the kingdom of the dead, allowing spirits to enter but never leave) slipped into the southern Gulf of Mexico. Local fore-casters dismissed Cerberus, calling it unorganized and no threat to any land areas except, perhaps, Mexico.

However, John Hope, the Weather Channel's hurricane expert and Nick's favorite TV weatherman ("He's a scientist, not a showman," Nick said, defending his choice over mine, Jim Cantore), said, "This is one storm we're going to have to watch. Conditions in the Gulf right now are very favorable for further development of this particular system. The water temperature is extremely warm—it's had all summer to heat up— and as you know, Jim, warm waters help fuel these storms. I wouldn't be surprised at all if by tomorrow morning we weren't dealing with a Category One, possibly even a weak Category Two storm."

"Well, where's it going? Where's it going?" I said, sounding as if I were a frightened four-year-old.

"Here," Nick said, staring fiercely at the Weather Channel's tracking map. He put his finger on the TV screen, tapped the tropical storm symbol, and brought his finger up to our little unidentified dot of land in the northern Gulf. "Right here."

Forty-eight hours later, after the storm wobbled, veered west, and then north northwest, Franklin County issued a mandatory evacuation order for all coastal residents. But I was to learn that this particular proclamation wasn't an order at all. Nor did it have the force of law behind it. In fact, a mandatory evacuation order is actually little more than an adamant suggestion wrapped in a tissue-thin veil of panic.

The sheriff explained as much as we stood on my front porch, watching Nick nail and screw the shutters over our windows. "You know I can't force you to leave, but I'm telling you, if you don't get off this island you're on your own once the storm hits. I strongly recommend you get the hell outta here before it's too late."

"Nick, honey, maybe we really ought to do what he says."

Soaking wet from the squall bands that blew in at random, Nick shook his head, his lips pressing on the three nails sticking out of his mouth like machined tusks. The nails were galvanized and shiny and the thought of them in his mouth set my teeth on edge. He gripped the nails and rolled them in his palm. He set the point of one against the plywood and hammered it in with two sure blows. "I'm sorry, sir, but I'll be damned if I'm going to leave this island. My family has been out here for nearly a hundred years and we've never run from a storm. I don't aim to start now."

The sheriff was a short man, his face ruddy with skin cancers. He breathed out hard, rubbed his hand on his lips as he thought, and then said, "You people are the stubbornest bunch I ever saw. Well, Nick. I hope you change your mind. And I hope you do it soon. At least make your mama leave."

He looked at Nick with a man-to-man toughness but Nick just went on hammering, leaving the sheriff little choice but to turn on his heel and walk down the drive to the pickup he'd borrowed from Vanessa, the mail lady. He climbed in, slammed the door, and took off without looking at us even though I politely waved.

"I hope this isn't the last of us he sees," I said as I watched him lurch down the sand road which was quickly becoming a muddy rut.

Nick set down the hammer and pulled me to him. "Baby, do you want to leave? I'll take you to the hill and get you a motel room if that's what you want."

His hair was matted against his skull which gave his bony features a stark skeletal prominence. Not caring that he would not understand what prompted my words, I blurted, "You're going to be a handsome old man."

He looked over my head in an attempt to hide his pleasure at my flirtation but I saw the glint in his eyes as they narrowed. "Well?"

"Only if you go with me."

"Sweetie, I—I just can't. Leaving during a storm, it doesn't feel right, it feels like I'd be throwing in the towel or something. And I don't think we're going to get a direct hit. It's not going to be all that bad. You know, those TV weather guys are always trying to frighten us."

"Really?"

"Really."

I flashed on an image of myself in some dark motel room, all alone in the middle of a hurricane. This wasn't exactly what I'd had in mind in my grilled Gruyère cheese storm fantasies.

"When are you going to move the boat?"

"Just as soon as I get this last shutter up."

"You're taking her upriver?"

"Yep."

"And leaving her?"

"Yep."

"Okay." I looked toward the Gulf. It was sunny but very windy and another squall band was spiraling in off the horizon. "Dem is going to help you?"

"He's meeting me here in about ten minutes. If you want, we'll take you with us and get you set up somewhere."

"Lillian is staying?"

"The whole gang is."

If I left and nothing bad happened, they'd never let me live it down. I'd forever be known as a big chicken. Now I admit, this wasn't a mature line of reasoning but I do believe my assumptions were accurate. And besides, I couldn't let Nick ride out the storm alone. "Nope. I'll just get things around the yard secured while you're gone and then go see if your mother needs any help."

Nick kissed me lightly. Rainwater dripped from his hair onto my face. I don't remember if I wiped it off or not.

Lawn chairs. Garbage cans. Flowerpots. Sprinklers. Outdoor tables. Buckets. Bird feeders. Wind chimes. Brooms. Rakes. Two small concrete statues—a pelican and a rat whose tail Nick had painted pink. I gathered anything that a hundred-mile-an-hour wind could turn into a projectile.

Object by object, item by item, I gleaned from my yard the bric-a-brac of my island home. And if the truth be told, I did this not out of any civic duty to properly prepare for the hurricane but because these every-day, take-them-for-granted knickknacks were the building blocks of my life. The concrete rat was an aberration, embarrassing, tacky. But every time I walked past it (I had tucked it just so amid a stand of wire grass), a smile slipped across my face. And a memory, too. A memory of walking onto the back porch one afternoon to find Nick in the yard ever so seriously painting the rat's tail that shocking, impossible-to-miss pink. So I moved through my garden slowly, methodically, and when it rained I did not seek shelter or pick up my pace. I simply continued on, piling everything in the shed, concentrating on imposing order on a world that would soon be subject to nature's primal revenge.

After I'd stacked my final lawn chair neatly at the rear of the shed, I wandered through my garden with its yarrow-lined pathways and fragrant plots of mint, lemon basil, and jasmine, worrying about how my carefully loved plants would fare in the storm. A hurricane was no good for a garden but I couldn't possibly dig up all my precious plants and bring them inside. And even if I could, the vegetables would never make it. My tomatoes and eggplants would simply give up and keel over. Let nature take its course, I told myself, pinching back the basil, there is little else you can do.

But I am nothing if not stubborn, and while I couldn't do much to protect what was in the ground I did manage to haul into the house with much grunting and great effort my many potted plants. Several geraniums, a thorny bougainvillea, two aloes, three colonnade apple trees (I had to shimmy them across the porch—made it as far as the northeast corner where they stayed because I couldn't lift them over the threshold without inflicting on myself serious physical harm), a plum, a dwarf peach, various petunias, basil, arugula, and a flat of striped German tomato seedlings.

Since early that morning, we had kept the TV tuned to the Weather Channel with the volume muted until the top of the hour when I would pause from whatever I was doing in order to listen to the storm update. By midafternoon, Cerberus' central pressure had dropped two points—a sign of strengthening—and its eye wall had become better defined—another sign that this storm was going to get meaner before it was all over. Its maximum sustained winds were 105 miles an hour, making it a Category Two storm, which meant, I thought gloomily, that my garden (and possibly our roof) was doomed. The hurricane center was predicting landfall somewhere between Cedar Key to our southeast and Mobile to our west.

"Damn it," I said to the TV, clicking on the mute button and then fussing once more over my plants, rearranging them on and around the wood-burning stove, testing the soil for dryness. This preoccupation with the aesthetics and health of my potted garden may seem ill-timed considering the fact that the sheriff was running up and down the island yelling that the sky was falling but the project centered me and eased my sense of impending doom. I nestled an aloe between two pots of petunias and stepped back to survey the composition. No, much too crowded. Perhaps the aloe with its striking succulent branches needed to be in its own space away from the cozy, nonthreatening petunias. I stood there tapping my toe, mulling over my next move, and then, either by force of habit or sheer luck, glanced at the TV screen.

"Oh my God!" I squealed and went scrambling for the remote.

Right there on our thirty-inch Magnavox, standing on our rickety dock in front of the *Mattie Fiona* with Jim Cantore, who was sporting his marine blue Weather Channel slicker, was my husband.

"So, what's your plan, Nick? What preparations are you making for the storm?" Jim asked, shoving the microphone at Nick.

"Well, Jim," Nick said, shirtless, wiping something off his bare beautiful shoulder, "I'm taking my shrimp boat upriver. Probably to Saul's Creek. That's the safest place for her. We'll tie her up real secure and just hope for the best."

Dem walked by in the background. He was on deck and he paused for a moment, his head between Nick's and Jim's, and grinned stupidly. I was afraid he was going to shout, "Hi, Mom!" but (and I was grateful for this) he moved out of the shot.

"Now, and I don't mean to alarm you, but what happens if the worst case scenario should occur and you get hit with the full fury of the storm and lose your boat?"

"I'd say I'm outta business."

"Well, let's all hope and pray that doesn't happen."

"You bet," Nick said and he looked dead at the camera as if he were an absolute natural.

"There you have it," Jim said and the camera moved in close, cropping out Nick.

I jumped up and down, hopped all over the living room. I do not know why seeing a loved one on TV is so exciting—it's as if it gives them an added dimension, somehow makes them more real than they were before their image was beamed to the heavens to a spinning satellite and then bounced into homes across the planet.

When Nick got home I kissed him wildly and he took out of his wallet a rain-soaked piece of paper (actually it was a receipt from Harry's Restaurant for two cups of coffee and a piece of pecan pie). He carefully unfolded it and said, "I got you something."

It was Jim Cantore's autograph. He wrote, "To Mattie, here's hoping for blue skies. Your weatherman, Jim Cantore."

"Thank you, sweetie," I said. And I tried to hide my pleasure—a TV weatherman's autograph—such a trifling, childish trinket to find joy in. Nevertheless, I had to struggle to keep my voice neutral, nonchalant, as I asked, "Is this his receipt?"

"No. It's mine. Dem and I stopped into Harry's and had some coffee before we moved the boat. That's where we met Jim."

Jim. My husband was on a first-name basis with Jim. "Is he nice?"

"Yeah. He seemed like a pretty good guy."

"You were terrific, Nick. I hope your mother saw it," I said, walking into the kitchen, carrying the autograph in my cupped palms and then carefully placing it on a plate in the cupboard to dry.

The world is a wondrous place in the hours before a hurricane. Nourished by offshore gales, the air feels energized, as if at any moment what we breathe but have never seen will become visible, something we could hold in our hands and contemplate. There is commotion in the sky. Birds of all ilk—songbirds, birds of prey, seabirds, shorebirds—take to the wing in search of refuge. The horizon no longer gleams in the unreachable, dream-like distance but looms disturbingly close. Clouds do not float by lazily. They zoom, constantly changing shape, propelled by the strengthening winds. And something happens to the light. A golden glow settles on the sea oats and rooftops and trees and dunes. Even the most ordinary objects—a wheelbarrel, a wooden fence, a pathway of worn stepping-stones—appear more vivid than they did the day before. Ahead of the storm, the natural and the man-made adopt a deeper hue.

But this paradise, this clean wind, this sky the color of faded berries is obliterated from time to time by the rain bands preceding the hurricane. In the blink of an eye, day turns to night. As if from a fire hose, rain pounds windows, cars, sidewalks, shutters. People pause in mid-sentence and ask tremulously, "Is this it? Is it here?" Their voices barely rise and fall before the squall passes, leaving them to wonder in awe at how petulant the universe can be. For the next few minutes or hours the world returns to its temporary state of grace. And we wait.

It was nearly three in the afternoon and Nick had gone over to his mother's to board up her house. I expected Beth, Maya, and Lucas to arrive at any time because they were going to ride out the hurricane with us since our house sat on the island's highest point of elevation and was situated well behind the dune line, unlike their Gulf-front cottage. Dem had decided to take Gaby to Tallahassee and had already left. They had reserved a room at the Quality Inn, and in my opinion, were the only members of the family displaying good sense.

I stood on my back porch and tried to think of what else I needed to get done. Everything, as far as I could tell, was secure. The wild cats could seek shelter in the shed. The boat was moored far upriver. Our windows and doors were shuttered. Whatever could be hurled by the wind was out of harm's way. The bathtub was full of water. Our ice chests packed with ice. The hurricane lanterns were topped off with oil and the flashlights all had fresh batteries. I had plenty of food, water, candles, drinks, and snacks. I mused that I might actually be as prepared as anyone possibly could be when I noticed that a squirrel was in the birdhouse I had nailed earlier that summer to one of the pine trees. It was fastidiously—perhaps even frantically—stuffing the birdhouse's opening with pine needles. I watched, amazed, as it created what amounted to a cork. At one point, the squirrel pushed aside the needles, stuck its head out, looked around, and then retreated back into the house, replacing what I hoped for its sake was a watertight seal.

"Unbelievable!" I said and then remembered Rhea's wives' tale about the beach building up before a storm. I'll just have to check that out, I thought. I went inside to slip on my flip-flops and to tie back my hair. As I guided the brush through my tangles, I heard Nick come home.

"Hey, where are you?" he yelled.

"In here!"

He came into our bedroom, shirtless and sweaty. I looked at him and considered making a move—you know, like in the movies—just walking over and laying one on him and fiddling with the waist button on his jeans and then the two of us falling onto the bed and making passionate love.

But instead, I said, "How'd it go?"

"Got 'em all boarded up. Even Charon's inside."

"That's good."

"What're you doing?"

"Going for a walk on the beach."

He held out his hand and I took it. "Let's go," he said but before we left the bedroom he kissed my fingers one knuckle at a time.

By five o'clock that evening, the heavy rains had begun and Beth, Maya, and Lucas had sought shelter at our house. Clouds blocked out any reception from the satellite dish so the Weather Channel wasn't of any use to us except that Nick's appearance on it made for a fine story.

"I was pinching off a spent blossom when for some reason I just happened to look up and there was Nick on the TV!"

Beth hooted with glee and slapped Nick on the back. "I always knew you'd make the big time one day."

Maya shook her head and said, "My gosh, and we missed it! Maybe they'll run it again. Maybe the satellite will come back on."

Lucas asked, "Did they put makeup on you?"

"No. It was just a quick twenty-second spot. Nothing fancy."

"Listen to him. He sounds like an expert."

"Yeah, Nick, you're not going to stop shrimping and become a TV star, are you?"

"I don't know. Depends on how good the pay is."

"Yeah, yeah, yeah."

So there we were, ushering in Cerberus—a potentially devastating storm—with music and fried chicken and drink and dance and laughter. Every once in a while the wind would blow particularly hard and we'd all fall silent, exchange glances, and then break into giggles.

"It's really blowing now," one of us would say.

"Shoot, this is a piddlin' wind."

"Yep. I bet it's going to get a lot worse before it gets better."

"Sure hope you've got hurricane strapping on your roof, Nick."

"This roof has more hurricane strapping than a stripe-ped assed ape."

"You think the chickee will make it?"

"Sure. It has seen far worse than this in its day."

About every hour or so we would cut off the music and listen to the weather on the radio. That's all the radio stations were broadcasting—emergency warnings from NOAA and the National Weather Service which were decidedly unnerving and left me feeling as if we were under siege. By 8 P.M. Cerberus had strengthened into a moderate Category Three storm with sustained winds of one hundred and eighteen miles an hour. It was lumbering at seven miles an hour due north which put the Big Bend directly in its line of sight. The storm surge was expected to be between nine and twelve feet above normal, perhaps higher depending on if it struck during high tide, which at Lethe was at 3:03 A.M. Our house was thirteen feet above sea level so if the surge was on the high end of the scale and if we got a direct hit, all of Lethe would be under water including our party of five.

This was not good news. I looked at Nick, who was listening intently to the report. He put his arm around my shoulders and kissed my temple.

"Don't worry," he said. "We're going to be fine. You know, it's sort of like having a baby. You're excited about it but also worried something awful because you don't want anything bad to happen. But nothing bad hardly ever does."

I looked at him, amazed at how he could babble on under the worst of circumstances. I started to say, "No, Nick, it's not anything like having a baby," but Beth chimed in before I could speak.

"I guess you're right. Just never thought about it that way before."

I threw my arms in the air and Nick asked, "What?"

"Nothing. Just forget it," and I reached for a Cheeto.

As static crowded his voice, the radio announcer gave an ominous rundown of what damage could be expected in a Category Three storm. "Denuded and/or toppled-over trees. Serious flooding at the coast and possible destruction of many smaller coastal structures. Mobile homes destroyed. Larger coastal structures damaged by battering waves and floating debris. Coastal evacuation routes flooded three to five hours before the eye of the storm hits. Land five feet or less above sea level flooded inland eight miles or more . . ."

"Maybe we should turn that off," Maya said.

"I agree." I tousled Lucas' hair. "You okay?"

He shrugged. "Yeah. Just a little scared."

"There is not a single thing to be scared about," Nick said. "This is just a little bitsy know-nothing storm."

"I'm going to remind you that you said that," quipped Beth.

The lights flickered on and off a half-dozen times and then went out for good.

"Well, so much for electricity," I said, grabbing a flashlight.

"Yep," Nick said and he went over to the front door, forced it open, and began fiddling with the small generator he'd topped off with gas earlier in the day. Maya and I lit candles and hurricane lamps. Once the generator was humming, Nick ran the VHF radio off it and called his mother.

"Why don't we run the lights off the generator?" Lucas asked reasonably.

"Yeah!" I agreed.

"We don't need the lights on. But we do need to be able to communicate with the outside world," Nick said, sounding just slightly priggish. "I can't run too much off this thing—it's not very strong."

Lillian must have had a generator, as well, because after several crackling seconds she answered Nick's call. "The Lillian Blue residence. Over."

She had been on the radio to the sheriff's department and provided us with a full rundown of local conditions. The bridges were all closed and Panacea, Alligator Point, Eastpoint, and Carrabelle were already experiencing minor flooding.

"You know what that means. Over," she said.

"Yes, ma'am, we must be flooding, too. Everybody okay over there? Over."

"We're just fine. Don't have any electricity, though. Over."

"Us either. Over."

"Don't use that generator for lights. You need to keep the radio going. Over."

"I know it. Now listen, Mama, if it gets rough at your place you call me, okay? Over."

"You, too, son. You hear that? Big-a-Mama is yelling about something. So I guess I'll talk to you later. Over and out."

For the next six hours, the weather grew steadily worse and there was no light beyond the flickering candle flames. The day had been brilliantly hued but the night was cloaked in an impenetrable iron-hard blackness, the color one associates with sleep or death. No stars. No moon. No lamplight. Only darkness so abiding that without the aid of a candle you couldn't see your hand in front of your face. I gazed out our only unshuttered door into the night and felt swallowed by it.

As the winds strengthened, our little house by the sea shook and groaned. Massive gusts buffeted the roof, clawing at Nick's blue shingles. And always, without end, the wind roared. But floating just underneath the roar was the sound of Nereus' bell. It clanged wildly, incessantly, on and on, like a warning to flee.

But there was no fleeing. We had waited too late. The normally placid Gulf and bay were churning with six- to ten-foot waves. We couldn't possibly navigate the bay in such weather. The *Poseidon* would be swamped before we even left the dock.

"What did we do with our boats?" I asked, feeling as if my bearings were being blown askew by the gale wind.

"Dem and I trailered them over to Mama's," Nick said. "They should be fine."

"Oh," and I wondered how the day got by me without my knowing that.

"Maybe we could take the *Poseidon* over to the hill," Lucas said hopefully as he sat on the couch slowly strumming his guitar.

"No way," said Beth. "We're keeping our butts right here. It's the safest place. That boat can't get across the bay right now."

A huge gust walloped the house. The trusses and two-by-fours and windows and doors and old pine planking shuddered and moaned. "Should we move into the bathroom or maybe the closet?" I asked.

"The house is just giving a little. That's all," Nick said. "If it wasn't moving, then I'd be worried."

"Oh, Jesus, look," I said, pointing at the floorboards. The wind was pushing the rain horizontally, causing it to seep through the windows and doors despite the shutters. I set about the task of mopping up the water with towels but soon discovered that my linen supply could not keep pace with the demand. So as I mopped, Beth wrung out the towels. For hours. Until my arms ached and my hands were rubbed raw.

Nick ventured onto the front porch to see if he couldn't somehow stop the flooding but hurried back inside, saying, "Whoa! A person could get killed out there."

Maya tried to keep her own panic in check by telling stories to Lucas. She told him about her grandfather, who had been a lector in the cigar factories in Ybor City in Tampa.

"What's a lector?" he asked.

"The lector read to the workers as they rolled the cigars."

"What did he read to them?"

"All sorts of things. Dickens to Tolstoy to the daily papers. But it was accounts of the Russian Revolution that got him fired. The factory owner said he was trying to start trouble."

"What kind of trouble?"

"Unionization."

"Hmmm," Lucas said.

Then Beth told him about his great-grandmama Rhea's notion that the beach builds up before a storm.

"And it's true," I said. "Today there were dunes I'd never seen before."

"It's been building for a week," said Lucas. "I noticed that."

Nick told him about the large pod of dolphins that followed him and Demetrius upriver.

"What were they doing?" Lucas asked.

"Getting out of the storm," Nick said.

"Cool!"

"Lucas, why don't you play us something?"

"Like what?"

"Something fast, something we can move to."

"Yeah, a foot-stompin' tune."

That is how the four of us came to rise to our feet—even while the water continued to seep into the house—and how we began to dance merrily through the wavering shadows, our faces blurred and dream-like in the frenetic candlelight. Beth tried to do the Russian dance in which you kick your legs cancan style from a squatting position but went sprawling onto her butt. We were howling with laughter when the VHF radio came back on and Lillian's voice filled the room.

"They're predicting a direct hit on us. So hang in there. It's going to get rough. What are you doing? Over."

"Dancing, Mama. Over."

"Dancing? Over."

"Yes, ma'am. Over."

"Whatever. Don't set the house on fire. Over and out."

Lucas set his guitar aside and said he didn't feel like playing any-more. Beth, Maya, and I tried to coax him. "Just one more tune!" Beth said.

"Yeah."

"Please? I'll give you a dollar."

But before Lucas could give in to our pleas, Nick stuck a CD in the boom box and cranked it full blast. Greek folk music suddenly com-peted with the wind. Nick shut his eyes, lifted his right hand to his chest, extended his left arm, and I said, "Oh-oh, here we go!"

Then, in a divine fit of selflessness, my dear Nick began The Dance. With his face aimed heavenward, he glided across the floor. His hips undulated. He swayed. He spun. Faster and faster as the song's tempo increased. He had no pride or shame when in the grips of The Dance. He was free. It was as if for a few moments he slipped past this world and all its self-consciousness. As I watched him sinuously shake his hips in time to that eastern rhythm, I decided that dancing was the closest thing humans had to flight. That or swimming. Take the manta ray, for instance, they fly through the water. They do not swim. Maybe each time our feet leave the ground we, for an instant, transcend ourselves.

Beth, Maya, and Lucas clapped in time to the music. Nick swirled past the couch, offered me his hand, and I shyly took it (why the sudden timidity, I do not know, but what a grand feeling—the surrender).

He put his hand on the small of my back and we dipped. Our audience cheered and then in rapid succession—one, two, three—something large hit the side of the house, thunder shook the walls, lightning slashed a path through the room, and the roof seemed to scream as the wind attempted to rip it off its trusses.

I gripped Nick tighter and looked at the ceiling, certain the roof was about to fly away and we would drown in the subsequent deluge.

"Are we gonna die?" Lucas asked.

"No, baby," Maya said tenderly. "We're going to live. Just you wait and see. We'll tell stories about this night one day."

I covered my face with my hands and tried to count to ten. Nick put his hands on my shoulders and whispered he was sorry. The roof continued to scream.

"It's not your fault, baby," I lied. Quarreling under these circumstances would only make things worse. But I promised myself that if we lived through this, I would give him what-for.

The VHF radio crackled to life. Nick shut off the boom box as the living room filled with the sound of Lillian shouting. "Charon's out in the storm. He's standing right out there in it. What're we going to do? Oh my God, he could die out there! Over."

"Mama, calm down. Is Big-a-Mama okay? Over."

"Of course she's not okay! Over!" Lillian barked.

"Everything is fine, Mama. Don't panic. I'll go get him. Over."

"You'll get yourself killed, Nick. Don't! Don't, don't, do—"

"Mama, just sit down and have some sherry. Over and out."

Nick snapped off the radio, ran his hands through his hair and down the sides of his neck. "Damn it all to hell."

"Nick," I said, "she's right. You can't go out there. It's too dangerous. You said so yourself."

He sighed and stared at the floor. No one spoke. We listened to the hurricane wind even as we tried to convince ourselves that things weren't as dire as they appeared.

"I don't see as how I've got much choice," he finally said and then went into the bedroom and grabbed his slicker.

"Well, you're not going alone," Beth said.

"Jesus Christ, you're both crazy."

"I think they'll be fine," Maya said, her optimism grating on me.

Nick pushed on the door but it wouldn't budge. The wind was pressing it shut, keeping us sealed inside. He stepped back and flung his full weight against it. The door popped open and he stepped into the storm, Beth at his heels. Before hurrying off the porch, he turned to his nephew and shouted, "Lucas, play something. I don't care what. Just don't stop playing."

I followed them out. "Go back!" Nick yelled.

"Okay!" I said and acted as if I were heading inside. But I did not. I stayed on the porch and peered into the blackness. The rain looked like steel slivers stabbing the night. I shielded my face but the wind and rain stole my breath. I tried to say, "Nick, Nick, come back," but the words were ripped from my lips before they were whole. And then—beyond the howling wind and Lucas' crazy playing and Nereus' incessant bell and my half-formed cry—I heard Charon. He was chanting, praying to the gods. His voice boomed across the bay, echoed onto the land, and whirled wildly across Lethe on the back of the wind. Maybe, I thought hideously, if he sacrifices himself, the rest of us will be saved.

The fear that I'd been doing battle with all night, the fear that resided in my belly like a white-hot coal, the fear that I had tried to deny while I rearranged my potted geraniums and fixed a fried chicken dinner and poured us each a merry glass of wine unleashed itself, striking me down, bringing me to my knees. A surprised gasp escaped my lips but was carried away on a gust.

Battered by wind and rain, I saw myself the way one does in a dream or a story. My mind hovered among the porch rafters, rigid and keen with the cold objectivity of the inhumane.

With a clarity that was both new and unforgiving, I saw that I was nothing more than a huddled speck of flesh and blood and bones. My love, inconsequential. My fear, worthless. In fact, in the context of this storm, my life had no meaning. I was as important as a crushed blade of grass, as vital as a grain of sand blasted into oblivion by the raging gales. I tried to stand but the wind knocked me down and it was then that I remembered George Blue, alone on the deck of the *Lillian B*, fighting for his life while unbeknownst to him his wife was giving birth to a boy they would name Proteus—a sea god, a shape-shifter, a divine being. Such was the dream spawned in the glow of post-birth joy. But the reality was that the baby boy born at sea in the clutches of a sudden storm was a mere mortal, nothing more. A vulnerable, helpless babe who in his thirtieth year would become my husband. My dear, dear husband.

"Oh my God, Nick!" I whispered. "Nick!" This memory of George

Blue, a memory that did not come to me firsthand but had been planted by his wife and altered by me to give it form and shape, to place it into the realm of narrative, to make it mine, tripped something inside me. The strength that George Blue summoned from his most primal recesses, the strength that had allowed him to defy nature and keep that boat afloat and save his wife and the son whom he didn't even know had been born, was transferred to me by the act of remembrance. I felt myself crash to the earth. No longer did I see myself from above. Such self-consciousness belongs to the gods, not frail humans who do not recognize their own strength.

Animal-like, I pulled myself up, flung open the screen door, and ran through the wind, chasing Charon's ravaged voice.

At 3:18 A.M., as we guided Charon inside our house and as Lucas played that guitar as if possessed, the winds shifted and it was then that we realized Cerberus' eye must have moved onshore to our west and that we were now experiencing the southeast quadrant of the storm.

We wrapped Charon in a sheet and sat him down at our kitchen table where we served him coffee from our thermos. His agitation decreased in concert with the winds and, though he made eye contact with no one, he nodded vigorously each time a gale pounded our roof.

I had been the first person to reach him. Nick and Beth had gone too far toward the bay, which was over its banks and lapping at the far border of my garden.

"Charon, come with me!" I had yelled but he did not acknowledge my presence. I screamed for help—three bloodcurdling howls—certain the wind would claw my voice into undetectable shreds. But it did not. Nick and Beth rushed out of the darkness and the three of us guided the old man, who was still chanting, aimlessly through the storm. Visibility was zero. In our own yard, we were lost. We wandered cold and beaten and fighting for breath. Finally Nick was able to hone in on the sound of Lucas' playing and by using its clamor as his North Star, he led us home.

But now, with all of us safely inside, other than for the darkness and the moaning of the wind, everything seemed nearly normal. Lucas, spent from the evening's events, set aside his guitar and lay down on a quilt on the living room floor. Maya and Beth were close to nodding off on the couch and once they realized that from here on out the storm would slowly subside, they drifted to sleep.

Nick and I kept watch over Charon. When the wind no longer howled at a constant, full-tilt screech, the old man fell asleep right there at the table. We had a hell of a time easing him out of the chair and onto the floor but we managed. I slipped a pillow under his head and said, "I feel terrible, leaving him on the floor like this."

"It's better than leaving him in the chair."

"I guess."

"He'll be fine. We'll probably have to push him out of the way come morning." Nick put his arm around me and rubbed his eyes. "I'm bushed," he said.

"Me, too."

The two of us threaded our way through the living room, blowing out candles as we went, and then entered our bedroom, shut the door, took off our clothes, and collapsed on the bed.

"We made it," I said.

"Yes, I think we did."

"I love you."

"I love you, too."

The words were automatic, a rote prayer leading us into sleep. Nick reached for my breast but before he could squeeze my nipple he was snoring. His leg straddled my belly. My stomach churned beneath the weight. His breath was sour with beer and coffee. Soon he was snoring with such gusto I was afraid he would wake the whole house, not to mention that I would never get a wink of sleep with all that clamor.

When I was young and heard adults complain about their marriages and spouses, I always wondered why they stayed married if their unions made them so miserable. As I lay there, pinned to the mattress, having survived into the far side of the storm, listening to my husband's nasal racket, I asked myself if this was the sort of closeness, sacrifice, bargaining, and compromise that made others gripe furiously, ad nauseam.

I, myself, could come up with a litany of charges. My husband had underestimated the hurricane's fury and as such put us all at risk. And now he was snoring so loudly I would never get to sleep unless I shook him awake, which I didn't have the heart to do. And even though the house was hot and close, he was lying on top of me—oblivious to the world and to my discomfort. And there were other things beyond the immediate situation. For instance, it drove me crazy the way every time he ate peanuts he first shook them in his palm and then popped them in his mouth as if he were tossing coins. And, of course, there was that morning breath that sometimes hung on all day.

After a night like ours, some couples would end the evening by having an argument. I was sure of it. Maybe even a knock-down-drag-out. Were Nick and I ignoring some essential facet of marriage? By simply accepting each other's foibles were we shortchanging ourselves, missing out on some grand, sexually infused passion?

Perhaps I could embark upon a campaign of bad habit alteration. I could demand that he sleep on the couch until he learned to brush his teeth every night. I could pitch a marathon fit that would cease only once he successfully underwent sleep disorder therapy in order to stop snoring. I could throw down the gauntlet and insist he see a psychiatrist to find out why he wouldn't leave Lethe even in the face of imminent peril. I could tell him that our marriage depended on it. "You have to change," I could say. And then I could beat my breast and emphatically cry, "I just can't live this way!"

That's what some women would do. And then they'd get on the phone to their friends and talk about their husbands as if they were stones in their shoes.

I lightly stroked Nick's leg. It was moist with sweat and his hair tickled my fingers. I lay there, irritated with the heat, and attempted to formulate pithy barbs that would stick in his heart. I came up blank.

Ultimatums and sarcasm, I supposed, were not my strong suits. Sterile correctness, not our lot in life. We were just humans, after all. I sighed. The thought alone was burdensome.

We had so much to worry about besides the piddling faults my bad mood illuminated. We didn't know if the *Mattie Fiona* was in one piece or not. It was very possible that all my hard work in the garden had been undone in just a few wind-wracked hours. Would I replant? Would the garden ever look the same? Would Nick decide that he'd like to help me as I continued in my quest to turn sandspur patches into visions of Eden, perhaps become a rosarian in his own right? Would I lose interest in trying to transform our small bit of this barrier island into an oasis? This was Lillian's fault, all this gardening mania. I'm sure she'd be in her yard at first light, saving what she could and cleaning up the rest. Well, at least I could gain comfort from the fact that I had successfully grown a plot of poppies and that they had withered months before the storm threatened and that even though Lillian didn't say a word about my startling success, I did catch her in my yard one morning fingering their extravagant blossoms.

I looked at Nick. He didn't have a clue that I was in such a snit. His face was slack, his muscles from head to toe dull and relaxed.

"I'm glad you don't know," I said. I closed my eyes and told myself that our marriage was not about exerting self-will. And that thought eased me. My irritability wavered. Yes, I decided, our marriage was about the journey, about making it through the night, about listening to each other's fears and doubts without those weaknesses igniting anger, about discovering that if one ran into the storm the other was compelled to follow.

Sleep-sodden, Nick rolled off me and onto his belly. He snorted three times and then fell silent. Despite my rant of a moment ago, I wasn't ready to be apart. I rested my head on his shoulder blade, flung my leg over his, trailed my fingertips down the crooked ladder of his spine, and listened to the rain herald the dawn.

.   .   .

September 25, 1997
The day after Hurricane Cerberus
Evening

I write this by candlelight as we still do not have electricity and have no anticipation of it coming back on any time soon.

I will try to record here just the facts.

Cerberus' eye went ashore nearly a hundred miles to our west, scouring away dunes and washing homes off their foundations and into the bay. This was near a village named Mexico Beach.

Property damage estimates for the Big Bend are in the billions.

Lethe, alone, lost eight houses and another twelve sustained serious damage. The sand dunes did their job—they staved back the water on our section of the island but they and the sea oats are scoured away. A light dusting of sand has settled on everything—looks like snow.

Highway 98 was washed out from Carrabelle to Eastpoint. The only way to Apalachicola from here is either by boat or through the logging trails of Tate's Hell.

The Mattie Fiona came through unscathed and any major damage on Lethe is mainly on the island's eastern end where the elevation is only a few feet above sea level.

Five shingles were blown off our roof. Nick replaced them about an hour ago.

Lillian's place survived untouched but Beth and Maya's front porch is severely damaged. Nick thinks that a downed tree acted as a battering ram in the wave action, destroying the porch's pilings. The wind took out their screens, which was to be expected.

Lucas' response: "We needed a new porch anyway."

All in all, I guess you could say we got lucky.

As for our sundry wildlife, last time I checked (about a half hour ago) the squirrel hadn't yet ventured out of his birdhouse. I hope he's just traumatized and not dead. Also, the cats, they are all accounted for and are as mean as ever.

Our front porch door blew open during the storm. The southwest screen was covered in butterflies and moths—don't know if the winds blew them or if they sought shelter there. Some made it—we released them as soon as we realized they were there—but many were dead.

Nick is over at his mother's taking down her hurricane shutters.

Earlier today, once the rains ended, we scavenged the beach. We found lumber and large garden pots and even a bench—all of it floating in the Gulf miles from where the storm first claimed them. The bench is now on my sundeck decorated with my potted geraniums (the garden is a mess and the trees are leafless, wind and salt burned—but it's not as bad as I feared—at least I have a foundation with which to start over and can correct some of my errors—coneflowers mixed with plumbago—ugh!—never again).

When I stood on the beach, looking out at the calm waters, it was hard to believe that this was the same place where we had feared for our lives just a few hours earlier. Cerberus scrubbed our world clean. The air was fresh and the sky the palest blue and the breeze gave no hint as to its violent side.

In its wake, the receding tide left behind all manner of sea life. Sand dollars blanketed the shore, sometimes four deep. The majority were dead but poor Charon returned them to the sea anyway. He was a frantic, crazy, dear old man, running ahead of the waves, playing beat the clock with the tides, the sand, the sun.

At Nick's suggestion I took over to the beach my pocket guide to seashells and marine life. I'm glad I did. I was able to identify scads of stuff. Here's a list (what I remember anyway): sea urchins, clams (several varieties), starfish, dog whelks, channeled whelks, lightning whelks, tulip snails, augers, oysters, cockles, alphabet cones (I made sure they were empty before even attempting to pick them up), conchs, sea pansies, sea whips, seaweed, sponges, crabs, jellyfish, blowfish, and innumerable other creatures—some worm-like and others bulbous—which I couldn't begin to name even with the help of my book.

But this was the best of all: Near the dune line, trapped in a stubbled tangle of sea oats, was the largest intact horse conch I have ever laid eyes on. I ran over, hoping with all my heart that it was vacant. I always observed the Blues' only religiously enforced beach rule—no shell can be collected if it's inhabited. I rolled the conch with my toe and cautiously peered inside. Its chamber was empty and so beautiful (coral to pink, then fading to ivory). I must have looked like a three-year-old, jumping up and down and shouting, "Yea!" I held the shell into the air and called to Nick, who was wrestling ashore a two-by-four. "Look at this!"

He dragged the board onto the sand and dropped it. When he saw what I was holding he gave me a thumbs-up sign and started toward me. He yelled something but I couldn't hear him because I had pressed the shell to my ear and was listening to the sea.

It was calm and steady, not anything like last night.

S eptember 26, 1997
Back porch
About 7 P.M.

Still no electricity but the squirrel is safe. He left his hurricane shelter sometime today and, last time I looked, was eating the seed I'd put out for the birds. I wonder how squirrels ended up on this island, anyway?

S eptember 28, 1997
Living room
Around 11 P.M.

We have electricity! Finally!

My roses already have new buds. Even Lillian was impressed.

S eptember 30, 1997
Front porch
Lethe
Early evening

Yesterday I saw a waterspout. Nick was at work. I was sitting on the beach staring out at the water, minding my own business. There was a big black cloud about two miles out and that's where it happened. I ran up to the house and radioed Lillian. She said I must be mistaken, that it wasn't the time of year for waterspouts. But I know what I saw.

November 1, 1997
Carrabelle dock
Eightish

Nick has stopped allowing me on the boat. He says it's too dangerous. I told him it isn't any more dangerous than the last time I went out but he won't change his mind. Says he doesn't want anything to happen to me.

I don't know what's causing him to act so spooked. He's probably hoping I'm pregnant. Which I'm not. But even if I were, that shouldn't make the boat off-limits to me. After all, Nick was the child born at sea by his mother's own will.

And another thing: He's been dreamy lately. In the middle of supper— maybe as I'm reaching across the table to refill his tea—I'll notice he's got this kind of faraway, glazed expression. He's somewhere else but I don't know where. I say his name. Sometimes two or three times before he drifts back. Then he smiles at me—that shy, sexy grin of his—and says, "I'm sorry, what were you saying?"

My best guess: the Indian summer. It's making him crazy. We haven't had even a hint of fall and here it is—November. The good weather has meant a long season on the water. Maybe it's getting to him. Maybe he needs a vacation. But I know him, he's not going to take a rest until the weather turns.

Gossip: Kelly has been practically living at Dem's. He's smiling again. All the time.

November 5, 1997
Our backyard dock
Near sunset

Nearly every day since the hurricane a mother dolphin and her baby come into the bay at dawn and again in the late afternoon to feed on the fish that school inshore. The mother sometimes rushes the mullet into the marsh grass and has her pick. They are east of me now, swimming slowly away from the sun.

Their daily appearances have renewed my interest in dolphin myths. I read today about Arion—a poet and musician whose crew tried to kill him as he sailed back to Greece. To escape danger, he summoned a pod of dolphins with his lyre and hitched a ride on the back of one. They protected him his entire journey home.

"Why aren't you going out?"

"Because I want to be with you tonight." He reached for my hair and crushed a handful in his palm.

"I could go with you. You said the shrimp are running real good."

"No. I don't want you out there. Too many things could go wrong. And besides, I want to *be* with you, not running around on deck hauling nets while you're below asleep."

He leaned into me, ran his lips across my cheekbone and the back of his hand along the hard angles of my jaw. "You don't want me to stay home?"

"Oh, no. I do. I do."

He held my face and kissed my forehead. I wrapped my arms around him and pressed my ear against his chest, searching for a heartbeat.

That night we ventured over to the chickee (the storm had claimed a few fronds—that's all—and filled it with a foot of sand), where we shared a bottle of wine and watched the full moon rise.

"We should do this more often," I said.

"Yes, we should." He stood and pulled me to my feet. "Come on."

"Where?"

"Let's go skinny-dipping."

"We can't. What if somebody sees us?"

"It's okay. They'll probably be related." He began unbuttoning my blouse.

"But Nick!"

He unsnapped my bra. It fell into the sand. He kissed my breast. "You win," I said and helped him strip off his jeans.

I shimmied out of my shorts and giggled again as I watched him strut naked in front of me. He was beautiful; his skin looked like alabaster.

Before entering the water, we played. We held hands and chased each other and dug for clams and terrorized the ghost crabs. Nick performed The Dance. He looked like a golden god spinning across the belly of the sea. I ran over to him and he held me and I whispered, "You're rapturous." We danced to music pulled from our memories, scattering footprints across the sand. We spun and dipped and sashayed until finally, breathless, we found that we had reached the water's edge.

"Come on, let's go in."

The surf lapped at my toes. "I don't know, Nick. Aren't sharks a lot more active at night?"

"Yes. But they won't bother us."

"Why not?"

"The dolphins. Sharks usually keep their distance from them."

"But how do you know there are any dolphins around?"

"I just do."

"And I'm supposed to trust you?"

"Yes."

I studied him, looking for a crack in his wide-open and honest face. But I did not find one. "All right then."

Against my better judgment, I slipped my hand into his and we waded in. The water was up to my knees when I felt something move under my foot. I leapt vertically, nearly clearing the water, screaming.

"Sweetie, it was probably just a crab trying to get the hell out of your way."

"I know," I said defensively, and then, "How far out are we going to go?"

"Until there's nothing but water."

"Nick, you know I can't do that."

"You can if you want to. I'll teach you. Swimming is easy. In fact, I should have taught you a long time ago."

"I don't know, Nick. Maybe we should wait and you can teach me during the day."

"Ahhh, come on, baby. Just follow me. Do what I do, like when we dance."

"But I'm kind of scared."

He touched my cheek. "Oh, Mattie, don't be. I'll keep you safe. Here, wrap your arms around my neck. I'll carry you. On my back. You'll be a pilot fish catching a ride on the whale."

I laced my arms over his shoulders and together, body to body, we ventured into deep water.

"You're not touching bottom anymore, are you?" I asked.

"No. We're in over our heads, as they say."

"That's not funny." I looked behind me. The houses were nothing but spectral forms wavering in the distance.

"Now listen," Nick said, and he faced me, keeping me in his arms, "if you think you're going to go under, grab hold of me. But if you just relax, the water won't take you. You'll float."

He let go and I panicked. I swallowed salt water. I flailed. I sputtered. I coughed.

"Easy, easy. Just move your legs back and forth, like you're riding a bike. Yeah. There you go. Nice and slow. See? There's nothing to it. Good. That's it. Now let's try floating on your back."

"No, no. I don't think so."

"Just ease into my arms and relax. Let yourself go. The water will carry you. That's it. Good. Are you relaxed?"

"Yes."

"You sure?"

"Uh-huh."

He let go of me and I immediately tensed which caused my body to drop like a concrete ball. The Gulf was dark and the salt burned my eyes but I was unafraid, certain that Nick would not let me drown. He pulled me to the surface. I spit up water.

"Let's try that again," he said.

"Maybe I have no natural buoyancy."

"It's not about buoyancy."

"Then what is it about?"

"Your mind. You just have to let it go." Again he slipped his arms under me, keeping me afloat as he talked about the sky, pointing out constellations and planets I hadn't noticed before. "See that bright, bright star that doesn't flicker? That's Venus. It'll be brighter tomorrow night with the new moon."

"Can you find Delphinus?"

"I think it's too late in the year. He's gone away."

"Where to?"

"I don't know. My great-aunt always told me that the stars spend half of their lives in the sea and half in the heavens."

"That's a beautiful notion," I said, and as the words passed over my lips, I realized I *was* floating. Without my knowing it, Nick had taken away his hands. For the first time in my life I felt weightless, as if I belonged in the sea.

"Wow."

"It's wonderful, isn't it?"

"Yes. Yes, it is."

Nick took me in his arms and we kissed, over and over. We remained buoyant even as we spun and glided. The moonlight sparkled on our wet skin. My hair trailed behind me. "Look at my hair. It's a stain! A long golden stain!"

"No, it's beautiful. And I love it." Nick dived beneath the surface, pulling me down with him, and when we reemerged we were making love.

I do not know how long we remained like that, joined together in the warm salty swells of the Gulf, our moans and sighs mingling with the high, lonesome cries of seabirds. I kept murmuring, "I love you, I love you, I love you."

Nick pulled me hard against him, his lips moving against my ear as he whispered, "Mattie, this is what we are about. Don't ever forget. Not ever."

The next day we slept until noon. My lace curtains billowed in the easterly breeze and sunlight filtered through their floral pattern with a harsh intensity not uncommon for that time of day. I rolled onto my belly and lightly rested my hand on Nick's back.

"Mmm," he said. "Good morning."

"You mean, good afternoon."

He shifted onto his side and opened his arms. I snuggled against him and he said, "Were we fabulous last night or what!"

"We should get an award we were so good."

"Absolutely."

We drank our coffee on the back porch. Mockingbirds and titmice flitted through my battered garden and a thrush sifted through leaf litter. On the bay, a lone pelican floated close to the shore.

I gathered my hair and lifted it off my neck. "We've got to do something soon with the garden. Your mother says fall is the very best time to transplant. And if the weather does change, I'd like to be ready for it."

"Well," Nick said, tapping his fingers on the arm of the chair, "let's go take a look."

If I had learned one thing from Lillian it was that gardening was not about the here and now. It was about trying to exert your will on the future. The best gardeners were visionaries. They could look at a plot of barren dirt and see tomorrow's potential: coneflowers in full bloom under a hot sun, autumn sedum rising to the fore when the days grow cool, and the changing texture of light and shade once the yellow rambling rose begins to mature. I gazed at my beginner's garden, tucked my hand in Nick's, and made a secret wish—that Nick and I and this earth from which I was trying to coax life would age in concert with each other, gaining dignity, maybe even some grace, through the years.

"You think we'll ever have a garden as nice as your mother's?"

Nick looked at the pine straw paths scattered with storm debris. "I think we already do. You still want some kind of pond back here?"

"Yes. But just a little one. And I'd like to fill it with papyrus. And maybe a lotus or two. What do you think?"

"Nice," Nick replied, giving in to his polite streak, and I realized he didn't know a papyrus or lotus from a daisy. "What if I build a stone pathway through here, Mattie? Right between these two beds and up to the steps?"

"That would be wonderful. We wouldn't track in so much sand. You know, I get tired of vacuuming."

He considered the dirt. "Yeah, a light-colored stone."

"The garden would look a bit more formal. But that's good."

Nick looked at the distance from the back arbor to the porch steps. "I can get started on it this week. I'll ask Dem if he wants to help."

"What do you think if we planted some fruit trees over there by the birdbath?"

"What kind of fruit trees?"

"I don't know. I was thinking about persimmons. They're native so they wouldn't require a whole lot of care. And also, we could sure use some citrus. The other day your mother told me about some new cold hardy varieties. Wouldn't it be nice to have a lemon tree? Just think— fresh lemonade. We could actually stand a little shade back here. Dappled light in the afternoon. Just enough."

"Where are you going to get the trees?"

"I don't know. Maybe at Just Fruits over in Medart. I thought that after class someday I could stop and see what they have."

"Sounds like a plan," he said absentmindedly and I was sure that in his mind he was miles away from any notions regarding fruit tree planting. He was probably engrossed in mental calculations regarding his stepping-stone path, utterly unconcerned with my current worry which was how to keep the birds out of what would surely—come spring—be a bountiful persimmon crop.

Nick was never a picky eater but after suffering through so many of my culinary failures he was well within his rights when later that same day he poked at his food with his fork and asked tremulously, "What is it?"

"Tomato pie."

Lillian had given me the recipe and I followed it to a T. *Four to five tomatoes, blanched for easy removal of the skins. Three quarters of a cup of mayonnaise (feel free to use light but not fat-free). Pillsbury refrigerated pie crusts (bake the bottom crust for ten minutes in a moderate oven, otherwise you'll have a juicy mess). As much garlic as pleases you (Nick, as you must know by now, loves garlic). At least one and a quarter cup cheese (I use feta). Plus fresh basil. Put it all together and bake at three hundred and fifty degrees for about thirty minutes.*

I served it with a green salad and sweet tea. I watched out of the corner of my eye as Nick balanced a bite-sized morsel on his fork, lifted it to his lips, and discreetly sniffed. His face betrayed neither surprise nor disgust. Having gotten this far—even if the savory smell had offended him—he had little choice but to go ahead and eat. He popped it in his mouth and chewed tentatively but within seconds his eyes widened gratefully and his face relaxed in that way men have—you know, when they are suddenly and unexpectedly content (I have noticed that this phenomenon almost always revolves around food).

"This is really good!" he said.

"Thank you," I said, ignoring the note of amazement in his voice.

That night, he chewed heartily. He ate two more pieces and I wrapped up what was left and handed it to him as he walked out the door. As always, I followed him onto the porch to see him off and, also as always, he kissed me deeply. People accused us of still behaving like newlyweds. I considered that a compliment.

"I love you."

"I love you, too."

"Call me if you need me."

"I will. Be careful out there."

"See you in the morning."

"Bright and early."

"Sweet dreams, baby. Sweet dreams."

I remember the details of what happened next with cinema-like clarity, as if each utterance and minor gesture were preordained in this dance — no, this battle — with fate.

Having exhausted myself with the triumph of my tomato pie, I went to bed early but awoke near midnight to the soft patter of rain. I got up, stumbled into the kitchen, poured myself a glass of water, went into the living room, and flipped on the Weather Channel. The rain was caused by a cold front, the season's first. It was a light, steady shower — nothing Nick could not handle — so I peed and went back to bed. I was not worried and slept soundly, unaware of my dreams. By morning, the sky was clear, the air crisp with the first hint of autumn air.

From my bedroom window, I gazed out at the Gulf, hoping to see the *Mattie Fiona* close inshore but she wasn't there nor were there any other boats. To the west I caught the faint outline of what was probably a trawler but couldn't identify it.

I crawled out of bed, fixed a pot of hot tea, fed the feral cats who were meowing at my kitchen door, pulled on a pair of jeans and a long-sleeved shirt, and rode my bike past Lillian's house (her kitchen light was on) and down to the dock. Before taking off for the hill, I looked for the mother dolphin and her baby — they had been making their rounds through the bay steadily for about a month — but did not see them. Maybe they'll be around tonight, I thought as I launched the *Medusa* and headed across the bay.

My teeth chattered in the cold wind but that did not dampen my appreciation for the season — the shockingly open sky, the sapphire water, the ospreys spiraling through the new air. I thought about Nick heading into port. In my mind's eye, I saw him standing at the helm, slightly bleary-eyed but also energized by the change in the weather. I was sure he was calculating pounds of shrimp into dollars and ruminating over how long it would be before a cold snap shut down the bay. After he docked, I would ask him how the night went and he'd either say, "Oh, fair," or "Pretty good," and then, still sporting his white rubber boots, his skin glistening with sea spray, he'd offer me his thickly callused fisherman's hand and help me aboard. We would kiss, and I'd caress his salty curls, and we'd whisper how much we missed each other, not caring if anyone was watching or not. After we finished kissing, we'd pack the Fordge with shrimp.

That is how every day unfolded and I counted on it. The continuity gave our lives structure, a framework that was both comfortable and desired. We need routines. I know that now. I know that without them, even the simplest decision, such as when to fix a meal or when to braid my hair, becomes monumental, beyond my grasp.

But back to that morning. I tied up at the dock in Carrabelle and began my daily wait. I sat on a towel to avoid the fish guts and bird poop, dangled my legs over the water, took my journal out of my backpack. *Waiting for Nick. Expect him anytime. This is the season's first cold front. Feels like we're in the upper sixties . . .*

I went on like that for a while, scribbling, my thoughts meandering from one subject to the next, when I thought I heard the *Mattie Fiona*'s diesel engine. I jumped up—my heart quickened as it always did when I watched our boat round the bend. As she came into view, I waved. But then I felt foolish because someone was waving back and it wasn't Nick. Nor was the boat the *Mattie Fiona*. She was the *Mayme Ellyn*, owned and operated by a husband and wife who were respected old-timers in Carrabelle. They ran a tight ship and usually docked beside us. A cloud of crying seagulls followed them in.

We said our hellos and joked that Nick must be hogging all the shrimp and then they loaded their truck with their haul and went on their way.

Sometimes our instincts are dead-on and mine were that day. As I watched the folks from the *Mayme Ellyn* pull out of the parking lot and head east on 98, a palpable sense of dread descended. I felt weighed down and inexplicably found myself fighting back tears. As the minutes ticked on I grew shaky and then sick to my stomach. Along my spine, vise-grip pressure began to build. I reprimanded myself for not bringing a watch. I glanced up at the sun. By its position in the eastern sky, I estimated that it was nearly nine. I wrote in my journal, *He just went out a little far, that's all. He's probably loaded down with shrimp and taking it slow.*

I thought I heard another diesel engine so I jumped to my feet and in the process dropped my pen in the water. My ears must have been playing tricks on me. I waited and waited but no boat appeared. Finally I gave up, sat back down, and knowing I needed to stay preoccupied, searched through my backpack for another pen but couldn't find one. Luckily, though, I had with me Rhea and Lillian's copy of *The Old Man and the Sea*. I didn't remember when I had put it in the backpack or why but was glad to have it. I rubbed my hand across the jacket and decided that when the weather grew cold enough to keep Nick in port, we would once again spend cozy evenings by the fire—me reading aloud from the novel and Nick listening intently, his eyes closed. In this way, Nick and I would begin a tradition, maybe one that we could pass on to our children, if we ever had any.

Once more, I gazed downriver and saw only sunlight and water. I tried hard to catch any hint of the low shuffling sound of the *Mattie Fiona's* engine but all I heard was traffic and seagulls. To ease my foreboding mood, I opened the book and started in the only logical place: *He was an old man who fished alone in a skiff in the Gulf Stream and he had gone eighty-four days now without taking a fish.* I tried to imagine what Nick would be like if he went eighty-four days without a decent haul. He'd probably go mad, I thought. His superstitious nature would run amok. A truck rattled down the highway and someone on the sidewalk yelled a greeting to a passing car. *He'll be here soon. He'll be here soon. He'll be here soon.* My stomach churned. I pressed my hand against my belly. I felt helpless. Alone. *Read the book, Mattie, read the book.*

And I did. I read. And I read. And I read. Until the old man was alone in the dark, far from land, lamenting that the boy was not with him.

I looked at the sky. I felt certain another hour had passed. The seabirds were all offshore. Pleasure boaters were leaving from the Carrabelle Marina and idling by. I noticed that the little secondhand store up by the road was open and it never opens until at least ten. What was I doing, just sitting here? What if something was wrong? The sun is hot. I'm dressed too warmly. Why doesn't that crow go away? "Shut up! Shut up your awful squawking!" None of this is right. My chest hurts. The pressure along my spine is so great I feel as if I might snap in two. My heart is beating out of sync. Much too fast. Breaking into shards, yes, glass shards. I can feel them, pricking my veins, bleeding me, privately, horribly. Don't let your fear gain the upper hand. Nick needs you. He needs you whole.

In the distance, softly at first, I heard that long-sought-after sound. The engine. Nick's engine. "Thank God," I said. I stood up and watched for the graceful curve of the *Mattie Fiona*'s bow as it made the turn into the channel. I smiled and started to wave and then saw that it wasn't the *Mattie Fiona* at all but a speedboat. It can't be, I thought, it just can't be. I looked toward the road. There were no schoolbuses rambling by, no early morning delivery trucks, no mothers driving their children to school. All of that had already happened. While I sat there on my butt the world had continued on and Nick was gone. Why hadn't I asked the people from the *Mayme Ellyn* if they'd seen him? They would have told me if something was wrong. But maybe they didn't know. Maybe he's hurt and can't reach the radio. And where are Beth and Maya? They moor over at the marina. I can't see it from here. Everybody is gone. Nobody knows what's happened. Nobody but me. No, dear God, no!

I ran down the dock, tripped on its uneven boards, ripped a hole in my jeans, pulled myself back up, and made my way over to Traders

Antiques. The front stoop was crowded with old picnic tables and pillars and a sideboard or two. I could not think clearly. My fear played havoc with the world—everything seemed to be moving too fast yet not at all. I flung open the door. I spoke—my tongue felt like rubber—but to my surprise, Debbie understood me. "Did a boat go down? Have you heard? Did something happen? Please tell me!"

"Why, no, honey, I haven't heard a thing. Not a word. Look at you, sweetie, you're white as a ghost. Come on back here and sit down. I'll get you a glass of water. Goodness, Miss Mattie, you're shaking like a leaf!"

Debbie contacted everyone for me: the sheriff, the Marine Patrol, the Coast Guard. They all had the same answer. They had received no distress call or any information that would lead them to believe that any of our shrimpers had experienced trouble overnight.

This news did not comfort me but only colored my panic, edged it toward the unthinkable, kept it alive with the worst sort of disbelief— that born of awful truth, that which is too horrific to admit to publicly, that which becomes a cancer in your belly, that which you're helpless to undo or make right.

I left Debbie's even though she urged me to stay. As I walked out her door, I heard her say, "I'll call Chester Mayo. He'll know. He shrimps every night."

According to the clock stuck on a varnished slice of cypress on Debbie's wall, it was nearly eleven-thirty. Even so, I could not allow myself to think of ridiculous possibilities that would explain his absence. That would waste time and time was precious. Time was my friend and enemy. The Gulf water temperature was in the mid to upper seventies. He could last awhile in water that warm. It wasn't like he was adrift in fifty-degree water where a man could die in minutes. And he was an excellent swimmer, a fish in the water. Go find Dem. He'll know what to do. If the tide is right, he might not have left Eastpoint yet. He might be just setting out.

I got in the Fordge and drove the old truck as hard as I could, wiping tears away, saying things like, "Goddamn it, Nick, where are you?" As I sped past old Carrabelle Beach a van with Jersey plates started riding my bumper and flashing its lights. I waved them around but I guess the curvy road frightened them. If this had been an ordinary day I would have slowed to a crawl but given the circumstances, I could not afford to take such a stand.

As I crossed over into Eastpoint, I got lucky. I spotted Dem's truck at a fish house. He was leaning on the driver's side door, jawing at some guy I did not know. I hit my brakes and pulled in. Gravel spewed and the idiot riding my tail blew his horn and shot me a bird. "Go to hell," I said.

I threw the truck in park and ran over to my brother-in-law. Dem was a good man. He knew by the look on my face.

We went inside and Dem got on the VHF to the Coast Guard. Immediately, they began giving him a runaround about no distress call and therefore no reason to send out a search boat.

I will never forget what Dem said. "Listen, you no-good cocksucker, my brother is missing. He should have been in port four hours ago. If you don't get your ass in gear and get some people out there, I will make sure you're out of a job. I will own your ass. Do you understand me! You people sat on your thumbs when my daddy was in trouble. You're sure as hell not gonna do that to my brother. Now get some fucking people out on that bay and find him!"

The man who owned the fish house patted Dem on the back. "Ease up, buddy."

I looked at my brother-in-law, grateful and amazed. I never knew he had it in him.

Dem wanted me to leave the Fordge in Eastpoint and drive back to the dock with him. But I couldn't. I would be faced with making conversation, and right then, that was beyond me. And besides, I told myself, maybe Nick will be waiting for me. He'll have a boatload of shrimp and if I leave the Fordge in Eastpoint I won't be able to drive our catch over to My-Way. The whole day would be shot.

When I pulled up to the dock and saw that the slip was empty—no shrimp boat, no Nick Blue, nothing but air and water—I slammed my forehead into the steering wheel and said, "No, no, no, no . . ."

Dem pulled me out of the truck, helped me into the *Medusa*, and together we sped back to Lethe.

Lillian met us at the dock. Lots of folks on the hill listened in to Dem's colorful rant to the Coast Guard and within seconds they were calling Lillian. I am deeply regretful that she heard about her son in this way. It is one of a handful of regrets that will stay with me to my dying breath.

She was much calmer than I. After all, she had been through this before and she was the type of woman who depends on her graciousness to see her through both the good and bad. "Everybody is out there. From Apalachicola to Spring Creek. The mullet fishermen, the shrimpers, the whole fleet."

"I'll go get Beth. We'll take the *Medusa*, if that's all right with you, Mattie. She goes faster."

"Beth is already out there."

"Let me go with you."

"No, Mattie. You stay here."

I looked at Dem. Each time there was a family crisis, he seemed to grow up. What a terrible thing. I wanted him to be wonderstruck. Forever. I wanted all of us to be normal again. I shut my eyes and saw Nick gazing at me, smiling.

Lillian put her hand on my arm. I opened my eyes. "Okay, Dem, but hurry back. Bring him home."

.   .   .

They found the *Mattie Fiona* drifting five miles offshore, her nets out. I do not know the man who first ran upon her but out of respect for the family, he did not pull the nets. Dem did that when he arrived. My hunch had been right. The nets teemed with shrimp. It had been a good haul. And I'm sure that as the sunburned, sober-faced shrimpers and mullet men looked on, they said a silent prayer or two when they realized that there was no human corpse in the nets—prayers thanking God for saving them from seeing that horrible sight and prayers asking God for the recovery of my husband's body.

For five days—from dawn to dusk—the awful drone of search planes filled the air. During this time, I did not sleep. While the planes searched from the sky, flying the same grid again and again, I stayed in my house and waited. When nightfall arrived and the droning ended, I put on my shoes, slipped into Nick's denim shirt—the one I hadn't washed yet, the one that smelled like him—left our house, and walked the beach, searching for Nick's body in the surf.

I was not alone during those hours. Charon was with me. We did not walk side by side nor did we speak, but nevertheless, we were together, the two of us patrolling the shore, me with a flashlight and Charon without, continuing to look for Nick once the planes had headed back to land. In this way, for those five days, the search never ended.

At first light, when the drone returned as nothing more than a dull throb at the far edge of the western horizon, Rhea would crest the dunes. She appeared mythic, rising from the sands, the wild morning sky stretched out behind her: a craggy old woman, hunched in the shoulders, her silver curls alive in the breeze, her cane waving crazily through the air. She would hobble across the dunes, navigate the sea oats and nettles, a thermos of coffee and two blankets in hand.

Tragedy had made her kind. She would drape the blankets over our shoulders, sit with us in the chickee, and pour us coffee.

"You need to sleep," she would say to me.

"I know I do."

Then she would put her thin arm around my waist, and her head would wobble on her little stem of a neck, and the three of us would gaze out at the water together, hoping, hoping, hoping, hoping, until we could stand the drone no more.

I needed a body. At first, only if it were intact and beautiful. As in life. I needed to lie down with him and trail my fingers over his skin and through his curls and whisper how much I loved him, would always love him. I needed to lead him to wherever he was going—that was my responsibility. I couldn't bear the thought of him journeying to a new and strange place alone. I had to ease his fear. I had to comfort my beloved in death. That's all.

After three days, however, my yearning changed. I wanted the body regardless of its condition. Just to touch him once more. To whisper, "I love you, baby." To hold his hand. To rub his feet. He loved to have his feet rubbed. I hoped they weren't cold. I hoped the water wasn't being cruel to him. To maybe say goodbye. Maybe.

By the end of the fourth day I could not close my eyes for fear of seeing what the Gulf had done to him.

If I had only said, "Baby, why don't you stay home tonight? We'll lie together in bed and I'll read to you."

That's all I had to do. He would have stayed. He always did. He never put up an argument or gave me any excuse as to why he needed to go out. If I wanted him at home, he was there.

But how could I have known?

How could I have gone to sleep when he was out there in some kind of terrible trouble?

How can I ever forgive myself?

How can I ever forgive God, if there is one?

Body or no body, I could not stand the sound of those search planes any longer. They were a constant reminder—as if I needed one—that Nick was gone. An official from the Coast Guard visited me. Actually came to my house. He said, "Mrs. Blue, we'll keep searching for as long as it takes."

This was on day two, when a few people actually kidded themselves into thinking he might still be alive (Lillian, for one). I thanked the kind man from the Coast Guard. I said, "I really appreciate it."

Dawn of day six found me on the beach again. All night, I had searched for Nick. But daylight brought with it a different yearning, one not centered on my husband's physical body. I wanted to find anything that would remind me of our happiness—a starfish, a mullet jumping, the graceful arc of a dolphin. I stood at the shore, staring seaward. Yes, a dolphin. Maybe I could believe the old tale. Maybe I wouldn't hurt so much. Maybe my sadness would ease.

I scanned the water, hoping for at least a glimpse of a silver gray fin, but all I saw was the endless Gulf. I closed my eyes and imagined myself swimming with a beautiful male bottle-nosed. I grabbed hold of his dorsal fin and we glided through the water, beyond the horizon, down to the Enchanted City at the bottom of the sea. There were stars there, just as Nick's great-aunt had told him there would be.

The gentle hum of the surf rose all around me and I thought that if I listened intently enough I might hear Nick's sirens. Maybe they lived there, too, in the Enchanted City. I opened my eyes and stared at the empty Gulf, my fantasy abruptly halted by the droning engines of the search plane.

I turned around and saw Rhea waving at me from the chickee. Charon was sitting on the bench, drinking coffee. Weary, my blood heavy with the weight of unrelenting grief, I joined them. I sat beside Charon and rested my hand on his leathery knee.

"That's it," I said. "I can't stand the sound of those planes anymore. I'll phone the Coast Guard today and ask them to call it off."

Rhea started in but I wasn't listening. I didn't care what people thought. In fact, I didn't much care about anything. I just sat there, looking around at a senseless world as Rhea jabbered and Charon drank coffee. I reached over and wiped away his tears.

That first week, Lillian and I stayed away from one another. Our individual grief ran too cold and deep for us to share it. And, after all, what was there to say in those early days? False hope sickened me. Disbelief hardened my pain. Sympathy both hurt and enraged me.

I suspect it was the same for her.

When the planes stopped buzzing overhead, we met in my garden. We didn't speak about Nick. At least not directly. We considered day-lilies. Casablancas, to be exact. Their big, pure white blooms on tall, sturdy stalks. Classically beautiful. "Everything a flower should be."

"I'll order you some."

"Fall planting, yes, you said that's best."

"These herbs could stand a good weeding, Mattie."

"Everything could."

"My tomatoes are pretty much done for—the storm took care of that. But your new ones are looking fine. You might get in a couple of harvests before it freezes. More if the weather holds."

"Lillian, I love you. I'm sorry if—"

"I feel the same toward you, dear. You're a good girl. Now get me a trowel. We've got a lot of work ahead of us."

I stand at the water's edge and consider death. It would be so easy. Nick taught me how. You simply step into the water and keep going. You let *it* take you, whatever it might be—a wave sweeps you under, or hypothermia claims you, or a shark attacks and then is joined by others.

Was it all a huge mistake or did he want to die? Did he fight against death until his last breath or did he go willingly? The prevailing theory is that he tripped on a rope or was knocked overboard by a sudden wave. Or a waterspout. That's it, a waterspout—it lifted him right out of that boat. He never wore a life vest. Not ever. Why didn't he swim back? Or grab hold of the rigging and pull himself aboard? Did he hit his head on something and pass out? Or was the Gulf just too much for him?

Visualize it, Mattie, every detail, and then maybe it will go away. Maybe, then, you can sleep. Maybe you'll be able to get your fingernail under a corner of this sadness and slowly chip away at it.

He is so surprised to be in the water. How did he get there? Perhaps he doesn't know. He is not afraid. Just swim back to the boat. That's all there is to it. But in the rain, he cannot find the *Mattie Fiona*. And it's a new moon and the storm has inked out the stars. Not one stitch of decent light in the sky. The waves are kicked up, kicked up real good— you could take a breath and end up with a gut full of seawater—not like last night, not like when we made love in the sea. No, this is rough. Keep your head up. Don't try to swim in this hard current. You'll exhaust yourself. You need all your strength. Try to float. Like you told Mattie. Just go with it. Salt water in the mouth and in the eyes and the cold. Very cold. Conserve your strength. Easy easy. Nothing to cling to. An ice chest—they float—that would keep me going. How long has it been? Just hold out till daylight. They'll find you come dawn. Yes, easy easy. What is that? I don't know where I'm at anymore. No. I'm at home, sitting at our supper table. A glass of water. Uh-huh. Iced tea. Right there. Didn't know I was going overboard. Happened so fast. There I go, under again. I'm so tired, so very tired. Where's the air? What do I breathe? No, God, don't let me die. I'll do anything. I'll be a better man. I'll take better care of my Mattie. Oh, Mattie, I'm sorry. I'm so sorry.

But did he say my name? Was there a moment—a singular piercing moment—when he knew he was going to die? That no matter what he did, death was imminent? Did he cry out? Did he curse the gods? Did he fight with every last ounce of strength he had until he became delirious? Did he drown fighting and angry and full of disbelief and fear at his fate?

No. No. That cannot be. I cannot have him die that way. Despite his big arms and rough hands and odd country manners, he was a man full of grace. Didn't he come into this world in the grips of a storm? And didn't I, myself, say he was reluctant to leave the womb, that watery realm where he spun and dived like a little dolphin god? He simply went full circle. He came from the sea and he has returned to it. Yes, he was surprised to find himself suddenly in the middle of a choppy sea. And did he think he could make it back to the boat? Of course he did. And yes, he struggled. I know he struggled. He did not want to leave me. I was his world. He'd said so himself a thousand times. He wanted to live because he loved me. He wanted to grow old holding my hand. He wanted life to unfurl in its expected way. We would turn gray and feeble together and we would love our wrinkles with the same purity with which we loved each other's smooth bodies. But at some point, alone in that vast sea, he knew that would never happen. And it saddened him beyond anything even I am experiencing. But he understood fate. He had come to welcome destiny and thus his return to Lethe. He was going home. Once he knew there was no returning to land, no ever holding me close again, he let himself be taken. He said, "Okay, take me home. But remember, it's Mattie I love. Mattie Blue. Remember."

Epilogue

His body escaped us. It did not float ashore. It did not become tangled in another shrimper's nets. It did not surface from the turbulence created by the entire fleet dragging their nets along the floor of Apalachee Bay. Not one bone. Not one cell. The Gulf took all of him.

I fought against that for a long time. As I've said, I needed his body. I needed to hold it near me just once more. I needed to whisper into the shell-like chambers of his ear, "I'm with you, Nick. Somehow, I am with you. I know this doesn't make sense. But it's true. We'll get through this together, honey, you, me, and our baby."

Five months have passed and so much has changed. I don't want his body to ever be found. I want him to remain in the sea. I want him to be part of every drop of water, every grain of salt, every foam-capped wave that washes ashore. He's not in his body anymore. He's here, in the Gulf, forever.

I cannot leave this place. Not with my current train of thought. If I left Lethe, I would be leaving behind all that I love, all that I know. They say Lethe was the river of forgetfulness, that before entering Elysium, spirits drank from its waters to forget the sorrows of their earthly lives. The legend says nothing of the joys of their earthly lives, however. Certainly, they are allowed that, to forever remember the joys of being human.

My sadness has not lifted but it is no longer the only emotion I feel. At times like these, when I am floating on my back in the Gulf's still waters with my swelling belly mimicking the lovely round form of the sun, I am peaceful.

A dolphin swims nearby. It comes every day and watches me and my unborn baby as we swim through the sea. Lillian says swimming is good for me, that it will strengthen my muscles and help me through my labor. I hope she is right. But that is not why I come out here. I'm here because in the water I feel close to Nick. In the water I talk to that dolphin as if it were human. In the water, I tell my baby stories—stories that have nothing to do with the century in which she will live: the diseases humans will or will not heal, the wars they will or will not fight. I do not mention the earth's dwindling diversity or humankind's death chase after the almighty dollar. The phrases *extinct species* and *nuclear proliferation* do not cross my lips. Neither does rattletrap about the promise of technology. Everything that I want her to understand is right here. The mystery is in the sand. And in the water. And in the air we breathe.

I feel her move in my womb, spinning just the way her father did when he was inside his mother. I close my eyes, envision my little sprout of a child, and whisper, "Let me tell you about your daddy, about the day we met."